Also by Kathryn R. Wall

In for a Penny

And Not a Penny More

Perdition House

Judas Island

Resurrection Road

Bishop's Reach

Sanctuary Hill

The Mercy Oak

Covenant Hall

Canaan's Gate

JERICHO CAY

KATHRYN R. WALL

 MINOTAUR BOOKS ⚸ NEW YORK

JERICHO CAY. Copyright © 2011 by Kathryn R. Wall. All rights reserved. Printed in the United States of America. For information, address St. Martin's Press, 175 Fifth Avenue, New York, N.Y. 10010.

www.minotaurbooks.com

Library of Congress Cataloging-in-Publication Data

Wall, Kathryn R,
    Jericho Cay : a Bay Tanner mystery / Kathryn R. Wall.—1st ed.
        p. cm.
    ISBN 978-0-312-60185-0
    1. Tanner, Bay (Fictitious character)—Fiction.   2. Women private
investigators—Fiction.   3. Hilton Head Island (S. C.)—Fiction.   I. Title.
    PS3623.A4424J47 2011
    813'.6—dc22

                                                            2011001268

First Edition: May 2011

10   9   8   7   6   5   4   3   2   1

To Norman:

For who you are. For who you've helped me to become.

A CKNOWLEDGMENTS

My thanks as always to the many professionals who take my fledgling manuscripts and guide them along to publication. It's sometimes a rocky road, and the bumps are most often navigated with grace and good humor.

I'd also like to acknowledge the generosity of the Morrisons and of the Tileys for their contributions to Literacy Volunteers of the Lowcountry. I trust they'll be happy with the characters I've created to honor the names of their loved ones.

I always dedicate the new book to my husband of nearly forty years. I just want to say again how much his love and faith in me have made this whole journey possible.

CHAPTER ONE

*K*ITTY. SUCH A QUAINT, INNOCUOUS NAME FOR THE deadly, screaming beast of a storm.

Most hurricanes begin life as gentle waves, slipping off the coast of Africa, drifting past the Cape Verde Islands and out into the Atlantic where they sit for a few days, spinning harmlessly and gathering strength. If conditions are ripe, they eventually move west, earning first the designation of tropical depressions before graduating to tropical storms and finally to category one hurricane status.

Back in the days before feminism and political correctness, all storms had female names. Now they alternate, so that both men and women can share the dubious honor of being associated with widespread panic and destruction.

Kitty was different. She had popped up unannounced and unexpected in the Bahamas, intensified in a matter of hours, hung a sharp left, and pointed herself directly at the Lowcountry of South Carolina. Those of us who have lived here all our lives expect a couple of scares every hurricane season, but we generally have a few days' warning while the unpredictable storms try to make up their minds exactly who they're going to crush.

If my husband Red and I had been the only ones we had to worry about, we probably would have refused to evacuate, opting instead to hunker down in our beach house to ride out Kitty. Though just a few yards from the ocean across a sheltering dune, the house had been constructed to withstand these threats. Built up high off the ground, it could weather a modest storm surge as well as strong winds. We also had functioning hurricane shutters to protect the windows and a gas-powered generator in case we lost electricity.

But we'd had other responsibilities. My surrogate mother, Lavinia Smalls, along with my half sister Julia and her caretaker, Elizabeth Shelly, had been huddled in the antebellum mansion where I'd grown up on St. Helena Island. Presqu'isle had stood tall and proud for the better part of two hundred years and had outlasted both Mother Nature and the Union Army. Still, they'd felt vulnerable—three women alone—so Red and I had battened down our Hilton Head beach house and raced north.

But those computer models, so beloved by weather forecasters, had missed it by a few hundred miles. That night, while we crept along roads growing more crowded by the minute with frantic tourists and fleeing residents, the predictions had her coming ashore at Savannah, which would have put us in the path of the deadliest quadrant. As Kitty neared the coast, however, she began a slow slide to the north, eventually devastating the poor folks along the North Carolina shore and dealing us only a glancing, but vicious, blow.

Almost two weeks later, I stood in the semicircular driveway of Presqu'isle and surveyed the progress of the repairs. All the live oaks had survived the onslaught of wind and driving rain, as they had done for a couple of centuries. The azaleas had been flattened, but they'd come back. The roof hadn't been so fortunate. One corner of it had been crushed, as if some giant fist had struck it, exposing the attic to the elements.

Even though the repairs had been completed, I figured it would be an unholy mess up there, but none of us had yet had the time or the heart to tackle the cleanup.

I did a cursory walk-around of the entire property. Despite some downed limbs that still had to be hauled away and a lot of foliage stripped from the shrubs, everything looked to be making a comeback. Even the short dock had weathered the pounding it had taken from St. Helena Sound. It could have been much worse. I left my damp shoes on the back verandah and slipped barefooted into the kitchen. Lavinia, our longtime housekeeper and the one solid presence left from my childhood, stood, as usual, at the stove. She turned when I let the screen door bang shut behind me.

"So how does it look?" she asked, the spoon she'd been using to stir the gumbo poised over the pot.

"Coming along," I said. "I think by spring you'll never be able to tell we took a hit."

I'd driven over from Hilton Head that morning to check that everything was under control at my childhood home after I'd gotten my own cleanup crew started on what I hoped would be their final day of work. Red and I had been camping out at Presqu'isle since the night of the storm, but things had progressed enough that we'd moved back to the island a couple of days before. The beach house my first husband Rob and I had lovingly planned and built had withstood the wind, but the surge that devastated the dune had roared unchecked into the lower portion of the house, filling the garage with a foot of sand and debris before receding.

I reached in the refrigerator and pulled out the iced tea pitcher. I carried a glass to the old oak table and slid into my assigned seat, the one I'd been using since I was old enough to leave the high chair. I took a long swallow and wiped a trickle of sweat from the side of my face.

"The roof looks good," I said. "I thought finding someone familiar with those old materials would be difficult, especially with every contractor in this part of the state already up to their eyeballs in work. But those guys from Charleston did a great job."

I sometimes felt guilty about being what most people would term *wealthy,* but money certainly came in handy when you needed to get things done in a hurry.

She lifted the spoon to her lips, tasted, then added a little pepper and stirred again.

"Have you been up there lately?" I asked, my eyes lifting to the ceiling. "Is it drying out okay?"

Lavinia wiped her wrinkled brown hands on her apron and joined me at the table. "I haven't done a real good inspection," she said, her smile rueful. "It's hard for my old knees to navigate those stairs. I just poked my head up and looked around while the men from the church were covering the hole with plastic, right after the storm. A lot of rain came in. That'll be the biggest problem, but I think most of it's salvageable." She sighed, and the smile faded. "I don't even want to think about movin' all those boxes around and sortin' through everything."

"Red and I'll take care of that. You just keep us all fed."

"You're a good girl, Bay, honey," Lavinia said, moving back to the stove. "You hungry?"

"For gumbo? Always," I said, "as long as you don't mind if I dig the peas and okra out of it first."

We shared a grin, memories of my childhood pickiness a warm presence in the familiar kitchen.

"It won't be ready for another hour or so," she said. "I expect Redmond will be back with Julia and Lizzie by then."

I smiled at her use of Elizabeth Shelly's nickname. At first, when the idea of the three women's sharing Presqu'isle had been broached, the two had been leery, addressing each other formally and circling warily. I wondered if it had been the shared danger of the hurricane that had finally allowed them both to unbend. Lizzie and Julia had been living in a rundown old rice plantation outside of Jacksonboro on the road to Charleston, but Lizzie's advancing years and the exorbitant cost of Covenant Hall's upkeep had made sharing Presqu'isle the only reasonable solution. I knew there would be problems with two such strong-minded women inhabiting the same domain, but recent events had proved they could work together.

Over the course of the past week they'd been gradually moving in. My husband was carrying them and the last of their belongings to their new home. I'm not a religious woman by any means—a backsliding Episcopalian, truth to tell—but I sent up a silent prayer that my half sister and her caretaker would find peace and harmony in their new home.

"I'm going to check upstairs. Just see how bad it looks," I said, rising.

"You put shoes on, you hear me? No tellin' what kind of critters might be up there."

"Yes, ma'am," I said, heading toward the hallway. "I've got a pair of old sneakers in my room."

Julia's room, I corrected myself as I climbed to the second floor and retrieved the shoes from the back of the closet. Already the place felt alien, some of my half sister's clothes now hanging on the metal rod, her childish pink jewelry box sitting on the tall dresser. The sight of it made me sad. Though we were nearly of an age, Julia's mental development had been stunted when, at the age of ten, she'd witnessed her mother's tragic death. An unusual form of childhood post-traumatic stress disorder, or so my friend and psychologist Neddie Halloran had diagnosed. She'd been working with Julia for several months and was optimistic about my sister's progress. I hoped the disruption of moving to a new home wouldn't adversely affect her treatment.

I was pleased to see that Lavinia had installed a new duvet and bed skirt as well as fresh towels in the adjoining bath. My late mother had been a fanatic about not changing a thing in the antebellum mansion her ancestors had built and furnished, and Lavinia sometimes seemed to have absorbed the same resistance into her bones.

But these were new times, with new inhabitants. Up until a few months before, I hadn't even known of Julia's existence, or the bizarre circumstances that linked us by more than blood. She had suffered, as a child and as an adult, and I wanted this to be a chance for her to start over, to begin to live the life she'd been cheated out of.

I walked down the long hallway and climbed the narrow stairs that led to the unused third floor where the house servants had slept back in the day. Up three more steps at the rear, I pulled open the door to the attic. As a child, I'd avoided its dark recesses and trailing cobwebs. I'd never been the kind of kid who enjoyed being scared—no horror movies or creepy comic books. Strange then, I thought, that I'd chosen private investigation for my second career. Accounting and financial planning had been safe, if unexciting. Erik Whiteside, my partner in Simpson & Tanner, Inquiry Agents, didn't go looking for mayhem and murder, and neither did I. It was just that sometimes they found us anyway. My new husband, former sheriff's deputy Red Tanner, had recently joined the team.

I fumbled to locate the dangling string for the lightbulb that I knew hung just above my head. My fingers finally closed around it, and I pulled. The weak shimmer illuminated only a fraction of the vast expanse. At the far end, I could see the pale eyebrow of the dormer window, just below where the roof had disintegrated. Scuffling my feet in the dust to announce my presence to anything live and wriggly that might have taken refuge from the storm, I moved down the narrow aisle, tugging on strings as they came into view. In a short time, I had lighted my path from the stairway to the end of the house.

At the height of Kitty, a giant limb from one of the live oaks had crashed through the roof, taking wood and shingles with it. It had required a block and tackle—and a few hefty men—to dislodge it so that repairs could begin.

The driving rain had soaked one corner of the attic floor. A few cardboard boxes had crumbled under the onslaught, mostly old clothes from the looks of them. They smelled damp and musty and would need to be taken downstairs to air out before Lavinia and I decided if they were salvageable.

Immediately ahead of me a humpbacked trunk, the kind with the leather straps my ancestors once used for long journeys, lay tilted onto its side. The lid had partially popped open. As I bent to right it, my foot kicked something hard, and it skittered away.

I used the toe of my sneaker to feel for it, unwilling to stick my hand into the dust and debris. The weak overhead light revealed a book, covered in dark red leather. I brushed away a few dead leaves and picked it up.

The rain had soaked the cover, which was swollen and warped, and many of the pages appeared to be stuck together. No lettering on the outside, but it reminded me immediately of the journal my late mother and Lavinia always consulted when considering any rearrangement of the furniture, especially in the formal parlors and public rooms of our antebellum mansion. Lavinia still used it religiously every Christmas when placing the holiday decorations.

This looked different, though. Gingerly, I pried apart a few pages. Unlike the "decorating bible," this was filled with solid writing—no drawings or recipes—in a formal, ornate script with dated headings. The ink had faded to a pale brown.

A diary. I turned back to the front, but there was no name, no immediate way to identify the author. I set it aside and righted the tilted trunk. Tissue paper rustled in the heavy stillness of the attic as I lifted out a dress carefully wrapped. It had once been white but had yellowed to a soft butter color. Not a wedding dress, I thought as I laid it gingerly across a pile of storage cartons. It had a flapper look to it, like something out of the twenties, with lots of fringe and a beaded pattern across the bodice. There were more clothes, and I removed them with great care, revealing the treasure trove in the bottom of the trunk.

What looked to be a dozen or more of the red leather journals nestled on the water-spotted paper that lined its bottom. With a slightly trembling hand, I stacked them one by one on the floor next to my feet. As I looked around for something to carry them in, Lavinia's faint voice drifted up the stairs.

"Bay? Did you hear me?"

I wove my way around the boxes and discarded furniture to the open attic door.

"No, ma'am," I hollered.

"Telephone," she said. "It's Erik."

"Tell him I'll call him back."

"He said it's important."

"Damn," I muttered, the stack of diaries pulling at me like a magnet. I glanced once over my shoulder. "Okay, I'll be right there."

I laid the clothes back in the trunk and set the books gently on top, but I couldn't resist another quick look. I selected one at random and eased it open.

"Madeleine Henriette Baynard," I read aloud.

I glanced again at the open door before sighing and replacing the slim volume on top of the others. I'd just take Erik's call and come straight back. I closed the trunk and slid it off to the side. Its passage left a trail in the dust, and I was sure I'd have no trouble finding it again. I pulled light strings until the whole place was plunged once again into murky twilight.

I knew it was only my imagination, but I thought I heard a faint rustle of crinolines across the pine boards just as I pulled the door closed behind me.

"I was in the attic," I said breathlessly, having skipped down three flights of stairs.

"Sorry," my partner replied.

"No problem. I need the exercise. What's up?"

"I got a very interesting call a little while ago."

"Client?"

"Could be. Does the name Winston Wolfe mean anything to you?"

I thought a moment. "It does, but I'm not sure why. Is that who called?"

"Actually, his secretary. A woman named Melanie Hearst. From New York."

Erik loved forcing me to wring information out of him, drop by drop.

"Is it bigger than a breadbox?" I asked, and he laughed.

"Okay. Wolfe is an author. True crime. He's done books on the OJ trial, Klaus von Bülow, and a couple of serial killers whose names I don't remember."

"Of course. Not my cup of tea, literature-wise, but I know who he is. What does he want with us?"

Erik paused dramatically, and I was just about to demand he quit playing games when he said, "Morgan Tyler Bell."

CHAPTER TWO

HE GUY WHO DISAPPEARED?"

I stretched the phone cord out to its full length and slid down the wall onto the floor. I pulled my knees up and rested my elbows on them.

"Couple of years ago, right?" Erik asked.

"More than that, I think. I don't remember that much about the specifics." I had a vague recollection of the sensation that was thereafter referred to as *The Bell Incident.* In capital letters. It had dominated the local news media for a couple of months and had even attracted some national attention. I tried to remember which case I'd been embroiled in at the time and couldn't put my finger on it. Whatever it was, I had definitely been preoccupied with other things.

"I looked it up online. There were two guys, the millionaire weirdo and his assistant who both disappeared about the same time. There was something hinky about the whole thing. Housekeeper found dead, and neither one of the men anywhere in sight. At first, they thought it was murder—the housekeeper, I mean—but eventually they decided it was suicide. Want me to print out some of the stories?"

"Slow down. What exactly does this Wolfe character want with us?"

"He's writing a book about the case, and he needs someone on the ground here to help him with his research. He heard good things about us." He paused. "His assistant offered us a contract at fifty percent above our going rate."

I had to admit it was tempting. The office had been all but closed for the past two weeks. Everyone was involved in some sort of cleanup effort, whether minor or major, and the phone hadn't rung more than half a dozen times. Erik had been checking voice mail and the answering service and dropping in once a day just to make sure everything was under control. I'd been up to my neck in trying to organize the restoration of both my own house and Presqu'isle. Our only ongoing case, aside from the usual background checks we did for local governments, schools, and charities, had been the battered women's shelter in Beaufort, but that, too, had been put on hold. It was basically Erik's baby, and I knew he'd been doing some preliminary computer work, but that was about the extent of our current responsibilities. A good paying client would be hard to turn down.

"What do you think?" I asked.

"It can't hurt to talk to him."

"I agree. Do you want me to call, or will you set something up?" I lifted my head at the sound of crunching gravel. *Red.* "I can be in the office first thing tomorrow. Maybe a conference—"

"The thing is, he's coming into town today. Flying into Hilton Head in his own plane this afternoon. His assistant said he'd be in the office at three o'clock, if that was convenient."

I could feel the hairs on the back of my neck bristling. "Well, it isn't. I've been sloshing around in the yard and crawling through the attic all morning. I need to shower and change and get back to the island. Besides, Red is bringing Miss Lizzie and Julia in as we speak, and Lavinia has been planning this huge welcoming lunch, and . . ." I let my voice trail off.

I hated being dictated to by someone else, especially someone arrogant enough to set an appointment time and expect me to jump through his hoop. I guessed Winston Wolfe was famous in a way and probably used to everyone's dancing to his tune. Not a good way to begin a relationship. On the other hand, one and a half times our normal rate for an unspecified period of time was nothing to sneeze at. The excellent state of my personal finances meant that the profits I took out of the agency didn't have to put food on the table, but I wanted my business to stand on its own. Besides, Erik—and, to a certain extent, Red—did rely on it for a livelihood, and I owed it to them not to turn down work just because the prospective client rubbed me the wrong way.

I looked up as the front door burst open, and my half sister Julia skidded to a stop on the heart pine floor. The sheer delight on her face brought an answering smile to my own.

"I'll do my best," I said. "If I'm not there right at three, keep him occupied."

"Will do," my partner said, and I could hear the excitement bubbling just beneath his words.

I hoped we'd both be that happy when all was said and done.

My husband, on the other hand, was not happy about it at all. We worked a sort of bucket brigade line with the luggage until it had all been stowed in the appropriate rooms before Lavinia shooed us all out to the scarred oak table. The babble of conversation as we spooned up gumbo made the kitchen come alive in a way it hadn't for a long time. I sopped up the last of the broth in the bottom of my bowl with my third baking powder biscuit before announcing my need to get on the road.

There were cries of dismay, especially from Julia, but I noticed that her emotions were less mercurial, less likely to swing from one extreme to another, and my promise to return for dinner mollified everyone except Red. I excused myself from dessert, the smell of warm sweet potato pie drifting behind me as he followed me out onto the verandah.

"You don't want me in on this?"

Since he'd turned down the assistant chief's job in Walterboro the night of the hurricane, he'd seemed at loose ends. The storm had pushed our personal troubles onto the back burner, but they still simmered there. I knew I needed to give my marriage my full attention and find a way to make Red a true partner in my business. One of the reasons I was willing to consider Winston Wolfe's offer was that it would give my ex-sheriff's sergeant husband a chance to make a significant contribution. We both needed that.

I turned and wriggled myself into his arms. "Let me get the details ironed out. I'll call you as soon as I have him signed on the dotted line, and you can get to work. There'll be a lot of catching up to do on the original investigation, I'm guessing, and you've got exactly the right contacts to get the stuff that didn't make it into the papers. Come back to the island, and we can discuss it on our way back here. That way we'll have only one car to worry about."

I could feel the tension drain out of his body a moment before he kissed me—long and tenderly. We were headed back onto the right track, and I'd work like hell until we got there.

"Be careful," he said and swatted me on the butt as I headed for the steps. "Don't get dazzled by the big-time New York writer."

A month, even a couple of weeks before, I would have taken offense. I'd learned a few things about Red—and about myself—in the aftermath of the hurricane.

I smiled over my shoulder. "I'll try not to swoon at his feet," I said, and my husband laughed.

I turned out to be only a few minutes late. I pulled into the lot on that glorious October afternoon in the Lowcountry and eased my Jaguar in beside Erik's big Expedition. The air hung lightly, a soft breeze with just a hint of coolness in it ruffling the tops of the pines that surrounded the row of offices just outside the gates of Indigo Run. The sun still had warmth in it. Nothing, of course, like the blistering heat of July, but gentler, almost a caress on my upturned face.

I heard voices a moment before I pulled open the outer door. Erik turned from his desk in the reception area when I stepped inside.

"Here she is," he said to the older man, who rose from the wing chair that was the only other piece of furniture in the waiting area. "Bay, this is Winston Wolfe. My partner, Bay Tanner."

I held out my hand as I crossed the short stretch of gray carpet, and he took a couple of steps to close the distance. I noticed a beautiful leather briefcase beside the chair drawn up to Erik's desk. He had a firm grip, not bone-crushing, and his palm was cool and dry. In the few seconds I had to assess his face, I realized he was older than I'd expected, perhaps late fifties, and his shock of pure white hair and ramrod-straight stance made him seem almost regal. That hackneyed word, so beloved of political commentators, flashed through my head: the man had *gravitas*. Still, his smile seemed genuine if perhaps a tad forced, and a sharp, aquiline nose saved him from being handsome.

"Mr. Wolfe. It's a pleasure. Please, follow me."

I led the way into what I still thought of as my new office, although we'd been settled into the expanded space for a few months now. I felt a small flash of pride at its spaciousness and décor, especially my late father's antique mahogany desk and high-backed chair. Erik settled in with his laptop on his knees, and I indicated our guest should take one of the client chairs.

"Good of you to see me on such short notice," Wolfe said, dispelling some of the annoyance I'd voiced to Erik a couple of hours earlier.

"Not a problem, although we haven't been in the office on a regular basis. You may have heard about our brush with Hurricane Kitty. We've been a little busy putting ourselves back together."

"Read about it, of course," he said. "Terrible business."

I wondered if he wrote like he talked, in staccato bursts that seemed to ignore completely the use of subjects in his sentences. I hoped not, as I figured I'd need to snag at least one of his books from the library or the bookstore, and I guessed it could get downright aggravating after a couple of hundred pages. Even after only a few minutes, the practice was already starting to grate on my nerves.

"Yes, well, we're coming along. Your secretary indicated you're interested in engaging our services. Can you tell me exactly what it is you'd like us to do?"

"Of course. I knew Ty. Makes it doubly hard, but someone has to write his story, and the family has decided on me."

"You mean Mr. Bell?" Erik asked. "I didn't realize he had any family."

Wolfe turned his intent gaze on my partner, but he held his own. Erik had come a long way from the shy computer geek I'd first encountered on the Internet.

"Been reading up on the case. Good for you, Mr. Whiteside. I like initiative in my colleagues. Not close family—parents, siblings, children. No, just a cousin on his father's side, but he is, so far at least, the next of kin. Ty didn't leave a will, at least not one that's been found. Everything's been tied up. Part of the reason I want to write his story now. Harold wants to have him declared legally dead so they can settle the estate. Or he could still be alive somewhere. That'll be your job, to prove it one way or another." He sighed. "Hell of a man. Threw the most shocking parties. Maybe you heard."

My head was spinning, and I tried to sort through the jumble of information for the kernel. "You want our agency to investigate Mr. Bell's disappearance and prove whether he's alive or dead?" I leaned back in my chair, a lot of the wind slackening from my sails. "The local and state authorities, with all their power and experience, were unable to do that at the time of the disappearance. Why would you think we'd be any more successful all these years later?"

"Ah, exactly!"

He reached for the briefcase he'd carried in with him and opened it. He leafed through a couple of papers before extracting a single sheet and laying it in front of me.

It was a photocopy of a driver's license issued in Ohio. The picture was blurred, as if the subject had moved just at the moment the shutter snapped. A fairly young man, maybe in his late thirties or thereabouts. He had light brown hair, and his tanned face looked as if he spent a lot of time outdoors. The name read GERARD, TERENCE EDWARD with an address in Grafton, a town I'd never heard of.

I swung it around so that Erik could get a good look.

"I don't understand, Mr. Wolfe. Of what significance is this?"

He smiled. "Notice the expiration date, Mrs. Tanner."

Erik said, "September 5, 2013."

We exchanged a look, and I knew he was as bewildered as I a moment before I saw something register in his eyes.

"Wait a minute. Gerard." He typed furiously for a moment on the laptop. "I know I saw that name in—"

"Ty's PA. Personal assistant. Bodyguard, gofer, and general hanger-on," Wolfe said with no effort to hide the contempt in his voice. "Disappeared the same time Ty did."

Erik stopped typing. "Yes. They suspected him right off the bat, but they never found him, either."

"Suspected him of what?" I asked. "The housekeeper's death?"

I felt completely lost. I should have postponed the meeting, taken the time to familiarize myself with the old case. I not only felt like a fool, I was certain I looked like one in front of this elegant New York literary lion.

"No, that was suicide. Officially," Wolfe said. "Induced by grief. Everyone loved Ty."

"Then I don't understand the significance of this photo. Have you located this Gerard man? Is he implicated in Mr. Bell's disappearance?"

Wolfe smiled again, and I realized he loved dropping these tantalizing hints without really telling me anything. Maybe that made him a good crime writer, but it was annoying as hell as a conversational gambit. *He and Erik should start a club,* I thought.

"Oh, I don't think so, Mrs. Tanner."

Again he paused, and I resisted the urge to leap across the desk and throttle him. Instead, I gave him what he obviously craved: a rapt audience.

"And why is that, Mr. Wolfe?"

He tapped the photocopy. "Because this is not Terry Gerard." He glanced over at Erik and back to me. Once again he rapped his index finger against the likeness. "It's Ty Bell."

CHAPTER THREE

WINSTON WOLFE HAD RESERVED A SUITE AT THE Crowne Plaza in Shipyard Plantation and a driver for the duration of his stay on Hilton Head. He'd offered us a retainer in an amount that staggered both Erik and me and a scant two days to develop a game plan before our next meeting. He'd balked at a formal contract, and I'd let it slide before heading home to meet Red.

"Sounds to me as if you don't really want him for a client," my husband said from behind the wheel of my Jaguar S as we sped along Route 278 back toward Beaufort. "Is it the money?"

I'd barely had enough time to use the bathroom and run a brush through my hair before we'd had to get back on the road. Lavinia expected punctuality, especially for meals.

"Partly," I said.

I'd pretty much convinced myself to send Mr. *New York Times* Best Seller back to his penthouse in "the City," but he'd proved himself a pretty good negotiator. The more he talked about the case of the missing millionaire, the more intrigued I became. Snatches of memories, culled from conversations and brief glances at headlines in the *Island Packet* back when the disappearance occurred, had helped to reel me in.

I glanced at Red. The primary motivation had been that it was a case that my husband could sink his teeth into. Our strange courtship and brief marriage had always been punctuated by sharp words and conflicting agendas, especially when Red still worked for the sheriff's office. I smiled at the image of Mr. and Mrs. North from the old mystery novels I collected. Or maybe Nick and Nora Charles. We needed to work together, without the bickering and carping we'd grown accustomed to. I'd made a vow to myself to do everything in my power to keep our relationship from falling apart, and Winston Wolfe had provided me with an opportunity to put my plan into action.

"What else?" Red felt me watching him and turned his head in my direction. "I Googled him when I got home. He's pretty famous. Are you sure that didn't have anything to do with it?"

I punched his arm. "Too smooth for my taste," I said with a grin. "Seriously, though, I need to do a lot of reading before we formulate an approach. Do you remember much about the original investigation into Bell's disappearance?"

He shook his head. "Most of that took place on the detective level. Way over my pay grade. Everyone involved was under orders not to gossip about the investigation. Papers and TV news people from all over the country were crawling around the story early on. The sheriff even held a couple of televised press conferences."

We exchanged a smile. Our longtime sheriff was not noted for his love affair with the media. He preferred tersely worded press releases, prepared by his spokespeople, to the give-and-take of a live briefing. He was smart and competent, but his jowly face and gravelly voice didn't lend themselves well to live media.

"Anyone still around who might be willing to share some insights?"

We took the ramp onto 170, and a lot of the rush hour traffic abated. Red relaxed back into the driver's seat.

"Lisa Pedrovsky," he said. "Ben Wyler might have been involved, too."

I shivered. Ben, a former New York City homicide detective, had been attached to the Beaufort County Sheriff's Office before being wounded on the job by a bullet meant for me. He had joined Simpson & Tanner, Inquiry Agents as a silent partner until his death on the deck of a boat in a small marina south of Amelia Island. He'd died saving Erik's life. And now Ben's daughter Stephanie and my partner were engaged to be married. Life works in strange ways sometimes.

"Pedrovsky wouldn't spit on me if I was on fire," I said, and Red laughed.

"I'm not her favorite ex-cop, either. Let me scout around and see who else might be willing to talk. There's always turnover in the department. Maybe I can find a disgruntled former employee."

"Wolfe would pay, I'll bet. Money doesn't seem to be one of his problems."

"What *are* his problems?"

I thought about it while Red maneuvered us through the traffic in downtown Beaufort and over the bridge to Lady's Island.

"Well, he's arrogant, but I guess he's entitled. I think every one of his books has been a huge bestseller, although Erik said he hadn't done anything lately. And he has this irritating habit of beginning all his sentences with verbs."

Red laughed. "That's it?"

"I don't know," I said, my mood darkening. "I don't think I trust him, not entirely. And I can't say exactly why."

We fell silent then, rolling over the causeway onto St. Helena Island. Neither of us spoke again until we were bouncing along the rutted Avenue of Oaks that led to Presqu'isle.

"How do you think this is all going to work out?" Red asked, startling me out of deep thought.

"I have no idea. It's early times yet."

"No, sorry. Not the case. I was thinking about Julia and Miss Lizzie. And Lavinia."

"I don't know. But they're going to have to figure it out. Some conservancy or other is making a bid for Covenant Hall. Elizabeth said they hope to raise funds to restore it and open it to the public. She sold off a lot of the old furniture and moved some of the antiques down here. They're in storage for now." I thought about the attics I'd been picking through that morning and wondered where they'd find room for more castoffs. I also made a mental note to retrieve the diaries I'd run across and stuffed back in the trunk when Erik called. I sighed. "So anyway, I think they're pretty much stuck with each other. I hope they're all prepared to make the best of it."

Red wheeled into the semicircular drive in front of the antebellum mansion where I had spent my less than idyllic childhood. So much had changed. So many people who had played pivotal roles in my life were gone. As if reading my mind, Red reached across and squeezed my hand.

"Ready?" he said, sliding out of the car.

"In for a penny," I muttered under my breath and unconsciously squared my shoulders as I mounted the first of the sixteen steps.

The force knocked me back into Red the moment I pulled open the heavy oak door. Before I realized what was happening, sharp nails dug into my shoulders, and a rough tongue was scraping against my face.

"Rasputin! No! Bad dog! Sit!"

My sister Julia tugged at the collar, and the slobbering beast dropped onto his haunches, huge brown eyes still fixed on me as if I were a hunk of meat. My mind flashed back to another place and another time, when the animal in question had been intent on separating my flesh from my bones, and I shivered.

"I'm sorry, Bay. He won't hurt you, honest he won't. He loves everyone, don't you, you big baby?"

She hugged the massive head and planted kisses on its droopy ears.

Behind me, Red laughed. "Is that why you named him Rasputin? Because he's so lovable?"

Elizabeth Shelly appeared in the entryway. "I told you to keep him outside, Julia." The stern look on her face matched her voice. "If you can't control him, he's going to have to go back to the Brawleys'."

The other two dogs that had roamed freely around the grounds of Covenant Hall had been adopted by a neighbor.

"Sorry," my sister said, and I cringed at her cowering demeanor as she led the dog away, its long tail twitching from side to side.

"He really is harmless," Elizabeth said, standing aside so we could enter.

A wave of something like resentment washed over me, and I pushed it away. Yes, Presqu'isle was my house, deeded over to me by my father on my fortieth birthday, but it was silly to feel like a visitor just because this strange, often hostile woman held the door open. Times had changed. I forced myself to smile.

"He just startled me is all," I said, thinking what a bloody, screaming fit my mother would have thrown to have that galumphing half-breed animal even drawing breath among her treasured antiques, its claws scratching across her original heart pine floors.

"Part Lab, is he?" Red asked.

"I suppose," Elizabeth said. "He wandered up to the Hall, half starved and limping. Not much more than a pup at the time. That's how we came by all the animals, except the horses."

I spared a moment of thanks that neither Miss Lizzie nor Julia had insisted on bringing them along, too.

From the kitchen, the smell of roasting chicken wafted out, and we trooped in that direction. A moment later Julia joined us, her head bowed so that I found myself staring at the top of her gray-streaked hair.

"I'm sorry, Bay. Rasputin just wanted to say hello. I know he's sorry if he scared you."

Before I could answer, Elizabeth spoke harshly. "You can't let him have the run of the house, Julia. We talked about this before we came. He's an outside dog. Miss Lavinia's friends have made a nice home for him in the back. He needs to stay there."

"Yes, ma'am. I'm sorry." My sister sounded very near to tears.

"It's okay," I said, draping my arm across her shoulder. "We'll get acquainted after dinner." I leaned closer and whispered in her ear. "Maybe we'll sneak some leftover chicken out to him."

"Everyone sit down," Lavinia said without turning from the stove. "I just need to dish up the potatoes, and we're ready to eat. Bay, will you get the gravy boat, please?"

I moved to the china cupboard while Red held chairs for the two women who had now become a part of our family. I glanced sideways at Lavinia, a thin line of perspiration glistening on her forehead.

"You okay?" I asked softly, my voice muffled by the scraping of chairs.

She knew exactly what I meant. "It'll be fine," she murmured. "Just take a little gettin' used to. For all of us."

I patted her shoulder as I set the piece of china on the counter. "I know. You're a good woman, Lavinia Smalls."

Her smile accentuated the wrinkles in her warm brown face as she turned toward the table. "All right, everyone, let's eat. Redmond, will you carve?"

We had lingered over coffee and tea, and Julia and I did manage to sneak a few scraps out to Rasputin, who seemed to be contented in the refurbished run and kennel my father had originally constructed for his bird and hunting dogs. I wasn't certain how the ghosts of Hootie and Beulah would feel about sharing their space with this interloper. But, like the women of Presqu'isle, I figured they'd just have to work it out.

Stuffed with apple turnovers and ice cream, Red and I left them to it shortly after eight and headed back to Hilton Head. Almost as soon as we'd cleared the driveway, I pulled out the sheaf of papers I'd carried from the office and flipped on the reading light on the passenger side of the Jaguar. My husband tuned the radio to a classical music station and settled into silence.

Erik had done his usual excellent job of research. Winston Wolfe had provided nothing more than the copy of the driver's license photo, although he'd hinted at more to come. Nothing had been culled or collated, so the data was coming at me in disjointed bits and pieces. I'd need to get it organized in some logical fashion before I could begin to draw any conclusions, but the basics were pretty stark and clear.

Morgan Tyler Bell had purchased Jericho Cay, an uninhabited island just off the coast of Hilton Head, from the estate of a local man who'd always intended to develop it into a golf resort, like those on Daufuskie. Finances, the economy, permits—whatever the reason, nothing had ever come of it. The heirs simply wanted it gone, and Bell had negotiated himself a pretty good deal.

He promptly set about constructing a home, a sprawling affair with numerous wings and strange angles, nothing like the multistoried, dormered architecture that dominated the Lowcountry. Those few who'd seen it called it a monstrosity of glass and steel that would have felt more at home in Manhattan than on a remote, wooded island off the coast of South Carolina.

There was mention of the parties Wolfe had referred to, speculation about high-powered businessmen and Hollywood types flying in for what some reports called orgies. There were even hints that some of the guests might have spent their time operating on the wrong side of the law. The fact that no one local had ever been invited seemed to stoke the rumor mill and no doubt engendered the nasty tone of some of the articles. Ty Bell had kept himself secluded on his private island, and the Lowcountry resented his lack of hospitality.

"Finding anything interesting?" Red's voice broke the spell.

"It's all a jumble at this point. Long on gossip and innuendo and short on facts—at least about Bell's life on Jericho Cay. I'm just getting to his disappearance."

"I remember the department didn't have many other priorities once they discovered he was missing."

"How did that happen? I mean, it sounds as if he didn't fraternize with the locals much. Who reported it?"

"A boat captain. Bell had supplies delivered every week. Stuff was left on the dock on Jericho, and they came out and collected it once the boat had gone. Captain came back to find the previous delivery still sitting there. He's the one who called the sheriff, best I can recall."

I flipped through a few more pages until Red made the turn into Port Royal Plantation. The security guard waved us through, and I straightened the pile of printouts and stuffed them back into my briefcase.

"I guess we know what I'll be doing for the rest of the night," I said, patting the rich calfskin case.

"We can split them up," my husband said, hitting the garage door opener as he swung into the driveway.

I was relieved to see that the workmen had finished up. Except for a thin line around the drywall that showed the high-water mark of the storm surge, the place was back to normal.

"I think I need to read it all. Maybe we could work out an assembly line. I'll get it organized, then read and pass it on to you."

Red flung his arm across my shoulders as we climbed the steps into the house. "Sounds like a plan. I'll make coffee." He peeled off toward the kitchen as I headed for the bedroom. "You want tea?"

"A gallon or so ought to do it," I called over my shoulder.

I changed into sweats and carried the briefcase across the hall into the third bedroom Rob and I had used as an office back in the day when I was his unofficial partner in his work for the state attorney general's office, tracking the flow of drug money into and out of South Carolina. I smiled to myself, remembering many evenings like this, when Red's older brother and I had settled in for an all-nighter. Of course that had been before his small plane exploded on takeoff, raining hot metal down on me and changing my life forever. A lot of people had looked askance when I'd married my former brother-in-law, and I had to admit it had taken me a while to get used to the idea. But Red loved me, and I cared deeply for him. It might take a little more effort than most relationships, but we were working at it.

I dropped onto the floor and set the stack of papers beside me. I decided to segregate anything having to do with the disappearance from the general background material, then sort through each of those stacks to get to the meat of the information. In moments I was engrossed in the task, looking up when Red appeared in the doorway. He carried a mug in each hand, and he, too, had changed into sweatpants and one of his ratty old Marine Corps T-shirts. He set the cups on the desk and squatted down beside me.

"How's it going?"

I pushed one of the stacks in his direction. "Can you put these in chronological order? They're not all dated, but do the best you can."

"Aye, aye, captain," he answered with a grin, handing over the steaming tea.

I set it beside me and continued sorting. "Does anyone know where this guy got his money?"

"No clue. It's probably in here somewhere."

"You don't remember anything from around town—rumor, gossip, supposition?"

"Nope. He wasn't a big topic of conversation, at least not until he disappeared. Oh, people asked about Jericho, mostly because of all the signs he had posted out there. No Trespassing. Private Property. Beware the Dogs. That kind of thing. I heard he even had a rolling dock, the kind you can swing back and secure on shore. To keep out the riffraff, I guess. Visitors who passed the island on those dolphin watch and sunset dinner cruises would get curious, but there wasn't much to tell them. We've got our own eccentrics, in case you haven't noticed. I guess folks just figured he didn't want to be bothered and left it at that."

When the phone rang, I glanced at the clock over the desk, surprised to see it was already after eleven. Red and I exchanged a look, and he rose to answer. My experience is that calls that late at night usually don't bring good news.

"Hello?" my husband said.

I watched his face for some sign, and my heart turned over when he frowned.

"Yes, sir. Good to hear from you."

I waited for him to enlighten me, but he looked away. I levered myself to my feet and went to stand beside him. I laid a hand on his shoulder, but he ignored me.

"Who is it?" I mouthed, and he shook his head.

"My wife did, yes. . . . No, sir, not that I'm aware of. . . . I see. I guess we could do that. What time?"

I fidgeted, and Red held up a hand.

"Ten will be fine. . . . Uh-huh, sure. . . . Okay. See you then."

He set the phone back in its cradle.

"What's going on?"

Red turned slowly to face me. "I wish to hell I knew. That was the sheriff."

"Is someone hurt? Was there an accident or—"

"No, nothing like that. He wants to see me. Us. Tomorrow at ten."

"Why?"

"He wants to know what the hell we're doing poking around in Ty Bell's disappearance."

CHAPTER
FOUR

$\mathscr{T}$HE CALL FROM THE SHERIFF EFFECTIVELY HALTED
work for the night. Red and I carried our mugs to the kitchen,
refilled them, and by unspoken agreement settled onto the sofa in the
great room. The air had grown chilly, and we briefly toyed with light-
ing a fire, but neither of us had the energy to deal with it.

"This reminds me of getting called into the principal's office," my
husband said, and I smiled.

Not too long before, Red's son Scotty had been involved in an
incident on the school bus that had necessitated his father's occupying
one of the hard, uncomfortable chairs at the middle school while he
pled the boy's case. He'd said then it had a familiar feel.

"I wouldn't know," I replied.

"You were one of those goody-two-shoes girls, the kind that never
got in trouble, weren't you?"

I laughed. "Oh, please! No, my claim to fame is that I rarely got
caught."

We let the silence settle over us again for a few moments.

"I don't like the idea of having to report to the sheriff. As far as I
know, they haven't done a thing with the investigation into Bell's dis-

appearance in a long time. It's not as if we're stepping on an open case," I said, snuggling down against the warmth of Red's body. "And besides, he doesn't have any right to order us around."

"Don't get yourself all worked up about it," my husband said. "He didn't *order* us to do anything. He asked—very nicely—if we could spare him a few moments to discuss things. Don't go in there with a chip on your shoulder."

He had a point. A moment later, I stretched and stood. "I should get back to reading through all that material. As long as we're going to have the ear of the guy who ran the original investigation, I'd like to be able to ask some semi-intelligent questions."

Red stood and took my hand. "It's not going to do you much good. You know the sheriff. I have a feeling the questions are only going to run in one direction."

I snapped off the lights, and we walked down the hallway toward the bedroom.

"We'll see about that," I said, half to myself, as I stepped into the bathroom.

We stopped briefly at the office to let Erik know what was going on.

"How did he even know we'd been hired to look into Bell's disappearance?" he asked as we all sipped our morning offerings from Starbucks around the desk in my office.

"One of the first questions on my list," I answered, earning a frown from Red.

"I wonder if Mr. Wolfe made a stop at the substation. It would be natural for him to want to interview the detectives involved," my partner said.

"Maybe. It would be good to know that."

"I'll call him," Erik said, pulling his iPhone from his pocket. He rose and wandered back into the reception area.

"You were up early," my husband said and pointed at my briefcase. "Reading?"

"Skimming," I said. I'd barely had enough time to get showered and dressed, and my stomach was growling in protest at having missed breakfast.

"Find out anything of importance?"

"Just more details, mostly from the newspaper accounts. A year after Bell disappeared, the *Packet* did a sort of retrospective of the case. That's going to be very helpful, having it all laid out in one place. There's even a time line." I looked up as Erik came back into my office.

"No answer in his room," he said, "and his cell is going to voice mail."

"Keep trying," I said, dropping my empty cardboard cup in the wastebasket, "and call me if you reach him."

Red stood and downed the last of his coffee. "Let's get this over with," he said, the first sign he'd given that he might be nervous about facing his former boss.

" 'Once more unto the breach, dear friends, once more,' " I quoted. "Shakespeare. *Henry the Fifth.*"

Both men smiled. My late father had invented the game, with points awarded for a complete citation, and we had often astounded both my husband and my partner with our joint ability to recall obscure passages. Meddling and cantankerous though he'd been, the Judge had dominated my life even into adulthood, and I missed him terribly.

As Red and I walked out into the cool October morning, preparing to face what would undoubtedly be the wrath of the sheriff of Beaufort County, I remembered my father's oft-repeated advice: *They can't roll over you if you don't lie down.*

"Let's go grab a cup of coffee over at Java Joe's. The stuff we cook up here isn't fit for human consumption."

The tall, rawboned sheriff gripped my upper arm, gently, and steered me back out the door we'd just entered. The substation on Pope Avenue was small and crowded with a couple of reporters studying the overnight crime sheets and deputies either delivering miscreants or checking in for assignments.

Red followed us out, and the sheriff dropped his hand. My husband and I exchanged a glance as we made our way across Lagoon Road to the island staple that had recently moved from inside Coligny Plaza. The chief law officer of Beaufort County insisted on buying, and I found a seat at a table in the far corner. At midmorning on a weekday after tourist season, we had the place almost to ourselves.

Red set the iced tea in front of me and took the chair on my left. He scooted it around a little until our shoulders were almost touching, a united front I was certain wasn't lost on the sheriff when he placed his coffee on the table and sat down.

"Now what the Sam Hill are you up to, Ms. Tanner?"

Known for his down-home speech and direct manner, the sheriff's good-ol'-boy façade concealed a sharp mind and a tenacious dedication to the welfare of his county and its inhabitants, both permanent and transitory.

We'd decided on the short drive over that I would take the lead. The agency had my name on it, and rumor had it that Red's resignation hadn't sat well with his boss. I leaned back in my chair and gave him my most dazzling smile.

"We're working for our client, Sheriff. It would be unethical for me to go into details, but he's interested in the Morgan Tyler Bell disappearance. We're basically doing local research into the case. Is that a problem?"

His deep brown eyes, locked onto mine, told me he wasn't buying my attempt to fob him off with generalities. "So I hear. This Wolfe character has a reputation for trying to make local law enforcement look like incompetent hicks. He's done it before. That what you're aimin' to help him do?"

"No, sir. I don't have a lot of recollection of the details, but I've read up on it. It seems to me your office did everything by the book. I don't see how he could portray you and the detectives otherwise."

That seemed to mollify him a little. He eased his considerable bulk against the back of the chair, and some of the frown lines in his weathered face smoothed out. "Good. That's good. Everything we got is public record, except for a couple of details we hung on to, in case we had to use them to confront a suspect." He sighed, and some of the wrinkles reappeared. "Hated like the devil to let it go cold, but there just wasn't anywhere else to go on it. Sticks in my craw. It's the only major unsolved case since I got elected."

His eyes narrowed, and I squirmed a little under his scrutiny.

"If you or this Wolfe guy come across anything I should know about, I expect to hear from you."

I straightened my shoulders and held his gaze without flinching, although the memory of the Ohio driver's license—with Bell's picture on it, according to Wolfe—made it more difficult. "Of course, Sheriff. That goes without saying. Any chance of taking a look at the official file?"

His snort ruffled the graying hairs on his bushy mustache. "I got a lot of respect for you, Bay, don't think otherwise. You got a good head on your shoulders, and I knew your daddy from the time he was on the bench, so I'm sure he taught you about doin' the right thing. But I'm gonna have to say no to that request."

He did sound almost sorry, or maybe that was just part of his aw-shucks persona.

Red finally spoke up. "How about if we examine the file in your office, without removing it? We could sign a nondisclosure agreement, if that would help smooth the way. It might keep us from blundering into areas you'd rather we stayed out of."

Way to go, Red, I said to myself, but the sheriff was having none of it.

"Sorry to lose you, son," he said, fixing my husband with his direct gaze, "but I understand you might prefer workin' alongside this pretty woman instead of having to look at my ugly puss every day." He stood and settled his gun belt more easily against his hips. Despite his bulk, there wasn't an ounce of fat on him. "Thanks for coming in. I do appreciate your time. Ma'am," he added, touching his finger to his forehead in an informal salute. "Keep in mind what I said."

With a wave to the young woman behind the counter, he ambled out into the sunshine.

"I think the guy watches too many *Andy Griffith* reruns," I said as we climbed into the Jaguar, and Red laughed.

"He does kind of overdo that country bumpkin routine sometimes, but don't underestimate him. He's as shrewd and sharp as they come."

"I know. He didn't exactly tell us to buzz off, though, did he?"

Red pulled out onto Pope Avenue and headed us back toward the office. "And that's significant. He'd never say it out loud, but he'd be happy to be able to resolve this case. And he's not above using us to get there."

"That's fine by me. As long as Winston Wolfe is willing to foot the bill."

I retrieved my cell phone from my bag and speed-dialed Erik. "Hey, we're on the way back. Did you get hold of our client?"

"Nope. I left another voice mail. How'd it go with the sheriff?"

I gave him an expurgated version of the morning's events.

"So he won't help, but he won't try to keep us from investigating, either?"

"That's it in a nutshell," I said.

"You tell him about the driver's license?"

"Nope," I parroted him. "Listen, I'd like to get out there. To Jericho Cay. Can you track down someone to take us? Maybe try Ron Singleton, see if his boat's still operating."

The excursion boat business pretty much died after Labor Day, but Ron had helped us out when we were investigating the grisly murders on Judas Island. He claimed he owed a debt to the Judge, something to do with his mother. That might have been canceled with my father's death, but I was certain Winston Wolfe's deep pockets would be willing to pick up the tab for a quick run to Jericho. I turned when Red tapped my shoulder.

"How about I call my old Marine buddy, Dave Reading? You know, the guy I was going to go into business with."

I shuddered, remembering the blazing row over those plans, which had ended with Red's storming out of the house, clothes and all.

"Let's try Ron first," I said.

"I'll get on it," Erik said. "Should we invite Mr. Wolfe along?"

"Sure, if you can reach him. We'll grab lunch and be back in the office by noon. You want us to bring you something?"

"Surprise me," my partner said. "I'll keep trying our client."

I had no reason to be concerned about Winston Wolfe or his whereabouts, but our inability to make contact sent a niggling little shiver up my back.

CHAPTER FIVE

HE PHONE RANG JUST AS I HAD FINISHED STACKING
the Styrofoam containers from the Chinese takeout place.
Erik picked up, then covered the receiver with his hand.

"It's our long-lost client." He hit the Hold button. "On one."

The knot in my stomach loosened. "Mr. Wolfe, thanks for calling
back. There've been a couple of developments."

"I understand you got taken to the woodshed by your illustrious
sheriff," he said in that slightly nasal, aristocratic accent that always
reminded me of Ben Wyler.

I laughed. "For a stranger in these parts, you certainly have a
great pipeline."

"I know you're accustomed to the power of money, Bay. And of
influence. I don't have much use for either except as tools to get me
what I want. I trust the gentleman wasn't too hard on you."

I didn't know whether to be irritated or amused. I also noticed that
Wolfe had suddenly turned loquacious, actually speaking in complete
sentences. I wondered why. "You've met?"

"Oh, yes. I stopped in yesterday to pay my respects. I've found it's
always good to establish the ground rules right up front. I told him

you'd be working for me on the investigation, so I fully expected him to haul you in for a good talking-to."

"I wish I'd known that," I said, fighting to keep the asperity in my voice to a minimum.

"I had every confidence you could hold your own," my client said flippantly. "Was there something else?"

I took a deep breath and reminded myself he was paying one-and-a-half times our going rate. "I've arranged for us to visit Jericho Cay. I know you've been there before, but I need to get a feel for the place. I've studied most of the newspaper reports, but I'd prefer to form my own impressions of the scene. Would you care to join us?"

"You'll need keys to the house. Fortunately, I obtained a set from the trustees before I came south." He paused. "Yes, I think I'd like to see the place again, although it holds nothing but sad memories for me." The sigh sounded genuine. "Poor Ty."

"We'll be leaving from Palmetto Bay Marina on the south end of the island at three this afternoon. Shall we pick you up?"

"My driver can find it. Or I could rent a helo. Have us there in no time."

"The boat transport's all arranged. If you have no objection."

"Fine, fine. Three, you say? Try to make it. No guarantees. Got some irons in the fire I need to pursue. I'll send my driver with the keys if I get held up."

"I'll look forward to seeing you."

Red and Erik looked at me expectantly.

"That guy is seriously weird," I said. "Anyway, he'll get us the keys to the house." A thought struck. "I wonder how it's managed to stay all in one piece, assuming it has. It sounds like the perfect place for kids to take over and destroy just for the fun of it. Any idea if it's still intact?"

Erik spoke first. "Ron Singleton told me they removed the dock. There's no good place to beach a small boat—too many rocks. Ron said he'd bring us in close to where the old landing was and use his gangplank to get us ashore." He glanced at my low-heeled pumps and black silk slacks. "You might want to change. Ron said we'll likely get wet."

We agreed to close down the office, change into something more appropriate, and rendezvous at the marina. I picked up my briefcase and checked to make certain I had all the papers we'd accumulated on the disappearance of Morgan Tyler Bell. I wanted to be able to envision just where all the players were when the housekeeper died and Terry Gerard followed his employer into the ether.

"Before we go," Erik said, "I want to talk a little about the battered women's shelter case. I feel as if I need to get back on it, and I talked briefly to Mary Jefferson, the director, this morning. The hurricane sort of put everything on hold. They had some damage, but nothing serious, and she's ready for me to try and track down these guys who've been harassing and threatening her clients."

"Understood," I said, slinging my bag over my shoulder. "You can skip this excursion if you want to—if you feel that needs your attention."

"It can wait until tomorrow. I know we need to get a game plan ready for Mr. Wolfe by then, too."

We trooped out, and Red locked the door behind us.

"If you can hold off until the first of the week, we should be in good shape. Red and I can take the point on this while you work with Ms. Jefferson."

"Sounds like a plan," my partner said as we split up and climbed into our vehicles.

I glanced at Red while he maneuvered out of the parking lot. "I'm getting kind of stoked about this case," I said. "I hope we can stay with it."

My husband didn't answer my smile. "You might want to be careful what you wish for," he said, and we both lapsed into silence.

The stretch Rolls-Royce looked entirely out of place sitting next to the dock in the small marina. The windows were tinted almost completely opaque, but I knew it had to belong to Winston Wolfe. We paused alongside, and the driver's door opened. I half expected to see someone in livery snap smartly to attention as he moved to the rear of the luxurious vehicle. Instead, a young woman in a crisp white shirt and black slacks smiled up at us a moment before the man himself slid out onto the pavement through the door she held open.

"Thank you, Brenda," Wolfe said. "I'll need you back here at . . ." He turned to me. "How long do you think this will take?"

I shrugged. "A couple of hours, I'd guess. I want to be back before dark."

"Be here at five. You may have to wait, but I need to leave the moment we're back on shore."

"No problem, Mr. Wolfe. Enjoy your trip."

She was blond and pretty, and her smile encompassed us all before she climbed back into the car. We watched her maneuver the big Rolls around and head back toward the main road.

"Lovely girl," Wolfe said. "And very knowledgeable about the island."

I controlled the urge to snort. I was pretty sure it wasn't Brenda's geography that had our client grinning like a schoolboy.

We moved down the narrow walkway single file to find Ron Singleton waiting for us. He'd maneuvered his excursion boat in at the far end of the small dock. After exchanging greetings and introductions, we followed him up the gangplank.

Erik, Red, and I took seats along the railing in the bow, but our client headed straight for the interior salon.

"The sun and I are not on the best of terms," he announced before stepping over the raised threshold and disappearing inside.

The engines rumbled, and the boat began backing away from the dock. The three of us exchanged a look, and I burst into laughter.

"I know," my husband said, glancing quickly over his shoulder to make certain we couldn't be overheard. "Do you believe that getup? Reminds me of the guy on that old TV show about being shipwrecked, remember?"

"Gilligan's Island," Erik supplied. "Where on earth did he find a hat like that? I can't believe he brought it with him from New York."

Our client did indeed look like Thurston Howell III, the Jim Backus character, complete with white slacks and ascot. "It's a yachting cap. I'm sure they sell them somewhere around here." I checked my own baggy cotton pants, old sneakers, and faded Northwestern sweatshirt. "No wonder he doesn't want to be seen with us."

Red stood and moved to the rail. "I wouldn't be surprised if he's got bearers and a litter waiting over there so he doesn't have to get his feet wet."

We watched Ron Singleton gain enough room to turn his boat and head us out toward Calibogue Sound. We slid past Brams Point in Spanish Wells with its multimillion dollar mansions, and my thoughts jumped to Bitsy Elliott, my best friend since childhood. Her home lay on the other side of the peninsula, and I wondered if I'd ever step foot inside of it again. My stomach churned at the thought of her negligent betrayal of my trust and at the confrontation looming on the horizon as a result. Red had cautioned me to wait, to let the hurt and anger settle a little. I almost blessed the hurricane that had kept us all so busy I hadn't had time to think too much about it.

"Buck Island," my husband said, turning back to where I sat lost in thought.

Ron turned us to the northeast, and the privately owned speck of land glided by. I wondered what it felt like to be master of your own kingdom, to be cut off completely from any connection to the mainland except by boat. I moved over to the port side to get a closer look.

It didn't appear as if the storm had done much damage. I knew there was a house there, but the screening palms and thick foliage still wrapped it in secrecy. Maybe that was the allure, I thought, the feeling that you were safe and unassailable.

It hadn't worked out too well for Morgan Tyler Bell.

I shivered a little in the cool breeze off the water and lifted my face to the sun. A few minutes later, I felt the beat of the engines slow and opened my eyes to see another island growing larger in front of me. Unlike Buck, this one looked as if the vegetation had completely retaken what man had destroyed. I knew there had to have been at least one road to the interior, but only an impenetrable wall of green faced me as Ron eased back on the throttle. Red and Erik joined me at the rail.

"Wow, maybe we should have brought machetes," my partner said.

"This might turn out to be a fool's errand," I replied.

Over the side, the fading afternoon light slanted into the water, revealing the stubs of dock pilings as we eased nearer to the shore. I jumped when Winston Wolfe spoke at my shoulder.

"How sad," he said, and I heard genuine regret in his voice. "It used to be so beautiful here."

It still was, at least to my eyes, but I didn't comment.

Ron maneuvered his ungainly boat close to the shoreline and dropped anchor. "This could take a little doin'," he said, speaking directly to me. "Looks to me like a lot of the water from the storm is still standin' close to shore. You folks are gonna get wet."

I glanced back at Winston Wolfe, resplendent in his yachtsman's outfit. "You might want to stay on board, sir. If you'll give me the keys, I'm sure we can find our way."

"Nonsense."

As Ron lowered the gangplank at a sharp angle toward the soggy shore, one of America's premier literary talents worked off his shoes and rolled his pants up to the knees. I glanced away from his nearly hairless legs, white and pasty as if they hadn't been exposed to the sun in decades.

"About as good as I can do," Ron said, eyeing his efforts, and I moved over to join him at the break in the rail.

I checked my watch. "It's three-forty now. We'll be back in an hour. That okay with you?"

A wide grin creased his whiskered brown face. "Take your time." He tilted his head toward the comic spectacle of Winston Wolfe. "I'm gettin' paid by the hour."

I patted his shoulder and returned his smile. "Okay. Thanks." To the rest of the landing party I said, "Ready?"

"I'll lead the way," Wolfe said and stepped out onto the gangway.

I pulled a notebook out of my bag and clipped a pen onto the spine. I saw Erik transfer his phone from his pants to his shirt pocket. Carrying our shoes, we trooped behind our leader down the metal walkway, the end of which had disappeared into the muck.

I had a sudden image of General Douglas MacArthur from World War II, wading ashore in the Philippines to flashbulbs and newsreel cameras. The only reception our little landing party received was the feel of cold pluff mud on our ankles and the startled screeching of hundreds of birds as they lifted in a multicolored cloud into the waning afternoon sun.

In spite of its warmth, I shivered.

CHAPTER SIX

ERIK WASN'T TOO FAR WRONG ABOUT THE MACHETES. The road—more a sandy path, really—was overgrown and nearly impassable in places.

We followed Wolfe through dense foliage that at times made it seem more like twilight than afternoon. He had stopped once we were clear of the soggy marsh to slide his bony feet back into his boat shoes, and the rest of us did the same. With the departure of the birds, the place had assumed a humming silence, the presence of insects heard but not seen. I wondered if I should have included some bug repellant, but it was too late to worry about it.

We'd gone about a hundred yards when his voice startled me.

"Damn shame! Plenty of money in the trust to keep this place decently cared for."

Wolfe seemed to be talking more to himself than to us, and Red and I exchanged a look. I wondered how the writer knew so much about Ty Bell's finances. He'd said there wasn't a will, so how could there be a trust for the care of the island? I filed the questions away for later and trudged on down the path. Here and there we encountered small pools of standing water—remnants of Kitty's passage, I guessed—but for the most part it was much easier going than I'd anticipated.

A few minutes later I began to detect what must once have been formal gardens. Although nature had retaken most of the land on either side of the road, I could tell that some semblance of order had once ruled here. I spotted a row of scraggly rosebushes almost swallowed by some sort of trailing vine, and here and there were patches of bright green that might once have been a lawn. So intent had I been on swiveling my head from side to side that I nearly ran our guide down when he stopped abruptly right in front of me.

I put out a hand to steady myself and looked over his shoulder. I didn't gasp, but it was a near thing.

The glass was filthy, of course, pocked with dirt driven hard by other storms over the years the house had stood empty. Still, there were a few places where the late afternoon sun glinted off the massive walls, and it wasn't hard to imagine it all clear and shining on a brilliant summer day. The support beams were metal, but they had weathered into the color of the trunks of the live oaks that bent lovingly over the roof so that the whole structure seemed to float unaided in the soft Lowcountry breeze off the water. Jericho's location on the leeward side of Hilton Head must have offered it a degree of protection, from Kitty as well as from other perils.

Red and Erik had moved up to stand on either side of me, and I could tell by their silence that they were as struck as I was by the crystal palace, in spite of the incongruity of its design and materials.

"I can't believe it's all in one piece," I said, breaking the spell.

No one replied, but Winston Wolfe shook himself and strode purposefully onto another path, this one lined with crushed oyster shells, that led directly toward the house. The rest of us scurried behind, but the writer had the keys out and the front door flung open by the time we caught up.

The air that drifted out smelled stale and moist, almost like the inside of a greenhouse. I hated to think that some stray limb or adventurous trespasser had opened up the interior to the depredations of the greedy vines and other vegetation that had overtaken the grounds. But a quick look past Wolfe showed an expansive room, still filled with what had once no doubt been expensive furniture, now reduced to moldy tatters. Even if the flora of Jericho Cay had been kept at bay, it seemed as if the fauna had somehow found its way in.

"Disgusting," Wolfe said, stepping aside so the rest of us could join him.

I listened for the patter of scurrying feet, the scratch of tiny claws on the cracked marble floor, but heard nothing. If the critters that had turned the seat cushions into cozy nests for themselves and their offspring were still in residence, they were staying put.

Wolfe walked farther into the room, his head moving from side to side, his heavy shoulders slumped. "My God," he said softly. "I never imagined . . ."

"It's a mess all right," I said briskly, mostly to break the spell that seemed to be holding us all in place. I skirted around the writer and turned in a circle. "There must be a breach somewhere. Looks like the swamp rats and squirrels have taken over." I walked toward the far end of the room where a massive stone fireplace took up an entire wall. "It's easy to see, though, that it must have been spectacular in its heyday."

"You have no idea," Wolfe said, running his hand over the warped surface of a side table next to the ruined sofa. "When Ty had his parties, the place was lit up like the inside of a lightbulb. I used to tell him I'd be surprised if it didn't show up on satellite images."

I let my imagination restore the house to its former grandeur, candles flickering, lights blazing, the massive room filled with conversation and laughter as beautiful people sipped champagne from sparkling crystal. I shook myself. Time for a reality check.

"Where exactly was the housekeeper's body found?" I asked, and the temperature seemed to drop a few degrees.

"In her quarters. I'll show you."

I tried not to show my surprise that an elite guest from "the City" would know how to find the servants' quarters, but I followed him past a huge mahogany table that could have seated thirty, down a long corridor off which doors opened every few feet. *Guest bedrooms,* I thought, *and baths.* It must have taken a hundred barge trips to haul all this stuff out to the remote island.

The door Wolfe pushed open led into a small room, its walls all glass like the rest of the house, except that here the tatters of heavy drapes drooped from rods affixed to the support beams. The housekeeper—

"What was her name?" I asked.

"Anjanette Freeman," Wolfe said. "Jamaican. Came with Bell from New York." He stepped aside and led us to an attached bath, mold now covering the floor. "She was there." He moved inside and pointed to where the tub must be, a patterned shower curtain still hanging in place. "She stabbed herself."

I could almost see the poor woman's body slumped against the porcelain, blood turning the water pink. I cursed my imagination, stoked by my fascination with crime novels and cop shows on TV.

"The reports say it was a week before anyone realized something was wrong out here. The body must have been . . . unrecognizable, don't you think?"

Wolfe apparently didn't have my squeamish stomach. "Not as bad as you might think. The air-conditioning was still running. But they checked dental records from New York to confirm her identity."

According to the papers, Anjanette Freeman had stabbed herself three times. The first two had been tentative, but the final one had severed the femoral artery, so the cause of death had been obvious. I wondered aloud if there had been enough left to allow the coroner to determine the exact time.

"We'd need to see the autopsy report for that." It was the first Red had spoken in what seemed like hours. "And the sheriff isn't going to let us get a look at that."

"I have a copy," Wolfe said, nonchalantly, as if he were commenting on the weather. "I'll have it faxed to you."

He turned abruptly, and we had to scramble to get out of his way. He walked briskly back into the great room. "Kitchen's there." He pointed to another hallway that led off in the opposite direction from the one we'd just used. "Ty's suite was on the other side. He had his own sauna and pool. I'm sure they've both been overgrown by now." He whirled to face me. "Anything else, Bay? I really need to be getting back."

I would have loved to spend an entire week exploring, not only the house, but the surrounding grounds as well. The place had a secretive air about it, despite its obvious transparency, and I had a feeling there was a lot more to discover.

"I wonder if I might have a copy of the key," I said, matching Wolfe's nonchalance and moving toward the front door. "In case I need to come back."

He hesitated, just for a moment, before handing it over. "Keep it. I have no further interest in this sad place."

"I'd like Erik to take a few photos, too, if that's okay."

"Suit yourself. I'll meet you on the boat. Please don't linger. I have business to attend to."

Red laid a hand on my shoulder as we watched the writer march down the shell path and disappear into the foliage.

"He's a strange duck," my husband said, and I nodded. "I can't figure out his angle."

Erik had moved up to stand next to us. "What do you want me to shoot?" He already has his phone open and waiting.

"Everything," I said, "especially the housekeeper's room. When you're done, I'm going to do a quick check to see if she left anything behind."

Erik entered the hallway, throwing open doors to snap pictures on his way. When he uploaded them to his computer, I'd have the chance to study things in more detail.

"What's on your mind?" Red spoke softly. "Anything in particular?"

"No. I just want to be able to get a grasp of the layout."

A moment later, Erik returned and started on the public rooms. Red trailed me down the hall.

"I wish we'd brought gloves," I mumbled as I stepped into Anjanette Freeman's room.

"Too late to worry about prints."

"I know. It's all the slimy stuff on the surface of everything. Gives me the creeps."

"Toughen up, Tanner," my husband said with a laugh. "It's only mildew."

I worked the sleeves of my sweatshirt down over my fingers and pulled open the drawers in the bureau and the small desk next to a cabinet that held a television. "Must have had satellite," I said, finding nothing at all. "The sheriff probably cleaned everything out during the investigation."

"Or maybe it got packed up and shipped to her family. It must have been a hell of a shock."

Red always had a soft spot for the victims and the ones they left behind.

"Well, we might as well get going. Wolfe seemed in a hurry to get back to Hilton Head."

As we moved back down the hall, I wondered briefly what kind of life it must have been for Anjanette Freeman there in that strange house, marooned with a man who had basically chosen to retire from normal life. Did she not long for a husband, perhaps children? Friends? Or was there more to her relationship with Ty Bell than Wolfe had been willing to admit? And had that been enough?

Erik joined us outside, and I locked the door behind us. No one spoke as we made our way single-file down the rutted path toward where the old dock had once been. Until we rounded the last gentle curve. Red had been in the lead, and he stopped short at the empty expanse of water lapping gently against the shoreline.

"Did we take a wrong turn?" he asked, looking over his shoulder at me.

"There aren't any turns," I said, the truth dawning on me the minute the words were out of my mouth. Squinting into the distance, I could just make out the retreating outline of Ron Singleton's boat. "That son of a bitch marooned us!"

CHAPTER SEVEN

AS IF WE WERE PARTICIPANTS IN SOME SORT OF BIZARRE ballet, all of us reached immediately for our cell phones.

Erik spoke first. "I've got bars. Who do you want me to call?"

"Try the prima donna first." I glanced at my own screen to see that it was searching for a signal. "If you get him, tell him I said to get his ass back here immediately."

"Maybe with a little more tact," Red added with a grin.

"It's not funny. I'm sure he intends to send Ron back for us, but that'll take the better part of an hour." I glanced toward the sky where the first rosy hints of what would be a spectacular sunset had begun to tinge the sky out to the west. "I'm not keen on sitting here in the dark."

"Voice mail," Erik announced, tucking his phone back in his pocket. "He's probably ignoring us."

"I'm going to have a few choice words for Ron Singleton, too," I said, turning and stomping back down the rutted road.

"Wolfe is paying the freight," my husband reminded me, but I wasn't interested in logic at that particular moment.

"I don't give a damn! You don't just abandon people on a deserted island with no access to food or water." I jumped and whirled back at the huge splash behind us.

Red looked, too. "Gator," he said calmly. "Big one."

"Wonderful."

"We might as well look around the house some more while we've got the chance." Erik sounded much calmer than I felt. "You didn't see the setup on the other side, did you? You could drop my whole condo down inside that guy's bedroom and still have space for a decent party."

The idea of rooting around in Ty Bell's personal space helped to mollify me. A few minutes later we stepped onto the shell path. I unlocked the door.

"Which way?" I asked, and Erik pointed to the left on the far side of the fireplace.

I followed the short hallway into a gigantic room—all glass like the rest of the house—that took up the entire width of the strange structure. A custom-made bed, larger than a king, dominated one wall. Another was taken up by a row of armoires, and I moved across the filthy marble to pull open one of the doors. I was surprised to find most of the clothing still intact. The fusty smell of mildew drifted out, but many of the things had been encased in plastic, and the thick mahogany must have repelled the invaders who had taken up residence in the furniture. I slid down a zipper and ran my hands over the soft cashmere of a navy blazer. I reached to the bottom of the hanging bag and retrieved a pair of tasseled loafers. The leather still felt supple under my fingers.

I put everything back and moved to a chrome-and-glass desk tucked into one corner. If there had been papers there, they'd obviously disintegrated. Or again, perhaps the sheriff had cleared everything out during his initial investigation into Bell's disappearance and Anjanette Freeman's death. They were probably stashed away in some cardboard box in an evidence room, and I spent a few moments trying to figure out how to get my hands on them. I wandered over to the fireplace, obviously the reverse of the one in the main room, and noticed that the grate was mounded over in ash. I poked the toe of my sneaker into it and pushed it around. It looked to me as if someone had burned a lot of paper at some point. Maybe that's where all the stuff from Ty Bell's desk had ended up. Unlike the detectives in some of the 1940s movies I loved to watch, I didn't find any unburned scraps with important clues overlooked by the bumbling cops.

Erik's voice in the doorway made me jump. "Wolfe just called. He apologized for the inconvenience, but he had an appointment he couldn't miss. He said Ron is on the way back for us. He'll be in touch."

"I'm about ready to kick his arrogant butt to the curb," I said, casting a final glance over the ruined splendor of Ty Bell's private sanctum. Through the filthy windows I could just make out the pool, accessed from a door in the far corner. It looked as if the island had retaken possession of what must once have been a magnificent garden.

I followed my partner back out into the great room. "Where's Red?"

"He wanted to look around outside. I told him we'll meet him at the landing."

Once again I locked the door, the mechanism working more smoothly now that it had been used a few times. I looked up through the overhanging branches of the live oaks to see that the sun had retreated over the mainland. It would be full dark in a very short time.

"Red!" I yelled. "Come on." I waited a moment but got no answer. "We're heading down to the dock."

"Right there!" His voice sounded muffled, as if he were down a well.

Erik and I turned for the path. In the lead, I walked slowly, waiting for Red to catch us up. In some places, the overhanging foliage coupled with the fading light made it seem almost like a long, dark tunnel.

"Are we sticking with this?" My partner's voice floated up from behind me.

"You mean the case?"

"Yeah. I don't see what we can do that the sheriff didn't already cover back when Bell first disappeared. If the woman's death was ruled a suicide, there doesn't seem to be any crime to investigate. If some rich dude wanted to cut and run and leave all of this behind, what business is it of ours? Or Wolfe's? I'm beginning to think he's trying to create some big conspiracy that doesn't exist just so he can make a few bucks writing about it."

I smiled into the gathering darkness. "My, my, my. You're getting almost as cynical as I am."

We rounded the last turn and stepped out into the twilight. Across the way, lights had begun to dot the mainland, and I could sense again that feeling of being shut away from the world that must have appealed to Ty Bell in some visceral way. Why else would he have expended so much time and money to create this haven on an almost inaccessible island so close to and yet so removed from the rest of civilization?

"So what do you think?" Erik spoke into the gathering darkness.

"About sending Mr. New York City packing?" I shrugged. "The money's good, and we don't have much of anything else going on at the moment. I'm inclined to run with it, at least for a few more days. There are a lot of unanswered questions. Especially that driver's license he showed us."

"I'd rather spend my time trying to straighten things out at the women's shelter. At least those people really need our help," my partner said, his gaze drifting past me toward the water. "Here comes Ron."

The excursion boat had all its running lights ablaze, and it looked like an apparition rising out of the mists beginning to swirl as the cool night air met the warmer water. I squinted down the dirt road, now almost lost in the lowering twilight.

"Where the hell is Red?" I took a couple of steps in the direction of the house, when my husband suddenly appeared out of the dark tunnel.

"Sorry," he said, huffing a little. "Did you know that place has its own generator? I wondered how they got electricity out here. There's a huge cistern, too. Must have collected rainwater. I found a pumping station they used to get it into the house." He paused to catch his breath. "There's a well, too. It's a damn ingenious setup. Bell could have survived indefinitely out here as long as he'd stocked up on food."

The blast of a boat's horn startled us all. Ron maneuvered the big craft alongside the space where the dock had once stood, and we stepped back while he swung the gangway out. I could see the anxiety on his face as we trooped on board.

"I'm sorry, Bay," he said the moment my muddy feet touched the deck. "Mr. Wolfe insisted. I wanted to let you know, but—"

"Don't worry about it," I said, most of my anger having dissipated and what little remained directed at our eccentric client. "I hope you held him up for more money."

Ron's shoulders relaxed. "He offered me a bonus to get him back to Hilton Head before five o'clock." In the fading light I could just make out his wide smile. "I charged him double."

"Good for you," I said, moving over against the rail while Red and Erik trooped aboard behind me.

"I'll have you back in no time," the captain said.

He hauled up the gangway and moved into the wheelhouse. A few moments later, the anchor rattled up, and we turned away from the island. In a matter of minutes, it had disappeared into the night.

My husband and my partner moved to flank me at the rail of the stern.

"Erik wants to take a pass on Wolfe." I turned to my husband. "Thoughts?"

"As long as we're getting paid, I say we stick with it."

I wondered how much of Red's interest in continuing the investigation stemmed from his old boss's inability to bring the case to a satisfactory conclusion, the opportunity perhaps for him to show up his former colleagues. The lights of Palmetto Bay Marina grew brighter as we neared the small, snug harbor.

"Let's do this," I said. "Red and I will continue to work with Wolfe. Erik, you take the women's shelter case and run with it. We'll give each other daily updates. I'll still need you to do the bulk of the computer work, but I think I can pick up some of the slack. I'm not nearly as hopeless as I was a couple of years ago." I smiled into the darkness. "I actually have been paying attention to what you've been trying to teach me."

I heard my partner's chuckle. "Okay, deal." He paused as the rubber fenders bumped up against the dock and Ron cut the engines back to idle. "Are we going to open the office tomorrow?"

Fridays were our swing days. Depending on how many cases we had going, we either made it a three-day weekend or hung out the CLOSED sign and caught up on paperwork.

"We promised Wolfe a plan of attack by tomorrow, so we'd better show up. I'll tell him we'll be ready around one, and we can take the morning to get all our ducks in a row. If you'll help out with that, you can get started on the shelter the first of the week, like we discussed before."

"Fine."

"Bay?"

I turned to find Ron Singleton hovering a few feet away.

"I'm really sorry about leavin' y'all out there," he said, and I waved away his apology.

"No problem. Thanks for being our chauffeur."

"Anytime you need me, you just holler." He paused. "I don't know if I ever said, but I was real sorry to hear about your daddy. The Judge was a fine man. He'll be missed."

I swallowed the sudden lump in my throat. "Thank you, Ron. You take care."

I scuttled down the shortened gangway onto the dock before anyone had a chance to see the tears pooling in my eyes.

We'd driven two cars, and Erik hurried off to meet up with Stephanie. Red and I decided to grab a quick bite at Jump & Phil's, our favorite pub on the south end of the island. Even though we looked slightly disreputable from tromping around in the mud all afternoon, no one there would give us a second look. Being a local had its privileges.

It was busier than I'd expected. From the voices drifting over from the bar as we took our favorite table beneath the massive head of Waldo the Moose, the crowd consisted mostly of visiting golfers. I knew from experience that the talk would get louder as the evening progressed and the beer continued to flow. So, too, their exploits on the many manicured golf courses that dotted the island would balloon, strokes shaved off scores and tricky shots becoming more spectacular with each telling.

"How come you never took up golf?" I asked when our thick cheeseburgers had been delivered.

"I tried it a few times. Dad liked to go out every once in a while, but none of us were very good at it." He smiled, remembering, I thought, his late father and brother. "Dad said he could go out in the street and get frustrated for free instead of paying a couple of hundred bucks for the privilege."

I nodded, my own thoughts drifting to my first husband, Red's brother. Strange how things worked out sometimes. After Rob's murder, I'd fought hard against my recently divorced brother-in-law's clumsy pursuit of me, feeling confident that I would adjust to spending the rest of my life alone. The fates, obviously, had had other plans.

I almost ignored the vibration of my cell phone in the pocket of my old slacks, but that Pavlovian reaction has been bred into all of us from early on. I checked the caller ID, but it was blocked. Red shrugged and stuffed the last French fry into his mouth as I answered.

"Bay Tanner."

"Wolfe here. I need to see you. Now."

I glanced at Red. He raised an eyebrow when I said, "It's almost eight o'clock, Mr. Wolfe. Can't it wait until tomorrow? We'll be in the office—"

"Now, Bay. It's urgent. Where are you?"

I chewed on my lower lip and smothered a desire to slam the phone shut. "We're just finishing dinner at a pub on the south end of the island."

"Give me the name. I'll meet you there."

"Look, Mr. Wolfe, I'm very interested in helping you with this investigation, but there are courtesies—"

"Don't dither, woman. Can't wait. The name?"

I ground my teeth together. Red laid a hand on my arm.

"Jump and Phil's. It's—"

"Brenda will know it. Stay there."

I drew a deep, calming breath before gently folding my phone closed. "He's on his way," I said. I could feel the blood pounding in my temples, and I very badly needed to kick something. Or someone.

"The customer is always right," my husband said with a grin, and I resisted the urge to move his name to the top of my hit list.

CHAPTER EIGHT

THERE WAS A COLLEGE FOOTBALL GAME ON ONE OF the large TVs and pro basketball on some of the others. I didn't give a damn about any of them, but it helped to pass the time. Jump, one of the proprietors, pulled up a chair and chatted with us for a while, but the steady stream of customers through the door kept drawing him away.

We talked occasionally, mostly about plans for the weekend. Red's kids, Scotty and Elinor, would be there as usual on Saturday morning, and we tried to think of something different to do with them. It was a cardinal rule that business, unless it was absolutely critical, did not interfere with our time together. Rob and I had always meant to start a family, but somehow we'd never gotten around to it. Ready-made children hadn't been exactly what I'd had in mind; but, at nearing my midforties, I'd decided they were as close as I was likely to get. If I thought about it too much, I began to wallow in self-pity, an emotion I despised—in myself and everyone else. I loved Red's kids, and, miraculously, they returned my affection. What could have been an awkward transition from my status as indulgent aunt to stepmother had gone off—so far—without a hitch.

"Where in the hell is the guy?" Red's voice had lost its amused tolerance of half an hour before. "Isn't he at the Crowne Plaza? He could have crawled over here on all fours by now."

The image made me laugh. "Wolfe would never crawl. He'd make someone else do it while he rode on their back."

That brought a smile to my husband's face. "Well, I'm giving the arrogant SOB ten minutes, and then we're out of here."

I checked my cell to make certain he hadn't left a voice mail and settled back into the chair. "I wonder what generates that kind of ego. I mean, I know he's a bestselling author and all, but it's not as if he's Stephen King. Do you think he comes from old money? Maybe he's been this way since childhood. In his blood."

"I don't care where he learned to be rude and overbearing. We don't need to deal with his crap." He stood suddenly and tossed his napkin onto the empty table. "Come on, let's go home."

I stayed where I was. "You said ten minutes."

He dropped back into his chair. "Eight," he growled and fixed his stare on the football game.

We'd paid the check and drained the last of our several glasses of iced tea when I heard raised voices at the bar.

"Hey, Phil! You guys expecting royalty or something?"

Heads swiveled toward the front of the restaurant where I could just make out the shape of the huge Rolls-Royce blocking several parking places as it idled in the driveway. Another murmur rippled through the group huddled around the bar when the striking blonde strode through the door. Brenda scanned the room a moment before she spotted us. More than a few male heads swiveled to follow her short progress to where we sat.

"Mrs. Tanner. Sir," she said. "I have the car right outside. Mr. Wolfe asked me to collect you."

Red spoke before I had a chance to open my mouth. "Collect us? We're not butterflies, honey. Is Wolfe out there?"

Her smile wavered a little at the anger in my husband's voice. "No, sir. He asked me to bring you to him."

"Where?" I asked softly. Whatever was going on, it wasn't this poor girl's fault.

"The airport. I just dropped him there a few minutes ago."

Red and I exchanged a glance. I patted his clenched fist to let him know I'd take it.

"Brenda, isn't it?" I asked with a smile, and she nodded. "Brenda, I know you're just the messenger here, but do you have any idea what's going on? Mr. Wolfe said he'd meet us here. What's he doing at the airport?"

"I think he's leaving. He had a suitcase with him, and I heard him talking to someone about getting his plane fueled up."

"Okay," I said, rising and hitching my purse over my shoulder. "We'll go out there, but we'll drive ourselves."

"Mr. Wolfe's instructions were very clear," she said, her confidence wavering a little along with her voice.

"That's fine. I'll be sure and let him know that you delivered his message. Thank you."

I moved around her, and Red followed me out the side door. I glanced back a moment later to see the tall blonde still standing at our empty table beneath Waldo's magnificent antlers.

It took us less than fifteen minutes to make it to the general aviation side of the Hilton Head airport just off Dillon Road. We passed the squat, darkened building which, back in the eighties, had been the main terminal for the small turboprops that delivered vacationers to the island. Now we had a modern, though still quite modest, public facility on Beach City Road where USAir and—sporadically—Delta offered service in and out of Charlotte and Atlanta.

Farther back in the trees, we spotted lights from another building.

Red pulled into the narrow lot, and I opened the passenger door while the engine was still running.

"This must be the private terminal. Why don't you wait here? I'll go see what he wants."

I jumped out before my husband could object. I really didn't want to see headlines in the next day's *Island Packet* about a former Beaufort County sheriff's sergeant having punched out a world-famous crime writer.

On the sidewalk, I spotted a couple of bags pushed back between two small bushes. On impulse, I stooped to examine them. The WWW engraved on a gold plate confirmed my hunch, and I spared a moment to wonder what the third *W* stood for. I glanced back at Red and pulled open the door to the terminal. Inside, I was astounded to find a beautifully decorated, modern facility, with pristine floors and paneling, a far cry from the utilitarian ugliness of the old building.

I didn't immediately see anyone on duty. To my right, an elaborate coffee setup had been shut down for the night. I moved left and poked my head into a small room with a computer monitor glowing. A quick glance showed what looked to be a fully equipped business center. At the end of the short hallway I could see through a large window a few lights sprinkled here and there. Farther off, toward what I guessed was the end of the runway on the public side of the airport, a plane glided in for a landing. I waited a few moments, but it touched down and taxied toward the opposite side of the field.

I emerged into a large space with a counter along one side, but there didn't appear to be anyone around. I could feel my temper rising as I realized that, unless Wolfe had barricaded himself in the men's room, he just wasn't there. *Maybe he's already taken off,* I said to myself, although I couldn't explain why he would have left his bags behind. I'd just decided to give it all up and go home when a young woman emerged from a door behind the counter.

"Oh, I'm sorry," she said in a soft voice thick with our peculiar

Lowcountry drawl. "I didn't know anyone was out here. How can I help you?"

"Hey," I said, startled by her sudden appearance. "I was supposed to meet someone here. Winston Wolfe. I understand he was flying out tonight on his private plane."

She cocked her head in the direction of the blackness outside the window. "Yes, ma'am, he sure was. Ordered her fueled and prepped for flight a little while ago." She paused, and I sensed a new wariness in her dark eyes. "Were you going with him?"

"Oh, no," I said quickly. "He just asked my husband and me to meet him here. Is he gone?"

She smiled then, relaxing a little. "Well, I guess you could say that. He was here for a little while, but he left."

"He left?" I repeated stupidly.

"Yes, ma'am, about fifteen minutes ago. He got a call. He said he'd take it outside, but then he never came back. I walked out there and looked around, but I didn't see any trace of him. Except his bags."

"Yes, I noticed them. And he didn't say anything about the plane? Or if he still planned to fly tonight? Did he by any chance leave a message for me?"

I fumbled a business card out of my bag and handed it across to her.

She studied the card for a moment before replying. "No, ma'am, Ms. Tanner, he sure didn't." She waited, the professional smile still on her round face. Finally she added, "I was just getting ready to lock up. We close at ten if no one's waiting to take off."

Through the stillness of the building and the Lowcountry night, I heard the sound of a car door slamming. A moment later, Red stormed into the building.

"What's going on?" he asked, his voice tight with anger. "Where is he?"

I gave him the phone call story.

"So what are we supposed to do? Hang around here all night until he decides to come back?"

"Miss . . . ?" I looked at the young woman, who had taken a step back in response to Red's outburst.

"I'm Latice. Latice Graves, ma'am."

"Miss Graves wants to lock up." I turned my best hundred-watt smile on the young woman, who seemed about ready to bolt. "What will you do with Mr. Wolfe's bags?"

"I don't know, ma'am. If he'd left them inside, we'd hold them for him." She looked confused. "Maybe I should call my supervisor. I don't know what our responsibility is for things left outside the building." She swallowed. "I'm kind of new here."

I stared hard at my husband, hoping we were on the same wavelength.

Red caught the look. He modulated his tone and managed a boyish smile. "Maybe we ought to take them along," he said. "Just for safekeeping."

I could tell Latice wasn't too keen on the idea. "I don't know," she finally said. "What if he comes back?"

"There won't be anyone here until morning, right?" I said. "I can call and tell him we've got his luggage."

I held her gaze until she cleared her throat and looked away.

"I suppose that'd be all right."

I pulled my cell phone out of my bag. "I'll see if I can reach him right now."

"You do that," Latice Graves said. "I'll try my supervisor."

She scooted back through the doorway while I found Wolfe's number and dialed it out. It went to voice mail after only three rings.

"No answer." I flipped the phone shut and moved closer to my husband. "What do you think the ethics of this are? You know I'm not going to be able to resist rifling those bags, especially the briefcase."

"Absolutely out of the question," Red said promptly. "Unless, of

course, we're worried about what's happened to him. Then we'd probably be justified in sorting through it all, just to see if it had any clues
about Wolfe's disappearance."

He tried hard to keep the smile out of his voice.

"I don't think it qualifies as a disappearance. At least not yet." I
sobered. "What in the hell could he be up to? Why would he order his
plane readied for takeoff and then just walk away? He didn't have a
car. Brenda said she dropped him off." I paused a beat. "And why
would he leave his luggage sitting outside?"

Red shrugged. "Got me. Anyway, I've had about enough of Mr.
Winston Wolfe, Esquire. Either we take the bags or leave them here,
but let's get this over with and get ourselves on home."

"Any luck?"

We both turned as the young woman stepped back up to the
counter.

"No, he's not answering, but I'd like to take his things with us
anyway. Mr. Wolfe is our client, and he's very particular about his
personal belongings. I'd be glad to give you a receipt, and you've got
all my numbers there on my card." I gestured toward Red. "My husband used to be with the sheriff's office. Believe me, we're pretty
trustworthy."

Latice Graves looked as if she wished she were anywhere but here.
"I couldn't reach anyone to give me authorization. I just don't know
what to do."

I took a notebook out of my bag, scribbled out a receipt, and
handed it to her. "I can assure you Mr. Wolfe will thank you for not
leaving his things where just anyone could walk off with them. Or
locking them up in here where he won't have access until tomorrow.
You'll be doing the right thing."

Either she believed my heartfelt assurances or she just wanted to
go home. She reached behind her to flip off the first of a series of
lights. "I guess that will be okay. You folks have a good evening."

"You, too." I urged Red toward the door before Latice could change her mind.

Outside, we wasted no time scooping up the two cases and hopping into the Jaguar. Red had us back on Dillon Road and pointed toward home before I had a chance to fasten my shoulder harness.

"I feel sort of like we just pulled off a heist," I said, and my husband laughed.

I felt the heft of the briefcase in my lap and resisted the urge to dump its contents out right there. Red had shoved the larger piece of luggage in the backseat.

"Try him again," he said as we slid up to the security gate at the entrance to Port Royal Plantation.

"Nothing," I said, closing the phone. "When we get home, I'll try to get hold of the lovely Brenda. Did you notice which limo service she was from?"

"No, but there's only a couple that have Rolls-Royces on hand. Shouldn't take too long to track her down."

We turned right into the driveway, and the garage door slid open. Inside, I carried Wolfe's briefcase to the third bedroom/office, and set it on my desk. Red had dropped the suitcase on the floor in the foyer. Out in the kitchen, I heard the slam of the refrigerator door. A moment later, Red stood in the doorway, a bottle of beer in one hand.

"You could just leave it alone," he said. "There's no law that says you have to go rifling Wolfe's papers."

"No law that says I don't," I replied and dumped the contents out onto the desk before my husband could remind me that yes, actually, there was.

CHAPTER NINE

ED WANDERED BACK OUT INTO THE GREAT ROOM, his instructions to keep trying Wolfe's numbers every fifteen minutes. He also had the yellow pages and would try to track down the limousine service that had provided the Rolls. And Brenda.

I pushed aside a twinge of guilt—a very minor one, I had to admit—and began sorting through the papers from our client's briefcase. The first few seemed to be computer-generated printouts of black-and-white photos. When I had them arrayed across the desk, it struck me that they looked like surveillance shots, the kind Erik might have taken if the agency had been hired to follow someone. On closer inspection, I thought they could almost have been taken from security cameras.

The venues might have been airports. A lot of glass walls, people milling around. Or maybe high-class train stations. *Europe?* I thought, but there was no immediate way to tell. In any case, in each one he carried the same bulging leather satchel, the kind with a long strap that he wore from left shoulder to right hip, bandolier-style.

I studied the pictures. Although his face was partially obscured by a baseball cap in all of them—and sunglasses in a couple—the general build was the same: slim, tall, slightly rounded shoulders, although that could have been from the weight of whatever he carried in the satchel. He wore jeans and sneakers in all of them, a T-shirt in one and a heavy leather jacket in another.

"Traveling through different climates?" I said aloud.

I concentrated on the views out the windows behind the central figure, but there was nothing to indicate where each one had been taken. Or maybe they'd been cropped to concentrate on the figure whose face always seemed to be just out of focus. Maybe the photographer wasn't very good at his job. Or maybe I'd been right in guessing that they'd been lifted from a surveillance tape.

I booted up the computer and connected to the office. I worked my way through the firewalls and passwords Erik had constructed on my office machine after the break-in a few weeks before. He'd assured me it would take the king of all hackers to crack our files. Once in, I accessed the driver's license photo of Terry Gerard—or Ty Bell, as Wolfe had claimed. The vital statistics could have matched the photos now laid out across my desk: Height, six-one. Weight, 195. The hair color—brown, and eyes—brown—weren't much help in the black-and-white shots, but they could have matched. No way to tell.

"No way to tell much of damn anything," I said and leaned back in the chair.

But Wolfe had been carrying them in his briefcase. They had to have some significance to the search for Ty Bell, at least to him.

I printed out the license photo. I gathered up the scattered images and placed Terry-Ty's official one on top. I'd let Red have a run at them. I stood and stretched, suddenly tired. I walked out into the great room to find my husband sound asleep on the sofa.

"Hey, Watson," I said with a smile, gently shaking his shoulder. "Falling asleep on your watch is a capital offense."

"Just resting my eyes," he said with an answering grin. "How come you always get to be Sherlock?"

"Because my name's on the stationery. And the bottom of the checks."

I let him pull me down beside him, and I nestled into the crook of his arm.

"I assume you didn't reach Wolfe."

"Nope, just voice mail. But I did find the limo company. Five-Star. No one answered, but I left a message for Brenda to call us when she comes in tomorrow. Any luck with the briefcase?"

I told him about the pictures. "There were other papers in there, but I didn't get to them. You want to take a look at the photos?"

"Can it wait?" He eased back so he could look into my face. "You're not seriously worried about Wolfe, are you?"

I thought about it. "A little. But he's shown himself to be pretty impulsive so far. And secretive. He could have called a cab and/or rented a car and be halfway to Atlanta by now. Let's give him until the morning. If he hasn't called back, we can decide what to do. He's supposed to be at the office at one. Let's proceed as if we expect him to show up, and see what happens."

Red stood and pulled me up next to him. "I agree. Let's get some sleep."

He held my hand as we buttoned the house up for the night. I stopped in the foyer to stare at Winston Wolfe's suitcase.

"What about that?"

"Frankly, my dear, right now I don't give a damn," my husband said, dropping an arm across my shoulder.

I laughed as we made our way into the bedroom.

I decided to take everything with me to the office. Erik looked startled when we walked in a little after nine, Wolfe's briefcase in my hand, and Red lugging the suitcase.

"You guys going on the lam?" he asked with a grin.

We dropped our burdens, and I took a few minutes to bring my partner up to date. "So we're waiting for a couple of things," I said. "Either Brenda to call and maybe give us some insight into Wolfe's mood or plans or whatever. Or the great man himself to answer his damn voice mails. Barring either one of those eventualities, I guess we'll just press on with organizing a game plan for how to prove whether Morgan Tyler Bell is alive or dead."

"We should check the suitcase," Erik said, moving around from behind his desk. "Want me to do the honors?"

I waved a hand in acquiescence, and he knelt next to the leather bag on the floor. He flipped the latches and threw it open. Clothes, neatly folded: shirts, socks, underwear. I was shocked to see that the flamboyant Wolfe favored boxers in plain white. A shaving kit, one pair of black tasseled loafers in separate shoe bags. And a flash drive tucked in between the folds of a maroon silk robe.

Erik held it up. "No label. Music, maybe?"

Red and I exchanged a look, and he shrugged. "Let's find out," my husband said.

Erik inserted the small cylinder into his computer as Red and I gathered behind him. A moment later, a series of files scrolled up on the screen.

"His books," Erik said. "I recognize some of the titles."

"A backup." I shrugged. "I guess that makes sense, although I would think his publisher has all that."

"Wait, here's something." I watched him click on a folder entitled RESEARCH. Inside, another series of files appeared.

"Is there one for Bell?" Red asked.

We waited while Erik paged through them. "Nothing that pops right out. Want me to start opening them?"

"Let's wait. What else is in the suitcase?"

He returned to removing the contents of the bag and setting each item on the floor. He picked up a single cloth bag and dangled it by the drawstring. "One shoe?"

I could tell by the shape exactly what it was, so there was no surprise when Erik eased it open and extracted a handgun.

"Glock," I said, recognizing the same model 9mm the Judge had bought so Red could teach me to shoot. I'd long since abandoned it in favor of the tiny Seecamp that could be concealed in the pocket of a pair of tight jeans without any detectable bulges.

Red took it from Erik's fingers and ejected the clip. "Empty. Not much use to him stashed in the bottom of his suitcase, especially with no bullets."

The phone rang then, and I reached to answer it. I felt a rush of relief mingled with guilt when the caller spoke.

"Mrs. Tanner? By what right have you taken possession of my private property?"

I turned to find Red and Erik staring at me. "Wolfe," I mouthed. Aloud, I said, "We did it for your protection, sir. It didn't seem prudent to leave your personal belongings sitting in plain view outside the airport office."

"I trust you haven't disturbed anything."

I suppressed a smile at his pomposity. "Of course not," I lied. "We have both your briefcase and your overnight bag here at the office."

I covered the mouthpiece with one hand and whispered, "He's pissed off. Better put it all back. But copy that drive."

"I'll be there directly," he said and hung up.

While Erik transferred Wolfe's data from the flash drive to his laptop, I carefully repacked the suitcase, taking care to put everything back in the same place. I hoped.

"Hurry up with that," I said when I'd finished. "We need to get that drive back in place. He could have been calling from the car."

"Got it." Erik whipped Wolfe's flash drive out and handed it over.

I slipped it back into the folds of the dressing gown and fastened the catches.

"I wonder if we have time to copy what's in the briefcase." I glanced over my shoulder toward the door. "Erik, keep an eye out for him. I'll get as much done as I can."

Red helped me remove the documents and load them, several at a time, into the copier. We managed to get through about half of it before Erik yelled, "Here comes the Rolls."

Red gathered up our copies and shoved them into a drawer in his desk just as I managed to get everything back in the briefcase and stack it neatly beside the other bag. Less than a minute after I'd stood and headed for my office, the outer door swung open.

Wolfe didn't say a word. He crossed to where his belongings were stacked and hefted each one as if testing to see if anything major had been removed. The three of us stood watching, and I had to force myself not to smile. I fixed my face in a stern look and cleared my throat.

"Where were you last night?"

Wolfe ignored me. I could tell he was itching to fling open his cases and check their contents, but our presence apparently held him back.

"Mr. Wolfe?" He looked over his shoulder at me. "You kept us waiting for nearly an hour, and then when we got to the airport you'd disappeared. You owe us an explanation."

Something passed across his eyes as he straightened and turned to face us. It was only the merest flicker, but it looked remarkably like fear. Something—or someone—had spooked our eccentric client. A moment later, his brilliant smile made me think I had imagined it.

"My dear girl, I do owe you an apology. And you as well, Mr. Tanner. I had a call. From my agent. You have no idea how tedious being a well-published author can be sometimes. It's not nearly as glamorous as it looks from the outside."

"But where did you go? We were concerned when we couldn't reach you."

"I am sorry. I had to go back to the hotel and receive a fax from my agent. Urgent business that couldn't wait. I called a cab."

"Where were you flying off to in the first place?" Red asked. "And what was so important that you had Brenda come to drag us away from dinner?"

I watched as Wolfe's phony humility deserted him.

"I had some information I thought might be pertinent to the case, but it turned out to be a false lead. The rest of my business is of no concern to you, sir. Again, I apologize for the inconvenience. Make sure you compensate yourselves for your time."

We could check it out of course, although I wasn't sure what the point would be. Not that I was buying his bullshit for a second. Something—or someone—had seriously rattled our client, enough so that he'd abandoned his briefcase and luggage and hightailed it away from the airport. Maybe it didn't have anything to do with the case, but I had a hard time believing that.

I glanced up to find Red staring across at me, and I realized I wasn't the only one who thought our client was lying through his well-cared-for and sparkling white teeth.

CHAPTER TEN

A FEW MINUTES LATER, AMID ASSURANCES THAT HE would return at one for our scheduled appointment, Winston Wolfe, a bag in each hand, disappeared out the door.

"You know, we've just committed about fifteen different felonies."

I tried to read from Red's voice whether he was serious or not. "Really? I'm willing to plead to rampant curiosity and an unforgivable breach of good manners, but we didn't actually *steal* anything."

"Tell it to the judge," my husband said with a smile, and I felt my shoulders relax.

"Time for a powwow." I turned, and the two men followed me into my office.

We all sat, Erik with his laptop resting on his knees, his fingers poised to take notes. We really needed a secretary, but my suggestion to that effect a few weeks before had caused some discord. I had in mind a young woman I'd met during our investigation into Cecelia Dobbs' accusations. Erik wanted us to hire Stephanie Wyler, his fiancée and my late partner's daughter. While keeping things in the family might not be a bad idea, I worried that so much proximity wouldn't be good for their relationship. *Look at Red and me. I* swallowed down that disloyal thought and decided to worry about it tomorrow.

"So where are we? Anyone care to recap?"

"I'll take a stab at it," my husband said. "We have Ty Bell, recluse millionaire, who apparently abandoned his private island a couple of years ago, along with his personal assistant who took off at about the same time. Both of them left behind Bell's longtime housekeeper, dead of apparently self-inflicted wounds. Enter crime writer Winston Wolfe, who has supposedly been sanctioned by Bell's only living relative to tell the story. But Cousin Harold is most interested in obtaining proof of death so the estate can be settled and he can inherit Bell's millions. Except Wolfe is in possession of a copy of an Ohio driver's license issued recently with a photo he claims is Bell but which is in the name of the PA, Terry Gerard."

I smiled. "Very good, Sergeant. Succinct and to the point." I looked at Erik. "Comments?"

"I keep coming back to motive."

"For what, the disappearance?" I asked.

"No. For Wolfe. I mean, what works best for him as a writer? If Bell is alive or dead? In the long run, it's no skin off his nose either way, is it? I mean, it's not as if he's going to profit from the estate." He paused. "Is he?"

"I don't see how. He's not a relative, and he says there's no will. He'll make his money from selling a million copies of his book. The only one with a vested interest in the eventual outcome is the cousin. I don't really see how that impacts how we proceed with the investigation." I pulled a legal pad from the right-hand drawer. Computer notes were all well and good, but I felt better with a pen in my hand. "Assuming we *are* proceeding with the investigation?"

Neither of them spoke for a moment. "I'm hooked," Erik finally said. "Especially after that stunt last night and all the stuff we found in his briefcase. There's something else going on besides a straight-out missing person's case. I want to know what it is."

I turned to my husband. "Red? How are you voting?"

"Well, I'm just the hired help, but I'm with Erik. At least for now. Let's play this hand out and see what other cards he's holding."

"Okay. So, we need a game plan. Erik, can you get into the database for the driver's license? Find out if it's legit or if he bought it on the street?"

"Could take a little doing. They've tightened up their protection everywhere since 9/11. Remember a lot of those hijackers used licenses as ID to get on the planes."

I shuddered at the memories any mention of that day always conjured up. None of us would ever be able to wipe away the images of the giant aircraft gliding almost gracefully into the top floors of the World Trade Centers.

"But you can do it?"

"Probably."

"Good. I'm going to search the newspaper archives and see if I can come up with a photo of Ty Bell. We have only Wolfe's word for it that he's the guy on the license."

I turned to my husband.

"And you can get on the copies we stashed in your desk." I reached into the center drawer and retrieved the magnifying glass, the one Erik had ridden me unmercifully about when I'd first brought it into the office. "Study the backgrounds, see if you can figure out where they were taken. The face in all of them seems to be obscured. Maybe it's Bell and maybe it's not. In any case, we need to know why this guy was so interesting to whoever went to the trouble to get the photos." I paused. "And why Wolfe is so paranoid about keeping us in the dark."

It amazed me that it was so difficult to find a decent photo of a man who had accumulated vast wealth at a relatively early age, who threw lavish parties for the rich and moderately famous, and who had been the subject of an intensive police investigation following his disappearance. The papers should have been full of them—but they weren't. I managed to scrounge up a single shot of Bell leaving a restaurant in New York City a couple of years before he disappeared. His head was slightly turned away from the camera as he spoke to the dazzling blonde hanging on his arm. I didn't recognize her, but then I'm not a follower of either the cult of celebrity or the carryings-on of high society.

I printed out the photo. Between the graininess of its reproduction in the newspaper transferred to the Internet and then further degraded in the copying process, I didn't think it would be much help. I looked up as Erik stepped into my office.

"The license is a phony. There's no record of it in Lorain County, where Grafton is located, or on the state database."

I scribbled on the legal pad, then handed him my recent find. "That's a start. This is the only picture I could find of Bell. What do you think?"

He picked up the copy of the license and held them side by side. "Could be. Same general shape of the face. The hair is parted on a different side, though."

I took the papers from him. "I didn't notice that. Good catch." I set them down on the desk and sat back in my chair. "But Wolfe says it's Bell. We may have to assume he's telling the truth."

"You find anything on Gerard?"

I shook my head. "Nothing. Do you have anything on your computer that could help with cleaning up all these images?"

"Remember the guy in Charlotte who helped us with that old picture Joline Eastman brought us?"

"Sure. Do we have to send the photos to him?"

"No. I was going to say, he gave me the program. I'll have to scan them into the computer, but then I can manipulate them to see if we can clean up the faces."

"Won't scanning them just distort the image more?"

"Maybe," he said, and I could feel his excitement from across the room. "Let me have a run at it."

"Hold on. Ask Red to come in, will you?"

A few moments later they both sat ranged around my desk again. "Any luck?" I asked my husband.

"Some." He handed across a sheet of paper with several lines of his precise printing. "I managed to pick out some partial signs. A few letters here and there. And in one of them, a woman in the background was carrying a magazine. *New Yorker.* Not much help. I think you can get those almost anywhere, can't you?" He looked again at his notes. "If we could enlarge it without too much distortion, we might be able to read the date. That would at least give us a point of reference for the rest of the photos."

"Good. Erik, take a run at that. What about the signs? English?"

"One is. The same one with the magazine." He pointed. "See? It's *n-t-a.* At the end. So I'm thinking Atlanta."

"I'd buy that. But it could be a restaurant or a shop name."

"True. But then there's this. What do you make of it?"

I turned it around so Erik could see it, too, but I had immediately recognized the single word: *été.* "It's French for summer," I said. I prayed no one would ask me how I knew that. I'd been pretty successful in putting my former Parisian lover, Alain Darnay, out of my mind. And everyone else's, I hoped.

"That doesn't necessarily mean France," I hurried on. "It could be New Orleans. Or a poster in almost any airport with international flights."

"Something else interesting turned up," my husband said, "among all those papers we copied."

"What?"

"The autopsy report on Anjanette Freeman."

I nearly jumped out of my chair. "Didn't Wolfe say he'd send it to us? You mean he had it with him all the time?"

Red nodded. "Looks that way."

"What does it say?" Erik asked.

"Pretty much what Wolfe told us. Ruled a suicide. Bathroom door locked from the inside. No drugs or alcohol in her blood. But Pedrovsky or Ben Wyler or whoever was in charge of the initial investigation certainly had to have questions about the whole scenario."

"What kind of questions?"

"Think about it," my husband said.

"Come on," I replied when he paused, "no games." I glanced at my watch. "We've only got a couple of hours before Wolfe shows back up."

"It's not a common way to commit suicide. Especially for a woman. For one thing, it has to hurt like hell. Most of the time, you'll find that women tend to use some combination of medication and alcohol. They don't like disfiguring their bodies. And even if she did decide to use a knife, why didn't she just slit her wrists?"

"So what are you saying? That she didn't commit suicide? If I'm following you, it would have taken her a while to bleed out. So if it was murder, why would she just sit there and watch herself bleed to death if she wasn't drugged or unconscious?"

Erik spoke for the first time. "Her body wasn't discovered for a week, right? So how could they tell? Even if someone did drug her, wouldn't it have disappeared from her blood by then?"

"All good questions. But Wolfe said the air-conditioning was left on. That would have preserved the body to a certain extent. Damn it, we need to see the sheriff's file. But anyway, that's the official report." Red shrugged. "We don't have much choice but to accept what the coroner put in there."

"Let's run it down," I said. "Bell leaves. Or disappears, at any rate. Then this Terry Gerard takes a powder. A week later they find the Freeman woman dead in the bathtub. We don't really have any provable time line, do we? It's a chicken and egg thing. Which came first, the disappearances or the suicide?"

None of us had an answer to that.

CHAPTER
ELEVEN

ERIK MADE A LUNCH RUN, AND WE SAT AROUND MY DESK eating pizza and trying to decide how to proceed.

My partner had fed the photos into the program he'd acquired from his friend in Charlotte, but the results had been inconclusive. I wondered aloud if Ty Bell had hired Terry Gerard because they looked a lot alike.

"What would have been the point?" Red asked, wiping a string of mozzarella off his chin.

"Maybe he liked to go out incognito, pretend he was Gerard to keep from being hounded by paparazzi or whatever."

"Seems to me he was pretty good at avoiding getting his picture taken," Erik said. "You had a heck of a time finding even that one photo online. And we don't know yet if we've even *seen* Gerard." He tapped the stack of photos on the corner of my desk. "These could all be him or Bell or a combination."

"True." I took a swig of Diet Coke. "Are all those loaded onto your computer?"

He nodded. "I double-passworded the file."

"So let's get these shredded before Wolfe shows up. We've only got half an hour."

"So you think we're ready to push forward?" Red asked.

"If Wolfe cooperates. We're going to have to rely on him to supply us with everything in his briefcase, all the stuff we're not supposed to know about. And he has to give us something concrete to go on. Right now we're just stumbling around in the dark."

The silence that followed my assessment was broken by the buzzing of Erik's iPhone.

"Steph," he said and rose to leave the room.

Red and I worked on polishing off the pizza without comment. I knew we were both wishing we could find something to hang an investigation on, and only a small part of that desire had anything to do with money. But we had to be realistic, I thought. If Wolfe continued to play games with us, I'd have a difficult time taking his cash without being damn certain I had a reasonable expectation of delivering.

I wiped my hands on a paper napkin and leaned back in my chair. What the hell was taking Erik so long? We had to resolve this before the great man descended on us. He should know better than to let his relationship with Stephanie Wyler interfere—

I shot forward in the chair, and Red jumped. "What?" he said.

"Erik!" I yelled. "Let me talk to Stephanie."

My partner appeared in the doorway, his face creased in an almost comic mix of question and aggravation. "Hang on," he said into the phone and handed it over.

"Stephanie, it's Bay."

"Hi! Is something wrong?"

"No, not at all. I have a question for you." I hesitated. "About your father's things. You still have them, right?"

After Ben Wyler's sudden death in the marina not far from Amelia Island, Stephanie had moved into his small house in Sea Pines

Plantation. Ben had spent a lot of time remodeling it, and I knew from things I'd heard afterward that his favorite daughter had inherited the property free and clear. Though she spent a lot of her time at Erik's condo in Broad Creek Landing, I had a feeling they might make the house their permanent home once they married.

"Not everything," she said, and I could hear the pain in her voice. "I gave the clothes and stuff to a couple of the thrift shops on the island."

"What about papers? Did he have files and notebooks—things like that?"

"Sure. They're in the attic." Again that pause that made my heart ache for her. "I just . . . I didn't know what else to do with them."

Across the desk, I could see my husband and Erik both looking at me strangely.

"Would you mind if Erik took a look?"

"Why?"

I mulled that over for a few moments. "It's to do with a case he may have worked on when he was still with the sheriff's office. Right toward the end before he retired."

"Wouldn't all that be there? I mean, at the office?"

Ben and I had gone around a few times during our brief association in the agency about his almost obsessive secrecy and unwillingness to share information. I had no way of knowing if he'd operated the same way in his official capacity, but it was worth a shot.

I glanced up at Red and saw understanding dawn in his eyes. A smile spread across his face, and he nodded.

"Probably. But he had his own system of working a case, and I'm betting he kept his own notes regardless of the rules."

That made her laugh. "You're right. Dad was never real big on rules."

"Are you home?" I asked.

"Yes. I'll be here all afternoon."

"Great. Erik will be over in a few minutes. If that's okay."

I could hear the smile in her voice. "Sure. I'll go drag out the boxes."

"Thanks, Stephanie. I really appreciate it. Here's Erik."

"No problem. Bye."

I handed the phone back to him, and again he stepped out into the reception area.

"You think Wyler may have some stuff on Bell's disappearance?" Red asked the moment we were alone.

"I think there's a good chance. He used to drive me nuts with holding his cards close to his chest all the time." I sobered. "It's partly why he got himself killed. And you said he was probably involved in the investigation."

"It's a good bet. Strictly speaking, it's against department regs to keep anything pertaining to an active case in your personal files." Red smiled. "I hope to hell he broke that one like he did so many of the others."

Erik appeared in the doorway. "What exactly am I looking for?"

"Anything that looks like it might be related to Bell's disappearance or Gerard's. And Anjanette Freeman's supposed suicide. Ben was a great one for scribbling in small lined notebooks. See if you can find any of those. Or even the official files. I wouldn't put it past him to have copied them so he could study them on his own time."

"Will do." My partner paused. "But what about Wolfe? Don't you want me here when he shows up?"

I checked my watch. "Since you're going to be working mostly on the women's shelter problem, I think Red and I can handle it. If you find anything at Stephanie's, call us right away. Use Red's private number."

"Got it. Want me to dump that on the way out?"

I handed him the empty pizza box and drink cups, then scooped up the copies from the corner of my desk and took them into the small storage room next to Red's tiny office. I had just fed the last of the photos into the maw of the noisy shredder when I heard the front door open.

Winston Wolfe had lost a lot of the bluster of earlier in the morning. He smiled and offered his hand to Red who had come out of my office to greet him. I breathed a small sigh of relief when I saw the briefcase swinging from his left hand. We assembled in my office.

"So," our client said, resting the leather case on his knees. "How will you proceed?"

Red sat back and crossed his arms over his chest. I straightened the legal pad on which I'd made a few notes and folded my hands on the desk.

"We have a couple of things to iron out first, Mr. Wolfe. I need to know if you have any additional information you're willing to share with us before we commit fully to pursuing this investigation. We have precious little to go on, as I'm sure you know. We've been denied access to the official reports. While I'm sure they're as accurate as possible, I hate relying on newspaper stories. You haven't really given us anything except your relationship with Mr. Bell and access to the house on Jericho Cay. And the Ohio driver's license." I paused to give him time to comment, but he merely smiled and nodded his head. "That's a phony, by the way. Probably bought on the street or from someone who's a pretty fair forger."

The smile faded from his aristocratic face. "I have it on good authority that license is genuine."

"My partner says there's no record in the official databases, and he's seldom wrong about these things. Where did you obtain it?"

Wolfe stiffened. "That's confidential. In my line of work, protecting sources is as imperative as it is for a reporter." The arrogance of the rich and famous was back in his voice.

"That's all well and good, but the fact remains that your star piece of evidence is a fake." I waited a beat before dropping the big bomb. "If you have no other information to offer, I don't see how we can help you. I'll have my bank send you a refund of your retainer, minus a modest amount for our time."

Red sat up straighter, and I could feel his intent gaze on my face. I had deviated from the script, but my gut told me this was the way to handle this pompous, aggravating man. He was obviously used to fawning acceptance of his proclamations. I needed him out of his comfort zone.

"I'm not used to having my assertions questioned," he said, echoing my own thoughts. "How do I know your young man is as good as you say?"

"You don't. You'll just have to take my word for it."

That stopped him for a moment. In the silence, I saw Red reach for his pocket and pull out his cell phone. With a nod, he rose and left the room.

"Your husband obviously has more important business than mine to attend to," Wolfe said with a sneer.

"Do you have anything else to offer us in the way of leads?" I asked. I let my breath out slowly. "Is there anything you haven't shared with us?"

I could feel him gathering himself to rise and march out the door, and I wasn't sure whether I felt bad about that or not. I knew what he had in that briefcase—a lot of it, anyway. What other information was contained in his files on the flash drive? We could certainly open them all and find out for ourselves, but that wouldn't establish the kind of trust I needed from a client. He had to offer it to us. The ball was in his court. I hoped to hell I hadn't overplayed my hand. I relaxed my shoulders and waited.

Wolfe fidgeted with the handle on his briefcase, and I wagered in my head about whether he was preparing to fling it open or let it swing by his side as he stormed out of my office. The line was running about sixty-forty in favor of our losing a potentially lucrative client when Red walked back into my office. I looked up to see him grinning widely.

"Erik has a lot to show us," he said, and Wolfe's head whipped around in his direction. "He's bringing everything back to the office."

I opened my mouth to tell Wolfe that we were definitely in, just a fraction of a second before his fingers snapped open the catches on his briefcase.

CHAPTER
TWELVE

$\mathscr{T}$HERE WERE A COUPLE OF SURPRISES IN THE DOCU-
ments Wolfe lifted from his calfskin case.

Copies of the photos already resided in tamper-proof files on Erik's
computer, along with the contents of the flash drive and Anjanette
Freeman's autopsy report, although our client was still holding that
back. I hoped our acting skills proved adequate in convincing Wolfe
that we'd never seen any of it before. Red surprised me with his talent
for dissembling.

"Are these all of the same man?" he asked when I'd handed them
over to him.

"I believe so," Wolfe said.

"And you think this man is Bell?"

Wolfe nodded.

"Where did you get them?" I asked.

"As I said, I'm not at liberty to reveal my sources."

I let that slide for the moment. "Where were they taken?"

"Various venues. Philadelphia. Montreal."

The French word for summer: *été*. Quebec. I should have thought of that. At least Wolfe might be telling the truth about that part. Although . . .

"Really? That doesn't make any sense. If it's really Ty Bell, why would he be hanging out in places like these? With his money, I'd expect him to be lounging on the beach on the Riviera or Bali or somewhere like that." I waited, but he sat mute, his gaze darting around the room. "And why would he be on the run in the first place? Do you suspect he had something to do with Anjanette Freeman's death?"

Wolfe's sputtering reply sent little droplets of saliva spewing from his lips. "Of course not! That never once entered my mind!"

"Really?" Red asked. "It's probably the only explanation that makes any sense. I'm surprised a man of your experience with crime didn't come to that conclusion right away."

I smiled at my husband. We were turning into quite a force to be reckoned with, tag-teaming Wolfe as if we'd rehearsed it all in advance.

"The poor woman killed herself." He rummaged in his briefcase and pulled out the autopsy report, slapping it down on the desk. "It's all in here. Your own people ruled it a suicide."

I picked it up and made a show of scanning through the few pages. I thought about calling him on his lie, then decided to let it go. "It says here she stabbed herself three times. That suggests either someone totally inured to pain, or . . ." Again I waited for him to fill in the blanks, and again he refused to rise to the bait. "Or," I finished for him, "she was murdered. Was Ty Bell capable of that?"

"Don't be ridiculous! Of course he wasn't. *Isn't.*"

"How about Gerard?"

Winston Wolfe slumped a little in his seat and ran a hand over his face. In that moment he looked old and tired.

"I don't know," he said. "Terry Gerard was something of a mystery.

Ty picked him up in New York sometime right after 9/11. I never heard anyone talk about his background, but Ty had complete faith in him. Relied on him for just about everything except his business dealings. Never traveled anywhere without him, and he controlled access to Ty with almost religious fervor." A small smile twitched at the corners of his mouth. "The mother hen, we used to call him. Guarded Ty like a she-bear with her cubs."

I let the mixed metaphors and similes slide, although they surprised me, coming as they did from a man who manipulated words for a living. "So do you think they left together? And, if so, why didn't you pick up his trail along with Ty's?"

"I've told you all I know. I believe that driver's license and those photos are of the same man. I'm convinced it's Ty. And that he's alive."

Once again his hand disappeared into the briefcase, this time producing a document we hadn't found or had time to copy. Wolfe handed it to me, and Red scooted closer to read it along with me.

"We have our own contract, Mr. Wolfe," I said after skimming over the two-page document. "Which you refused to sign."

"Of course. But this contains some clauses pertaining to contingencies I'm certain don't usually arise in your normal business dealings. Paragraph six."

I found it. "You want us to guarantee that any information we obtain in the course of the investigation will be shared exclusively with you and with no one else." I glanced over at Red. "If we discover something that pertains to a crime, we're bound by professional ethics to turn it over to the sheriff. Surely you know that."

"*Pah!* Ridiculous. I pay you. You work for me. The civil servants can dither around on the taxpayers' dime, not mine."

The condescension in his voice made Red's shoulders stiffen. I jumped in before he could rise to the defense of his former colleagues.

"That's not open for discussion, sir. Our license is granted by a bunch of those civil servants in Columbia, and I'm not about to jeopardize my business by spitting on their rules. That's a deal-breaker."

We stared at each other for a long moment before he nodded. "That clause can be amended to exempt law enforcement. But I insist on being the first one informed of any leads you encounter. This is *my* livelihood, Mrs. Tanner, and I won't have some local newspaper reporter scooping me. I trust that's acceptable."

I looked to Red, whose nostrils were still flaring, and raised an eyebrow. He drew in a long breath and nodded once.

"Agreed," I said and initialed my changes to the offending paragraph.

Wolfe studied the document when I handed it back, retrieved a gold pen from the breast pocket of his immaculate tan blazer, and scribbled his name with a flourish. I followed suit and leaned back in my chair.

"The first order of business," I said, "is for you to come clean. Now that we have a contract in place, there's no longer any reason for you to hold out on us."

Wolfe sat up straighter in his chair. "I have no idea what you're talking about." He gestured to the papers spread across my desk. "That's everything."

"I don't think so. The questions you haven't answered are legion. For openers, how did you get onto Bell's trail? What made you think he was still alive? Where did you obtain those photos? How did you get a copy of the Ohio driver's license? Why would Bell steal his employee's identity? And if he's using it, where is Gerard? Why are there no pictures of either Bell or Gerard anywhere on the Internet? How do we know these photos are really the missing millionaire?"

Wolfe leaped on my last question. "Because I'm telling you! What reason would I have to lie about that?"

I ignored his rising anger and kept my voice low and controlled. "I have no idea. I don't know you, Mr. Wolfe, except by reputation, and by our brief interactions of the past couple of days. You haven't given me reason yet to trust you—or your pronouncements. I need some independent corroboration before I or my partners go haring off in pursuit of what could turn out to be a publicity stunt designed to gin up interest in your forthcoming book."

To my complete surprise, he laughed. "Damn it, I like you, Bay." His shoulders visibly relaxed. "All right, cards on the table. Do you remember Howard Hughes?"

"You wrote a book about him," I said, recalling the listing I'd scanned on Amazon.com right after Wolfe's first appearance in our office.

"Yes. One of my earlier efforts. Not so much a true crime work as a character study. The man was an absolute recluse, rich as Croesus, but paranoid about privacy. In his last days he became totally unhinged, refusing to bathe or eat, letting his fingernails grow into talons. Such a brilliant mind. To see it reduced to that of an idiot child was almost too sad to write about."

"Are you saying that Ty Bell is crazy?" Red asked. "And that's why you want to write about him?"

"No, nothing of the kind. But he developed, over the past few years before he disappeared, something of that same paranoia for privacy as Hughes. He'd throw the lavish parties you read about but never make an appearance. He'd lock himself in his private wing of the house and never show his face. Of course his guests found it odd, but not so much that they stayed away. The cachet of being invited to Jericho Cay more than made up for the strange behavior of their host."

I leaned forward over the desk. "Are you saying that no one saw him? For how long a period of time before he disappeared?"

Wolfe shrugged. "Several months. I was present at the last big party he threw, a few weeks before he left Jericho. Terry Gerard expressed Ty's regrets, said he was involved in a big deal that needed his personal attention, and that he'd try to look in before the weekend was over. But he never did."

Red and I exchanged a look. "So you don't know if he was there or not," my husband said.

"Of course he was there. I spoke to him myself." Wolfe paused. "Through the door to his suite."

"And you're sure it was him?" I asked.

"Of course," he repeated. "What are you suggesting?"

"It occurs to me that Ty Bell may have been gone long before his official disappearance."

"Nonsense! Who would I have been speaking with if not with Ty? He told me he'd enjoyed my last book and was looking forward to the next. He said he'd call next time he came up to the city and we'd have a drink. I knew—*know*—his voice, Mrs. Tanner. And his face." Again he reached to tap the photos on the corner of my desk. "And I'm telling you, this is Morgan Tyler Bell. I'd stake my reputation on it."

"I believe you already have, Mr. Wolfe," I said quietly. "And mine. I hope, for both our sakes, that you're right."

CHAPTER THIRTEEN

ERIK STEPPED BACK INTO THE OFFICE JUST AS WINSTON Wolfe rose to take his leave.

We certainly had a lot more information than we'd been privy to a few hours before, but not all of it by any means. First and foremost, Wolfe had made no mention of the flash drive concealed in the folds of his dressing gown. Nor had he offered any plausible explanation for his strange behavior of the previous evening when he'd led Red and me on the wild-goose chase to the airport on Dillon Road. Still, I felt fairly comfortable in pursuing the investigation. I hoped Erik, who nodded at Wolfe as they passed in the doorway, had mined some gold from Ben Wyler's cache of papers.

We all pulled cold drinks from the small refrigerator and settled around my desk. I scooped up the papers our client had left behind and stuffed them all in one file folder. We'd have to get them organized and labeled, but I was too excited to delve into the box Erik had carted in to worry about it right then.

"So what happened?" he asked, setting the carton on the floor.

I gave him a rundown of our conversation. "I signed the contract, so we're on. Still a ton of unanswered questions, but I'm hoping what you've got in there will help solve some of the mysteries."

Erik leaned over and began unloading his treasure trove. Folders and several of the small notebooks I remembered began to pile up in front of me. I pulled one of the spiral-bound pads toward me and flipped it open. Ben Wyler's crabbed, almost indecipherable handwriting brought a flood of memories, and I had to blink back the tears that sprang suddenly into my eyes. Red caught my stricken look and reached to lay his hand gently over mine. I sniffed and cleared my throat.

"Did you have a chance to look through any of this?"

"Just enough to determine they had something to do with Bell and Jericho Cay," Erik said. "You were right about the official reports. I think Ben must have copied what he had access to." He tapped the pile of three folders. "It's loose and not in order, as far as I can tell, so I don't know if he had everything."

I itched to open them and get started, but I was also mindful of my promise to myself not to shut my husband out. Reluctantly, I handed them to Red.

"Do you want to take a run at these? You'll know better than either one of us what's important. Try to gauge if anything's not there that should be, too. I'm a little familiar with Ben's god-awful scribble, so I'll tackle the notebooks."

"You want me back on the shelter?" Erik asked.

"Yes. Unless we run into something computer-related we can't handle. Anything I can do to help you with that?"

"I want to set up an appointment with Mrs. Jefferson, over here this time. I think maybe she'll be more forthcoming if she's sure we can't be overheard."

I remembered then Erik's tale of his first meeting with the director of the shelter at the Fig Tree in Beaufort. He'd commented on her cloak-and-dagger behavior in handing over her list of suspects in the attempted break-ins and her fear that their computer system, with its records of the residents, might have been compromised.

"Do you want me to be there?"

"Let's play it by ear." He paused. "But it would be good if we could use your office."

"Done. Just let me know when you have the time firmed up."

Erik nodded. "I'm going to get going on that list she gave me, then. I'll see what I can find out about the guys she has on her radar screen. Call if you need me."

Red rose as well, picking up the folders as he stood. "I'll get started on these."

A moment later, I was engrossed in deciphering my late partner's chicken scratch, working hard to suppress the memories that kept threatening to overwhelm me as I followed the twists and turns of the investigation into the disappearance of Morgan Tyler Bell and the supposed suicide of Anjanette Freeman.

When Red appeared in the doorway of my office, I had absolutely no idea how long I'd been at it. I had filled several pages of a legal pad with notes, and my hand felt as if someone had crushed it in a vise when I dropped my pen and looked up at my husband.

"Quitting time," he said, smiling. "Unless the boss is going to chain us to our desks."

I removed my reading glasses and rubbed the bridge of my nose. "Is it five already?"

"Closer to six," he said. "I didn't want to disturb you. You looked pretty engrossed."

I began shuffling everything together and sliding it into my brief-case. "How did you make out with the sheriff's reports?"

Red stretched his arms over his head and stifled a yawn. "There are some gaps, unfortunately ones that might have proved useful, but he had a lot on the initial investigation. And before you ask, I can't see anything they did—or didn't do—that would indicate a less than professional job by everyone involved. A couple of surprises, though."

"Like what?"

"They did a pretty thorough search of the grounds. Even brought in SLED and some of their fancy equipment."

"What kind of equipment?"

"Ground penetrating radar," my husband said.

"Looking for another body?"

"That's my guess, although what Ben had didn't go into specifics."

"It makes sense, I guess. One corpse and two missing men might lead anyone to think they might never have left the island." I shoved the last of the notebooks into my briefcase. "I'm assuming they didn't find one."

"Nope. Although, they did consider that it could have ended up in the water. Or maybe gator food." He ignored my shudder. "You have any luck with Ben's notebooks?"

"Not much new information, but I didn't get through them all. I can say that he wasn't thrilled with the suicide verdict. Same reasons you gave. Not the usual choice for a woman." I locked the file cabinets and turned back to my husband. "You up for cooking? I sure as hell don't feel like it."

"Let's go out. You need to change?"

I felt grubby from handling all the paper that had been stored in Ben's attic for the past few years, but I didn't want to waste time going back to the house. "I'll just wash up and run a brush through my hair. Where to?"

"Your call."

I slid past him and across the reception area to the restroom. Erik's desk was buttoned up and cleared off, and I wondered when he'd made his escape. A few minutes later and several layers of grit cleaner, I met Red at the door. He handed me my bag and briefcase.

We walked out into the warm fall evening, the hazy twilight good for another couple of weeks before the loss of daylight savings time plunged us once again into early darkness. We'd driven two cars to work as usual, and I tapped the remote control for the locks on the Jaguar. Red had just pulled open the door to his Bronco when the Rolls-Royce limo careened into the driveway and slid to a stop just inches from my bumper. Brenda threw the giant vehicle into Park and leaped out, almost in one motion. I waited for her to scurry around and open the door for Winston Wolfe, but she bypassed the passenger side and trotted up to where we stood staring. It occurred to me then that she'd never returned our call of the night before.

"Hey, Brenda," my husband said, but she ignored him.

"Something's happened to Mr. Wolfe," she said in a breathless rush. "You need to come right now."

"Slow down." I laid a hand on her trembling shoulder. "Tell it slowly. Where is he?"

"He wants me to take you to him."

Red closed my door and spoke softly. "You need to tell us what happened. We're not going anywhere until you do."

The young woman drew a deep breath and let it out slowly. "Okay. After we left here, he told me to take the afternoon off. I went and got the limo washed and cleaned out and waited for him to call. He's paying a daily rate whether I actually drive him or not, so I need to be on call whenever he needs me. That's the deal."

"Good," I said in imitation of Red's calm voice. "You're doing fine."

"So anyway, he called about four thirty and said to pick him up at the Crowne Plaza, which I did. I got there a little before five. He wasn't out front, so I asked the bellman if I could leave the car and ring up to his room. I went inside to the desk, but Mr. Wolfe didn't answer. I didn't know what to do."

Her speech rate had increased, and again I reached out to touch her. "Slow down. You're doing great."

"I went back out to the car and got in. I was going to park somewhere and wait for him, you know? But when I closed the door, he was already in the backseat. Lying down, like he was hiding from someone. He scared me to death. Before I could ask him anything, he told me just to get the hell out of there. So I drove out toward the exit on 278. He wouldn't tell me where to go, so I turned right. I was so scared, you know? I mean, he acted like someone was after him or something."

Red and I exchanged a look while the poor girl caught her breath.

"What did he say?" my husband asked.

"Nothing! That's the thing, he didn't say anything after he told me to drive away. So I just headed down 278 until we were almost off the island. Then he said, in a real shaky voice, he said for me to turn around and go back. Then he said he needed to find another place to stay, somewhere he wouldn't be expected to show up. So I took him back down Pope Avenue and let him out at the Holiday Inn on Coligny. He jumped right out of the car and told me to come and get you and bring you to him. He said it was a matter of life and death."

And with that the poor child slumped against the side of the Rolls and burst into tears.

We spent the next few minutes soothing the distraught young woman until I felt confident she could make her way back to the limousine company offices in one piece. We assured her we would head immediately for the Holiday Inn as soon as she felt comfortable on her own.

"What the hell's going on?" Red asked as he slid into the driver's seat of the Jaguar. "What has that weirdo gotten himself into now?"

"*Weirdo* is a little harsh, don't you think? Eccentric, certainly, but that probably comes with the territory. And who knows how much is real and how much is cultivated to create an image?"

"I don't really give a damn," my husband replied. "This is beginning to get just a bit too strange for my taste. Who could the guy think is after him? The ghost of Ty Bell?"

The smile faded quickly. "Maybe there really is someone on his tail. It could explain why he disappeared so suddenly from the airport last night."

As soon as I said the words, it occurred to me that Wolfe had used the Rolls to show up at our office only a few hours before. He hadn't seemed the least afraid or even nervous then, so maybe I was just manipulating the facts to suit my theory. God knew, Red had accused me of that often enough. Either way, we'd know soon enough.

Red tapped his fingers on the steering wheel while we waited at the light at Gumtree Road. A moment later, we roared onto the Cross Island Parkway, heading for the south end of the island. When we'd merged with the heavy traffic flow, he said, "I suppose he's made some enemies over the years with his books. Have you read any of them?"

"No. Not exactly my cup of tea. I prefer my crime in fiction form, with all the loose ends neatly tied up at the end."

"Strange profession you've chosen then," he said without humor.

"Maybe. But back to Wolfe. You're right. I suppose he could have made some enemies with his tell-all books about real murderers. Besides, he's got the kind of attitude that could piss people off without too much effort."

"Yeah, I noticed," Red muttered, as we cruised through the toll gates in the Palmetto Pass lane.

We lapsed into silence during the drive down Pope Avenue, the usual traffic heavier on a Friday night with a good many of the locals headed out to dinner, so it was close to seven when we spun around the Coligny circle and into the parking lot of the Holiday Inn. Inside, the staff was unable—or unwilling—to confirm that Wolfe had registered, let alone give us his room number.

I rang his cell, but of course there was no answer. I slammed mine shut and stomped outside, Red right behind me.

"Okay, now what?" he asked.

"Now I'm getting seriously concerned. He was here an hour ago, at least according to Brenda. You don't think he just used this as a blind, do you? I mean, he sent the girl back to get us, so he must have expected her to bring us here. Maybe he went to another hotel." There were several down South Forest Beach Drive and a couple in the opposite direction. "And he could be using another name to check in."

"Not without showing some form of ID he couldn't. Every hotel requires that now."

We stood under the overhang, off to the side to stay out of the flow of people moving in and out.

"Let's try the beach first." I whirled around and headed toward the side of the building closest to the newly revamped beach park with its dancing waters. I'd taken only a couple of steps when I felt Red's hand on my shoulder. "What?"

"Hang on a minute. Over there by the sidewalk. No! Don't turn around." He pulled me quickly into his arms then slowly pivoted so that our positions were reversed. "Guy with the red baseball cap leaning up against the palm tree."

I spotted him, and my stomach clenched. Tall and slender, he wore a faded yellow T-shirt with some kind of logo on it, and khaki shorts. His long legs looked tanned, and his running shoes had seen better days. I jerked my gaze back to his face, but it was obscured by wraparound sunglasses.

I stiffened in Red's arms, then eased myself out of his embrace. "You don't think—?" I began just as the man turned, and I caught a glimpse of some sort of strap hanging on his left shoulder a moment before he walked briskly across the street.

CHAPTER FOURTEEN

BEFORE I COULD TAKE THE FIRST STEP, A TOUR BUS
rounded Coligny Circle, stopping in front of the park entrance
and blocking out my view.

"Come on!" I grabbed my husband's hand and pulled him after me.

In the old days, Red would have balked, holding me back while
we discussed the pros and cons of chasing after a complete stranger
who happened to be dressed like someone we might be looking for.
Apparently, hanging out with me had extinguished some of his cop
caution, because I could feel him pounding along behind me as I
sprinted across the parking lot and onto the sidewalk. The circle was
full of traffic, and we had to wait an agonizingly long time before we
found a break. We dived into the copse of trees that filled the inner
ring, taking the most direct path to the other side. We emerged into
fading sunlight and more cars whizzing past.

But our quarry had disappeared.

"Damn it!" I shouted, and a couple with two young kids in tow,
waiting to cross a few feet away from us, shot me a disgusted glance.

I whirled 360 degrees, but the man in the red baseball cap was
gone.

"How'd he do that?" Red was puffing a little.

I did another scan of the area, but there were a lot of places he could have disappeared into—shops and restaurants and even the dense foliage that bordered the old Smokehouse Restaurant. A little shiver ran down my spine at the memory of Cecelia Dobbs and the slimy lagoon just a few yards away.

"We have to find Wolfe," I said, turning back toward the hotel. "I'm damned if I'm going to lose another client."

Red caught up and took my hand. Under its pressure, I slowed a little.

"Don't even go there," he said softly. "We'll find him."

Once again dodging traffic, we headed left to the public entrance to the beach. Though the sun was sliding down over the mainland, its dying rays lit the sky over the ocean with faint hints of orange and pink. Out on the beach, a few diehard tourists still splashed in the cooling water, and one of the locals loped along behind a pair of panting golden retrievers, their long blond legs crusted with saltwater and matted with sand.

We cut right toward the Tiki Hut and the hotel's pool. The outdoor bar was doing a brisk business, and it took us some time to scrutinize the clientele jammed around the entire area. Most of them were younger, and no flowing white hair caught our attention. Red tilted his head toward the pool, and we began a visual grid search, my husband scanning the left while I took the right. Very few chaises were occupied, and it took only a minute for us to admit defeat.

I flopped down on the sand and fought the longing for a calming hit of nicotine. "I suppose we should try inside again," I said. "He has to be here somewhere. Unless he saw the ghost of Ty Bell, too, and decided to take off."

"Insufficient data," my husband said, mimicking Erik's favorite expression. "We don't know for sure it was him, ghost or not."

I blew out a long breath. "True. But it's pretty damn strange that someone who looks exactly like all those photos would show up in exactly the same place we're supposed to meet Wolfe. I've never been a fan of coincidence, and this one just strains imagination way too far."

"True," Red surprised me by repeating, "but you can't jump to conclusions, either." He stood and held out his hand. "Let's go track down the great man. Maybe he'll have some answers."

I reached in my pocket. "Let me try his cell again."

I punched in the numbers from memory. God knew I'd dialed them often enough in the past couple of days. My head snapped up a second later when I heard the faint strains of "New York, New York."

"Do you hear that?"

Red cocked his head to one side. "Yeah." He listened intently, turning until he faced the thick stand of palmettos that shielded the far side of the pool from the beach. "Over there."

We looked at each other. "Is that his ringtone?" he asked.

"I have no idea. It would be like him, though, don't you think?"

"Hang up and try it again."

I hit End, and the music stopped. Without words, we moved together in the direction from which we'd heard the sounds. I redialed, and immediately the song wafted out from the bushes.

"Be careful," I called as Red gingerly separated the razor-sharp leaves of the huge plants and disappeared from view.

Suddenly, the music stopped again, and I heard Red's voice.

"The phone was here on the ground," he said in a somber tone.

"Wolfe?" My voice cracked a little on the single word.

"Nothing," my husband said and emerged from the tangle of bushes with the phone held high. He carried it to me, and we stood for a moment staring at each other.

"Now what?" I asked, the fear—and the memories—making it come out in a breathless rush.

"Now we call the sheriff."

But we didn't. Not right then.

After the initial shock of finding Wolfe's phone abandoned among the palmettos, we did another sweep of the area, our task made more difficult by the encroaching darkness. We found nothing more to indicate where our client might have gone or how he ended up separated from his cell. We walked silently back up the beach path to the front of the Holiday Inn.

"We've done just about all we can do." Red ran a hand through his short, straight hair. "I think we need to get the pros involved."

"And tell them what? That Wolfe seemed to be afraid of someone and changed hotels? That he might have dropped his phone on the beach?" I almost smiled. "Think back to when you were wearing the uniform. If I came to you with this story, what would you have said?"

He took a few moments to answer. "Fair enough. I would have told you to go home and wait, that you'd probably hear from him before the night was out. Not to jump to conclusions."

"Ever the voice of reason," I said dryly. "That was you. Things look a little different from this side of the fence, don't they?"

He nodded. "So what do you suggest? We can't make the front desk people give us his room number. If he's even registered here. And they certainly wouldn't let us into his room."

"We could try a bribe." I reached in my bag for my wallet. "How much do you have on you?"

"Forget it. Besides, what do you expect to find? He didn't have anything with him."

"We don't know that for a fact."

I sighed and glanced at my watch. "We should have asked Brenda. She's probably gone home by now. And we don't even know her last name. Do we?"

"No, at least I don't."

"Wait!" I pulled Wolfe's cell out of my pocket and powered it up. "She said he called her to come pick him up."

I pushed buttons on the unfamiliar model until I found the right screen. The last outgoing call was a local number. I held the phone to my ear and waited.

"Damn it," I said when it went to voice mail. "Brenda, this is Bay Tanner. We haven't been able to locate Mr. Wolfe, and we need to speak to you urgently. Please call me as soon as you pick up this message." I left both Red's and my cell numbers.

"Good work, Sherlock," my husband said.

"Fat lot of good it did us. Do you know anyone at the Crowne Plaza? Anyone in security?"

Red hesitated, and I could tell by the look on his face that my changing gears had confused him for a moment.

"You want to get into his room?"

"It would tell us whether or not he had his briefcase or suitcase with him. Besides, he may have had other luggage than what we swiped from the airport. There could be lots of clues that could have a bearing on who he's running from or where he's gone."

"Possible. Let me think about it."

"Can we grab something to eat on the way over? I'm about to crash and burn here."

"That's one of the things I love about you, Bay Tanner. Nothing puts you off your feed."

"Go to hell," I said with a smile as we headed for the car.

It turned out that Red did have a contact at the Crowne, although he had to make a couple of calls to get the right name. Friend of a friend of a former deputy, he explained as we waited in the drive-thru lane at McDonald's. One of these days the cheeseburgers were going to come back and haunt my hips, I thought, but it didn't keep me from enjoying every last juicy bite. It was just after eight when we pulled up into the jammed parking lot of the resort hotel inside Shipyard Plantation. As we approached the main entrance, I saw Erik pacing near the bellmen's stand. With Stephanie right beside him.

"What's she doing here?" I whispered to Red as we made our way through the rows of cars.

"They were out to dinner. What was he supposed to do, take time to dump her at home?"

"This isn't a double date. We have business to take care of."

"Chill," my husband said, squeezing my arm a moment before we reached them.

"Hey." Erik looked a little sheepish. "Steph wanted to tag along. She'll stay out of the way."

"Fine," I said, moving around them and into the tiled lobby with its soaring atrium. "Red, go see if you can scare up this Cooper guy. We'll wait here."

He shot me a look before he walked over to the front desk. A young man in a smart blazer smiled brightly, then picked up a phone. I moved into the center of the lobby to where a number of chairs and love seats were clustered and flopped down. Erik and Stephanie followed, seating themselves on one of the small sofas, their hands clasped firmly together.

"I know you're not happy about me being here," the trim young woman said. "I can go wait in the car if it'll make things easier."

I let my breath out and ordered myself to be reasonable. "It's fine, Stephanie. Really. It's just that I'm concerned about our client."

It wasn't totally true. Something about the young woman—aside from my guilt about her father's death—made me uncomfortable in her presence. Chances were it was more me than Stephanie. I needed to get past it.

I looked up as Red appeared in front of us.

"He'll be right out. Have you filled Erik in?"

I shook my head. "Why don't you do that? Stephanie and I are going to check out the bar. Maybe someone's seen or talked to Wolfe recently. Come and get us when your contact shows up."

The surprise showed on her pretty face, but she leaped immediately to her feet and followed me down the wide hallway with its bank of windows reflecting our own images back at us as darkness enveloped the grounds.

"Okay, here's the plan. We're just two ladies out for the evening." I looked down at her. "Do you drink? Alcohol?"

"Wine mostly."

"Okay. We'll sit at the bar. Just follow my lead."

I could feel her excitement, and it brought a smile. I remembered the last time I'd sashayed into this lounge, dressed to the teeth and looking to flush out a rapist who preyed on escorts. I'd found the hunt exhilarating until the whole thing turned deadly. Stephanie might be pumped by the *idea* of being part of an investigation, but I hoped she was never forced to confront the darker side of the job.

The room was fairly full on that Friday evening, a combination of couples, a few tables of what were probably golfing buddies on vacation, and one or two single guys at the bar. We found two stools and slid onto them. The bartender moved quickly to stand in front of us. Young and not at all bad-looking, he zeroed in on Stephanie. It stung a little, but I could understand. As long as he didn't assume I was her mother.

"Ladies?" he said. "What can I get you?"

"I'll have a Pinot Grigio," Stephanie said.

"Perrier and lime," I chimed in.

"Coming right up."

I swiveled around and did a slow scan of the rest of the room. No long, flowing white hair. And no red baseball cap. I turned back when the bartender slid our drinks in front of us.

"Want to run a tab?" he asked, again directing his attention to Stephanie.

"No, thanks." I handed him my personal credit card. No sense advertising our business unless we had to.

We sipped until he came back with the slip, which I signed, adding a more than generous tip. That brought his attention back to me.

"Pretty crowded tonight. Is there something special going on?" I asked in a tone that implied the answer wasn't important to me.

"Seafood buffet in the restaurant. We always get a lot of spillover on Friday nights. Folks waiting for tables."

I nodded. "Are most of them guests?"

"Some," he said, his voice sounding a touch more wary.

"We were sort of hoping to run into a friend of ours." Stephanie leaned a little closer to the young man, and I nearly laughed. Maybe I had been wrong about Erik's fiancée. In a lot of ways.

"I guess you don't see her. Or him," he added with a matching grin.

"My aunt's sort of got a crush on the guy." She giggled effectively. "He's a crime writer. Aunt Lydia's kind of a groupie."

I was astonished at her quick mind and improvisation. Yes, I had seriously underestimated Stephanie's capacity—for playacting as well as for outright lying.

"Oh, yeah, I know who you mean. Older dude. Long white hair. Yeah, he's staying here, I think. At least he's been in here the last couple of days. Vodka martini, straight up. Haven't seen him tonight, though." He turned his megawatt smile on me. "Sorry, ma'am."

A couple climbed onto stools a little way down the bar, and our informant moved away to serve them. I took a long swallow of the carbonated water.

"You're good," I said softly, and Stephanie smiled.

"Did I do okay?"

"More than okay. Do you think you can pump him a little more?" I told her what I had in mind. I gulped down the rest of the glass. "I'm going to make a trip to the ladies' room."

I slid off the stool and made my way out of the lounge. Outside in the hallway, I stepped back out of the bartender's line of sight just as Erik and Red surrounded me.

"What's going on?" my partner asked. "Where's Stephanie?"

"Working," I said and smiled.

CHAPTER
FIFTEEN

ICK COOPER SLID HIS PASS CARD INTO THE SLOT ON
room 422 and stepped back.

"I need to go in with you," he said, opening the door just a crack. "It's going be my job if anyone finds out."

"No problem." Red patted him on the shoulder. "And no one's going to hear about it from us. Just a quick in-and-out to make sure Wolfe's okay."

The security man paused, again checking the hallway in both directions before pushing the door fully open. He held it for me, and he and Red followed me into the room. It was huge, the bathroom just to the left as you entered, with the expansive bedroom/sitting room opening out at the end of a short hall. The drapes were open, revealing the entire back wall as floor-to-ceiling glass. It was oceanfront, and the view in the daylight would have been spectacular. I moved into the main expanse and stopped short. The two men crowded around me.

"Jesus!" Rick Cooper said. "What the hell happened in here?"

The place had been searched, and by someone who obviously didn't give a damn if anyone knew it. Empty drawers and clothing littered the plush carpet, along with hangers and several books. The closet stood empty, and the bed had been stripped down to the mattress. I moved a little farther into the room until Red's hand on my arm stopped me.

"Don't touch anything," he said in the cop voice I hadn't heard in some time.

"I know." I took a few more steps and turned in a circle. "No suitcase or briefcase that I can see. Bathroom?"

Red turned and retraced his steps, returning in a moment. "Clean," he said. "Two used bath towels. No toiletries. The shower's dry."

"I need to report this," Cooper said, reaching for a walkie-talkie attached to his belt.

Red held up his hand. "Hold on a sec. Just watch us. We're not going to do anything to disturb the scene. We just need to see if there're any papers he might have missed." He nodded to me. "Carefully, Bay."

I tiptoed around, making certain I didn't dislodge any of the mess. "I don't see anything. Whoever did this looked in all the right places. If there was something to find, I'm betting he found it."

"When would the room have been made up?" Red asked. "I mean, is there a schedule or something?"

"Sort of. Housekeeping has specific floors and rooms assigned, but they have to skip one if the guest is inside or if the Do Not Disturb sign is out."

"It is," I said. "I saw it while you were unlocking the door."

"So they would have left it until later?" Red asked.

"They would have kept trying, but they're mostly gone by now. They would have reported it to the front desk, though. If they couldn't get in."

I didn't want to discuss our business in front of Rick Cooper, helpful as he'd been. I stared at Red until he looked my way, then flicked my head slightly toward the door.

"Well, thanks, Rick. I appreciate you letting us in. You go ahead and do what you have to do." As he spoke, he moved toward the doorway. "I hope we can keep our little excursion here to ourselves."

Out in the hallway, the security man let the door close behind him. "I'll do my best, Sergeant. Can't promise anything, though. You understand."

"Of course." Red held out his hand. "Thanks again. Give my best to Will when you run across him."

"I'll do that. Probably see him this weekend. Bunch of us usually get together and take my boat out if the weather's good." He glanced back toward room 422. "Maybe not, though. We'll see how it goes."

I looked back as we stepped into the elevator to see Rick Cooper speaking into his walkie-talkie.

We met up with Erik and Stephanie in the lobby, and the four of us beat a hasty retreat out to the parking lot. We stood around the Jaguar, and I could feel the two young people's tension level rise as Red told them what we'd found upstairs.

"So let's meet up at the office," I said. "We have a lot to sort through and not a lot of time to do it in."

I glanced at Stephanie, who'd managed to learn from the eager bartender that Wolfe had drunk alone the past two nights. No one had seemed to recognize him, but that hadn't kept him from expounding to his captive audience of one about his fame and fortune. Of course, he could have been overheard by others sitting close by, but that didn't necessarily mean one of them had taken the opportunity to trash his room. Whoever had searched his things had been messy but thorough.

I held Stephanie's gaze for a long moment. "You want in?" I asked, and her face lit up.

"Yes, ma'am," she said without hesitation.

Erik squeezed her shoulder, and I realized that he wasn't as thrilled about the prospect as his fiancée.

"We could use an extra pair of hands and eyes on this," I said matter-of-factly. "Red?"

"Fine by me. It's your call."

"Good. Then let's get moving."

Red and I spoke very little on the short ride up-island. Erik must have been right on our tail, because he pulled in beside me almost immediately. I grabbed my briefcase out of the backseat, and we trooped inside. Erik assembled chairs so that all of us could gather around my desk. I spread out the papers I'd intended to carry home with me.

"I don't know quite how to begin," I said, eyeing my team. I have to admit it gave me something of a rush to think that we might need more space one day soon. "I wish we had a whiteboard."

"I've got one at home," Stephanie offered. "I got it at Wal-Mart. I could run over there and pick one up. It'd only take a few minutes."

"Good idea. Erik, give her some money out of petty cash. We'll get organized." I looked up to find her intent gaze on me. "We'll wait for you," I said, and she smiled.

Erik handed over the keys to his Expedition along with the cash, and Stephanie hurried out. When the door had been locked behind her, I turned to my partner.

"Stephanie could be helpful on this. We won't let her get involved in anything dangerous, but she's used to putting together a story for the magazine. She has good organizational skills and a logical mind. Print out an employment contract, and let's get her official so she can be privy to all the information." I gestured to the piles of paper on the desk. "Agreed?"

"I thought you just wanted a receptionist." Erik's voice was calm, but there was an undercurrent of disapproval he couldn't quite hide.

"Everyone around here has to do double duty. You of all people should know that. If she wants the job, she's going to have to be involved in the cases, at least peripherally. That means she has to be bound by the confidentiality clause. If you don't want her here, *you* tell her. As far as I'm concerned, she's hired."

I felt bad for the confusion I could read in his eyes, but it was something he and Stephanie would have to deal with. Suddenly, it seemed important for us to have her on the team, and she and Erik would have to work it out between them.

"Okay," he said finally. "But nothing dangerous. I have to have your word on that."

"You've got it," I said. I breathed deeply and squared my shoulders. "Okay. It seems to me we have only one priority right now, and that's to find out what the hell happened to Wolfe. As soon as Stephanie gets back, we'll write out a time line. Erik, is she a fast typist? I mean, can she take notes while we brainstorm?"

"Absolutely." He turned at the sound of a soft knock on the door and rose to let his fiancée in.

I smiled at the look that passed between them and hoped to hell I knew what I was doing.

We set the whiteboard on top of the mini fridge. Stephanie had also bought a package of dry erase markers in several colors, and she laid those out on the desk. Without even thinking about it, I picked up the red one and divided the pristine surface of the board into three columns. Behind me, I heard Erik chuckle. This was the process I'd learned from my late husband Rob in the days when we'd worked together on money-laundering cases: What do we think, what do we know, what can we prove. It was a tested method I fell back on whenever I felt overwhelmed with information, and my partner had seen these three columns on all kinds of paper, from lined legal pads to the backs of envelopes, whatever I could lay my hands on.

"Let's skip the 'prove' column," my husband said. "No legal matters here, at least not right at the moment. I think what we need is a time line of Wolfe's movements, as far as we know them."

Stephanie had slipped out and returned with some paper towels from the restroom. I wiped out what I'd written and turned to the group.

"Okay, somebody get us started. Steph, will you be the scribe?"

I handed her the marker, and she moved to take my place by the board. "When do you want to start? From the time he first contacted you—Wednesday, wasn't it?" she asked.

"Right," Erik said. "He came to the office at three on Wednesday afternoon."

Stephanie printed the information at the top and waited.

"Then he met us on Thursday at the marina," I offered, and that seemed to kick things loose.

We worked steadily, each of us chiming in, until we had a fair representation of Winston Wolfe's locations and activities as we knew them, right up until his last encounter with Brenda. I must have conjured her up, because my phone rang at almost that exact moment.

I fished it out of my pocket. "Brenda," I said, and everyone's heads turned in my direction. "Thanks for getting back to me."

"I hope it's not too late," she said. "I'm out with some friends and just picked up the message."

"No, you're good. I wanted to ask if Mr. Wolfe had any luggage with him when he got out of the limo at the Holiday Inn."

I could hear the concern in her voice. "Didn't you find him?"

"I'm afraid not. He may have changed his mind. I'm sure we'll hear from him. If we knew what he was carrying with him, though, it would help us . . ." *What?* I thought. It sounded stupid, even to my own ears, but I didn't want her worrying about what might have happened to her passenger. "It would just help," I finished lamely.

"Sure. He had his briefcase. I remember, because he wasn't holding it by the handle when he got out of the limo and sent me to get you and your husband. He was sort of clutching it to his chest with both arms, you know?"

"Thanks, Brenda. I appreciate your getting back to me so quickly. Have a good evening."

But the young woman wasn't about to let it go at that. "You're worried about him, aren't you? I mean, because he thought someone was following him?"

"He might have been overreacting just a little. You know how these artistic types can be."

"I guess," she said, not entirely convinced. "I'm still on call for him until next Wednesday. He paid for a week up front."

"Let us know if you hear from him, okay?"

"Yes, ma'am," she said, "I sure will."

"Thanks again." I closed the phone and relayed the gist of the conversation to my colleagues.

"So whoever ransacked his room wouldn't have found the documents he always carried," Red offered. "That might explain why the room was trashed. If that's what they were looking for."

"Then where's the suitcase?" I asked when no one offered a comment. "If Wolfe didn't have it, whoever searched must have taken it away with him."

"Unless he put it somewhere else. For safekeeping." Stephanie's voice was just a shade above a whisper.

"Could be." I smiled at her. "So where would you stash a big piece of luggage you didn't want anyone to find?"

"The concierge desk?" she offered. "In New York hotels, they have a room where you can put your bags if you have to check out before you're ready to catch your plane. They give you a claim check, and you can go to your meeting or whatever and then come back and collect your luggage."

Red had already taken out his phone. "I'll see if Rick Cooper can find out."

He stepped out into the reception area, and I found my eyes drawn back to the board and its time line.

"Here's the thing. He left here, and Brenda took him back to the Crowne Plaza. That would have been around two thirty or three, agreed?" I didn't wait for Erik and Stephanie to comment. "Then he called her around four thirty to pick him up and then went through his hiding in the backseat routine when she got there. So sometime in those couple of hours something changed. Either he saw someone, or he got a call . . ."

I refrained from smacking myself in the forehead, but it was a close thing. I picked up Wolfe's cell phone from the desk and checked the incoming log. He had received no calls after he left the office. But he did have one at 6:37, just about the time we were fighting traffic on our way to the Holiday Inn. It was a 440 area code. I scribbled the number on a notepad and handed the sheet to Erik.

"Can you find out who this belongs to?"

"Sure. Just take a minute."

He used his iPhone rather than power up the laptop. As his thumbs raced over the keys, Red came back into the room.

"Rick checked with the concierge. Wolfe didn't leave a bag with them."

"Damn! Then either he stashed it somewhere else, or—"

"Or whoever searched his room took it." Red noticed Wolfe's phone in my hand. "Did he get a call?"

I opened my mouth to tell him about my brainstorm when Erik looked up from his miniature keyboard. "This is weird," he said.

"What?" I asked.

"The call came from Ohio. At least that's where the area code is." That made my head snap up.

He paused, as he often did, for effect. "And the number's registered to Terry Gerard."

CHAPTER SIXTEEN

WE KEPT AT IT UNTIL WELL AFTER MIDNIGHT, BUT NO scenario we could come up with gave us the first clue about where Wolfe might have disappeared to—either on his own or at someone else's insistence.

Of course, we tried Gerard's number, and of course there was no answer. No voice mail, either. Erik downloaded all Wolfe's numbers, both in and out, onto a flash drive and promised to work on them at home. It was a slim chance that one of them would lead us to our missing client, but it had to be checked out. Once the information had been dumped, I tucked the phone in my purse so I could secure it in my floor safe at home.

Just as we were locking up, Red took a call from Rick Cooper at the Crowne Plaza. He told my husband he'd contacted the sheriff's office, using the excuse of no activity around Wolfe's room all day as his rationale for letting himself in with the passkey. Detective Mike Raleigh had been on scene, so I knew we had a chance of prying some information loose about what they'd found. If we played our cards right. Had it been our old nemesis, Lisa Pedrovsky, we could have kissed any opportunity for cooperation good-bye.

The four of us had stood in the parking lot, mulling over our lack of success on finding Wolfe and brainstorming a game plan for the next day. Red and I were handcuffed by our commitment to Scotty and Elinor, my stepchildren, who spent every weekend with us, so we'd have to leave a lot of it in the hands of our younger associates. It might have been a good exercise for them, working on a case together, if I hadn't had that sinking feeling in the bottom of my stomach. My thoughts kept sliding back to another case and another missing client. That one had not turned out well. Not well at all.

It was pushing one o'clock when Red and I finally set the alarm system in our house on the beach in Port Royal Plantation and tumbled into bed. I snuggled against the warmth of my husband's body, my mind racing a mile a minute. I squirmed a little, and Red's arms pulled me closer.

"Let it go, honey," he whispered against my hair. "There's nothing else we can do."

"There should be," I said, flipping over and fitting my body into the curve of his.

"The sheriff's aware of the problem now. They'll be on the lookout for Wolfe." He stroked my bare arm, and I felt myself relaxing. "You going to the game with me tomorrow?"

Red's son Scotty had failed to make the middle school football team. Reluctantly, he'd abandoned his dreams of glory on the gridiron, opting instead for the speed and grace of soccer. He proved to be a natural and more than once had scored the winning goal. Having been raised on football, I was generally confused by all the running back and forth on the soccer field without much tangible result, but lately I'd found myself getting more and more into at least the spirit of the game—even if I didn't yet understand all the rules.

"Maybe I should stay here," I mumbled, sleep stealing over me in spite of my mental gymnastics. "In case . . ." I tried to hold on to the thought, but I could feel myself slipping away.

"We'll see," I thought my husband said, but I was gone before I could mount an argument.

As it turned out, the decision was taken out of my hands. I awoke to an empty bed and sun streaming through the French door that led onto the deck. I squinted at the clock, dismayed to find it was already after nine. I bolted up and out to the kitchen, but I could tell Red had already left. His coffee cup sat in the sink, and toast crumbs littered the counter. The note was propped up against the canister that held the tea bags.

Back by noon. Let's picnic on the beach. I'll bring the food. Love you. R

In the bathroom, I brushed my teeth and decided a run would help clear the cobwebs. As I tucked my phone into the zippered pocket of my running shorts, I detoured back into the bedroom and opened the safe in the floor of my walk-in closet. I powered up Wolfe's cell and checked for messages. A blinking cursor told me he had a voice mail. I fiddled with buttons, but I couldn't figure out how to retrieve it. There probably isn't a techno-challenged person on the planet that could hold a candle to me. Try as I might, I couldn't seem to wrap my head around the logic—or lack thereof—of all the shiny new gadgets that kept appearing every fifteen minutes to confuse and confound.

I tried Erik and got him on the second ring.

"Any flashes of illumination since last night?" I asked, stretching out as I talked.

"Not yet. You?"

"Do you remember Wolfe's phone? I mean, the model and all? He's got a voice mail, but I don't know how to retrieve it."

I stopped working on my rusty muscles and followed Erik's instructions. "I need a password," I said once I'd found the proper screen.

"I could probably break it if I had the phone," he said. "Want me to pick it up?"

I toyed with the idea, but I didn't really want to have it floating around. I preferred it to remain in the safe. "Can you do it here?" Inspiration struck. "Red is bringing the kids back around noon, and we're going to have a picnic on the beach. You and Steph want to join us?"

I had no real idea how Erik felt about being around children, or if he and Stephanie had discussed the possibility of a family once they were married. Not that that had to be the sequence, especially these days. I tried to remember when it had become socially acceptable to bear children first, then decide if marriage seemed like a good plan. I was definitely getting old.

"Thanks, but we thought we'd spend some time on trying to crack those files I copied from that flash drive Mr. Wolfe had hidden in his suitcase. I've got them on my laptop, and a lot of them are passworded."

I'd completely forgotten about those files we'd raced to copy after we'd swiped Wolfe's luggage from the airport.

Airport! That's what came of trying to work out problems with only half your brain functioning.

"Can you call the general aviation office and see if his plane is still there?"

"I should have thought of that," my partner said. "I'll do it as soon as we hang up."

"Let me know if it's gone." I paused. "Listen, why don't you and Stephanie stop over later this afternoon, then? We'll be down on the beach just at the end of our boardwalk. If you find out anything, we can talk about it then, and you can take a look at the phone."

"I think we can do that. You know you can check the caller's number without accessing the actual message," my partner said.

"No, I didn't. Tell me."

Again Erik talked while I punched buttons. "It's the same one with the Ohio area code," I said. "You really think you can crack the passcode?"

"I'll give it a shot, but you never know. They're always coming up with new ways to keep people like me from meddling," he added with a chuckle. "We'll see you later this afternoon."

I hung up and returned the phone to the safe, stretched out my hamstrings for a few more minutes, then trotted down the steps and over the wooden walkway onto the beach. The air held a slight chill, but the sun beat down from a cloudless sky. I mourned the destruction of a good portion of the dune, the sea oats flattened and dead. Kitty may have missed hitting us directly, but she'd certainly left her mark. I swung onto the hard-packed sand, turned off my mind, and gave myself up to the joy of the run.

My hair was still damp from the shower when the troops came whooping into the house a little before twelve. Scotty, who had shot up over the summer, gave me a fleeting hug, and headed for the bathroom he shared with his sister. He was growing up. Maybe we'd have to think about reconverting the office back into the bedroom it had originally been. He would soon be at the stage where even sharing the same air with his little sister would be anathema to him. Or so I'd heard. Having had no experience of growing up with siblings, I had to rely on my friend Bitsy Elliott's tales of the trials and tribulations of having four children in the house, one or all of whom continually whined about the trauma of having to share anything with each other.

And that thought led immediately to another as I accepted a more enthusiastic hug, this one from tiny Elinor, whose beaming face never failed to cheer me up. I poured her a glass of her favorite peach iced tea and spoke to Red while he unloaded sandwiches.

"Do I have time to call Presqu'isle? I haven't talked to Lavinia since we were there on Wednesday night. This Wolfe business put it right out of my head." I pulled the nylon cooler out of the pantry and set it on the counter. "I hope they're getting along okay."

"Are we going to see Miss Lavinia?" Elinor piped up from her place at the glass-topped table. "You said we could."

I looked at Red. I'd mentioned that we might bring the kids by, and Julia had seemed pleased at the prospect. It might be good for her.

"Maybe. We'll see," he said. "She's pretty busy right now."

"And will the other lady be there, too? Is she my aunt now?"

Red and I exchanged a smile. The dynamics of my family would be confusing, even to an adult. The kids had decided to keep on addressing me as Aunt Bay, even though I was now technically their stepmother. We had left it up to them, and I was fine with their decision.

"I think if you just call her Miss Julia that will be fine. And Miss Elizabeth is her friend who's going to be living at Presqu'isle, too."

"And they have a dog, right? Mama won't let us have a dog. Or even a kitty. It's not fair."

The sunny smile immediately morphed into a puckering of the small, perfect lips, and Red reached over to ruffle her light brown hair. "That's your mother's call. Now finish your tea and go wash your hands. You need to get your bathing suit on, too. But put your shorts on over it. It might be chilly down there."

Elinor gulped down the last swallow of tea, wiped her mouth with her forearm, and bolted down the hall.

"And bring a jacket. Tell your brother."

I laughed and reached for the phone. "Will you pack up? I've got tea in the thermos."

I turned away and waited. Elizabeth Shelly shocked me by answering.

"Presqu'isle."

"Hey, Miss Lizzie. It's Bay."

"Good afternoon. Did you wish to speak to Lavinia?"

I hesitated for a moment, finally deciding I needed to establish a relationship with this woman who had now become, for better or worse, an integral part of our family circle. "No, ma'am, that's okay. I was just calling to see how everyone was getting on."

It might have been my imagination, but it seemed as if the stiff disapproval I'd detected on most of the occasions when we'd spoken was missing—or had at least been ameliorated a little.

"Well, I think we're doing just fine. Julia is outside with Lavinia in the garden. They're staking out some flower beds that Julia can take care of herself. I was just getting ready to call them in for lunch."

It sounded so normal and domestic. Lavinia had apparently unbent enough to allow someone else access to her kitchen. I smiled to myself. Progress, indeed.

"Just tell them I said hello. We'll try to stop over tomorrow on our way to drop off the kids. Probably early afternoon."

"We'll look forward to it. Good-bye now."

Like Lavinia, Elizabeth Shelly apparently liked to have the last word. Before I could ponder too much on the strange ways things sometimes worked out, I found myself surrounded by babbling children eager to be out on the beach.

"You-all go ahead," I said to my husband. "I'll bring the food."

As they clattered down the steps and out toward the boardwalk, it occurred to me that I had gone an entire half hour without once thinking about Winston W. Wolfe.

CHAPTER SEVENTEEN

THE LUNCH HAD BEEN DEVOURED AND CLEANED UP, and I was drowsing on the blanket when I felt the shadow fall over me. I jerked up onto one elbow to find Erik and Stephanie grinning down at me.

"Sorry if we woke you," the young woman said, dropping onto her knees at the edge of our makeshift dining area. "We brought some Cokes," she added, setting a plastic bag down beside me.

I moved over and sat up to make room for them. "That's great." I glanced toward the ocean across the wide expanse of beach exposed by the ebbing tide. "They're all out there boogie-boarding."

We passed around drinks, and Erik pulled off his shirt. Stephanie wore shorts and a bright yellow T-shirt that showed off the tan she'd acquired over the summer. She slid off her sandals and wiggled her toes in the sand.

"So what did you find?" I asked, shading my eyes against the sun to watch Red and the kids gliding along on the shallow surf. Scotty lost his balance and jackknifed easily back into the deeper water. Their laughter drifted up to where we sat.

"First off, Mr. Wolfe's plane is still at the airport."

I wasn't sure if that was good news or not. "What about the files?"

"I concentrated on the ones in the research folder," he said, his eyes, too, focused on the kids. "Not much to help us with finding him. It's mostly stuff related to his books. There is one on Ty Bell, but it doesn't have much more than what we already know. Did you get a chance to decipher Ben's notes?"

"I spent most of yesterday afternoon going through them." I felt the smile drift from my face and glanced quickly at Stephanie. It felt awkward talking about her dead father with her sitting right next to me. "He wasn't entirely sold on the suicide theory of Anjanette Freeman's death, but there wasn't much he could do about it after the coroner's ruling came down."

"Any particular reason?" Erik asked.

"Pretty much what Red had to say. The method mostly. The fact she left no note. And I guess, too, that no one could seem to shed any light on why she might have done it. According to her family in Jamaica, she loved her job and got paid enough that she was able to send a lot of money back home."

"I wonder if she had any friends." Stephanie spoke tentatively, and I nodded to urge her to continue. "I mean, it sounds from everything Erik told me that she was stuck out there with Mr. Bell and Terry Gerard. No other women around. She must have been lonely."

I remembered then the fleeting thought I'd had as Red and I searched through Anjanette Freeman's room. Something about whether or not her relationship with Ty Bell had been strictly one of employer and servant, or if perhaps they had been involved in some way. Or maybe it had been she and Gerard. Either way, their proximity and isolation would have made a liaison understandable. And might have provided a possible motive for her suicide. Or her murder.

I jumped as cold, wet arms snaked around my neck, and Elinor giggled in my ear.

"Daddy says you guys should come in the water. You, too, Mr. Erik."

I swung her around and onto my lap. "You're freezing! You-all need to come up here and get warm."

"The water's nice. Come on, Aunt Bay. I need a girl to play with."

It was hard to resist the plea in her wide eyes, but Stephanie rose to my rescue. "I'll come with you, honey, if that's okay."

Elinor ducked her head, her innate shyness making her snuggle a little more deeply into my loose embrace.

"Go ahead with Miss Stephanie. It'll be okay."

The young woman rose and held out her hand. I lifted Elinor onto her feet and gave her a gentle nudge, but still she held back.

"Race you!" Stephanie yelled and took off across the beach.

Elinor hesitated for just a second before she, too, went tearing off, crying, "No fair! You got a head start!"

I turned to find my partner smiling widely. The question of children leaped again into my head, but I squashed it before it found voice. None of my business. We sat in silence for a few moments, the waning afternoon bringing with it a cooler wind off the ocean, overwhelming the fading strength of the October sun, and I shivered.

"We're nowhere on this, aren't we?" Erik didn't look at me but continued to stare after his fiancée as she romped in the shallow surf with Elinor.

"That we are," I said. "I don't see any point in pursuing the Bell thing until we know what's happened to Wolfe."

"Agreed. What does Red think?"

With his daughter in good hands, my husband had taken his son out farther into the water, hoping for a wave they could ride into shore. A few yards beyond where they paddled on their boards, a dolphin flashed into the sun in a powerful leap that took him high above the surface. He seemed to hang in the air forever before knifing back into the sea. No matter how many times I witnessed it, the beauty and grace of the creatures never failed to move me.

"Bay?"

"Red and I haven't had a chance to discuss it. Having the kids around is a full-time job. But I'd be willing to bet he'd see it the same way." I hesitated. "I'm thinking that we ought to bring Mike Raleigh up to speed on the whole deal."

"Really? That doesn't sound like you."

I wasn't sure if I could put the feeling in the pit of my stomach into words, but I gave it a shot. "I have bad vibes about Wolfe. I don't think he disappeared on his own, and I really don't believe he staged this whole thing as some kind of publicity stunt, even though I wouldn't entirely put it past him." I rubbed my arms and reached behind me to retrieve my jacket. I pulled it on and hugged my knees. "I think something's happened to him, and I don't want anything we do to impede the sheriff from finding him."

Back at the house, the four of us sat around the table in the kitchen for a makeshift conference while the kids were showering and changing. Strangely enough, Red was the one who put up the biggest fight. In the end, though, he relented. We agreed to consolidate all our files and store them in the floor safe until such time as we knew for certain what had become of our client. Red would call Detective Raleigh in the morning while the kids were in Sunday school and explain our involvement. If he wanted our files, we were prepared to hand over everything we had and to help in any way possible with his investigation into Wolfe's disappearance.

"I know you don't like it," I said, rising to take the huge casserole dish of lasagna from the refrigerator. My part-time housekeeper and sometime cook, Dolores Santiago, had left it for us to warm up for dinner. The kids loved it, and all I had to do was throw it in the oven, along with some garlic bread, and toss a salad. It was the perfect way to end a day at the beach. "But I'm not comfortable with our sitting on any information we may have that could help them find him. And it might even give them a little kick in the butt to take it seriously."

"Oh, they're taking it seriously," Red replied after a long swallow of iced tea. "This isn't some runaway teenager or flaky town drunk. Wolfe has a reputation. Believe me, the sheriff isn't going to be sitting on his hands. Especially since it's all tied up with the Bell disappearance. It'll be a full-court press, you can count on it."

I slid the casserole into the oven and smiled at Erik. "You sure you guys won't stay for dinner? As you can see, there's enough here for the entire block."

Erik stood and reached for Stephanie's hand. "Thanks, but I think we should go get all our stuff in order. I'll try to put everything onto one drive so Detective Raleigh doesn't have to wade through a bunch of CDs or paper files. We'll stop at the office and then grab something on the run. Should I—?"

The sound of feet pounding on the hardwood floor in the hallway interrupted him as Scotty and Elinor bounded up the three steps into the kitchen. They skidded to a halt when they realized we still had company.

"Sorry, Aunt Bay," my stepson said.

"Hey, buddy." Erik held out his hand for a knuckle tap, which had apparently replaced the high-five among the cooler folk when I wasn't paying attention. "We're just heading out." He turned to me. "Should I bring them by in the morning?"

"That'd be great," I said, pulling the iced tea pitcher from the refrigerator. "The kids leave for church around nine forty-five."

"Do we have to?" Elinor looked tired, and her voice had dropped into the whine that usually accompanied her crabby moments.

"Yes," her father said, ruffling her still-damp hair. "Now say good-bye to Mr. Erik and thank Miss Stephanie for playing with you today."

"Yes, sir," she said meekly and did as she was told.

"We'll get onto the women's shelter on Monday," I said. "And we have background checks to run. We'll make do with that until we see what shakes out."

Red escorted them out to Erik's Expedition, and I put the kids to setting the table. When my husband returned, he sank back down into his chair. "You guys can go watch something if you want. Dinner in . . . ?" He looked at me.

"Half an hour," I said. I slid the foil-wrapped bread into the oven beside the lasagna and took salad ingredients from the fridge. "No MTV," I hollered after them as they took off for their room.

"Meanie." Red laughed at the scowl I turned on him.

"Hey, I have a certain reputation to uphold. Stepmothers are always wicked. Don't you read your fairy tales?"

I busied myself with chopping and slicing while my husband seemed content to study the wet rings made by his tumbler on the glass-topped table. I reached to set the salad bowl in front of him and let my hand settle on his shoulder.

"What's the matter? What are you so glum about?"

"I feel helpless," he said, leaning back in his chair. "I feel like we should be doing something to find Wolfe."

"Like what?"

"Where's his phone?"

"In the safe. Why?"

He stood and headed down the steps. "I want to look at it. Is that a problem?"

I held up both hands in mock surrender. "Hey, knock yourself out. You know the combination."

I picked up his glass and sipped from it, my mind a chaotic jumble of maybes and what-ifs. Did the man we'd seen lurking around the

Holiday Inn have anything to do with where Wolfe might have gone? Had our client just gotten spooked by something and taken off? Had he dropped his phone by accident, only realizing later that he'd lost it? Or had there been some kind of struggle there in those tightly packed bushes at the rear of the hotel? Could someone really have made off with our client in broad daylight, surrounded by all the patrons of the Tiki Hut bar?

Saved by the bell, I thought when the phone rang shrilly in the relative silence of the house. I reached it on the second ring, but it had already switched to a dial tone. I stared at the handset a moment before shrugging and setting it back in the cradle. I crossed to the oven and checked on the lasagna, which was bubbling away. *Another few minutes,* I thought, just as the phone rang again. I decided to let the machine pick up and stood staring at the built-in desk, prepared to wait through the five programmed rings. But it stopped at four.

"What the hell?" I mused out loud just as Red came back up the steps, Wolfe's cell in his left hand.

"What's going on?" he asked. "Who was on the phone?"

"Nobody. Dial tone the first time, and it stopped before the machine could get it just now." I shrugged. "Could be kids just screwing around."

"I thought Erik wanted to take this and check the voice mail someone left last night."

"He did. He looked at it while you were getting the kids organized for showering, but he couldn't crack the password. I didn't want to let him take it with him, so . . ." I let my voice trail off. "If it comes down to it, the sheriff's tech guys can have a run at it, I guess."

"I don't like the idea of just giving up," my husband said, then whirled at the sound of the house phone again. Before I could move, he'd snatched it up. "Who is this?" he demanded in his sternest, former-cop voice. Then, "Lavinia? I'm sorry, I didn't realize—What?"

"What's the matter?" I could feel the fear gripping my chest, not only at his tone but at the stunned look on his face.

"Bay will be right there. I'll drop the kids at Sarah's . . . Yes, we'll meet you there. Stay calm."

"What is it? God damn it, Red, what's happened?"

He shook his head, and it took him a moment to gather himself. He reached out and grabbed hold of my arms, and I could feel myself swaying.

"What?" I whispered.

"It's Miss Lizzie. She fell down the stairs. Lavinia says it's bad. We have to meet her at the hospital." He swallowed hard. "They think she might not make it."

CHAPTER
EIGHTEEN

HE NEXT HOURS PROVED TO BE EXACTLY THE KIND of nightmare I'd envisioned as we sped in two cars toward the latest calamity that had befallen my family. Red veered off just past the new bridge over the Beaufort River to take the shortcut to Sarah's. He'd called her while we hurriedly gathered the kids' things together. We'd tried not to frighten them too much, but it was impossible to shield them entirely from the fear and anxiety that pulsed through my veins in time with my heartbeat. They were completely subdued as we hustled them into Red's Bronco, and I hoped they'd be able to shake it off without too much lasting effect.

I found Lavinia and Julia huddled together on plastic chairs in the emergency room when I rushed through the door. Lavinia stood and gathered me into her arms, more, I thought, for her own reassurance than for mine. I disengaged myself and looked at my half sister. Her face showed nothing, no trace of anxiety or fear. I moved closer and laid a hand on her shoulder.

"How are you doing, Julia?"

"I'm fine," she said, then turned to survey the room with its bland walls and functional décor. "I don't like it here. It smells funny. Can we go home now?"

Lavinia moved to her other side and took her hand. "We have to wait and see how Miss Lizzie is doing. She got hurt, remember?"

Julia seemed to have reverted to her former, childlike self, all the progress she'd made in her many visits with her psychologist, Neddie Halloran, apparently wiped out by the sudden tragedy.

"Okay," she said and leaned back in her chair.

I motioned Lavinia to step a few feet away and bent my head closer to hers. "What happened?"

Pain flickered across her weathered brown face. "I don't know. I heard the noise and came running from the kitchen." I saw her shudder. "Elizabeth was lying . . . all twisted and bent, and there was blood coming out of her mouth. I leaned down and . . . and checked for a pulse. She was barely breathing. I ran for the phone, to call the paramedics. Julia had been out with the dog, but when I got back from calling she was standing there, just looking at Elizabeth. She never made a sound. I got her away as soon as I could, but it must have been terrifying for the poor child." She let out a long, ragged breath. "I kept her in the kitchen until the ambulance arrived."

I hugged Lavinia again and felt the tremors running through her body. Over her shoulder I watched my half sister idly pleating the hem of her white blouse, her head bent in concentration on her task. *Dear God,* I thought, *we may have lost her for good this time.*

Lavinia stepped back and wiped her eyes with a sodden handkerchief she clutched in one hand. "We'll need to be strong for her if . . ."

"What do the doctors say? Have you talked to anyone?"

"Not since they first brought her in. She was . . . alive when we got here. That's all I know for sure, except that the paramedics who came with the ambulance seemed to think it was bad."

"Maybe it's not as serious as they thought," I said, not believing my own words. "We'll just have to wait and see what the doctors have to say."

"I don't expect they'll talk to me," Lavinia said.

Here was something I could sink my teeth into. "They'll damn well talk to *me*."

I led Lavinia back to her seat beside Julia and headed for the glassed-in opening behind which I could see movement. I slid the split pane aside and cleared my throat. A heavyset black woman turned from her keyboard and smiled.

"Yes, ma'am?"

"My name is Bay Tanner, and I'm here with my friend Mrs. Smalls and my sister Julia. My sister's caregiver was brought in a couple of hours ago. Elizabeth Shelly. She fell down the stairs."

The woman glanced back to her computer screen but didn't reply. I pressed on.

"Miss Shelly lives in my house with Mrs. Smalls and Julia. She has no family in the area, so we need to be kept apprised of her condition and to be consulted about any medical decisions that need to be made."

The woman had probably heard all these songs before, and I had to give her credit for patience. "Do you have her medical power of attorney?"

I had no idea what provision Miss Lizzie might have made for this kind of eventuality—if any. Surely she would have been aware, especially before Julia and I discovered each other, that any illness or accident would have left my sister in a very precarious position. She must have made arrangements, but no one had had the time or the foresight to worry about that.

"No, I don't. Miss Shelly just recently came to live in Beaufort, and I don't have access to her personal papers."

"Can you contact anyone who might know?"

The truth was that we knew very little about Elizabeth Shelly,

other than what she'd told us herself. For all I knew, she had brothers
and sisters, nieces and nephews, cousins, whatever.

"Not at the moment. But we're concerned about right now. Can
you at least ask her physician to keep us informed of her condition?" I
turned to glance over my shoulder at Lavinia huddled in her narrow,
uncomfortable chair. "Legally or not, she's part of our family, and we
need to be here for her."

"I'll see what I can do." She turned back to her computer just as
the wide double doors whooshed open and a woman in surgical scrubs
walked through into the waiting room. I whirled and intercepted her.

"We're with Elizabeth Shelly, the woman who fell down the stairs
out on St. Helena. Do you have any news for us?"

Lavinia jumped up to join me, leaving Julia studying the backs of
her hands.

The woman pulled the pale green skullcap from her head of
straight brown hair. I knew what she would say by the look on her
face, and I reached for Lavinia's hand.

"Are you the family?"

I didn't hesitate. "Yes."

"Let's sit down," she said, cupping my elbow with her hand, but I
shook her off.

"Just tell us," I said.

"I'm sorry, but Ms. Shelly didn't make it. Two broken ribs punc-
tured her lung, and she had serious internal injuries. She bled out before we could get it stopped. I'm sorry."

Lavinia gasped and clutched a hand to her chest. "Oh, that poor,
poor child."

We all turned as if on cue to stare at Julia. Sensing our gazes, she
raised her head and smiled.

"I'm hungry. Can we go home now?"

———————

I don't know what I would have done without Red. He arrived at the emergency room just minutes after the doctor had offered her condolences and disappeared back into the nether regions of the hospital. While I tried to compose myself, my mind whirling with all the arrangements that would need to be made, he dealt with the paperwork.

Back outside, Lavinia convinced us she was perfectly capable of driving her van. I insisted on taking Julia with me while my husband led our strange caravan back through the darkness to Presqu'isle. Lavinia went immediately to the kitchen, her place of solace and refuge, while Red and I took Julia into the morning room. She seemed to have snapped out of her lethargy to some degree, jumping up from the settee almost as soon as I had gotten her seated.

"Julia, come and sit down," I said, patting the delicate brocade upholstery. "I need to talk to you."

"Is Miss Lavinia making spaghetti? I love spaghetti."

She roamed the room, reaching out a finger to touch the various pieces of porcelain my late mother had collected and running her hand across the smooth surface of the spindly-legged French escritoire Emmaline had used for her correspondence.

"Julia, please!"

Red shook his head and crossed the room to take my sister by the hand and lead her back to me. She smiled up into his face and dropped down beside me.

"Do you understand what happened?" I said softly. "To Miss Lizzie?"

"Miss Lavinia said she fell. There was blood on her mouth. I don't like blood."

Tentatively, I put an arm around her shoulders. When she didn't flinch, I drew her closer. "Miss Lizzie died, Julia. I'm so sorry."

A series of unreadable looks passed across her face before she said, "And I can stay here?"

I glanced up at Red. "Of course you can. This is your home now."

I had no idea how Lavinia would cope, and I knew how patently unfair it was for me to expect her to. The proper thing for me to do would be to take Julia home with us. She was *my* family, *my* responsibility. But dear God, how would we manage? Maybe I could hire someone to come in and help. Dolores?

"Time enough to worry about that," my husband said softly. "Let's go see what Miss Lavinia has got for us to eat, okay?"

He held out his hand, and Julia immediately leaped up and took it. I watched the two of them walk out into the hallway. It was easy to see which of us had the experience of dealing with children, even if this one happened to be a middle-aged woman.

It was nearly midnight by the time Julia had been coaxed into bed. I used the bathroom across the hall to sluice my face and neck with cold water. The image staring back at me from the mirror looked as if it had aged ten years in the course of the evening.

I came back downstairs, carefully skirting the dark patch on the heart pine floor where Elizabeth Shelly had bled to death. Lavinia had obviously found time to try and scrub the worst of it away, but the stain would, no doubt, be added to the tales of the long and checkered history of Presqu'isle.

I found Red and Lavinia still sitting around the oak table in the kitchen. The remains of the dinner she had hastily thrown together littered the counter. It was a measure of the depth of Lavinia's shock that she had not immediately begun putting things to rights.

"She's asleep," I said, dropping down into my chair.

Without asking, Lavinia reached for the teapot and poured me a fresh cup. "That's a blessing," she said softly.

"What the hell happened? Did she trip on something?"

For once, Lavinia didn't chide me for profanity. She sipped her own tea and squared her thin shoulders. "There was nothing on the steps. After . . . when the paramedics had gone, I looked."

Red asked, "How about what she was wearing? Anything there, like shoelaces, maybe?"

Lavinia shook her head. "I don't know. I didn't pay any attention to what she had on her feet. But she did like to wear an old pair of slippers around the house. She could have stumbled or gotten her feet tangled up. Those steps are steep, and she wasn't a young woman." She sighed. "I really have no idea."

"Maybe she had a stroke. Or a heart attack. Or she might just have gotten dizzy for some reason and lost her balance." I looked at Red. "Do you want us to take Julia back to Hilton Head? Not tonight, of course, but I mean, it's not your—"

"Julia will stay with me," Lavinia said, some of the old authority back in her voice. "Don't you even think about uprootin' that poor child again."

"She's not a child, Lavinia." Red spoke gently, much as he had done with my sister in the morning room. "And, from the looks of things, she's going to need some serious help to get past this."

"All the more reason for her to be somewhere she's used to." She rattled her cup into its saucer and stood abruptly. "Bay, give me a hand with this mess. You know I can't abide an untidy kitchen."

I pushed myself to my feet. Crossing behind Red, I laid a hand on his shoulder, and he covered mine briefly with his own.

Lavinia snatched up the nearest pot and clanked it into the sink. "Julia will stay with me," she said again, whipping her head around to stare directly into my eyes.

. I picked up two plates from the table and carried them to the counter as a flood of emotion, equal parts guilt and relief, washed over me.

"Yes, ma'am," I said.

CHAPTER NINETEEN

ED LEFT EARLY ON SUNDAY MORNING TO MAKE HIS meeting with Detective Mike Raleigh. The tragedy at Presqu'isle had kicked most of my concern about our client to the far recesses of my consciousness. I'd had plenty of other worries to keep me tossing until well after four thirty, and I'd awakened late and still exhausted.

I could hear voices in the kitchen as I stood at the top of the stairs. I had crawled and scampered and trotted up and down them thousands of times over the years, as had my parents and Lavinia and her son Thad. I had even tottered awkwardly down them in my first full-length prom dress and high heels. No one had so much as stumbled before, at least not that I could remember. The more I stared, the more convinced I became that Miss Lizzie must have suffered some kind of incident that had caused her to lose consciousness and tumble to her death. A horrible, stupid accident.

The smell of frying bacon wafted up, but I turned away, back toward the bedrooms that lined the long hallway. Elizabeth Shelly had occupied the one directly across from my old room which Julia had taken over. With a silent apology, I pushed open the door.

It still looked like a guest room. Miss Lizzie had done little to put her own stamp on it aside from a couple of pictures on the tall oak dresser and a book on the side table next to the bed. Idly, I picked it up. *The Mysterious Affair at Styles*. Agatha Christie. I wished I'd known of her interest in classic mystery fiction. It might have given us something to talk about, some bond that might have overcome her ill-concealed discomfort around me. Not that I didn't understand it. She blamed both my parents for the death of her beloved friend, Julia's mother, and for the tragedy of my half sister's stunted mind. Still, she'd been willing to give up the home she and her ward had shared for decades to come and live in the house that had been the home of those she despised. For Julia's sake.

I moved closer to the dresser and picked up the larger of the two framed photos. It was an old print, much faded, but the two girls who stood self-consciously in their bathing suits at the edge of the ocean, arms flung around each other's shoulders, still radiated the innocence and joy of youth. *Probably Elizabeth and her friend Brooke, Julia's mother,* I thought. I shivered despite the warmth of the sun flooding through the room's tall window.

So much tragedy. And all because of love. My father's for Brooke, Elizabeth's for Julia, my parents for me. It shouldn't turn out like that. Love shouldn't be the cause of such misery. And yet so often it was.

The other picture was of Julia, sometime in her early twenties, it looked like. Dressed in the plaid shirt and jeans that had become her uniform after her mother's death, she stood beside a chestnut horse, a carrot dangling from one hand. She wasn't smiling, but she looked . . . contented. Maybe that was all someone in Julia's condition could hope for—contentment. The thought of her wandering through this strange house, feeling abandoned by the only parent figure she could remember, filled me with such sadness I could hardly bear it.

I shook my head, set the photo back on the dresser, and yanked open the first drawer. If I was going to rifle through Elizabeth Shelly's things, I needed to get at it. I swallowed back the hovering tears and set to work.

I poked my head around the doorway of the kitchen, relieved to find Lavinia alone. Julia, it seemed, had gotten into the habit of spending a good part of the morning outdoors, especially now that she had her own plot of garden to tend. She also liked to romp around the backyard with Rasputin, who seemed as gentle with her as a kitten. I spied them through the back window as I moved farther into the room.

Lavinia turned from the stove. "Oh, good, you're up. Eggs in two minutes. I've been keepin' the bacon and the biscuits warm in the oven."

I really didn't even want to think about food, but I knew there was no point in refusing. Lavinia firmly believed that a full plate could solve just about any problem. Or at least take your mind off it for a while.

"You skipped church," I said, the realization bringing home once again how drastically the accident had affected our lives in such a short time. Lavinia never missed a service. Never.

"God understands," she said.

No arguing with that. I laid the brown envelope on the table and took my seat. "I found Miss Lizzie's papers," I said. "She did have a medical power of attorney." I swallowed hard against the thought that she'd never needed it. "And a will. Everything goes to Julia."

Lavinia whirled. "You read it? Is that proper?"

I shrugged. "Proper or not, I thought it was necessary. She hadn't changed it since they made the deal to sell Covenant Hall, but that shouldn't matter." I paused as Lavinia slid the plate in front of me. In spite of myself, I felt my stomach rumbling. I lifted the fork and dug in. "There's also two small bequests. Cousins on her mother's side. Sisters."

Lavinia's head snapped up. "Cousins? She never mentioned any family."

"I know. Not to me, either. But she names them. Mrs. Patricia Rieth and Mrs. Matilda Tiley. Same address, so I'm guessing they're widows who live together. I don't know if they're older or younger, but they have to be at least in their sixties, I'd guess."

She seated herself across from me before speaking. "Where do they live?"

"Pawleys Island. Up near Myrtle Beach. Probably some sort of retirement home."

Lavinia bristled. "No reason to assume that. Not all of us who manage to survive this long are ready for the home, Bay Tanner."

For the first time since I'd heard the tragic news about Elizabeth Shelly, I smiled. "Well, *you're* certainly not."

She nodded. "We need to contact them right away. This morning. They'll need to be consulted about arrangements."

"I'll do it."

I thought that Miss Lizzie's relatives would want to be more than *consulted* about her funeral. Technically speaking, it was their responsibility to make those decisions, not ours. Julia may have been the person the dead woman had been closest to, but she was in no condition to decide much of anything. I sighed, my gaze wandering out the back window to the narrow yard sloping down toward the water, where my half sister and the dog Rasputin sat quietly at the end of the short dock.

"How are you going to manage?" I asked softly, and Lavinia's head snapped up.

"You mean with Julia?"

"Yes. She's reverted back to where she was when I first met her. I don't see how you're going to handle it on your own, Lavinia." I held up a hand to stem the indignant reply I knew was coming. "I know you're not ready for the scrap heap, as you've so eloquently put it before, but this is different. She can be . . ."—I fumbled around for the right word—"difficult," I finished.

"Julia has been nothing but docile and loving since I first met her.

Dr. Halloran will get her back on track, once all this . . . Once the funeral and all is done with." A ghost of a smile touched her creased brown face. "You know, there are times she puts me in mind of you when you were younger."

I forced myself to smile back. "Not surprising, I guess. We share half the same gene pool."

I looked up as the screen door onto the back verandah banged shut.

"I watered the garden, Miss Lavinia, and I made sure the new seeds had a really good drink. I'm thirsty, too."

Julia crossed to the refrigerator and pulled out the iced tea pitcher, poured herself a glass, and joined me at the table. There was no denying that she seemed to feel right at home at Presqu'isle. Her eyes had lost some of the blankness of the night before, and I had to admit she looked healthy and not the least distraught. I added a call to Neddie Halloran to my list of things to do on that beautiful October Sunday morning.

Julia smiled at me across the expanse of weathered oak, and I found myself wondering if maybe being oblivious to the pains and miseries life so often visited on us wasn't, as Hamlet had pondered, "a consummation devoutly to be wished." I mentally awarded myself two points and pushed back from the table.

"I need to make a couple of calls," I said. "I'll be back in a few minutes."

As I turned for the doorway, I heard Lavinia say, "Would you like to help me with the dishes, Julia?"

"Oh, yes, ma'am," my half sister replied. "I'm real good at drying."

I left the two of them busily clearing the table and went in search of my cell phone.

Both Elizabeth's cousins were listed in directory assistance, but no one answered. And I certainly didn't intend to break the news of Miss

Lizzie's sudden death in a voice mail. *Probably at church,* I told myself, glancing at the ormolu clock on the mantel in the main drawing room. I'd slipped in there for some privacy as it was a place no one much ventured into in the normal course of events at Presqu'isle. The deep blue-and-gold color scheme on the upholstery and drapes of the most formal setting in the antebellum mansion, along with the Italian marble fireplace and my mother's most precious treasures and paintings, had intimidated me for most of my life. It had always been a good place to hide out.

Dr. Nedra Halloran's service promised to forward my message to my old college roommate, and I knew she'd get back to me as soon as she received it. Neddie, though technically a child psychologist, had initially taken on Julia's case as a personal favor to me. Over the past several months, however, she'd become committed—both personally and professionally—to giving my half sister the best possible chance at a normal life. I had to believe that she could help Julia overcome this latest blow. The only other alternative—I shoved the idea of some sort of residential care facility completely out of my head. Lavinia would never stand for it. Never.

I'd been sitting for some time, staring into the black void of the fireplace, when the phone jangled in my hand. Without checking caller ID, I flipped it open.

"Bay Tanner."

"Thank God! You have to help me. Please!"

For a moment, I didn't recognize the voice. Then it struck. "Mr. Wolfe? Is that you? What the hell's going—"

"Don't talk! Listen! I'm in trouble. I'm at a rest stop on 26, just south—"

His words stopped abruptly, but I could hear background noise, gears grinding as if an eighteen-wheeler were just pulling out. There were voices, too, but they sounded like children's, boys' mostly, I thought, and a lot of laughter.

"Wolfe! Where are you? Just south of where?"

I waited, straining to catch anything that might help me figure out what was going on. Then I heard the distinct sound of a toilet flushing. *Men's room.*

"Talk to me!" I yelled into the phone. "Wolfe!"

"Have to move."

The background voices faded, and Wolfe's labored breathing filled my ear. A moment later I heard a car door slam.

"If you're in trouble, call nine one one," I said as calmly as I could manage. "Or tell me where you are, and I'll call the highway patrol."

The roar of an engine's starting up drowned out his next words.

I could feel my own heart racing, and the phone slipped a little in my sweaty hand. "Say again."

". . . burg." A crackle of static, then something unintelligible and, ". . . Ty. Can't—"

Silence. I thought for sure I'd lost him, but I leaned forward, like a sprinter before the gun, the phone jammed tightly against my head as if I could, by sheer force of will, bring him back. A moment before I gave up, one final word made it through on the fading signal, and I jumped to my feet. That one had been perfectly clear.

Wolfe had nearly shouted, "Dead!"

CHAPTER TWENTY

I FORCED MYSELF TO A CALM THAT THREATENED AT any second to desert me and pulled up my recent call log. With a trembling finger, I punched the key to redial the last number received. I expected the canned voice telling me the number was not in service, but I had to be certain. I disconnected and immediately speed-dialed Red. I looked up to find Lavinia standing in the doorway.

"Any luck?" she asked.

"No answer." I turned on the settee to face away from her. "Come on, come on!" I muttered under my breath a second before Red picked up.

"Hey, honey. How's it going?"

"Hold on." I moved across the faded Persian carpet to stand at one of the long windows overlooking the side yard and the two-hundred-year-old live oak whose limb had crashed through the roof during the brush with Kitty. A quick look over my shoulder told me Lavinia had retreated back to the kitchen.

In a few words, I relayed my strange conversation with Wolfe. "He was in an all-out panic," I finished.

"God, Bay! We don't need this right now."

I could almost see my husband running his hand through his short brown hair, no doubt leaving tufts of it standing straight up. Exactly like his brother used to do. For some reason, the image helped to dispel the knot of anxiety twisting in my chest.

"I know. But we have to do something, though I'm damned if I know what."

Red sighed, and his voice dropped a couple of levels. "Okay, he was on I-26. Hang on a sec."

A few moments later, the sound of the Bronco's engine died. "Where are you?" I asked.

"Just coming back from meeting Mike at the sheriff's office. I pulled off into the parking lot at Aunt Chilada's."

The Mexican restaurant was only a block or two up Pope Avenue from the substation.

"Why?"

"Map," he said, and I could hear paper rustling. "Okay. A roadside stop on 26 with a restroom." He fell silent. "There's one just outside Orangeburg. A little southeast."

"That must be it. But what the hell is he doing up there? And who's chasing him?"

"I have no idea. Presumably whoever he was running from when he jumped in the backseat of the limo at the Crowne on Friday. You said he mentioned Bell?"

"Just the one word: Ty." I thought a moment. "Or it could have been the tail end of a word. Maybe I just assumed it was a name because of the case."

"And nothing before 'dead'?"

"Nothing I could hear. Are you going to tell Detective Raleigh?"

I heard the Bronco start up. "Yeah. I'm turning around now. I'll call you after I talk to him."

"But shouldn't we do something? I mean, we can't just leave him out there."

"There's nothing we can do from here. Give me that number Wolfe was calling from."

"I'll have to get it off the phone. I'll call you back from the land line."

"Hurry up," my husband said and disconnected.

I pulled up the screen as I walked out into the hallway. From the kitchen, I heard Lavinia and Julia talking. I picked up the house phone and gave Wolfe's new cell phone number to Red. He promised to get back to me as soon as he'd spoken with Mike Raleigh. As I turned to go make my peace with Lavinia, my cell chimed.

"Wolfe?" I nearly shouted.

"It's me, Bay. Neddie."

I let out a long breath. "Sorry. Different crisis."

"More than one? Sounds like a typical day in the life of Bay Tanner, Girl Detective. What's up?"

I moved back into the drawing room. In a few short sentences I relayed the circumstances of Elizabeth Shelly's death and my half sister's strange reaction to it.

"Damn it!" my friend nearly shouted into the phone. "She was doing so well."

"I know. But what's bugging me the most is that she doesn't seem to grasp that Lizzie is dead. I mean, her . . . affect, is that the right word?"

"Yes."

"Her affect is one of almost . . . indifference, I guess. Like nothing happened. Shouldn't she be, I don't know, traumatized or something?"

"She is," Neddie said immediately. "She's coping with it in the same way she did when she saw her mother die." She paused for a moment. "I'm coming over. Everyone's at Presqu'isle?"

"For now," I said, thinking about Winston Wolfe and his frantic flight from who knew what. Or whom. "I may have to leave."

"The other crisis?"

"Yeah. How long do you think you'll be?"

"I can leave in a few minutes. Say an hour. Two at the most."

"I'll try to hang in. But if I have to go, you'll be able to handle things, right? Lavinia will be here."

"I'm on my way," she said and hung up.

Lavinia was relieved to hear that Neddie was in transit. I paced the rooms of the old mansion, my cell clutched in one hand, while the two women donned gardening gloves and retreated to the backyard. I wished I had the smallest interest in grubbing around in the dirt. Instead, I found myself flipping open the phone on every pass through the kitchen to make certain I hadn't missed a call. Neddie. Red. Miss Lizzie's two cousins. Where the hell was everybody?

I decided I was just making myself crazy with the pacing and fretting. I shoved the phone in my pocket and let the screen door onto the back verandah bang shut behind me. Lavinia, her wide-brimmed sun hat shading her face, looked up as I trotted down the steps.

"Anything?" she asked, sitting back on her heels, and I knew she was thinking of Neddie.

"No. But she said it might take a couple of hours. How's . . . ?" I inclined my head toward my half sister who was picking dead leaves off the row of mums that lined the west side of the house.

"Quiet. Content," Lavinia said softly.

I moved closer and lowered my voice. "I may have to leave. The phone call earlier. Will you be able to handle things here?" The look she turned on me almost brought a smile. "Of course you will. Sorry."

"I don't know about dealing with the cousins, though," she said.

"Don't worry about that. I gave them my cell number to call back. I'll let you know as soon as I hear from them."

The sharp ringing made me jump. I jerked the phone out of my pocket and whirled back toward the house. I didn't recognize the number.

"Bay Tanner." I moved around to climb the steps onto the verandah.

"Good afternoon. This is Patricia Rieth. You left a message for my sister and me. Something about our cousin Elizabeth?"

I steeled myself for hysterics as I settled into my father's old rocker and set it gently into motion. As succinctly as possible, I relayed the circumstances of Miss Lizzie's accident, along with the connection, through Julia, that had put her at the top of Presqu'isle's stairs in the first place. It took longer than I thought, but the woman never once interrupted, either with an exclamation or a question. When I finally wound down to the horrible outcome, there was nothing but silence.

I waited a few moments. "Mrs. Rieth? Ma'am? Are you still there?"

"What do you want from us?"

Her sharp tone took me aback, and I sputtered a little before answering. "Well, first of all, I wanted to inform you of your cousin's death. I assumed you'd want to know. And there are arrangements to be made."

I heard another voice in the background, then Patricia Rieth's saying, "Cousin Elizabeth is dead." A moment later, she spoke into the phone. "We haven't seen Elizabeth for nearly twenty years. You certainly can't expect us to be responsible for her now."

I opened my mouth, but she overrode me.

"How did you get our names? And how do I know this isn't some sort of scam you're trying to run on us? We're not dotty old women, I'll have you know. If you're trying to get us to pay for some bogus funeral expenses, you've picked the wrong pigeons. My son is with the state police, and I'll—"

"Ma'am!" I said forcefully, cutting her off. "Hold on a minute. I got your name from Miss Lizzie's papers. She has been the caretaker of my half sister for most of her life, and they've recently come to live in my family's home on St. Helena. I can assure you that what I'm telling you is completely true and accurate. Feel free to have your son check me out."

I'd spoken more forcefully than I'd intended, and I backed off a little before continuing.

"I'm not suggesting that you and your sister are responsible for any funeral costs. Miss Lizzie had sufficient funds, at least as far as I can tell from the documents I found. I thought you might wish to be consulted on the service. If not, we'll be glad to take care of all that. If you don't wish to attend, that's certainly your prerogative."

Again I heard a muffled exchange away from the phone. I could feel my heart thumping in my chest, anger warring with anxiety. Why hadn't Red called? What was taking Neddie so long? And where was Wolfe? My head pounded in time to my pulse, and I massaged my temples with my free hand.

"Give us your direction," the woman finally said. "Tillie and I will be there by evening."

"I beg your pardon?"

"We're coming. Now, where exactly are you located?"

I pulled Lavinia away from the garden long enough to relay the message that we had guests on the way. She insisted that they would stay at Presqu'isle, but I overrode her.

"We've all got enough on our plates without playing hostess," I snapped.

She fought me for a while, but not too hard. "Well, we can at least feed them. It's a long drive, and they're not young. I'll see to everything."

As she spoke, I followed her up the steps and into the kitchen, where she pulled open the door to the refrigerator and peered inside.

"Something simple. Perhaps a quiche. Light enough, and I've got some crab, fresh yesterday. And a salad. That should do it."

"I'm sure whatever you fix will be fine. I may have to leave before they get here," I reminded her.

"We'll be just fine, Bay Tanner," she said, her head still stuck in the refrigerator. "Don't fret about it. Now what for dessert? Banana pudding, that's always welcome."

I left her to her menu planning and wandered back onto the porch. Julia still picked at the mounds of chrysanthemums, their russet and tawny heads swaying in a light breeze off the Sound. I wondered when the full impact of the tragedy would finally find its way into my sister's muddled mind, and what the long-term effects of it might be.

I glanced at my watch, startled to find that it had been nearly two hours since I'd spoken to both Red and Neddie. I flipped open my phone. My husband answered on the first ring.

"Bay, honey, I'm sorry I didn't get back to you. I'm on my way there right now."

"Here? Why? What did you find out from Mike Raleigh?"

"We'll talk about it when I get there, honey. Try to stay calm."

"Don't patronize me, Red. What are they doing about Wolfe? God Almighty, don't I have enough damn things to worry about right now?"

"Take it easy, Bay," my husband replied, his voice tightening. "I know you're upset, but let's not get into it in the middle of downtown Beaufort. I'll be there in fifteen minutes."

I stared at the phone for almost a full thirty seconds before I realized he'd hung up on me.

CHAPTER
TWENTY-ONE

R. NEDRA HALLORAN AND RED ARRIVED ALMOST ON each other's heels. Julia seemed ecstatic to see them both, bouncing back and forth in her excitement. With one arm around my sister's shoulders, Neddie raised an eyebrow as we trooped into the house.

"Use the morning room," I said, indicating the door opposite my father's old study.

"I'll bring you some tea." Lavinia laid a hand on Julia's arm before turning toward the kitchen.

Red and I hadn't spoken except for a cursory acknowledgment of each other when he'd climbed the steps onto the front verandah. I spun on my heel and marched into the back parlor, the one we'd always used for less formal gatherings. I flopped myself down on the settee and folded my arms across my chest.

"Don't start," my husband said as he settled his rangy body into the Judge's favorite armchair and slouched down to rest his head on the back. "You're not going to like what I have to tell you, but there's not a damn thing you can do about it, so try to keep from biting my head off. I'm just the messenger."

I expelled a long breath and offered him a tepid smile. "Okay. But I'm due a little slack. It hasn't exactly been one of my better weekends, in case you hadn't noticed."

"Point taken," he said, tucking his hands behind his head. "Here's the deal. Erik dropped the flash drive off to me outside the sheriff's office."

I jumped in my seat. "Oh, hell and damnation! I forgot he was coming to the house this morning."

Red held up his hand. "I took care of it. He said to tell you to let him know if there's anything he or Stephanie can do."

I nodded. "So what did Raleigh say?"

"I gave him the high points, particularly about Wolfe's being afraid of someone, his cell phone turning up in the bushes by the Holiday Inn, and his call to you this morning. Of course he already knew about the search of Wolfe's hotel room." He sighed and leaned forward to rest his elbows on his knees. "I have to say I don't think he was as concerned as we are."

I made myself speak softly. "So he's not going to do anything about it?"

Red reached across to take my hand in his. "That's just the point. What is there for him to do? There was no sign of forced entry at the hotel. Wolfe could have torn the place apart himself. Besides, we don't have a clue where he is. Even if we're right that he was calling you from a rest stop south of Orangeburg, that was hours ago. We don't know what he's driving or which way he's headed. There isn't a whole lot for them to go on."

Of course I knew he was right. And I had a strange sense of déjà vu, as if we'd had this same conversation in another place, at another time. Which we probably had, when Red was the official voice of law enforcement, handing down the logical and reasoned argument against my burning desire to ride off to someone's rescue. I'd learned a few things over the years, many of them the hard and painful way, and I wasn't all that much surprised at the detective's response. Still . . .

"That doesn't mean we can't do something," I said, turning to hold his gaze with my own. "You believe he's in some kind of serious trouble, don't you? Wolfe, I mean. Don't we have a responsibility to him as our client?"

"Of course we do, sweetheart. But Mike is right. What is there for us to do? Even if we hopped in the car right now and headed for Orangeburg, what would you expect to find? Anyone who might have seen him would be long gone by now. We just don't have anything to latch onto. It would be pointless."

I sighed and let go of his hand. "You're right." I forced a smile. "And you know how much I hate it when you're right."

I reached into my pocket and pulled out my phone. I scrolled to the number Wolfe had called from and dialed it out. Nothing. I flipped it closed and tossed it onto the cushion beside me.

"Miss Lizzie's cousins are coming," I said and told him about my conversation with Mrs. Rieth. "Lavinia wants to feed them, but I'm hoping they'll stay in a hotel in Beaufort. I've had about all the drama I can take for one day."

My husband scooted out of the armchair and knelt beside me. This time he took both my hands in his and leaned in to kiss me gently on the lips. "My poor Bay. Why don't you lie down there and take a little nap? I'll sit right here in case Neddie or someone needs you." He smoothed my hair away from my brow and settled one of the back cushions against the armrest. "Things will look better when you're rested."

I didn't want to take a nap, but I didn't want to fight him, either. I felt as if every last ounce of energy had been sucked out of me by the circumstances of the past few days. I slipped out of my sandals and swung my legs up onto the settee.

I vaguely remember the softness of the afghan settling over my arms before I dropped off.

I was dreaming about my childhood, something to do with hiding out from my mother in the concealing branches of the big live oak in the side yard, when someone jerked me back to reality with a hand on my shoulder. I tried to shake it off, but my attacker was insistent. I groaned and blinked into the soft sunlight of late afternoon. My eyes finally focused on Neddie's hovering over mine.

"I'm sorry, honey, but I need to talk to you before I head back to Savannah."

She moved aside as I swiveled my legs around and sat up, rubbing my face to chase away the heaviness I always felt after napping in the middle of the day.

"What time is it?"

"A little after four. You missed lunch, but Red said to let you sleep."

"I feel like crap," I said, stretching, and she laughed.

"You always had such a way with words." Neddie dropped into the chair my husband had occupied when I'd dozed off and worked her head around on her neck. "I'm not exactly on top of the world at the moment, either."

"How's Julia?"

She hesitated a moment before replying. "I'm concerned, but not overly so. I believe she's already coming out of it. The immediate trauma, I mean. I think the fact that she's here, in somewhat familiar surroundings, with you and Lavinia, is helping a lot. I don't believe it will take too much time and effort for her to get back to where she was." Again she paused. "You know, I don't like to speak ill of the dead, but I always thought Miss Lizzie—may she rest in peace—was a big part of your sister's problem."

"What do you mean?"

"The way she treated her, like some naughty child that always needed correction. Julia couldn't seem to do anything right. We spent a lot of time, Julia and I, talking about her feelings about that. It's horrible to say, but I think your sister may make significant strides now that Lavinia will be the guiding force in her life."

Something in me wanted to defend Elizabeth Shelly. After all, she'd taken in an orphaned child and raised her as her own for nearly four decades. Julia had had emotional issues even before witnessing her mother's death, and that tragic event had only magnified them. It wouldn't have been an easy job. And Elizabeth had sacrificed any chance for a full life of her own—home, husband, children—to fulfill her commitment to her dearest friend.

Of course, another part of my brain argued, she could have contacted my father at any time during all those years. She certainly knew where to find him. Julia might have grown up here, at Presqu'isle. With me. *No,* I reminded myself, *not while Mother was still alive.* But she might have had a chance to know us. We might have been able to get her help long before now. I shrugged. Water over the dam.

"Miss Lizzie probably did the best she could," I offered. "Under the circumstances."

"Granted. But I have a feeling she wasn't the kind of woman destined for motherhood. Some aren't, you know."

We shared a long look. Both of us approached our midforties still childless. I wasn't sure what that said about us. But that was a topic for another time.

"So you think she should stay here? At Presqu'isle?"

Neddie nodded. "Lavinia and I have already discussed it. I think she'll blossom with the kind of attention she'll get. I think you'll be amazed at how much progress she'll make. And rather quickly."

I was trying to digest this information, which seemed terribly

disrespectful of all that Elizabeth Shelly had sacrificed on Julia's be-
half, when Red wandered into the room.

"Am I interrupting?"

"No, I think we're done here." Neddie stood. "I need to be getting
back."

I rose, too. "I don't know how to thank you. Send the bills to me
on Hilton Head. What kind of schedule are you going to set up for
Julia's visits?" Suddenly, Winston Wolfe's disappearance roared back
into my head like an oncoming train. "I don't know how we'll manage
it, but we'll make sure she gets there. Whenever you say."

"Lavinia and I have that all worked out. We'll keep the trips to
Savannah to a minimum, for both their sakes. I'll come up like every
other weekend and spend some extended time with Julia, at least at
first."

Red moved farther into the room. "That's a hell of an imposition,
Neddie. I mean, you've got a life of your own."

My old college roommate laughed. "Not so's you'd notice. And
besides," she added, picking up her bag and heading toward the doorway, "I'd drive a lot farther than this for one of Lavinia's meals. In fact,
we might even work out some sort of barter system. I think her sweet
potato biscuits are easily worth at least an hour of shrink time."

We said our good-byes, Julia hugging her psychologist before
turning to bound back up the stairs to wash up for dinner. I added my
own embrace.

"Call me if anything happens," she said from the verandah. "And
let me know when the funeral arrangements have been made. I'd like
to be there."

"You're the best," I called after her before closing the door.

Red slipped an arm around my shoulders. "She sounded pretty
upbeat," he said as we walked back into the parlor.

I folded the afghan and laid it across the back of one of the overstuffed chairs that flanked the cold fireplace. "I hope she's right. Any word from Wolfe? Or Mike Raleigh?"

"Nope. I took your phone and kept trying that cell number Wolfe called from. No voice mail. It just says the number is not in service."

"That's what I got. What are we going to do?"

"Find you something to eat and let it go for now," my husband said with a warm smile. "And I could use a beer. Don't forget, we still have the 'cousins' to contend with."

"God save us," I replied and followed him into the kitchen.

They arrived in a whirl of light, feminine perfume and no-nonsense practicality that would have been delightful under different circumstances. There was no doubting their relationship, although neither bore the slightest resemblance to Elizabeth Shelly. Both had silvered hair, Matilda Tiley's bouncing in curls around her square face while Patricia Rieth's was cut in a severe style, close to her head and straight as a string. I towered over both of them, neither sister topping much more than a few inches over five feet. But what they lacked in stature they more than made up for in vitality. In spite of the long drive down from Pawleys Island, both seemed fresh and ready for battle. *Feisty* was the word that popped immediately into my head after introductions had been made.

Lavinia had put on one of her church dresses in a pale lavender, always one of her favorite colors. Julia looked more than presentable in khaki slacks and a cotton sweater in a soft rose that flattered the tan she never seemed to lose. She shook hands solemnly and hung back a little as we escorted our guests to the front parlor. When Lavinia left to retrieve a pot of restorative tea, my sister leaped up and followed.

Having slept in my clothes with no opportunity to freshen up other than to wash my face and run a comb through my hair, I probably appeared to the well-dressed sisters like the slightly unbalanced member of the family. Red had turned up his considerable charm full blast, and we made convivial small talk until Lavinia returned with the tea tray. I helped her settle it on the coffee table, the one my mother always claimed had been purchased in Paris by one of my aristocratic forebears, and inclined my head to indicate she should pour. No second-best Royal Doulton for this occasion. The delicate Spode cups and saucers, nearly transparent, gleamed in the light of the crystal chandelier.

Pat finally broached the subject we'd all been skirting around. "Tillie and I were saddened to learn of Cousin Elizabeth's passing, even though, as I said before, we hadn't been in touch for many years. I hope you don't think ill of us, but . . ."

She let the rest of it trail off. In an obviously long-standing habit, her sister picked up her unfinished thought.

"But it was mostly Elizabeth's choice. We received very dutiful notes at Christmas, but that was about the extent of our contact." She shifted a little on the settee, her short legs not quite able to reach the floor so that she looked almost like a wrinkled child among the grownups. "Our mothers were sisters, you know. Elizabeth's came to the States long before we emigrated. Our father was Scots."

That explained the slight burr in their speech, most noticeable in Pat, but underlying the soft Southern drawl they'd both adopted in their years in South Carolina.

"We're very sorry for your loss," I said, feeling, despite my disheveled appearance, that the role of hostess had passed to me. "We'd only known Miss Lizzie—Elizabeth—for a short time, but we were all immensely grateful for her care of Julia."

My sister had sunk back into the wing chair, her head lowered so that all that could be seen of her was the top of her head. She'd refused tea and almost seemed to be shrinking under the increasingly frank glances the elderly sisters cast her way.

"I have to say the whole family was shocked when we learned Elizabeth had taken on that responsibility." Patricia Rieth spoke matter-of-factly, but there was an undercurrent of disapproval in her tone. "Of course, we all offered to help in any way we could, but Elizabeth was quite adamant that she could handle the situation on her own, in spite of her being an unmarried woman." She frowned and stole a glance at her sister. "Quite adamant."

I wondered if Miss Lizzie's rebuff of the sisters' overtures might account for their seeming indifference to her sudden death. Or maybe they just weren't a demonstrative family by nature. I could relate to that.

"Yes, well." Tillie set her cup back on the tea tray, her face coloring, perhaps in embarrassment at her sister's plain speaking. "We've made arrangements to stay at a very nice bed-and-breakfast in town. I suppose we should be settling in."

"Lavinia has prepared a light dinner for all of us. We'd be very pleased if you'd have a bite before you venture back out."

"How kind," Pat Rieth said. She exchanged a look with her sister and apparently received unspoken agreement. "We'd be happy to accept."

"I'll just get things organized," Lavinia said, almost leaping to her feet. "Julia, will you help me, child?"

My sister nearly sprinted toward the kitchen, leaving Red and me to carry the conversational load with the two strangers. We learned that both, as I had surmised, were husbandless—one widowed, one divorced—and had decided to set up housekeeping together, both for companionship and for the economic benefits. Both painted, Tillie specializing in florals while Pat preferred landscapes. They gardened and traveled, mostly with groups of similar age and interest. Tillie, like Elizabeth to judge by the Agatha Christie I'd found on her bedside table, loved mysteries. We spent a few minutes comparing libraries, discovering that we shared a passion for the Golden Age British classics as well as the more hard-boiled American novels of the early twentieth century.

Red chatted idly with Pat about current events and local points of interest they might explore while they were visiting the county, and the time passed easily enough until Julia, in a halting, almost inaudible voice, announced that dinner was ready. I cursed Lavinia for having parked us around the huge mahogany table in the sterile dining room. Red seated everyone. I had just dropped onto the hard-backed chair at the foot of the long table when my phone rang in my pocket. Excusing myself, I retreated into the hallway and nearly gasped when I recognized the number.

"Wolfe!" I shouted into the phone, heedless of who in the dining room might be able to hear me. "Where the hell are you?"

CHAPTER
TWENTY-TWO

NLIKE OUR EARLIER CONVERSATION, THIS ONE CAME
through loud and clear.

"Where are you?" I repeated.

"Safe." Unlike earlier in the day, his voice sounded calmer.

I moved down the hallway toward the kitchen and pulled out my usual chair. "What's going on, Mr. Wolfe? Who are you running from?"

"I hope you haven't involved the authorities."

"Really? After that frantic phone call this morning, you just expected me to say 'Oh, well' and move on? After you finished the conversation with the single word *dead,* you thought I'd just have Sunday dinner and forget about it? Jesus! I've had my own personal crisis to deal with, and your sounding as if the hounds of hell were nipping at your heels sure hasn't helped any."

"Apologies for that. Afraid I overreacted."

The merry-go-round that had been my relationship with this aggravating man almost right from the start was making me dizzy. I let out another long breath. "Okay. I'm glad you're all right." I hesitated, but I had to know. "Are you aware someone searched your hotel room?"

He didn't answer for some time. I waited. I'd had the feeling right from our initial meeting that the complete truth wasn't high on Winston Wolfe's list of priorities, at least in his dealings with us. I was eager to hear what kind of story he'd concoct. He surprised me.

"Yes. What initially spooked me, actually."

"And you know who did it?"

Silence. I debated telling him we'd found his phone in the bushes outside the Tiki Hut and that we'd spotted someone who looked remarkably like the photos of Ty Bell with which Wolfe had reluctantly parted, but something held me back. Two could play his game.

"Mr. Wolfe?"

"It doesn't concern you. Please carry on with the investigation. Notify Miss Hearst if you require additional funds. I'll be in contact with you periodically to check on your progress. It's become imperative that I have an answer to my inquiry immediately, certainly no later than the end of the week."

I was about to comment on his sudden loquaciousness—and his imposition of a nearly impossible deadline—when I realized he'd hung up.

Back in the dining room, conversation abruptly ceased when I appeared in the doorway.

"Sorry about that," I said, seating myself. "Business."

"And what kind of business is it that you're in?" Matilda Tiley canted her head to one side like a pudgy bird.

"Bay owns an inquiry agency," my husband answered, and I smiled my thanks. "We actually work together."

"How . . . interesting," Patricia Rieth said from the opposite side of the table. I could tell from her tone that *interesting* probably hadn't been the first word that popped into her head, but she was too much of a lady to give voice to her real thoughts. She'd told us earlier that she'd been headmistress of an exclusive girls' school, and I could well imagine her charges withering under the stern stare she'd turned my way.

Her sister, on the other hand, jumped right in. "You mean a detective agency? You're private eyes? Why didn't you say so? Good Lord, I must have made a complete fool of myself, rattling on like I was some sort of expert, when all the time—"

"You did no such thing," I interrupted her. "Believe me, the reality of it bears little or no resemblance to most crime novels. It's actually quite boring a good bit of the time."

Red and I exchanged a look and a brief smile. "Wolfe?" he said softly, speaking almost against my shoulder.

"Fine," I whispered back. Then, eager to change the subject, I said more loudly, "The quiche is wonderful, Lavinia."

The gambit worked, and there were murmurs of agreement around the table. We moved on then to safer, more mundane topics for the remainder of the meal. Over coffee and the promised banana pudding, the ladies got down to the purpose of their visit—Miss Lizzie's funeral arrangements. Before they could discuss too many details, I hustled Julia out of the room, ostensibly to check on Rasputin and to take him his nightly meal. The three of us ended up walking out onto the dock and my sister and I dangled our feet over the side while the big dog settled himself between us. The sun had nearly disappeared off to the west, but the soft glow of its last rays cast a lovely amber haze over the still waters of the Sound.

"Are you okay?" I asked, not sure how much to probe. I wished Neddie had given me some guidelines, but her only advice had been to use my best judgment. I thought about Winston Wolfe and his crazy quest, and wasn't sure how much to trust my own instincts these days. About anything.

"It's pretty here," my sister finally said. "I like being by the water."

"Me too," I answered cautiously. "You're going to stay here with Miss Lavinia. Is that all right with you?"

"Sure. She's nice. She's the nicest lady I ever knew."

The smile she turned on me was so sweet it nearly melted my heart. What went on behind that nearly unlined skin, those guileless eyes? Did Julia understand more than she let on? For a brief instant, I wondered if she was more aware than any of us gave her credit for. Including Neddie.

"When are the children coming? You said they'd be here today."

I'd completely forgotten that we had promised to bring Scotty and Elinor by on our way back to their mother's. Funny that after everything that had happened, my sister still remembered. Cautiously, I put an arm around her shoulders.

"Maybe next week." I steeled myself for a reaction, of what kind I wasn't sure. "After Miss Lizzie's accident, we didn't think it would be a good idea."

"I hope she went to heaven," my sister said, her gaze focused on the water now lapping gently at the pilings below us.

"Miss Lizzie?"

"Uh-huh. She didn't like to go to church. Not like Miss Lavinia. Miss Lizzie said God was just a crutch for people who couldn't manage their own lives."

I had no idea how to respond to that, so I let the words hang there.

"If you don't go to church, you go to hell. That's what someone on TV said. I'm glad Miss Lavinia goes to church. I'm going with her next week. I need a good dress, though. All I have are pants, and pants aren't good enough for church."

I leaned away a little and studied my sister's face. She seemed perfectly at ease talking about her dead caretaker, almost as if Elizabeth Shelly were someone she'd just met or knew casually. I shivered. Probably just the cooler air drifting up from the Sound now that the sun had fully set, I told myself. I stood and offered my hand to Julia.

"Come on, let's go in. It's getting chilly."

She let me help her up, and together we settled the dog for the night. Back inside, Julia said her goodnights and left five relative strangers to make arrangements for the burial of the only parent she'd known for the better part of four decades. I watched her gray-streaked hair bouncing behind her as she trotted up the stairs, seemingly oblivious to how those few worn oak steps had altered her life forever.

I shook my head in amazement at the inexplicable workings of the human mind, then straightened my shoulders and went to join the others.

It took remarkably little time to agree on a simple interment to take place on Tuesday. Lavinia had already been in touch with her pastor, who'd agreed to officiate at the graveside service. On Monday, Pat and Tillie would select a coffin and a burial plot. I assured them all their expenses would be immediately reimbursed. I'd worry about settling up with Elizabeth Shelly's estate after her will was probated. I had a fleeting memory of Winston Wolfe remarking that I of all people should understand the value of money and its ability to smooth out the rough edges of life, but I thrust his arrogant face out of my head. I couldn't think about his insistence that we solve Ty Bell's disappearance in a matter of a few days. On advice from Scarlett, I decided to worry about that tomorrow.

With our assignments understood, Red and I led the elderly sisters in a caravan back into Beaufort and saw them safely to their B and B just off Bay Street. It was nearly eleven by the time we finally rolled across the second bridge onto the island. We pulled both cars into the garage and trudged wearily up the steps.

Red went immediately to the refrigerator. "I need something cold. You want a tea?"

"No thanks. I'm heading for bed."

I had peeled off my sticky clothes and tossed them into the hamper by the time he appeared in the bedroom.

"So what happened to Wolfe?" he asked, flopping down on the bed.

"Shower first," I said on my way to the bathroom. "Just a quick one."

I took longer than I'd expected, letting the blessed hot water pound some of the knots out of my shoulders, but Red was still dressed and wide awake, sprawled across the duvet when I finally emerged.

"He wouldn't say where he was or who was after him," I said, rubbing my hair with a fresh towel. I shivered in my light nightgown, the air having grown decidedly cooler.

"Come over here and let me warm you up."

I had no trouble interpreting the lascivious smile on my husband's face, and I laughed. "Nice try. Later." I sat down at the end of the bed, out of his reach, and began working a comb through my mass of hair. "Listen, something's seriously screwed up here. Wolfe isn't telling us the truth—at least not all of it—and now he's imposed this crazy deadline of solving the whole case by the end of the week."

Red jerked himself up. "*This* week? Like five days from now?"

"Yup." I told him the rest of it, then wandered back into the bathroom. "And he absolutely refused to tell me where he was or who he was running from," I hollered over the hum of the hair dryer. "What if we gave him his money back and washed our hands of the whole thing?"

I looked up to see Red standing in the doorway. "You can't be serious. I thought you were hooked."

I shut off the dryer and turned to face him. "I am. But there are all these undercurrents and hidden agendas."

I thought about Julia and how she'd cope without Elizabeth Shelly. About the sessions with Neddie and how Lavinia would handle the day-to-day responsibility, especially at her age. And how much more involved in Julia's life I would need to become. I sighed, and the weight of it seemed almost more than I could bear.

"I'm just not sure I'm up to dealing with Wolfe on top of everything else."

He stepped closer and enfolded me in his arms. "I know. It's hard to believe so much could happen in such a short amount of time."

I let him soothe me, his strong hands massaging my back, and I felt myself relaxing under his touch.

"Let's get some rest," he finally murmured, stepping back and following me into the bedroom where he paused to plant a long, lingering kiss on the tender skin just behind my left ear. "Things will look better tomorrow," he whispered, his lips following the line of my neck and beyond, to the scar tissue that was a permanent reminder of our mutual loss.

I turned into his embrace and allowed the thin straps of my nightgown to slip down over my arms. I had serious doubts about his optimism, but I couldn't argue with his methods.

CHAPTER
TWENTY-THREE

E CONVENED AT THE OFFICE AT NINE ON MONDAY morning. I was surprised to see Stephanie precede Erik through the door until I remembered that I'd hired her. My first thought was that it might have been a bad idea. The second was where in hell was I going to put her?

But while I had been occupied with Elizabeth Shelly's death and its aftermath, Erik had taken charge of the office logistics. "They're delivering another desk this morning," he said, rightly interpreting my look of dismay. "They had a good sale going at my old employer's, and I got one of the guys to give me half the staff discount. I also got a chair and a couple of other things." He smiled down at Stephanie. "I charged it on the company credit card. I hope that was okay."

"Perfect," I said. "Did you give any thought to how we're going to arrange things?"

"I thought Steph would take the receptionist's place here. I'll take the new desk, which is smaller, and should fit over in the corner. She brought her own laptop, so we won't have to buy a new one. I've already loaded it up with some of our software. I just need to show her how the phone system works, and we're in business."

I thought of how, even a few weeks ago, I might have resented my partner's initiative, his taking the lead on something like this. The new Bay Tanner thanked him with sincerity, grateful to have been spared the worry of the details on top of everything else.

A few minutes after I plopped my briefcase down, everyone gathered in my office. Red opted to hitch one hip onto the corner of my desk. I glossed over the nightmare of Miss Lizzie's death and concentrated on briefing my staff on our interaction with Wolfe. I nodded at Red, who brought everyone up to date on his conversation with Detective Mike Raleigh.

"So, bottom line, I let him know that we'd heard from our client, and they've abandoned the search," my husband concluded. "They're still investigating the trashing of his hotel room, although Mike isn't convinced Wolfe didn't make the mess himself in his rush to get out of there."

"Based on his lack of candor with us and his impossible deadline, I propose we calculate what we've earned so far and refund the rest of Wolfe's retainer. Stephanie," I said, and her head snapped up from where it had been bent over her laptop. She'd been taking notes.

"Yes, ma'am?"

I smiled at the formality. "You should find a form in the Word file for a termination letter. Fill in what blanks you can, print it out, and bring it to me for completion. Then you can prepare a check. I want to get this thing off my mind as soon as possible."

"Yes, ma'am."

"Hold on a second," Red said.

I looked up to see both him and Erik looking at me strangely. "What?"

"I thought we were going to discuss this." He glanced at my partner. "Erik has some say in this, too, even if I don't."

I'd slept fitfully, visions of Elizabeth Shelly tumbling down the stairs at Presqu'isle playing over and over again every time I closed my eyes. I consciously relaxed my shoulders.

"You're right. What do you think, Erik?"

He took a moment to gather his thoughts. "Well, I have that appointment with Mary Jefferson this morning." Erik glanced at his watch. "At ten thirty." He hesitated. "You said we could use your office."

"I remember. I planned on taking some background files and making myself scarce. I also need to check on how things are going with the cousins. Maybe I should have offered to take care of dealing with the funeral home."

I let my head settle onto my hand and unconsciously rubbed my temples. The silence stretched out.

"Maybe this isn't a good time to be making decisions," my partner finally said. "Why don't we table it until later on today? You've got enough things on your mind."

I looked up into his kind, handsome face, and some of the tension seeped out of the room. "Okay." I pulled my briefcase onto my lap and selected several files from the stack on my desk. "But I want Stephanie to prepare that letter anyway." I stared at my husband. "Just in case."

"Fair enough." Red offered me a smile.

"You know," I said to Erik as I took a legal pad from the desk drawer, "now that I think about it, next time you're at the computer store, pick me out a laptop, will you?" I had to grin back at the astonishment on my partner's face. "Might as well get all the way into the twenty-first century."

"They've got a great deal going on BlackBerrys," he said. "Bluetooth, G4, all the latest stuff. Or maybe an iPad. I've had my eye on one, just waiting for the price to come down a little."

"No thanks. One learning curve at a time is all I can handle."

"Think about it," Erik said as he and Stephanie retreated to the reception area.

"I think I'll wander over to the substation and see what they've come up with on Wolfe's hotel room. Just out of idle curiosity," he added when I raised an eyebrow. "Unless you've got something else for me to do."

"Nope. I think I'll take my work and go find a bench in Jarvis Park. It's a glorious day, and I can make phone calls from there."

"See you later then. Call me when you're ready for lunch."

It took me only a few minutes to stuff all the paperwork pertaining to Morgan Tyler Bell, Terence Gerard, Anjanette Freeman, and Winston Wolfe into the drawer that held the closed files. In my mind, I'd already given up the case, even if my partner wasn't yet on board. Later, I'd put Stephanie to work organizing everything so we had a coherent record of our failed efforts to solve one of the Lowcountry's most intriguing mysteries.

I heaved a sigh as I slid the drawer closed and shot a glance at the whiteboard, still covered in writing and propped against the wall, mute testimony to our efforts to work out a time line on Friday night. There was so much we'd never figured out. I hadn't read completely through Ben Wyler's notes, and we hadn't investigated all the files we'd copied from Wolfe's flash drive, either. We should erase those, I thought. Erik hadn't been able to crack the password on our client's voice mail, either. I had to remember to return the cell phone, if Wolfe ever came back to Hilton Head. I hesitated to send it through the mail, but it might come down to that. So much was still up in the air. I knew that when all the dust had settled—on the tragedy of Elizabeth Shelly's death as well as on our frantic search for Wolfe—I'd regret that we no longer had a reason to chase down the answers. I also knew that Red would be disappointed not to have an opportunity to do what his compatriots at the sheriff's office had been unable to do and solve the case. But there was nothing to say we couldn't still do a little digging on our own, I thought. Just for our own satisfaction.

On my way out, I reviewed the termination letter Stephanie had prepared, filled in a couple of blanks she'd been unsure about, and left her to reprint it for my signature. I also left her with a packet of tax forms and other paperwork she needed to fill out to complete her new personnel file. All in all, it had been a good decision to add Erik's fiancée to the staff. She was personable and competent, and her presence would free my partner up for more off-site participation in our cases. And there would be other cases. Hopefully with more candid, cooperative clients than Winston W. Wolfe.

In the car, I tossed my briefcase onto the front seat beside me. If I hadn't been in a skirt and low heels, I could have jogged over to Jarvis Park, set behind Wendy's and the new day care center that had just been completed. At that hour of the morning, the sprawling grounds were nearly deserted, only one car pulled up in the circular parking area. An older couple strolled along the paved path that circled the manmade lagoon, created during the construction of the Cross Island Parkway, along which the distant buzz of traffic could be faintly heard. I smiled as the gray-haired twosome passed me, a sadly obese poodle huffing along beside them at the end of a leash.

On impulse, I locked my handbag and briefcase in the trunk and set off after them. A couple of turns around the lagoon would be a good way to get the final Wolfe cobwebs cleared out of my head. I'd slacked off on my running regimen lately, and I could feel the pull in my calves as I maneuvered around my only other companions. The sun shone down from a cloudless sky of unbelievably clear blue; and, aside from the drone of trucks on the parkway, the silence was broken only by the songs of myriad birds. I breathed deeply and congratulated myself on my decision. Fresh air, beautiful surroundings, and the peace of a crisp October morning had been the perfect choice.

Wolfe would find someone else to take up his cause, I had no doubt. We weren't by any means the only agency in the county, or even on the island, for that matter. It would have been nice if it had been a straightforward missing persons case, without all the baggage our former client had brought to the table. But that was the nature of the business, or so I'd discovered after a few years of dealing with the people who sought us out. I supposed it wasn't all that different from my accounting practice. "Everyone lies," my father often said. "Some just do it better than others." In my CPA days, they were trying to skate the IRS and hoping to use me to do it. Wolfe, too, had his secrets, and he was determined to hold them close. I drew in a deep, cleansing breath and expelled it. Not my problem anymore.

I nodded to the old couple when I passed them for the second time. A great blue heron glided in toward the shore, and just past his landing spot I caught a glimpse of a small alligator slithering into the water. I watched the ripples he generated as he worked his way in a series of lazy *S* curves toward the middle of the lagoon. *The ducks and Canada geese will be back soon,* I thought, slowing a little as a sheen of perspiration began to pop out on my forehead.

Back at my car, I retrieved my stuff and found a wooden swing, the kind you might put on your front porch, and settled myself in the shade. I spread the papers out next to me, slid my reading glasses onto my nose, and immersed myself in the reports I'd generated from the many databases we subscribed to. The subject was a young woman who had applied for the job of counselor at the Boys and Girls Club. They were extremely cautious about potential employees, especially those who would have direct contact with the kids.

Behind me, I heard a car start up and turned to see the older couple backing out into the driveway. The pudgy poodle had his head hung out the open passenger window, and he seemed to be smiling at me. I smiled back, then bent my head to my paperwork. I worked steadily, the slight breeze that ruffled the leaves overhead a soft backdrop to the birdsong. Susan McNally would make an excellent addition to the staff of the nonprofit, I decided, and took out a blank legal pad to begin writing up my recommendation to the board. As I turned to rifle my bag for a pen, a sudden shadow fell across my line of vision.

Before I could react, a leather satchel with a long strap dropped from behind me onto the empty space on the swing. I leaped to my feet, my heart pounding, my hand reaching back into my bag for the Seecamp I now carried as a matter of course.

"Please don't be alarmed, Mrs. Tanner." The voice came from behind and sounded innocuous enough. "I didn't mean to startle you."

I whirled, my bag in one hand, the other clamped firmly on the grip of the tiny pistol. Before I could respond, he moved around in front of me. The glare off the water and the red baseball cap pulled low over his forehead kept his face in shadow, but I had no doubt this was the elusive man who had successfully dodged us outside the Holiday Inn on Friday night.

I jerked back when he held out his hand, but again he spoke softly.

"I thought it was time we met. I think you've been looking for me. My name is Terry. Terry Gerard."

CHAPTER
TWENTY-FOUR

E STEPPED BACK AS IF TO PROVE HE WASN'T A threat, and I let loose of the gun. I didn't, however, drop the bag. He sensed my intention not to shake his hand and let it drop to his side.

"Can I sit down?"

His voice held an edge of Midwest flatness, but it had been softened, perhaps by his stay in South Carolina, although his isolation on Jericho Cay couldn't have given him much contact with the locals. I could feel the questions stacking up in my mind like storm clouds gathering for an assault.

I gestured toward the swing, and he picked up his satchel and set it down beside him on the ground before easing himself onto the hard seat. With the sun behind him still rising toward noon, I had to shade my eyes to bring his face finally into focus. No doubt this was the man in the blurry photos Wolfe had reluctantly parted with that last day in my office.

"I'm sorry if I shocked you by just showing up," Terry Gerard said.

I bent down to retrieve a stray paper from the file I'd been studying and slipped it all back into my briefcase. It gave me enough time to put my jumbled thoughts into some sort of order.

"Do you have any identification?"

He looked puzzled as he stared up at me. "Sure."

I stiffened, my fingers reaching toward the Seecamp still nestled in my bag, when he half rose and stuck his hand in his back pocket. He came out with a worn wallet, extracted a driver's license, and handed it up to me. My reading glasses were still perched on my nose, but I didn't need them to recognize the original of the photocopy that had been the first piece of information Wolfe had parted with less than a week ago.

"This is a fake," I said, tossing it carelessly onto his lap.

That rattled him. I could see it in the sudden tensing of his shoulders.

"No it's not."

I shifted from foot to foot, uncomfortable at not being able to see his face clearly. "Follow me," I said, slinging my bag over my shoulder. I tucked my briefcase under my arm.

I didn't wait to see if he was behind me. I marched across the small playground, the gravel crunching under my shoes, and dropped onto the seat of a picnic table in the pavilion. A moment later, Gerard—or Bell, or whoever the hell he was—slid in across from me.

"Why do you think it's a fake?" The hard bite had crept back into his voice.

"My partner can access just about any database on the planet. That isn't on record, either in Lorain County where you supposedly applied for it, or in the state records. Ohio doesn't realize you exist, Mr. Bell."

The smug confidence drained from his face, and his eyes blazed with anger. "Is that what that old goat, Wolfe, told you? That this is Ty?" His bark of laughter held no humor as he waved the license around. "That son of a bitch is nuts. You oughtta be more careful about believing everything you hear."

"Still, that license is bogus, and you know it as well as I do."

We stared across the expanse of picnic table for a long moment. Gerard was the first one to drop his gaze.

"Okay. Yeah, this is a fake. I bought it off some guy that was recommended to me by . . . a mutual friend. There were reasons I couldn't get my old one renewed. But I *am* Terry Gerard. Wolfe is a meddling old fool who wouldn't know the truth if it walked up and bit him in the ass."

Though I'd harbored similar thoughts myself, I didn't intend to let him sidetrack me. I gestured toward the wallet he hadn't replaced in his pocket. "Anything else in there to prove who you are?"

He flipped it open and spread out an array of credit cards, all with the Gerard name. I picked up several of them and checked the expiration dates. "These all have at least two years to run. They could be brand-new."

He pulled out an American Express gold card from the pile and nearly shoved it into my face. "There! See? It says 'member since 2001.' Is that good enough?"

"So you stole them. Or borrowed them from the real Terry Gerard. That doesn't prove a damn thing."

"You're really starting to piss me off, lady." He scooped up the credit cards and began jabbing them back into the slots in his wallet.

"Get used to it. Have you ever been arrested, Mr. Gerard?"

I could tell by the way his face immediately closed up that I'd hit a nerve.

"None of your damn business." He shoved his wallet into his back pocket as he rose. "I thought maybe we could help each other. But I can see you're not any better than that vulture that hired you." He grabbed up the satchel and whipped the strap over his head. "You can both go straight to hell."

I'd been anticipating his reaction. I lifted my hand above the level of the table and pointed the Seecamp at his navel. "Sit down,

Mr. Gerard." When he didn't move, I leaned in a little closer, careful to keep the gun steady and out of his reach. "Sit. Down."

His legs folded and dropped back onto the bench attached to the table. "You got some nerve waving that thing around in a public park," he said. "That could land your own ass in jail."

"A place I assume you're familiar with? I don't give a damn about your record, Mr. Gerard, if that's in fact who you are. Except that would mean you've been fingerprinted." I eased back a little and relaxed my grip on the gun. "Give me your AmEx card. That should have a good set of your prints on it. We'll go back to the office and wait while my husband gets one of his old sheriff buddies to run them. That should settle your identity to our mutual satisfaction."

We both jumped at the low rumble of a big vehicle as it down-shifted behind me. I risked a darting look over my shoulder at the bright yellow school bus lumbering into the parking lot. The windows were down, and the excited chatter of a lot of children drifted over to us on the still air. I turned back to see Terry Gerard stand slowly, a satisfied smile spreading across his face.

"I think you better put that peashooter of yours away," he said with a sneer. "Lots of little witnesses about to come to my rescue."

I had no choice but to slide the pistol into my pocket. The bus ground to a halt, and I could hear the raised voice of a grown-up trying to be heard above the clamor of the giggling and shouting. I looked up at the man who might be the only key to what had happened all those years ago out on Jericho Cay and cursed. Threatening him had proba-bly been a mistake.

"Why did you follow me?" I asked, intentionally keeping my voice low and calm. "What do you want from me?"

"Information," he said simply, "but now I'm not sure you have any." He stepped back away from the picnic table, and again his face was lost in the glare of the noonday sun.

"I have a lot of information on Ty Bell. And you. Come back to the office with me, and let's talk it over." The idea of losing him had set off a wave of panic that made my words come out in a breathless rush. "Wolfe's gone, out of the picture. I just need to be sure you're who you say you are. Let's try to work this out together."

He hesitated, and I thought I might be persuading him.

"I don't think so."

"Wait!" I jumped up and held out an empty hand. "Where are you staying? Is there a way to reach you?"

He turned away without answering, then stopped abruptly and looked at me over his shoulder. His eyes were unreadable in the shade of the red baseball cap, but his voice had lost its anger. "None of it really matters now. It's almost over."

His last statement stunned me to silence. Behind me, I could hear the raucous shrieks of the children, ecstatic at escaping the rote and boredom of the classroom as they tumbled out of the bus, momentarily distracting me.

"What do you mean it's almost over?" I finally managed to croak out as Terry Gerard's long strides took him farther and farther away from me.

I stood staring at his back as he disappeared into the thin strip of woods that separated the usually tranquil park from the bustle of traffic on 278. A moment later, I was engulfed in a sea of shrieking children.

CHAPTER
TWENTY-FIVE

CURSED MYSELF ALL THE WAY BACK TO THE OFFICE. I detoured first to take a few runs up and down the short stretch of 278 that bordered the park on the off chance I might spot the man in the red baseball cap. I supposed I might as well think of him as Terry Gerard. If he was, in fact, Ty Bell masquerading as his former personal assistant, as Wolfe had implied, he had gone to a lot of trouble and expense to carry it off. Either Gerard had had a car stashed somewhere out of sight, or he'd become a master at disappearing into thin air, because I found no trace of him anywhere in the vicinity.

Erik's Expedition was gone from the parking lot when I pulled in. I couldn't remember what Stephanie drove, but Red's Bronco was also missing. I hesitated, the low rumbling in my stomach reminding me that it was past lunchtime. I thought about calling around to see where they all were, then decided a little quiet contemplation would probably do me more good. I reached for my phone and turned it off. I needed time before I sprang my strange encounter in the park on them. I knew this would change everything, at least as far as Red and Erik were concerned, and I wanted to think about my response. I accelerated and swung back out onto Lafayette. A large slice of Giuseppe's pizza would give me the fortitude I'd need to admit to my colleagues that I'd had the key player in Wolfe's drama in my sights—literally—and lost him to a gaggle of third-graders.

Of course, I told myself, none of it made a damn bit of difference if it wasn't our case anymore. If I signed the termination letter, we had no more legal or moral obligation to pursue the Bell disappearance. Was that what I wanted? Really? I wasn't sure anymore, I told myself. In fact, I wasn't sure about much of damn anything. Simpson & Tanner was a business, not a hobby I had decided to dabble in for my own amusement. It may have started out that way, but now other people's livelihoods depended on my making sound decisions.

The parking lot of the shopping strip right next to the Mall at Shelter Cove was about half full, and only one table on the outside patio of my favorite pizzeria was occupied. I stepped inside to indicate I'd prefer to eat out there, then slid out a chair and dropped into it. The sun felt good, and I determined to let the whole Bell/Gerard thing go and just enjoy the solitude. I ordered and leaned back, tilting my face up to the warmth, and felt my eyes drifting closed. The sudden scrape of hard plastic on concrete jerked me upright.

"Sorry."

I squinted across the table at the small woman who plopped down without invitation into the chair opposite me.

"Hey, Gabby," I said. "Long time no see."

The ace reporter for the *Island Packet* dropped her bag on the ground and shoved her sunglasses onto the top of her head.

"You're a hard woman to track down. Don't you ever check your phone for messages?"

"Once every six weeks or so," I quipped, stung a little by the accusatory tone of her voice.

Gabby Henson and I had known each other briefly in college, though our paths had crossed much more frequently since she had moved with her kids back to the island. While we had been of mutual assistance to each other on a couple of Simpson & Tanner's early cases, I was always wary of her reporter's instincts for any sort of trouble brewing in the county. There was no doubt she had a nose for scandal, and she had no qualms about sticking it into my business whenever it suited her purposes.

"I talked to your handsome husband, and he said you were over at Jarvis. I missed you there but managed to pick up your trail back at the office."

"You followed me?" There seemed to be an epidemic of that, I thought.

She shrugged and glanced around the now-deserted patio. "What do you have to do to get a little service around here?"

I was just about to tell her she had to go inside first when the door opened, and my server carried my slice-and-salad special over to the table.

"Oooh, that looks yummy." Gabby patted her slim waistline and sighed. "I'll have that, only hold the pizza."

I had to laugh as the waitress turned back toward the restaurant. "Pizza and salad, hold the pizza? I'm sure they don't run across that order every day."

The sun glinted off the blond highlights in her brown hair, and I realized that she'd been highly successful in her campaign to lose the pounds that childbearing had piled onto her hips. Her makeup, nonexistent when I'd first encountered her back on the island, had been expertly applied.

"Go ahead," she said, tilting her head toward my steaming pepperoni and mushrooms. "I'll just enjoy the aroma while you eat."

I took her at her word. "Sort of like secondhand smoke, eh?"

"At least cigarettes aren't fattening."

I swallowed and wiped my mouth with a paper napkin. "You look good."

"Thanks. You, too. Just so we're clear, I still hate you for being able to eat like that and not gain an ounce."

"Get over it." I speared some lettuce. "So what do you want?"

"I'm stung by your implication. Why do you always assume I'm after something?"

"Because you generally are." I thought a moment. "No, let me guess. Word is out that Winston Wolfe has been in town, and I've been seen in his company. You probably got it from someone at the sheriff's office. I'll make it easy for you," I said, pausing to stuff more pizza into my mouth. "I'm not telling you jack, even if I knew anything you might be interested in. See how easy that was? Now we can just enjoy each other's company. So how are the boys?"

Her braying laugh ricocheted off the wall of the restaurant. "Whoever said you were witty was only half right," she fired back. " 'Seen in his company'? Don't insult my intelligence, Bay. Or my contacts. You've been running all over the damn island—and beyond—with the great man in tow. Word is he's going to write about Morgan Bell's disappearance."

I ate in silence, avoiding direct eye contact with the reporter, who in the past had demonstrated an uncanny ability to tell when I was lying through my teeth.

"That was my first big story, you know," she went on. "After I came home." She paused. "After the divorce."

I glanced up to see her eyes had lost the mocking look she usually wore. I remembered how devastated she'd been by her husband's desertion and decided to back off a little. Too bad I hadn't paid more attention to the bylines on the stories Erik had printed out for me. If we had still been in Wolfe's employ, Gabby might have made an excellent source for information. While she never gave me much credit for it, I had become pretty adept on prying things out of her, too.

"Ancient history," I said, applying myself to my lunch. "He's gone back to wherever, and we're on to other things."

"You went out to Jericho Cay." It wasn't a question.

"So?"

"So what's it like out there? I managed to tag along once with a buddy of mine who runs fishing boats, but I never actually got onto the island." She reached into her bag and pulled out a notebook. "Is the place still standing? We ran an artist's rendering of it based on some plans I managed to dig up at the courthouse, but I've never actually seen it in person. Too bad we didn't have Google Earth back then."

"What's Google Earth?"

"What planet have you been living on, girlfriend?" Gabby asked just as the waitress deposited her salad and iced tea in front of her.

I continued to shovel food into my mouth, hoping that the distraction would allow me to avoid answering her more pointed questions. I should have known better.

"It's got something to do with satellites and lets you zoom in on specific places, even individual houses, from your computer. Quit trying to sidetrack me. Did you get inside the house?"

I wiped my hands and leaned back in my chair. "Gabby, listen to me. *If* I had been working with Winston Wolfe, and *if* I had been to Jericho Cay, all of it would be confidential and none of your damn business. I'm not telling you anything. Zip. Zilch. Zero. *Nada.* Got it?"

She shrugged, and I was happy to see the keen light of the reporter back in her eyes. "Bullshit. You know I'm irresistible when I get on the scent of a juicy story. You'll see. Eventually you'll be powerless to resist me."

"Shut up and eat," I said, laughing.

To my utter surprise, she did.

We parted company half an hour later with vague promises to get together for lunch again soon. I knew she would never give up trying to pry information out of me as long as she was convinced I could offer her a pipeline to the famous author. She, in turn, would be a treasure house of background on the original investigation into the disappearance of Ty Bell.

Maybe . . .

I shook my head and climbed into the Jaguar.

It was after two o'clock when I stepped into the office to find that everyone else had made it back before me. Red looked up from his small desk off the reception area when I walked in.

"Something wrong with your phone?" he asked, following me in as I dropped my bag on one of the client chairs. "I've been trying to reach you for a couple of hours. That reporter from the *Packet* was trying to track you down, too."

I turned back to where Erik and Stephanie huddled together around the single desk. "I turned it off. When is the new furniture arriving?" I asked my partner.

"They said between two and four. I'm showing Steph how the phone system works."

"I have all the paperwork filled out," his fiancée said, handing me a folder. "And here's the letter for Mr. Wolfe."

I carried the papers back into my office and dropped into my chair, Red right on my tail.

"Why'd you turn your phone off?"

"Because I needed a little peace." I heard the snap in my voice and dialed it back a notch. "Get those two in here, will you? I have a report to make."

A moment later, they were all ranged around my office, Stephanie with her laptop balanced on her knee, and Red perched again on the corner of my desk. In a few brief sentences, I related my encounter with the supposed Terry Gerard. I held up my hand to forestall any interruptions, but they all erupted into questions the moment I sat back in my chair.

"Hold it! There's no point badgering me, because I've told you everything that happened." I tapped my index finger on the letter Stephanie had handed me. "If we were still working for Wolfe, we'd have a strategy to plan and a million things to discuss. As it is . . ." I glanced at my husband to find him staring at me intently. "What?"

"You actually tried to hold him at gunpoint?"

I let out a long, slow breath. "That's what I said. For God's sake, Red, I wouldn't have *shot* him in the middle of Jarvis Park."

"Never point your weapon at someone unless you're prepared to pull the trigger."

I sighed again. "I know, Gun Handling 101. So lock me up. I was just trying to pin him down, make him talk to me." When no one responded, I said, "Damn it, I just wanted to know who the hell he really is."

Erik cleared his throat and spoke quietly. "So shall I tear up the termination letter, or would you like to do the honors?"

I stared at him and waited.

"Don't you see, this changes everything," Erik said in that same soft tone. "Whether this guy is Bell or Gerard, he's the key to a lot of the questions we've been asking ourselves. If we could find him—or if he finds you again—we might be able to earn the rest of Mr. Wolfe's retainer. And a lot more besides."

My mind flipped back to my interior monologue on the way to Giuseppe's. I'd told myself I had an obligation to these people to see that the agency was profitable and continued to be a viable business. Did I have a right just to toss away tens of thousands of dollars in potential earnings?

"Let's discuss it," my husband said. "Rationally. All in favor, say *aye.*"

"When did this become a democracy?" I asked, allowing the hovering smile to break out in full force. "I thought I was running a benign dictatorship."

"There's been a coup." Red's shoulders relaxed, and he looked at Stephanie and Erik a moment before they all murmured, "Aye."

"Motion carried," my husband said and reached for the termination letter still lying on the top of my desk.

I watched in silence as he ceremoniously ripped it in half.

CHAPTER
TWENTY-SIX

UESDAY DAWNED HOT AND CLOUDY, THE THREAT OF
rain hanging in the low clouds that blanketed the Lowcountry. A perfect day for a funeral.

Lavinia and Julia arrived at the cemetery just ahead of Red and
me. Erik and Stephanie had offered to accompany us, but I'd convinced them to stay and man the office. After we'd kicked around
possible moves to locate the elusive Terry Gerard, my partner had
brought us up to speed on the women's shelter case. His meeting with
Mary Jefferson had resulted in a signed contract and a modest retainer. We agreed to cut our usual fees due to the nature of the business she ran. Erik had given her a program to upload that would allow
him to *trap* any intruders into their system, and he was confident that
he could produce results in fairly short order.

I offered my sister and Lavinia a half smile as Red and I approached. For the first time in the short while I'd known her, Julia
wore a dress, black, with matching pumps. With her wild hair tamed
into a neat coil at the nape of her neck, she suddenly looked more like
the middle-aged woman she was in body, if not in mind. I wondered
when they'd had time to go shopping.

"Good morning, honey," Lavinia said, then nodded at my husband. "Redmond."

We turned toward the area where a green awning covered the raised bier holding the simple oak coffin, sprays of white gladioli cascading down its sides. I'd offered to take care of this detail, but the sisters had waved me away. All the arrangements had been of their choosing. I was simply footing the bill until Elizabeth Shelly's estate was settled. She'd used a local attorney in Jacksonboro, and I had added being in contact with him to my growing list of things to take care of.

"Lavinia," I answered, stopping next to my sister. "Good morning, Julia. Are you doing okay?"

Her smile was tentative, and she looked much more subdued than she had when I'd last seen her on Sunday.

"I guess."

I thought that the gravity—and finality—of Miss Lizzie's death might finally be sinking in. I turned away to speak softly to Lavinia. "Is Neddie coming?"

"She'll try. She had an emergency with a patient, but she said she'd do her best. I told her it wasn't necessary." She sidled a little closer to my sister. "I told her Julia and I would be just fine, won't we, honey?"

Julia laid her head briefly on Lavinia's shoulder. "I guess."

The sound of a car door slamming made us all turn. Patricia Rieth and Matilda Tiley, both dressed in almost identical navy blue suits, picked their way carefully along the gravel path that led to the gravesite. Red moved over to offer his arm, and Matilda took it gratefully. Patricia politely declined and led the small cavalcade up to where we stood waiting.

"The minister isn't here?" she asked, scanning her surroundings as if the Reverend Henry Chaplin might have been lurking behind one of the headstones.

Lavinia bristled a little, and I watched her take a deep breath before replying. "The service is set for ten o'clock. We're a little early."

"Of course you're right," Mrs. Rieth said, and I noticed that she seemed to be holding herself in tight check. "I'm just hoping we can finish before it rains," she added more gently, and Lavinia reached over to pat her arm.

"Here he comes now," she said.

The white hair, cut to a soft cap, contrasted sharply with the deep brown of his kindly, wrinkled face. "Sorry to keep you waiting," he said, his smile at once warm and somber.

Lavinia made the introductions.

"Shall we begin?" he asked, and we ranged ourselves on either side of the bier.

Julia clung to Lavinia and seemed to look everywhere except at the coffin.

The service itself was short and generic. Reverend Chaplin's voice, which I had heard on other occasions booming out across the packed congregation in Lavinia's church, fell to a soft baritone that made the simple, familiar words more comforting. At one point, he asked if anyone had anything they'd like to say about Miss Lizzie, any personal remembrances they'd like to share. From either side of the casket, we all stood and looked at each other, perhaps embarrassed that none of us had known her well enough to offer anything in the way of a eulogy. At some point, all eyes slid to Julia, the one person among us who had shared the life of Elizabeth Shelly, but she remained mute, her head bowed in respectful silence.

Finally, I said, "Miss Shelly was a devoted friend and protector of my sister, and for that I will always remember her with fondness and gratitude."

At the final *amen,* Reverend Chaplin shook hands with all of us. I walked a little way with him toward his car so that I could discreetly hand him the check I'd prepared in advance. He thanked me, and I expressed our appreciation for his willingness to perform the ceremony for someone he'd never met.

He smiled up at me. "Miz Smalls is one of our most faithful congregants. Any service I can render to her or her family I'm happy to do. I wish the occasion weren't such a sad one, but I hope everything met with your approval."

I thanked him again and turned back to the group now making its way toward me. Overhead, thunder rumbled out over the water, and I caught a glimpse of two men standing discreetly back in the trees beside a small backhoe. Once we'd left, they would complete the process of consigning Elizabeth Shelly to the ground.

Lavinia touched my arm. "Do you want to visit your mother's grave while we're here? I have a small bouquet in the van."

"No. Thanks. We should get back to the office."

There was no hint of recrimination on her wrinkled face, although I knew she was disappointed in me. I couldn't help it. Standing over my mother's headstone always brought back a flood of painful memories I'd spent most of my adult life suppressing. I sent up silent thanks to the Judge for insisting on cremation. His ashes had joined the great flow of water to the ocean, and I often found myself staring out over the vast expanse and smiling. *Nowhere and everywhere.* That's what he'd said in his detailed instructions that I'd followed to the letter. It wasn't a bad epitaph.

We halted at the small group of cars pulled up under the sheltering limbs of a huge live oak just as another clap of thunder reverberated across the open grass of the cemetery, and a fork of lightning followed quickly on its heels.

"Would you like to come back to Presqu'isle?" Lavinia asked. "I've prepared a small lunch for us. It won't take a moment to put it all together."

Patricia Rieth and Matilda Tiley exchanged a look. Tillie spoke for both of them. "It's very kind of you, Mrs. Smalls, and we appreciate everything you've done. But we should be heading back north." She tilted her curly head toward the lowering sky. "It's a long drive, and we'll probably run into this rain somewhere along the way."

"Yes, thank you so much for your kindness." Pat held out her hand to Lavinia, who took it in both of hers.

"I'm sorry it took something like this to bring you into our home. Please know that you're always welcome. Anytime."

Matilda stepped forward and hugged Lavinia and then me. "I'm so glad Elizabeth had such good friends." She made a move toward Julia, who shrank back against Lavinia. "I hope everything works out for you, honey," she said.

In unison, the two sisters moved toward their sensible sedan. Red hurried to open the doors, and in minutes their taillights had disappeared into the gloomy morning.

"Well," Lavinia said, reaching for Julia's hand. "We'll just make a quick stop at Emmaline's grave and then meet you at the house."

She stared straight into my eyes and almost dared me to refuse. I glanced at Red, who shrugged, then nodded.

"That's fine," my husband said. "We'll go ahead, and Bay can get things started."

I knew it was pointless to fight both of them, so I let my husband lead me to the Jaguar. I'd learned a long time ago that graceful surrender was the only course when you were outnumbered.

As we crossed the bridge onto Lady's Island, I turned my phone back on so I could check in with Erik and Stephanie and discovered a message waiting. Neddie had called just before ten to tell me she was hung up with a patient and wouldn't be able to make the service. She apologized several times and asked me to let her know how Julia had come through the ordeal.

I dialed her office and got Carolann. I told her to let Neddie know that everything had gone smoothly and that I'd talk with her later in the day. Erik said he and Stephanie had gotten all the new furniture arranged and that he was showing her how to access some of the databases we used in our background checks.

I tried to still the niggling little thought worming its way into my head that perhaps I wasn't as completely indispensable to the smooth operation of Simpson & Tanner, Inquiry Agents, as I thought I was. I glanced over at Red, who seemed to pick up on my disquiet. He reached across the console and captured my hand in his. We rode that way in silence all the way into the semicircular driveway in front of Presqu'isle.

Inside, I tucked my cell phone into the pocket of my suit jacket and began pulling dishes and cutlery out of the cupboard. Since we weren't having guests, I opted for the everyday china and glassware. And we definitely weren't going to sit around the long mahogany table in the dining room. I arranged everything on the old oak table in the kitchen. With all the lights turned on, the homey room did a lot to dispel the gloom of the morning's business as well as that of the darkening sky.

That task completed, I looked around for some hint of what Lavinia had planned for lunch. The refrigerator was, as usual, crammed with covered dishes. I lifted a couple of lids, but I decided the best course was to wait for her to do the cooking. Even though she'd apparently unbent enough to allow Miss Lizzie into her private domain on a couple of occasions, I knew she preferred for the rest of us just to stay out of her way.

I wandered into the back parlor to find Red, his jacket draped over one of the wing chairs and his tie loosened, half sprawled on the settee. He looked up from the newspaper spread in front of him and smiled. He patted the cushion next to him.

"Come sit down and relax," he said. "I'll share the paper."

Neither of us had had time to more than glance at the headlines in our rush to be on time for the funeral. I took the front section he held out to me and settled in beside him.

"You know," I said, scanning the leads and turning to the inside pages, "if we're still going to pursue Wolfe's case, I need to pick Gabby Henson's brain. She said Bell's disappearance was her first big story after she came back to the island. She probably has a lot of notes, things that maybe didn't make it into her articles, that might be useful."

"Let's not worry about it right now, okay? Have you talked with Lavinia about Julia?"

I continued to skim the newspaper, unwilling to meet his eyes. "You know I have. And you know perfectly well she wants Julia to stay here. She thinks it will be the best thing for both of them. So does Neddie." I cast a quick glance, but he had his nose buried in the sports section. "Do you have a problem with that?"

"Technically it's none of my business. I just feel as if we should be taking more of the responsibility. Lavinia's not as young as she used to be."

"No one is," I snapped back, then ordered myself to back off a moment before a short lead on page four of the paper caught my eye: BODY FOUND IN BURNED CAR

"The point is," I heard Red say as I scanned the two-paragraph article, "that it's not fair to expect—"

"Wait! Listen to this." I folded the paper back and read aloud. " 'The body of an unidentified male was found by hikers in a wooded area near the Monticello Reservoir yesterday just outside Sumter National Forest. The couple, whose names have not been released, discovered a late-model sedan partially burned in a clearing beside the water. Preliminary indications are that the victim, estimated to be in his late fifties or early sixties, had been shot once in the head before his vehicle was set on fire. No identification has been released, but sources close to the investigation say an expensive briefcase, partially burned, was found nearby. The Fairfield County Sheriff's Office is in charge of the case.' "

"What—?" Red spluttered.

I jumped up and nearly ran into the hallway. I yanked open the drawer in the console table and fumbled until I found a tattered South Carolina road map. Back in the parlor, I dropped down onto the heart pine floor, spreading the map carefully in front of me. With a trembling finger, I traced Interstate 26 from just south of Orangeburg, through Columbia, and on toward Newberry. I jabbed my finger on the small splotch of blue that represented the reservoir, located a few miles off the highway. I looked up as Red tossed aside the newspaper and joined me on the floor.

"What in the hell are you talking about?" He nudged me aside and looked at the spot I was pointing to.

"It's just off 26. Going north from Orangeburg."

I saw it register in his eyes. "You don't think . . . ?"

"Yes, I do," I said with a shiver, sitting back on my haunches. "I think we just found Winston Wolfe."

CHAPTER TWENTY-SEVEN

NEITHER ONE OF US REGISTERED LAVINIA AND JU-
lia's arrival until they walked into the parlor.

"What on earth are you doing?"

Red and I both jumped. I shot him a look that I hoped conveyed
the message that we should keep our mouths shut.

I snatched up the map and began refolding it. "Just checking out
something from the paper." I stood and tossed it onto the settee. "I
have the table set, but I wasn't sure which of the dishes in the fridge
you wanted out."

"I'll see to that." She turned and put her arm around Julia's shoulders. "Why don't you go up and change, honey? Get into something
comfortable. Then you can go and check on Rasputin. I'll bet he's
missed you this morning. Then we'll have some lunch."

"Yes, ma'am," my sister replied, a little light finally creeping into
her eyes. "He doesn't like it when it storms. He's probably afraid without me."

She turned a dazzling smile on Red and me before sprinting for
the stairs. We listened in silence to the unaccustomed sound of her
high heels clicking on the oak steps. I wanted to call out to her to be

careful, but I held my peace. I wondered how long it would be before I could exorcize the image of Miss Lizzie tumbling to her death.

"So." Lavinia looked from Red and back to me. "Is something wrong? You two seem on edge."

I avoided glancing at my husband. "Just some business we need to take care of. How long before we're ready to eat?"

"Give me about half an hour. The shrimp are all peeled and de-veined, and I just need to make some rice. You can come out in a few minutes and toss the salad for me." Again she studied me for a long moment. "I want to make things as normal as possible for Julia. So don't let whatever this business of yours is get in the way of that, hear?"

"Yes, ma'am," I said, echoing my sister. "I'll be there in a minute."

Lavinia nodded once and slipped into the hallway. The moment her back disappeared toward the kitchen, I made a dive for my cell phone.

"Who are you calling?" Red moved a step closer and laid his hand on my arm.

"Mike Raleigh at the sheriff's office. He can get in touch with the Fairfield County authorities. If the briefcase has Wolfe's initials on it, we'll know for sure."

"Slow down, Bay. Let's talk about this."

I forced myself not to fire back at him, mindful of my resolution to steer our sometimes shaky relationship onto firmer ground. I lowered the phone.

"Okay. Tell me why we shouldn't assume the worst. Because I have to tell you, Red, I'm as sure as I'm standing here that someone's put a bullet into Wolfe's brain and set his car on fire to cover it up. For whatever reason, they botched the job. So it probably wasn't a professional hit. That means—"

"That means that you're all over the map with this thing, Bay. Slow down a minute. You're basing this on so many unfounded assumptions I don't even know where to start." He nodded at my cell phone. "Try that number you've got for Wolfe, the one he called you from on Sunday. Let's try to tackle this in some sort of logical order."

I bit my tongue and accessed the call record. "No service and no voice mail," I said a moment later. "Now what?"

Every fiber of my being screamed out to do something, to leap in the car and get up there. If the body hadn't been burned beyond recognition, maybe we could make an official identification, although the idea of it made me shudder. I wondered if Wolfe's prints were on file anywhere. Unless the remains were too badly charred. Or maybe dentition. That's how they'd positively identified Anjanette Freeman's body. Or—

"Bay? Did you hear what I said?"

I blinked and came back to the parlor. "Sorry. What was it?"

"I said that I can call the sheriff and see if anyone has any connections up in Fairfield County. I'll just ask if there's been an unofficial identification yet."

"Okay, that's good. Here." I thrust my phone at him.

He took it from me and sat back down on the settee. "Why don't you go help Lavinia? Let me handle this."

I bit back a retort. "Fine. But tell them to check for his initials on the briefcase. And let me know the second you have an answer."

I found Lavinia, as usual, at the stove, a voluminous apron tied over her suit. Plastic bags filled with cut vegetables rested beside her on the counter, and I carried them to the salad bowl and began dumping them in.

"I see you decided on the everyday china." Lavinia spoke without turning around.

"Yes, since it's just us. Is that a problem?"

"No, honey. In fact, I think it's good if we try to get things back to normal as soon as possible. For Julia's sake. You did exactly right."

My motives hadn't been nearly as altruistic as she was giving me credit for, but I let it slide. "Has she said anything more about Miss

Lizzie?" I asked while drizzling on the homemade vinaigrette Lavinia
had prepared in advance.

"No. And I'm not sure if that's good or bad. I need to speak with
Dr. Halloran."

"She left me a message, by the way. She apologized for not being
able to make it up here. I told Carolann to have her call when she gets
back to the office. Is there anything specific you want me to ask her?"

Before she could reply, Julia bounded into the kitchen. She wore a
plaid shirt and jeans, and her feet were bare. It was the outfit she'd
worn almost every day of her life since she'd witnessed her mother's
death more than thirty years before, and Lavinia and I exchanged a
look of alarm. Part of her progress under Neddie's tender guidance
had been her willingness to break out of that morbid obsession with
dressing as she had on that tragic night at the beach when Brooke
Garrett died.

"I'm going out to see Rasputin," she said. "Can I take him one of
those bones you got for him from the butcher? He loves those, and it'll
make him feel better about the thunder."

"Hadn't you better put on some shoes?" Lavinia spoke softly, but I
could see the concern in her eyes. "And don't you want to wear any of
the new clothes we bought for you yesterday? You look so pretty in
those."

Julia took a couple of steps and threw her arms around Lavinia.
"Oh, they're much too nice for playing with the dog in. I want to save
them for best. Like when we have company."

It made perfectly good sense to me. But we'd have to let Neddie
know and see what she thought.

"Well, put on some shoes anyway, honey."

"Okay." Julia turned and hurried from the kitchen.

"Trouble?" I asked as I carried the salad bowl to the table.

"Maybe," Lavinia answered. "We'll have to see."

I watched her square her shoulders, and once again I thanked God that she was in our lives. I absolutely believed that, under her loving guidance, my sister had her best chance at claiming a normal life.

The meal passed uneventfully, the talk around the table centering on mundane things, including the weather. The skies had opened up barely a minute after Julia returned from comforting her great brute of a dog, and the sound of the rain beating against the roof made the warm coziness of the kitchen all the more welcome.

When Red joined us, he'd handed over my phone with a brief shake of his head and a quick lift of his shoulders, which I took to mean he hadn't gotten any satisfaction on the question of whether or not it was Winston Wolfe's body in the burned-out car upstate. I itched to hear the details, but it certainly wasn't a fit topic for table conversation, especially with Julia right beside me.

"This is so good, Miss Lavinia," she said a couple of times. With Miss Lizzie no longer glaring at her across the table, she seemed much more relaxed, and we certainly couldn't fault her table manners, although she did tend to eat faster than anyone else. Since I'd been the previous holder of that title, I couldn't very well criticize.

We'd just sat back, pleasantly full, when Red's cell phone rang. We exchanged a look before he excused himself from the table and stepped out into the hallway. I helped carry the empty plates to the counter with one ear cocked for any snatch of his end of the conversation, but the thick walls of the old mansion defeated me. Thinking of that, I wondered how the roof repair was holding up under the onslaught of the autumn storm and decided I should take a quick peek in the attics before we headed back to the island. And that thought led to the memory of the red leather diaries I'd hurriedly stuffed back in the humpbacked trunk the week before.

Madeleine Henriette Baynard. I wondered how we were related and whether or not she'd actually lived at Presqu'isle. It would be fascinating to see the house through the eyes of someone who had experienced it in its initial glory, who had sat on the settees and spindly-legged chairs when they were new, who perhaps had had a hand in acquiring the china and silver we still used to this day. For the first time in my life, I began to understand how my mother might have become so caught up in the past.

I'd just picked up a dish towel to help Julia with the drying when Red came back into the kitchen.

"A word?" he said, tilting his head toward the hall.

I dropped the towel and followed him out. "Did you get an answer?"

"Not yet. But Mike's in touch with the sheriff up there. There seems to be some question about who's got jurisdiction."

"The paper said it was the Fairfield County sheriff."

"I know, but the crime may have taken place inside the national forest. That apparently makes it a little iffy. I'm pretty sure the sheriff has jurisdiction over any local or state crime, even if it's committed on federal land. But there's a discussion going on that could delay things. I guess we'll just have to wait until they iron it out."

I sighed and leaned against the wall. "Why does everything always have to be so damned complicated? So you're saying they're going to keep us hanging while they duke it out over who gets possession of the corpse?"

"No, honey. It's a question of who will conduct the investigation and therefore have control of the evidence. In the meantime, no one's willing to divulge anything that might compromise the case."

"That is such bullshit," I said, and my husband winced. "All someone has to do is look at the damned briefcase. It either has Wolfe's initials on it or it doesn't. It's not as if we're asking them to reveal state secrets."

He ventured a smile. "You know, sweetheart, your life would be a lot simpler if you quit trying to make the world march to your notion of the way things ought to be and just learned to deal with the way things actually are."

My father would have been proud of my indignant snort. "If everyone felt that way, we'd still be living in caves and scratching pictures on the walls."

We turned at Lavinia's voice. "Dessert is ready. It's just leftover apple pie, but I warmed it up. And there's tea."

I pushed away from the wall. "Well, let's get this over with and get back to the office. Maybe we can rattle some more chains from there."

Red draped his arm over my shoulder as we walked back to the kitchen, and I thanked the gods that our harsh words hadn't led to a wider argument. Maybe I was actually learning from past mistakes. Maybe.

CHAPTER
TWENTY-EIGHT

EDDIE HALLORAN CALLED WHILE WE WERE EN route back to the island. I'd jumped at the sound of the phone and did my best to conceal my disappointment that it wasn't Mike Raleigh or someone else with news of the murder in Fairfield County.

"Everything went fine," I told her as Red stopped for the light at Burnt Church Road. I relayed the information about Julia's reversion to her old wardrobe, but Neddie shrugged it off.

"I don't think it's necessarily a sign that she's regressed. It does make sense that she wouldn't want to go out to that muddy dog pen in anything new. How did she seem during the service?"

"Quiet. Reserved. Reverend Chaplin asked for remembrances, but Julia didn't speak. She conducted herself the way Miss Lizzie would have expected of her, I guess. Which is way past ironic, now that I think about it."

"Well, just have Lavinia keep an eye on her. Hopefully they'll establish a routine. I'll stop in and see them Thursday night."

"You don't need to be making house calls, Neddie. Lavinia is perfectly capable of driving to Savannah. If she can't, either Red or I can do it."

"I'm going to be on Hilton Head anyway, so it's no big deal to go on over to Presqu'isle. I'll try to get myself invited to dinner."

I laughed. "Even if you get fed, you need to bill me for your time." I paused. "What are you coming to the island for? If it's patient related, just tell me to mind my own business."

"No, nothing like that. I'm looking at some condos. I need to have some beach time, especially on the weekends, and I didn't find anything I liked on Tybee. I just want a little hideaway. You know, somewhere I can kick off my shoes and wriggle my toes in the sand."

"You're always welcome to stay with us," I said, wondering where I'd put her since we had the kids every weekend.

"Thanks, but I need my own space. I'll let you know how it goes. And how my session with Julia works out. I'm very hopeful we'll be making steady progress from here on out."

I thanked her and hung up, relaying her news to Red.

"It's the right time to buy, I guess, although beachfront property is still pretty pricey. The shrink business must be good."

We pulled into the agency parking lot about fifteen minutes later. I stopped dead in the doorway at the strange sight of the reception area, now completely rearranged with the new desk and chair. Stephanie looked up from Erik's old space, a welcoming smile on her pretty face. There was a new plant in the corner, and the wingback chair had been set beside it, along with a low table with a few magazines fanned neatly on its gleaming surface. A divider had been added to screen Erik's new setup from the casual observation of a visitor.

"Am I in the right place?" I asked just as my partner stepped out from behind his desk.

"Do you like it?" Stephanie had leaped up to stand with her hands clutched tightly in front of her. "I thought it might look more inviting, less intimidating if we moved some things around. And I had some art and a couple of tables of Dad's stored away. If you hate it, we can—"

"Whoa, slow down. It looks wonderful." I watched her visibly relax. "If the detective business slacks off, we can always hire you out for interior decorating."

Erik crossed the carpet and stood next to his fiancée. "I told Steph you'd be okay with us sprucing the place up a little." His smile faded. "How did it go this morning?"

"The funeral service was fine. I mean, everything went as planned." I sighed and glanced at Red. "We have another problem. Bring the laptop, and let's talk."

They all followed me into my office. When everyone was settled, I nodded at my husband. "You want to do the honors?"

He told them about the article in the paper and about his conversations with Detective Mike Raleigh. I gave him credit for not downplaying my own conviction that the body in the car was Winston Wolfe.

"I hope you're wrong," Erik said. "But it does seem to be a pretty big coincidence, given everything we know about his being on the run from somebody." He reached across and lifted the laptop from Stephanie's hands and typed for a minute. "Okay, this is what I was thinking of. Didn't he call you on Sunday and say that he was safe? At least that's what I have in my notes."

"That's what he may have thought." I paused a moment. "We need to find Terry Gerard."

"You think he might have been the one after Mr. Wolfe?" Erik asked.

I tried to reason it out. "Maybe. But we don't know yet when Wolfe died." I forestalled Red's interruption. "I know, *if* it's even Wolfe at all. Gerard was here on Hilton Head yesterday, we know that for sure." I grimaced, remembering how close I had been to the answers we'd been searching for. "But if it happened Sunday night, after I talked to Wolfe, there's no reason it couldn't have been Gerard."

Red spoke quietly. "There's no point in speculating. But I agree that finding this guy should be at the top of our priority list. Until we know something for certain."

Stephanie raised her hand to shoulder height, like a schoolgirl afraid to interrupt the teacher, and I smiled.

"There's no need to ask permission to speak, Stephanie. If you've got an idea, throw it out there."

"Okay, sorry. I was just wondering if Mr. Wolfe's secretary would be someone to talk to. I mean, maybe she's heard from him."

"Melanie Hearst," Erik said, beaming at his fiancée. "Good call." He glanced at me. "Should I try to reach her?"

"Do it. But don't alarm her. Just say we think Wolfe's cell phone may be out of range, and we need to talk to him. Ask her if she has another number we can try, or if she knows of anyplace he might go for some privacy. See if she'll pass on a message if she hears from him."

Erik stood and walked back out to the reception desk.

"Anything happening on the shelter case?" I asked Stephanie.

"All the computer work is done and set up. Erik downloaded their e-mails from the past few weeks, but it's a lot to get through. I've been helping a little."

"Good. Keep me posted on how it goes." I turned to my husband. "Any bright ideas on how to go about tracking down Terry Gerard?"

"I think we need to check the hotels. You saw all his ID. If he's got something in another name, we could be screwed, but it makes more sense for him to be registered under his own name."

My mind shot back to my search for an accused rapist and the difficulties I'd encountered in trying to wheedle guest names out of the hotel staffs. "I think that's something Erik needs to take care of. He can hack—I mean, access—the registrations." I held up a hand as Red opened his mouth to object. "I know, it's not strictly legal, but you know we're not doing it for nefarious purposes."

" 'Not strictly legal'? It's as illegal as hell, and you know it."

"Remember which team you're playing for," I said with a grin. "Even though we don't have badges, we're still the good guys."

"I don't think the county solicitor would agree with you."

Erik stepped back in. "Melanie Hearst hasn't heard from Mr. Wolfe since Friday morning. He told her he would be out of touch for a couple of days, but she expected him to have called in before now. She said he sometimes does these disappearing acts when he's on the trail of something hot for one of his books, but she's getting a little concerned."

No one spoke. I racked my brain for a time line, then realized we still had one up on the whiteboard leaning against the far wall of my office. I pointed to it. "Set that back up on the filing cabinet, will you, Red?"

My husband looked at me quizzically but did as I asked.

"Okay. We saw him briefly on Friday morning when he came to retrieve his luggage, and we had a meeting on that afternoon. So he knew then, for some reason, that he'd be out of the loop for the weekend. Or at least that's what he told his secretary." I paused, but no one jumped in to correct me. "But by that evening he was on the run. And no one's seen him since Brenda dropped him off at the Holiday Inn."

"No one we're aware of," Red added.

"Right. We don't know if he ever checked in, but someone ransacked his room at the Crowne Plaza, either before or after he got back from our office." I looked around at three faces scrunched up in concentration. "So what do we think? Does any of this help us figure out what Wolfe was up to? Or exactly what the hell is going on?"

"Remember he left us stranded out on Jericho Cay on Thursday?" Erik seemed to be talking as much to himself as to the rest of us. "When he apologized for that, he said he had an important business meeting back on Hilton Head that he couldn't miss."

I nodded. "And right after that he packed up and had his plane readied for takeoff." I whirled toward Red. "I wonder if he filed a flight plan. We never followed up on that. Maybe it would help us if we knew where he was going."

"But he never left," Stephanie offered, her eyes on the board. "Something must have interrupted him. Or scared him off, because that's how you got his luggage. From the aviation terminal."

I'd been unconsciously twirling a pencil around in my fingers, my preferred substitute for occupying my hands since I'd quit smoking, and I tossed it onto the desk. "None of this is any use at all. We just don't have enough information even to formulate a working hypothesis. We need to find out a lot more about his movements on Thursday and Friday."

Red cleared his throat. "Does any of it matter if he's the guy with a bullet in his head?"

That stopped me, and for a long while none of us spoke. Finally, I leaned back in my chair and let out a heavy sigh. "You're right. We need to know the answer to that before we waste any more time speculating. Can you call Mike and see if he has anything new?"

Red expelled a long breath. "I hate to keep bugging him. He promised to get back to me as soon as anything shook loose. Let's not screw up a good contact by making ourselves a pain in his butt."

That made me smile. "Okay. Just in case we get the news, I want Erik to check the hotel lists for Terry Gerard. Even if Wolfe has been murdered, we need to talk to him."

"Why?" All three of them said it in unison, like some Greek chorus.

"Because I want to. Good enough?" I stood and reached for my bag. "And I've about had it with funerals and disappearing suspects and possibly murdered clients. I'm going home."

No one argued with me as I picked up my bag and wove my way back into the reception area. As I approached the door, Red reached around me and pulled it open.

"We'll see you all tomorrow," he said and followed me out.

At home, we decided, in deference to our unusually hearty lunch, to settle for salads and garlic bread. As I moved about the kitchen, the image of Winston Wolfe with a bullet in his head, his pasty white body perhaps charred beyond recognition, kept floating to the top of my consciousness. My efforts to stuff it back down met with limited success. After we'd eaten and cleaned up, we retired by unspoken consent to the chaise longues on the back deck.

Red, a beer in one hand, stretched out and exhaled loudly.

"What?" I asked, arranging myself with my arms tucked behind my head.

"I'm not sure I'm cut out for this," he said softly, his head turned away from me.

"Not cut out for what?"

The soft shushing of the waves on the other side of our battered dune made my eyes demand to slide closed. I had to force myself to concentrate on his next words.

"All this murder and mayhem you seem to attract."

I bit back the retort that sprang immediately to my lips. "You're blaming this on me?" I said as calmly as I could manage. When he didn't answer, I added, "And how many years have you spent in law enforcement? Between the Marines and the sheriff's office? Don't tell me that was some kind of cakewalk."

It was some moments before he answered. "You're right. It's not that I haven't seen my share of blood and guts." He paused. "But I never got personally involved with the people. I mean, sure, I had a lot of dealings with the survivors of some kind of tragedy. But I only came on the scene—and mainly as support—after someone had already been killed. I never had a personal relationship with the victims."

I gave my response careful consideration before I spoke. "I guess I

can understand how that might get to you. Maybe it's because it's happened to me before that I'm not as shocked about the idea of the dead
guy being Wolfe as you are."

"It's not just that. There don't seem to be any rules."

"Rules about what?"

"When I was an MP and then a deputy, we had procedures.
Guidelines. This . . . this seems to be all over the place." He turned
and looked at me. "You seem to make it up as you go along."

I thought about that. "You're right. There's no operating manual.
But I don't know how else to play it. I mean, there's no one up the food
chain to hand off to when things get complicated. I'm it. So I just try to
be logical, to think things through even though you think I don't." I
moved my head and held his gaze. "Is it my wanting Erik to hack into
the hotel databases that's bugging you?" He didn't reply, so I pushed on.
"I know you don't like it that we sometimes break the letter of the law,
but it's part of the deal. I don't go looking for ways to step over the line.
It's just that sometimes it's necessary."

"I guess."

I took a deep breath. "Look, Red. You had the chance just a couple
of weeks ago to get out of this and back to the kind of policing and investigating you're obviously more comfortable with when they offered
you the job up in Walterboro. Why didn't you take it?"

He turned away from me and gazed out across the rail toward the
ocean. "Truth time?"

"Absolutely. Nothing but."

"I was . . . I *am* worried about us. I'm not sure we'd survive living
apart for most of the week." His laugh held no humor. "Hell, I'm not
sure we'll make it like this, come to think of it."

A part of me wanted to jump in with reassurances, with soothing
words to make him see how silly he was being. But he had said it
himself: *Truth time.*

"There's no guarantee either way."

The only response I got was a tightening of his jaw. His eyes still avoided mine.

"Nothing's ever engraved in stone when it comes to a relationship, Red. This isn't a news flash. Look at you and Sarah. I thought you two had everything in the world going for you: high school sweethearts, a nice house, two great kids. And then, poof! It's all gone to hell." I paused. "If you're looking for sure things, you came to the wrong place."

For a long time he remained silent, the nearly empty bottle of beer resting on his tight stomach. Then his head turned, slowly, and I waited for an outburst that never came.

"You're right," he said and reached for my hand.

I released the tightness that had gathered in my chest and blinked back the treacherous tears I'd been determined to hold in check. As the sun disappeared behind us, spreading its pink and orange glow across the far horizon, we sat, our fingers entwined until the stars slid out from beneath the shredded clouds.

CHAPTER
TWENTY-NINE

E MADE LOVE, AND BOTH OF US FELL INTO EX-
hausted sleep sometime after midnight. Though my eyes
popped open almost exactly on the hour, every hour, until just after
seven, no one called.

I scrambled some eggs while Red put in a call to Detective Mike
Raleigh.

"He's out" was his only report when he'd hung up the phone.

We wolfed down our breakfast and arrived at the office just after
eight thirty. Inside, it took me a moment to reorient myself to the new
décor and furniture arrangement before I walked into my office and
set my bag on my desk. I checked for messages and found none.

"Well, this is just great." I dropped into the chair and folded my
arms across my chest. "What the hell are we supposed to do now? We
don't know if our client is alive or dead. We don't know where the hell
Terry Gerard is." I tilted my chair back to a precarious angle. "And
where the hell are Erik and Stephanie?"

My husband knew better than to laugh, but I saw him struggle to
suppress a grin. "That's an awful lot of *hells,* even for you."

I looked up as the outer door opened. My partner and his fiancée walked in, hand in hand, then jumped apart when they realized they weren't alone.

"Good morning," my husband said to cover their embarrassment. "We're at it a little early today."

They both mumbled greetings and moved to their separate desks. The red flush on Erik's face made me smile and helped to smooth out my rough edges.

"No messages," I said in my most businesslike tone. "Did you have any luck with the hotels?"

His head jerked up, and he awarded me one of his dazzling smiles. "You know me too well. Yes. I hit it on the third try last night. The Sea Crest. On North Forest Beach."

"Really?" I'd been convinced—maybe by Terry Gerard's scruffy clothing and that satchel that looked as if it had been through the wars—that he would have opted for something much more low-key. And cheaper.

"Under his own name. He's been there since last Thursday. He's paid up through today."

I took a moment to mull that over. "So he arrived a day after Wolfe. What do we think about that?"

Without instruction, everyone settled in front of my desk.

"That he was following Mr. Wolfe?" Erik suggested.

"My best guess." I glanced at Red. "Or do you think it's just a coincidence?"

"No. The timing's too tight. Either Gerard followed him, or he knew where he was going ahead of time."

I hadn't considered that. "Inside information? The secretary?"

"Maybe," my husband said. "Do we know anything about her?"

"I can Google her," Stephanie offered.

"Do that," I said. "And maybe check Amazon for the dedications and acknowledgments in some of his books. He might have thanked her somewhere along the line."

"You read all that stuff?" Red asked.

"If I'm going to read a book, I'm going to get every last word I paid for," I answered with a smile. "Even the author's bio and end-notes." I sobered. "I thought of something else last night. We need to talk to Brenda again. She probably drove Wolfe to that meeting on Thursday." The date struck me. "You don't suppose he was hooking up with Gerard, do you? The timing's right."

Erik spoke up. "But why? I mean, if he was in touch with Gerard . . . And if we're convinced he's the one in the photos Wolfe had, why was he bothering with us? I mean, we're pretty sure Terry Gerard is the key to what happened out on Jericho Cay, right? If Wolfe had him, what did he need us for?"

No one responded, because it was a damn good question, one to which none of us seemed to have an answer.

"Okay," I said, shaking my head to clear out all the disconnected thoughts bounding around in there, "here's what let's do. Stephanie, you investigate Melanie Hearst, Wolfe's secretary. Print out anything that looks as if it might be pertinent, especially anything that would tell us how long she's been with him. Erik, you see if you can track down Brenda at the limo service. We need to know where she took Wolfe on Thursday after he stranded us on Jericho. Also, push her on anything she might know about where he planned to go when he ordered his plane fueled up."

Both of them nodded and hurried out to their respective desks. I turned to my husband.

"Red, go over to the general aviation side of the airport and nose around. Find out if anyone saw Wolfe after he left his luggage sitting outside the building. Or if he filed a flight plan."

"No one is going to just hand over that information, Bay."

"Use your boyish charm," I said, and he laughed.

"What about you?"

I thought about all the disparate threads our association with

Winston Wolfe had unraveled. "I'm going home to get his phone, the one we found on the beach. Erik needs to crack his password so we can access that voice mail. And I want to know who he talked to before he got snatched or scared off or whatever happened to him."

"Aye, aye, captain," my husband said, rising.

"Wait!" I held out a hand to stop him. "Before you do that, stop at the sheriff's office and see if you can locate Mike Raleigh. I need to know if we're just spinning our wheels here. We have to have a positive identification of that body."

I picked up my bag and watched Red make his way out the door. I stopped at Erik's new desk. "Everything working out okay?" I asked when he lifted his hands from his keyboard.

"Sure. By the way, all this stuff came to around twelve hundred dollars. I hope that was okay."

"Fine. Do you need anything else?"

"No, we're good now for a while. I have a couple of laptops picked out for you. When things slow down a little, we can go over to the store and check them out. You need to try them and see which one is comfortable for you to type on."

"No problem. Listen, we really need to get into Wolfe's phone and see who that voice mail was from. I'm heading home to get it out of the safe. Do you need another program or something?"

His face colored slightly. "I feel kind of stupid I couldn't get it on the first try. I'm usually pretty good at that stuff."

"I know. So download or buy whatever you need to make it happen."

"You got it."

I nodded at Stephanie and stepped outside. The air had cooled after the storms that swung through on Tuesday, and the temperature had to be hovering around seventy. Perfect October weather on the island. It would have been a great day for a leisurely stroll on the beach. Or to stretch out on a chaise with a good book. I sighed. *No rest for the wicked,* my father used to say when he was buried in legal briefs up to his elbows. The thought of him made me smile. As I slid into the front seat of the Jaguar, I realized that it was times like these that made me miss his counsel, even though it would have been peppered with criticism of the way I'd been handling things. Compliments never sprang readily to his lips, and he always thought he was smarter than just about anyone else he knew.

"And you were, Daddy," I whispered to the warm, empty air of the interior. "You were."

I saw Dolores Santiago's head appear at the kitchen window when I pulled into my driveway. Once the business had taken off, our paths rarely crossed anymore. She came twice a week to keep the house in order, and I didn't hold her to any particular schedule. She had other clients. Even though her husband's landscaping business had survived the recent recession, she had two kids in college and another one on the cusp. Sometimes I didn't see her for a couple of weeks at a time, although I could always tell when she'd been there. The house sparkled, and there was almost always something wonderful waiting for me in the refrigerator or the freezer.

I waved as I slid out of the car and found the tiny Guatemalan woman standing in the doorway when I climbed the steps from the garage.

"Ah, Señora, *bueno*. Is good to see you."

I hugged her and she stepped back, as always feeling awkward at any overt display of affection.

"You, too, *amiga*. How's everyone? The kids doing well?"

"*Sí*. And Mr. Red? He is good?"

"Fine. Listen, I can't stay. I just need to get something from the safe."

"No time for tea? I make fresh."

I checked my watch. "Okay, maybe a couple of minutes. I'll be right back."

I skirted the vacuum cleaner standing sentinel in the hallway and worked the combination on the safe concealed in the floor of my walk-in closet. A moment later, I dropped Wolfe's phone into my bag and returned to the kitchen. Two frosted glasses of iced tea sat on the blue flowered place mats on the round table in the alcove. I pulled out a chair. Before I could pump Dolores for more information about her children, she broke the silence.

"A man was here today, Señora. He come to the office?"

I frowned, and I could feel my antennae, the ones that always signaled trouble, begin to quiver. "What man?"

Dolores shrugged. "He say you have for him the package. He ask me to give it to him."

The hackles on the back of my neck had joined in the alert. "I didn't send anyone here. What did he look like?"

She thought a moment. "Tall, like you, Señora. And . . . how you say, no *gordo?*"

My Spanish left a lot to be desired, but I'd managed to pick up a modest amount from Dolores. "Not fat? You mean, skinny?"

"*Sí,* Señora. *Skeeny.*"

"What was he wearing?"

"The hat, for the baseball. *Rojo.* Jeans. And he have the bag, like this."

She pantomimed something that crossed from left shoulder to right hip.

A red hat and the satchel. Terry Gerard. But what in the hell was he doing at my *house?* And how did he get inside the plantation? Probably walked up the beach, I told myself. No real mystery there. And anyone with a computer and access to Google Earth could pinpoint the location. At least according to Gabby Henson.

I sipped tea and let my eyes wander around the room. I didn't want to frighten my housekeeper and friend.

"Can you remember exactly what he said?"

She gave it her full concentration. "He say you need package at office. You send him to pick up. But I say, no package. No note from my Señora. He . . ." She couldn't come up with the word, so she made an exaggerated shrug. "Like that. Then he say, thank you."

"And then he left."

She nodded. "*Sí.*"

"Did you see which way he went?"

"No. I close door, I go back to work." She studied me closely. "Is *problema,* Señora? Did I do wrong?"

I reached across the table and gripped her two hands, clasped tightly together in front of her. "No, of course not. It was just a mix-up." She raised her eyebrows in confusion. I fumbled for the right word in Spanish, then gave up. "A mistake," I finished lamely. I gulped down the remaining tea and stood. "Don't worry about it, my friend. I have to get back to the office. Give my best to the family."

I bolted out the door and trotted down the garage steps. What was Terry Gerard doing knocking on my door? Had he expected to find the place empty? Had he intended to do a little B & E to see if maybe I had Wolfe stashed in one of the closets? But if he was looking for my client, did that mean he didn't know he was probably dead? I shook my head. Too damn many questions and not enough answers.

As I backed around and pulled out of my driveway, I reached into my bag, and my fingers brushed against Winston Wolfe's abandoned cell phone. I moved on to my own, flipped it open, and dialed the office.

Come hell or high water, the sun was not going to set until I'd had a few choice words with Mr. Terence Edward Gerard.

CHAPTER THIRTY

ERIK STOOD THE MOMENT I STORMED INTO THE OFFICE. "He checked out. About seven thirty this morning. No forwarding address."

"Damn it!"

I restrained myself from flinging my bag onto my desk. Instead I set it down gently and retrieved Wolfe's phone.

"Here." I waved it in Erik's direction, and he took it gingerly from my hand.

"I've been working my way through the e-mails from the women's shelter," he said, moving back a little out of the line of fire, then held up the phone. "Is this the priority?"

"Yes!" I drew in a long breath and let it out slowly. "Yes, please," I said more softly. "I'm betting there's some clue to Gerard's whereabouts in there. I want him." I held my partner's gaze. "I want him bad."

"Understood."

I picked up the phone on my desk and punched in Red's cell number. He answered on the second ring.

"Where are you?" I asked without preamble.

"Just coming back to the office." He paused. "I have news."

My heart jerked a little in my chest. "Was it Wolfe?"

"No positive ID on the body, but the briefcase sounds like it might have been his."

My legs folded under me, and I dropped down onto my chair. I'd been 99 percent certain the blackened corpse would turn out to be Wolfe, but the confirmation still shocked and saddened me. I realized Red had been talking in my ear.

"What?" I said, coming back to the present. "What did you say?"

"I said, don't jump to conclusions. The bag was empty, and the monogram, if it was even there, was unreadable."

I didn't have to feign confusion. "But it's his, right? I mean—"

"They're not ready to make a call on the . . . remains." He swallowed hard and continued. "Mike Raleigh's been in touch with the sheriff up there. They finally settled jurisdiction, and Fairfield will take the case. And Mike told them we might be able to identify the body." He paused a moment. "Apparently the face wasn't totally . . . gone. Just pretty messed up."

I gulped down the revulsion that leaped into my throat. "*We?* As in you and I?"

"Hold on. I'm just pulling into the parking lot. I'll be there in a minute."

I hung up and sat staring into space, the image of a burned body imprinted front and center on my mind's eye. I hardly noticed when Red walked into my office, Erik and Stephanie trailing behind.

"Bay? Honey? You okay?"

I shook myself, both mentally and physically, and offered him a wan smile. "Fine. When do they want us up there?"

Everyone sat down, and Red pulled one of his long legs across his knee. I noticed that his foot was shaking, bouncing up and down, the only real manifestation of his own nervousness.

"You don't have to go. I can do it. I told Mike to let them know

I'd be on my way as soon as possible. I should be able to be up there by noon or shortly thereafter."

A part of me sagged in relief that I wouldn't be forced to come face-to-face with the horror that must be Wolfe's remains. But another voice told me I was being a coward.

"I'll go with you," I said, squaring my shoulders, but my husband was already shaking his head.

"There's no need. I know what the guy looks—looked like. You have other things to take care of, right?"

I suddenly realized he had no idea that Gerard had been at our house. I took a moment to fill him in. A second after I finished, his foot hit the floor with a thump.

"The bastard! I'll rip his goddamned heart out!"

Red's outburst broke through the pall of fear and sadness that had settled over me at the thought of having to view Wolfe's body.

"He checked out of the Sea Crest this morning. We're going to have to locate him some other way." I paused. "But seriously, Red, I don't want you to do this thing alone. It's not fair. It's not your job."

For a moment, his eyes held my gaze. "I'm making it my job." He stood. "Should take me a couple of hours to get up there. I'll call when I know anything."

Completely ignoring our unspoken office protocol, he walked around the desk and kissed me, hard, on the lips.

"Be careful," I said to his retreating back. "And thank you," I mumbled under my breath.

No one spoke for a few moments after Red's departure. Finally, Stephanie cleared her throat, and I forced myself to smile in her direction.

"I couldn't find anything about Mr. Wolfe's secretary online, so I took on calling Brenda Carter. From the limo service? I hope that was okay. I took notes." She glanced over her shoulder toward her desk.

"And I have a number you can reach her at if you want to speak with her yourself."

"Excellent. Get your notes." I looked at Erik. "Get on that phone, okay?"

He nodded once and left the room.

Stephanie took her seat again and flipped over a page of a steno pad.

"Go ahead." I leaned back in my chair and closed my eyes.

"Okay. Thursday. After she picked up Mr. Wolfe from the marina at Palmetto Bay, she took him back to his hotel. To the Crowne Plaza. He told her to wait in the parking lot and went inside. She says it was about half an hour before he came out. He had his briefcase and one piece of luggage with him." She paused and looked up.

"You're doing fine, Stephanie. I'm assuming these are the things we found outside the general aviation building. So she took him to the airfield. Go on."

"No, see, that's the thing. She didn't take him straight there. He had her drive to the Sea Crest, and—"

I jerked upright in my chair. "The Sea Crest? Where Gerard was staying?" I ran my fingers through my hair, tangling the long strands. "Wait, let me think about this. We're talking Thursday, late afternoon, right?"

She nodded.

"Erik!" I yelled, and a moment later he stood in the doorway. "When exactly did Gerard check in at the Sea Crest? What time?"

He held up one finger and turned back toward his desk. He punched a few keys and was back in less than a minute. "Three thirty on Thursday."

"Thanks. Did you see these notes Stephanie took?"

"No. I was working on the shelter's e-mails. Why, is there a problem?"

"Wolfe marooned us on Jericho Cay so he could meet up with Gerard."

"We don't know that for a fact, Bay. All we know for certain is that Gerard had checked in by the time Wolfe showed up, right? Whether or not they actually connected is just an assumption."

"A pretty damn good one, though, don't you think?"

"Better than fifty-fifty, I guess, but not a sure thing." He paused, and I tipped my head at him. "I mean, it's certainly possible. That is, if we can come up with a scenario, with everything else we know, that makes any sense of it. Why would the two of them be meeting?"

Again I twirled strands of my hair in my fingers. "I don't know." I sighed. "Anyway, go ahead, Stephanie. What else did Brenda have to say?"

Erik's fiancée bent her head again to her steno pad. "He left his suitcase in the limo but took the briefcase with him. He was gone about twenty minutes."

"Time enough for a meet," I said, then waved my hand at her.

"When he came back," Stephanie continued, "he told her to take him to the drive-thru of McDonald's."

"McDonald's? Wolfe?" The idea of that arrogant, fastidious New Yorker eating food out of a cardboard box left me nearly speechless. No accounting for taste, I told myself. "Strange. Then what?"

"He told Brenda to get something for herself, too. They ate in the car, and then he had her take him to the airport. The part where his plane was." She hesitated. "She also said he was making phone calls the whole time they were driving, but she couldn't hear anything he said."

"Okay, what happened when they got to the airfield?"

"He left his bags outside, went in, was gone a few minutes, then came back out and told her to go get you and Mr. Tanner." She looked up. "I guess you know what happened after that. That's about all for Thursday."

"Great work, Stephanie," I said absently. "That's really helpful."

I let the new information percolate in my brain, only vaguely aware that the young woman had stood and returned to her own desk. Did Wolfe have a meeting with Terry Gerard at the Sea Crest? Or did he spend those twenty minutes looking for him and never making contact? Why was he leaving the island? And what happened between the time he sent the limo to Jump & Phil's to collect Red and me and the time he disappeared from the aviation building? Where did he go? And how did he get there? And why did he leave his bags—especially his briefcase— behind?

I could feel the stirrings of a headache. I closed my eyes and leaned my head against the back of the chair. I consciously slowed my breathing and lay my hands loosely in my lap. It had been a long time since I'd meditated, but I tried to settle myself into that calming state where my brain could filter out all the confusion and conflicting thoughts racing around inside it. I could feel the tension draining from my neck and shoulders as I sank more deeply into controlled re- laxation. The sound of two sets of hands clicking on computer keys faded, and I let myself drift.

The faces arose, one at a time, misty and hazy, as if I saw them through a veil of gauze. Winston Wolfe. Terry Gerard. I tried to con- jure up Ty Bell, but his countenance remained the most obscured of all. Why were there no pictures of him? Surely somewhere, someplace, he'd been photographed. There had to be a time before his reclusive- ness surfaced and was honed to an art form. As a child? A teenager on his first prom date? In sports, maybe? College yearbook?

The images floated in front of my mind's eye, my inner sight al- ways returning to the blank face. Had he resembled Gerard, as I had earlier suggested? I concentrated. Had Wolfe ever said as much? Even if he had, was it the truth? When you came right down to it, we had only our client's word for any of it. Bell. Gerard. Even Wolfe himself.

I jerked upright. "Stephanie!"

She appeared in the doorway. "Yes, ma'am?"

"Did you ever meet Wolfe? Face-to-face?"

"No, ma'am."

"See if there are pictures of him on his Web site. Or on Amazon. Something current. If not, take some money from petty cash and run over to Barnes and Noble. See if any of his books have his picture on the back flap."

Erik stepped up behind his fiancée. "Something wrong?"

"Go on, Stephanie."

She whirled and ducked under Erik's arm.

"Do you know for a fact that the man we've been dealing with is Winston Wolfe, the true crime writer?"

"We didn't ask for ID, but—"

"But what?" I ticked off the points on my fingers. "One, he didn't give us a check, something that would have had his name on it. He transferred funds directly into our account. Two, he hasn't been acting like any legitimate researcher I've ever heard of. He's been evasive, and we've had to pull information out of him. Three, all the stuff we've seen has been superficial, something he could have set up before he showed up here. We don't have one iota of evidence to prove he's who he says he is."

Erik's face reflected his skepticism. "But why? I mean, why would someone want to impersonate Winston Wolfe? What would be the point? What would he have to gain?"

"I haven't figured that out yet. But I keep coming back to the body up in Fairfield County. Why set the car on fire if not to disfigure the dead guy so he couldn't be identified? And then leave a briefcase that sounds exactly like Wolfe's out there in plain sight?"

"Maybe we're not dealing with a sophisticated killer. Those are amateur mistakes, ones someone in a panic might make."

I thought about it for a moment. "Or someone who knew exactly what he was doing."

CHAPTER
THIRTY-ONE

STEPHANIE MATERIALIZED BESIDE MY PARTNER. "No photos on the Web site or anywhere else that I could find."

"That alone is weird," I said. "Get over to the bookstore."

Erik turned to watch her dash out the door, then pulled out a client chair and sat. "I still don't get where you're going with this."

I rubbed my hands across my face. "Neither do I, for certain. I was thinking about there not being any pictures of Ty Bell. And it occurred to me that all this data we've been chasing has mostly been provided by Wolfe. You asked the question a couple of days ago: How does finding out if Bell is alive or dead benefit Wolfe? I mean, think about it. He says he's been commissioned by the sole relative who stands to inherit—what? Millions? Maybe even a billion or two? Why would the cousin be concerned about a book that wouldn't make him a cent? Wouldn't you be putting together a team of top-notch lawyers and begin legal proceedings to have Ty declared dead? I don't know what the statutes are in South Carolina, but if no one's heard from him in all this time, the cousin would have a pretty good shot at it, wouldn't he? And Wolfe seems to be trying like hell to convince us Bell is alive. That can't make the cousin very happy."

Erik steepled his fingers and rested his chin on them. "I see where you're going, but I'm still coming back to his motivation. I mean, assume you're right, that the guy we met was someone impersonating Winston Wolfe. Why? What's the upside for him?"

I slapped my hand down hard on the desk. "I don't know! But we need to find out if we've been dealing with the real deal or an imposter. That's the first step."

We sat in silence for a long time. I was sure Erik's brain was buzzing with the same questions that were rattling around in mine. We both jumped when Stephanie hurried back into the reception area. A tan Barnes & Noble bag dangled from her left hand.

"Here." She thrust it at Erik, who took it and passed it off to me.

It was a book about the two crazies who had terrorized the Washington, D.C., area—the snipers who had nested in the trunks of cars in order to pick off their victims. I flipped to the back cover flap. It was an old photo, not a studio portrait but an outdoor shot taken on a street with the packed buildings of a city rising behind him. Traffic had been caught in a blur in front of the author, and the whole thing had the look of an arty pose meant to appear as if the photographer had caught his subject in mid-stride on the way to an important meeting.

I pulled my magnifying glass from the right-hand drawer and zeroed in on the face. I studied it for a moment before thrusting the glass at Erik.

"What do you think?"

He looked. "It could be. Hard to tell. This guy is a lot younger. And the picture's blurry."

"Sound familiar?" I asked, thinking of all the supposed photos of Terry Gerard—or Ty Bell—that Wolfe had been carrying around in his briefcase.

I took back the book and turned to the front matter. "His publisher's listed here." I jotted notes on the desk pad. "Let me check the acknowledgments. Okay, he thanks his agent, Maury Lance, and his editors, Kerry Styles and Charles Poitiers. Get me numbers for all of them."

Stephanie moved to her desk.

"It's more important than ever that you crack that cell phone."

Erik nodded. "I'm gaining on it. Give me another half hour."

"Do it," I said, my hand reaching for the phone. A moment later, I had Red on the line.

"I'm making good time," he said. "Won't take as long as I thought. Not much traffic on the interstates on a Wednesday morning."

"Listen, I had a brainstorm. Or a complete break with reality, one of the two."

I talked my way through my thought process, trying my best to put it all in some sort of logical order. I finished with the inconclusive author photo in his latest book and sat back to await the verdict.

"It's an interesting scenario," my husband said, obviously unwilling to commit himself one way or the other. "Have you managed to work out what his motive might be? I mean, it's a pretty elaborate scheme to work up if there isn't a big payoff."

"That has to be it," I said softly. "The money. Somehow or other, it comes back to that. Bell was a millionaire. And everything he owns has been sitting around accruing interest or gaining value."

"Unless he had it all in the market."

That made me smile. My own portfolio had taken a serious hit in the recent madness on Wall Street, and I was just beginning to dig out of the hole created, for the most part, by some bad government decisions and the shenanigans of some super high rollers.

"Even so, all the stories in the papers at the time of his disappearance said he was loaded." I paused. "So you don't think I've totally lost my marbles?"

Red laughed. "Maybe. But you've got a point about all of us taking his word for everything. Any luck finding Gerard?"

"We haven't really gotten that off the ground. Any suggestions on where to start?"

"Let me get through this ID first. Can you scan that author photo from the book and send it to my phone? It might be helpful when I'm viewing the body."

Again I forced the images out of my head. "Erik can. I'll get him on it now."

"I'll call you as soon as I land in Winnsboro. That's the county seat. They don't have an official morgue, but the body's at a local funeral home."

"I need to know as soon as you do. One way or the other."

"I'm on it." He paused, and his voice sounded much more confident than I felt. "We'll figure it out, sweetheart. Don't worry."

I hung up just as Stephanie walked into my office. "I've got those numbers for you. The agent and the editors. I called, and all three of them are in. Shall I get them back for you?"

I smiled. Ben Wyler's daughter had obviously inherited his brains as well as his tenacity. If I didn't watch out, I thought, she could be running the place soon.

"Yes. Let's start with the agent." I glanced down at my notes. "Maury Lance." I handed her the book. "Give this to Erik and ask him to scan Wolfe's photo and send it to Red's phone."

"Yes, ma'am," she said, and I wondered if I'd be able to break her of the *ma'am* habit anytime soon.

A moment later, she buzzed me on the intercom. "I have Mr. Lance on line one."

I punched the button and picked up. "Mr. Lance. Thanks for taking my call."

"My secretary said you're a private detective. That's a very persuasive young lady you've got working for you. She swore it wasn't about a project. I'm not taking on any new clients at the moment. So how can I help you?"

"You represent Winston Wolfe, is that correct?"

The pause told me a lot about Maury Lance's integrity. "I guess you could get that from any of his books, so yeah, he's a client. I won't discuss him—or his work—though."

"I understand. My firm was retained by Mr. Wolfe a week ago to assist him with research into the disappearance of Morgan Tyler Bell. Are you familiar with the project?"

Again he waited to respond. "I'm a little confused, Ms. . . . Tanner, is it? Winston doesn't have anything going right now, at least not that he's discussed with me."

I could feel the wariness in his next words.

"Where did you say you're located?"

"Hilton Head, South Carolina. You can check me out if you like and call me back. We're a legitimate agency, licensed by the state. One of our associates is a former Beaufort County Sheriff's sergeant. And my late partner worked homicide in New York City before he was killed."

I waited to see if that was enough provenance for the literary agent.

"Then if this isn't some kind of scam, there has to be a mistake."

The hand gripping the phone tingled, and I could feel my breath growing shallow. "Why is that, sir?"

"Because Winston Wolfe is currently . . . incapacitated."

I felt a surge of excitement radiate from my chest over my entire body. "Can you be more specific?"

He didn't want to tell me. I gave him almost a full minute before I put on my most reassuring voice.

"Someone purporting to be Winston Wolfe has sat in this very office at least three times in the past week. He wired a considerable amount of money into our office account as a retainer. He claimed to have been close personal friends with Ty Bell. He also claimed to have been engaged by Mr. Bell's sole surviving potential heir to write the story of his disappearance. In order to do that, he told me, he needs to determine if the man is dead or alive. That's supposedly what he hired us for. If I wasn't dealing with Winston Wolfe, you'll need to convince me."

I distinctly heard his long sigh. "I'm going to trust you, Ms. Tanner, if for no other reason than that I've been in this business a long time, and I've seen my share of con men and bullshitters come and go. I've got pretty good radar for it." Another sigh. "The truth is, Winston is in a care facility under a false name. We've been keeping it under wraps, out of respect for his privacy."

A care facility? I thought. Was the real Winston Wolfe a drunk? Addict? Nutcase? Before I could find a way to ask the question tactfully, Maury Lance continued.

"This whole thing you're laying out here doesn't make any sense. Why would someone be impersonating him?"

"It's a long story, Mr. Lance, and one whose details I haven't worked out yet. I don't like being scammed any more than you do, but I have to tell you the guy is good. It never occurred to us, until quite recently, that he might not be who he claimed to be."

I toyed with whether or not to tell him about the charred body in the burned-out car but decided he didn't need to know that. At least not yet.

"What can I do?" Lance sounded more angry than upset. "Do you have the cops involved? Do you want me to do an affidavit or something attesting to the fact that your guy can't be Winston Wolfe?"

"That might prove helpful down the road, but for right now it's enough to know that we've been had by an imposter. Thank you so much for taking my call and for being so up-front with me."

"Is there any other information you can share? This thing has thrown me for a loop, I have to tell you. I can't make heads or tails out of it."

Join the crowd, I thought. What I said was, "I'll be glad to keep you informed as much as I can. It's going to end up an official investigation before long, and we'll be out of it. But I'll do my best." I paused, not really needing the information, but bursting with curiosity nonetheless. "Can you tell me what's wrong with the real Winston Wolfe? It might be helpful in pursuing the imposter," I lied.

He kept me waiting for a few beats. "It has to be strictly confidential, Ms. Tanner. If it gets out, it could ruin his career. What's left of it."

"You have my word," I said. "Only on a need-to-know basis within my organization. And law enforcement, if it becomes relevant to their investigation."

"Good. Fine." He sighed. "After his last book bombed, Winston took it hard. Got mixed up with some bad people trying to find a hook for his next manuscript. I'm afraid he came up dry. Nothing was working for him. He got messed up with some prescription medication for depression and moved on from there. Basically, he crashed and burned. He's been in a private sanitarium for the past two months."

CHAPTER
THIRTY-TWO

NO ONE FELT LIKE LUNCH, BUT STEPHANIE VOLUN-
teered to fly for takeout from Wendy's. I ate about half of
my burger and fries and tossed the rest back into the bag. Erik managed a little more, and his fiancée toyed with her salad long enough for
it to get too soggy to eat.

We kicked around the astonishing news about the real Winston
Wolfe. The moment I hung up the phone with his agent, I called Red
and filled him in. He was as shocked as the rest of us. Why none of us
ever thought to vet our client said a lot about the lure of money in
large chunks. I tried to tell myself that hadn't been the driving factor,
but I would have been lying. At least a little. And, if we admitted it,
all of us had been a little starstruck by the phony Wolfe and his supposed credentials.

Erik carried the bags of half-eaten food out to the Dumpster, then
resumed his seat in front of my desk. "What now? I think I'm close to
cracking the phone. And we need to start hunting for Terry Gerard,
don't we?"

Stephanie wriggled a little in her seat. "I was thinking about
something."

I smiled in her direction. "Go ahead."

"The secretary. Melanie Hearst. If Mr. Wolfe isn't . . . wasn't . . . I mean, if it wasn't him, then she must be in on it."

"You're right. You said you didn't have any luck with Googling her?"

"No. And I used a couple of the databases Erik was showing me to see if I could get any information about her. There's no record in New York or New Jersey. I could try some of the other surrounding states."

"Don't bother. I think she's probably just another cog in the scheme. But I wonder." I paused. "Get her on the line. I'd like to speak to her myself."

Both of them rose and returned to their desks. Two minutes later, my phone buzzed.

"She's on," Stephanie said.

"Thanks." I pushed the button. "Ms. Hearst? This is Bay Tanner."

"Yes?"

I may have imagined the caution in her voice, but I didn't think so. "We're still unable to make contact with Mr. Wolfe, and we're all quite concerned. Have you heard from him?"

"No, I haven't."

"You told my associate he left a message on Friday saying he'd be out of touch for a few days, is that correct?"

"Yes, exactly. He does that sometimes, especially if he's on the trail of something for one of his books." She paused. "But he's never been out of touch for this long. I . . . I'm really starting to worry."

Wolfe's being out of the loop had seriously rattled the woman, or else she was a damned good actress. The tremor in her voice sounded genuine. If the dead man in Fairfield County really was the Wolfe imposter she was working with, I could understand why she'd be getting more than a little nervous not to have been in contact with him for nearly a week.

"Maybe we should check with his agent. Mr. Wolfe might have been in touch with her. Do you think that's possible?"

I waited for the phony secretary to take the bait, but she'd obviously been well coached.

"Oh, I don't think that's a good idea. Mr. Wolfe wouldn't like us bothering Mr. Lance."

I tried another tack. "I have some reports that Mr. Wolfe asked us to send directly to his office so you could deal with them. May I have the mailing address?"

She hesitated, and I wondered if my claiming that the imposter had asked for anything to be mailed had tipped my hand. There was a little more confidence in her voice when she responded.

"Just fax them. I believe you have the number."

Score one for the bad guys. I gave it one more try. "It's quite lengthy. I could overnight it to your office."

"Mr. Wolfe doesn't actually maintain an office outside his apartment. I do work for him occasionally, when he needs secretarial skills. The fax number you have will send it directly to his home phone. That's how he prefers things to be done."

It sounded lame to me, but I couldn't press her without giving the game away. "Fine. We'll do that. And you will call as soon as you hear from him, won't you? We're beginning to worry about his safety."

That shook her. In as unguarded a statement as she'd made during the entire conversation, she said, "Me too."

I thanked her and hung up. I rose and walked out into the reception area. "She has to be in on it," I said, as both Erik and Stephanie paused in their work. "And she's worried. I don't think the fake Wolfe was supposed to be out of touch for this long."

"I think I've got something." Erik spoke softly.

"The phone?"

"Not yet. I have a new program running on it, and I'm close.

While that was working, I reran the hotel registers. Terry Gerard moved down the street to the Metropolitan on South Forest Beach."

"Call them and ask for his room," I said, whirling around and striding back into my office. In a moment I had my bag slung over my shoulder and was standing in front of Erik's desk.

He hung up the phone. "No answer."

"But he's registered?"

He nodded.

"Okay. I'm going down there and scout around. He doesn't seem to care much about altering his appearance, so I should be able to spot him if he's in the vicinity."

"It's kind of a long shot," my partner said.

"I know, but I'm sick of sitting around here waiting for the next shoe to drop. Call me when you've gotten into the phone. And don't forget, I want to know who Wolfe was calling on Thursday after he was at the Sea Crest. And who was calling him back. If Red checks in, route it to my cell." I turned to Stephanie. "You can get back on the e-mails for the women's shelter unless Erik has something else for you to do."

I didn't wait for either of them to acknowledge my instructions before I was out the door.

The noon rush of locals was over by the time I pulled into the parking lot of Coligny Plaza. Only a few tables at Market Street Café's outdoor seating area were occupied. None of the diners was a lanky man in a red baseball cap. I took a quick look inside before I moved down the line of stores and restaurants that faced the ocean side of the street. The plaza itself is a rabbit warren of narrow sidewalks weaving their way around small lagoons and a hodgepodge of shell and jewelry shops interspersed with small eateries, a movie theater, and several clothing stores. A few late-season tourists ambled along, window shopping, but my quarry was nowhere to be seen.

I retraced my steps and decided to walk toward South Forest
Beach by way of the businesses on the other side of the street. I mean-
dered in and out of T-shirt shops and bathing suit stores, checking in
the few restaurants before heading around the Coligny Circle. I
glanced at the Holiday Inn rising out of the glare of the October sun
and found myself shuddering a little at the thought that this was the last
place we'd known for certain that Winston Wolfe—or whoever he was—
had been seen alive. I pondered over the strange phone calls I'd received
from him on Sunday, the first sounding completely panicked and de-
manding help, and the second telling me he was safe.

If the body in the burned-out car was in fact his, he'd been dead
wrong about that last part. Literally.

I crossed back over to the west side of the street and headed toward
the Metropolitan, a small hotel that had at one time been part of a
chain, but I couldn't remember which one. Almost as if I'd conjured
him up, I spotted the figure of Terry Gerard moving across the hotel
driveway toward the lobby.

I slowed and lowered my head, fumbling in my bag as if I'd lost
or forgotten something. I glanced up briefly to confirm that my quarry
had in fact entered the building, then pulled out my cell phone.

"Stephanie, give me Erik."

She didn't ask questions, and a moment later my partner picked up.

"Listen," I said, "I've just spotted Gerard going into his hotel.
Give me his room number."

"One fifteen," Erik said. "I'm on my way."

"No!" It was a gut reaction, but it took my better sense only a second to override it. "Okay, yes. I'm going to scout around and make sure
there isn't another way out, then I'll wait for you out front. Hurry."

He didn't reply, and I knew he was already dashing out the door.
It would take him close to ten minutes using Marshland Road and the
Cross Island, a little less if he hit the lights on Pope Avenue just right.

I forced myself to walk slowly past the small hotel. Since Gerard's room was on the first floor, I didn't want to expose myself in case he happened to look out a window, so I kept going, casting long glances from side to side in what I hoped made me appear to be a tourist out for a stroll in the warm afternoon. I'd just turned to retrace my steps toward the hotel's driveway when Gerard emerged back out into the sunshine.

Again I bent my head, thankful that I'd left my hair loose that morning. It cascaded down and hid my face. Through the thick chestnut curtain I watched Terry Gerard turn, not toward the street but back into the parking lot. I cursed under my breath. If he had a car, I was screwed. Mine sat on the other side of the circle, and even if I sprinted I'd never be able to reach it in time to get on Gerard's tail.

I flipped open my cell phone and speed-dialed Erik.

"I'm almost there. Two minutes."

"He's on the move. Pull past the hotel and off the road. Maybe we can still catch him."

"Got it."

I raised my head a fraction in time to see the red baseball cap on the driver's side of a white Toyota Camry. The car stopped to wait for traffic to clear, then pulled across to head back toward the circle.

"Damn it!" I yelled out loud a moment before Erik's big Expedition screeched to a halt in front of me. I jerked open the door and leaped inside. "White Camry. Just coming out of the circle onto Pope. Go!"

Erik stole a quick glance in his rearview mirror before executing a sharp U-turn, cutting off a startled woman in a dark gray van. If the blast of her horn caught Gerard's attention, he didn't show it, continuing up Pope Avenue well within the speed limit. Erik waved his apologies to the angry driver and set off in pursuit.

"Don't crowd him," I said, working hard to get my breathing under control.

"I'm on it," my partner said, shooting a wide grin in my direction. "I've done this before, you know."

I couldn't return his smile, remembering another time when he'd tailed someone all the way through Georgia and into Florida. That chase had ended in a tiny marina amid a hail of gunfire that had left my other partner, Ben Wyler, bleeding to death on the deck of a small boat.

Erik was right, though. He had perfected the skill of allowing a few cars to move in and out between us and Gerard's Camry, making sure to stay close enough that he wouldn't be able to leave us behind at one of the traffic lights. I'd been prepared to bet he'd head out Palmetto Bay Road toward the Cross Island Parkway, the fastest way off the island from the south end, but he clung stubbornly to the right-hand lane. At the Sea Pines Circle he swung onto Route 278, and Erik and I exchanged a look.

"Where could he be going?" I asked.

"We'll find out," was Erik's sage reply. We rode in silence for a moment before he said, "I got into the phone."

I jerked my head in his direction. "Why didn't you say so? What did you find?"

"Not a lot, for all the trouble it took. He talked to Hearst, up in New York, a couple of times. And she called him. The voice mail was a man. He didn't say anything except to leave a number with an 843 area code."

"Here," I said, surprised that it was our own. "Or somewhere along the coast. That's it? No other message?" Erik shook his head. "Did you try it?"

We rolled through the light at Arrow Road, past the Wexford Shopping Plaza, on northward.

"I was just about to do that when you called." He reached into the breast pocket of his short-sleeved shirt and handed me a slip of paper along with Wolfe's phone. "Use this if you want to do the honors so whoever it is won't get spooked by a strange ID."

Traffic was heavy on the main business road that ran from one end of the island to the other, and we had closed until only another small SUV with Pennsylvania plates stood between us and the Camry. I flipped open Wolfe's phone and punched in the numbers.

"Well, that's interesting," my partner said as I glanced back up.

"What?"

He smiled his enigmatic grin and looked over at me.

"Gerard just picked up his cell."

CHAPTER
THIRTY-THREE

HO IS THIS? WHAT THE HELL KIND OF STUNT ARE you trying to pull?"

Terry Gerard's voice, the one I remembered from our exchange in Jarvis Park, thundered through the ether from a few yards in front of us. I held the phone between Erik and me so he could hear.

"God damn it, say something."

I looked at Erik, not sure what to do. Answer and give ourselves away? Hang up and maybe arouse his suspicion even more? I made the decision and snapped the phone closed.

Up ahead, we could see Gerard fling his own cell onto the seat beside him.

I dialed the office. "Stephanie. We're tailing Terry Gerard up 278, just passing the mall. Has Red called in?"

"No, but I'll have him reach you on your cell the moment he does. Is there anything I can do?"

"Just hang close. I'll get back to you."

I fastened my gaze on the white Camry, now a few cars in front of us, and tried to make sense out of the mess we'd gotten ourselves into. Were Gerard and the phony Wolfe in on this together? He'd left a voice mail on the phone Red and I had found in the bushes the day the supposed writer disappeared. And he'd certainly recognized the caller ID a few moments ago. But was it the real Wolfe or the phony one he thought he was dealing with? What the hell was their game? It had to be about money—Bell's money, of course—but what was their plan? Our imposter client had mentioned a trust that administered the home on Jericho Cay. They'd given him a key. But how much of that had been a part of the scam? I massaged my temple, the unanswered questions whirling so fast I couldn't grab onto them as they flew by inside my head.

I glanced at Erik and checked the digital clock on the dashboard. "It's after two. What the hell is taking Red so long?"

Erik shrugged. "Who knows? Paperwork, maybe? Or it could be the sheriff up there isn't all that keen on cooperation. You never know."

He was right, of course, but that didn't make things any easier. I flipped open my own phone and dialed my husband's number. After four rings, it went to voice mail.

"Hey," I said, "what's going on up there? Things are breaking, and I need to talk to you ASAP. Call me."

Through the Folly Field/Mathews Road intersection, traffic thinned out a little. Erik and I sat in silence. There really wasn't much to talk about that wouldn't have involved rank speculation, and we'd already had more than enough of that. The whole investigation had been turned on its head, and I didn't have the foggiest notion how to proceed. Following Terry Gerard seemed as good a course of action as any while we waited for Red to tell us whether or not our so-called client was dead or alive.

Finally, as we approached the intersection with Gumtree Road, the Camry moved into the far right lane, and its turn signal flashed.

"Why didn't he just take the Cross Island?" I asked. The whole point of building the four-lane bypass was to avoid all the traffic and lights on business 278.

"He must not be that familiar with the island," Erik said, slowing to allow Gerard to move farther in front of us.

"He managed to get around pretty good the other day," I said, remembering how he had materialized in front of me at Jarvis Park and disappeared just as quickly.

"The Boathouse," my partner said out of the blue.

"What?"

"I'll bet that's where he's headed."

"Why?" I asked a moment before it struck me. "He's going out to Jericho Cay."

Erik cocked a finger at me. "Bingo. I'd lay money on it."

A few minutes later I was glad I hadn't taken him up on the bet. The Camry slowed at the entrance to the Skull Creek Boathouse restaurant and pulled into a parking space alongside the huge boat storage building that shared the lot. Erik cruised on by and turned in among the throng of cars in the area reserved for those taking the Melrose ferry over to Daufuskie Island. Both of us jumped out and hurried back the way we'd come in time to see our quarry striding purposefully toward the water.

"We're screwed if he's already arranged for a boat to take him out there," I said, matching my partner's long gait step for step.

"So we'll get our own. If we're certain that's where he's going."

"Where else?" I asked, both of us slowing as we neared the entrance to the popular seafood place on the water.

"You should go inside," Erik said. "He knows you. He's never seen me."

"You hope," I replied tersely, but I moved up the shallow steps and into the nearly deserted interior.

I asked for a table by the windows and followed the trim hostess. I chose the chair that gave me the best vantage point to keep an eye on the boat storage building, then watched Erik wander down the long cement pier to stand gazing out across the water toward Pinckney Island.

A few moments later, Terry Gerard walked out of the boat build-ing and down toward the dock. Erik turned casually to lean his back against the rail and follow Gerard's progress. A lanky young man in shorts and T-shirt met him there, and they shook hands. Erik shifted his gaze back out toward the horizon and did his best to appear a ca-sual tourist admiring the scenery. I hoped I was the only one who no-ticed the tenseness in his shoulders and his head cocked to one side in the hope of picking up on the conversation.

A waitress stopped at the table, momentarily blocking my view.

"Just an iced tea for now," I said, willing her to move on.

"We've got some great specials today. The shrimp—"

"Just the tea." She spun on her heel and marched away.

Back on the dock, Gerard and his companion had disappeared. I frantically scanned the area just as the faint whine of an engine start-ing up drifted through the glass. I saw Erik move closer to the edge of the pier a moment before a sleek white boat edged away from the pil-ings and cut a smooth arc toward the bridge spanning Skull Creek, one of the two that gave access to Hilton Head from the mainland.

I jumped up and nearly collided with the waitress, who managed to keep my glass of iced tea from toppling off the tray and onto the floor.

"I'm sorry," I mumbled. "I have to go." I whipped out my wallet and tossed a twenty onto the tray.

I forced myself to walk quickly rather than run down the long cement pier. Erik met me at the dock.

"We have to find a boat," I said in a rush.

"Taken care of. It's going to cost us an arm and a leg, though. The kid is willing to let us use his, but he wants cash. How much do you have on you?"

I fumbled for my wallet and did a swift count. "Two hundred and ten dollars. How about you?"

"About a hundred."

"Will that be enough?"

"We'll make it work."

"Gerard's got a big head start." I paused. "How is he going to get onto the island? Ron Singleton said you couldn't just beach a small boat because of the rocks. That's how the house has remained in one piece all this time."

Erik shrugged. "Beats me. But maybe him being ahead of us is a good thing. We'll just find wherever he goes ashore and follow him in."

My cell phone chimed, and I grabbed it from my pocket. "Bay Tanner."

"Hey, it's Mike Raleigh. From the sheriff's office."

I glanced at Erik and shook my head.

"Hey, Mike. How's it going?"

"Okay. Listen, have you heard from your husband? I mean, in the last couple of hours?"

My heart rate kicked up, and I swallowed hard. "No, I haven't. Is there a problem?"

"No problem. I mean, not really. I just got a call from the Fairfield County sheriff wondering why Red hadn't shown up to view the body."

My knees wobbled, and I had to force myself to speak calmly. "He hasn't? I talked to him around lunchtime, and he said he was almost there. Maybe he had trouble with the Bronco."

"Wouldn't he have called?"

"I'll try him again. It could be a flat tire or something like that."

"You're probably right. I'm sure it's nothing to worry about. When you reach him, tell him they're still waiting for him at the funeral home in Winnsboro. Take care."

"Thanks, Mike. You, too."

Erik stared at me as I tried to draw enough air into my lungs. "What's the matter?" he asked, taking my arm and guiding me to one of the wooden benches built into the side of the dock. "Is Red okay?"

In a few halting words, I gave him Mike's end of the conversation. "Even if he had car trouble, why isn't he picking up his phone? Something's wrong."

I punched in my husband's number and swore when it again went to voice mail.

"It could just be he's out of cell range, or there isn't service for his provider," Erik said. "Don't assume the worst."

I managed a smile. "That's what I do. Haven't you figured that out by now?"

"Here comes our guy."

I turned to see the young man, little more than a teenager really, trotting back down the dock. I handed Erik the twenties I had crumpled in my fist. The boy skidded to a stop, a key dangling from one hand.

"We've got three hundred cash," Erik said, holding out the wad of bills. "And plenty of insurance."

"You sure you know how to drive a boat?" the boy asked, his gaze darting around as if this were a drug deal going down in some dark alley in the heart of the city. "If anything happens to her, my dad is going to murder me."

"No sweat." Erik thrust the money at the kid and snatched the key out of his hand. "Which one is it?"

"The Grady White. You want me to give you a quick rundown on how she operates?"

"Sure." Erik followed the boy toward where another white boat lay rocking in the midafternoon sunshine.

I couldn't move. Images of my husband's restored Bronco, smashed and crumpled on the side of Interstate 26, his body flung against a tree, glued me to my seat.

"Bay?" Erik's hand on my shoulder broke through the waking nightmare. "Bay?"

"Yeah, okay." I stood and let him lead me toward the boat.

"You can stay here and let me handle this. Get on the phone to the state police and get them looking for Red."

I shoved my fears down deeper into my chest. "I'm okay. We'll call Stephanie and get her working on tracking Red down. I'm sure he's fine." I expelled a long breath. "Let's find out what Terry Gerard is up to."

"Your call," my partner said, and I hoped to hell it was the right one as I followed him to the boat.

CHAPTER
THIRTY-FOUR

ERIK DID A CREDITABLE JOB OF MANEUVERING US OUT into the creek and around any obstacles on the short ride out to Jericho Cay. He told me he'd handled small speedboats on some of the lakes during his teenage years when he and his friends had spent weekends skiing and horsing around on the water, and he apparently hadn't forgotten everything he knew.

We approached the island this time from the opposite side, and I could see why most people would assume it was uninhabited. Unless you were looking for the reflection of the sun off some of the glass panels of the house, a casual observer wouldn't even have known it was there.

Erik throttled back the engine and began a slow circuit. Even from a hundred yards out, we could see the gentle lapping of the water against the large rocks that spilled off the land and into the water. None of the other small islands in the area had such a natural barrier, and I wondered if Bell had added them purposely to construct another layer of protection to his privacy. Neither of us spoke until we'd come nearly halfway around.

"There." I pointed to where Terry Gerard's boat rocked gently on the slight swell.

"Well, that answers that question," Erik said, idling the engine and holding us in place. "He's anchored."

"You think he swam in?"

"I don't see how else he could have done it. Look."

I followed his extended arm to a slight break in the otherwise continuous rock formation. You'd miss it if you weren't looking for the tiny square of sand amid the tumbled stones.

"What do you want to do? Can you swim that far?"

"Sure," I answered, remembering the warm waters of Bishop's Reach and how my ability to keep myself afloat had literally saved my life. "But what I'd really like to do is get on that boat."

"Why?"

"Because he had his satchel with him when he went down the dock, and he sure as hell wouldn't have had it strapped to his shoulder while he swam in." I looked at my partner. "Can you get me close enough to jump onboard?"

"Probably. What if he sees us?"

"What if he does? We can get away a lot faster than he can swim back out."

"I thought you wanted to talk to him."

"I do. But I'll have a lot better chance of getting the truth out of him if I've got some ammunition. Like who he really is."

Erik eased the throttle forward without any more questions. While we approached Terry Gerard's boat, I tried Red on my cell phone again. This time I got the "no service" message. I shook off my fear. In a few minutes we were alongside. While my partner looped a rope around the cleat, I hopped across.

"Give me a shout if he starts back," I said and dropped down onto the deck.

It didn't require any special detecting skills. The satchel lay front and center on one of the cushions that ringed the open area of the boat along with the shorts and T-shirt I'd seen him wearing when he came out of the hotel. I searched the pockets and found a few coins and his cell phone. I flipped it open, but I had no way to copy any of the numbers in the memory. The same wallet I'd seen Gerard take from his pocket when he'd confronted me in Jarvis Park sat right on top in plain sight. It held the Ohio driver's license and the credit cards along with a wad of bills I didn't take time to count. No photos or small slips of paper with cryptic notes or telephone numbers. I set it aside and pulled the satchel onto my lap.

"Damn!" I said.

"What?" Erik moved away from the wheel to lean over the side.

"Clothes." I spread them out on the seat around me. All neatly folded, they looked as if they'd seen a lot of wear. "This must be his luggage." I emptied the leather case and searched for any hidden compartments or pockets but found nothing. "Damn," I said again and began refilling the case.

"So now what?" Erik once again sat behind the wheel of our hastily rented boat.

"I'm going to take a quick look around. Just in case."

"We shouldn't hang out here too long, unless you don't care if he spots us."

"Right back," I called over my shoulder as I eased into the tiny cabin. A moment later I was back on deck. "Nothing."

I stepped back across onto our own craft while Erik unwound the rope from the cleat. "I don't get it," I said, flopping down onto one of the vinyl-covered seats.

"What?"

"Why did he bring that satchel along?"

"It looks like he's got everything he owns in the world in there," Erik said.

"I know. So why not leave it in the car? It would sure as hell be a lot safer there than sitting out here on an unattended boat. Anyone who happened along could steal his wallet, if nothing else."

"You want to head back to the boathouse, or are you going to try and swim in?"

Before I could answer, a faint shout erupted from the shore. We looked over to see someone waving frantically from the tiny patch of beach nestled among the rocks. We were too far away to hear any words, but it wasn't a stretch to deduce he was angry. Bare-chested, he kept jumping up and down, and it looked as if he had a cell phone in his right hand.

"Is that Gerard?" Erik asked.

"I can't tell. But who else—?"

My question was cut off by a sharp *crack,* and it took only a fraction of a second for the bullet to whine over my head and disappear into the water.

We both hit the deck. I felt a stab of pain as my elbow connected with the smooth wood, and all the air rushed out of my lungs.

"You okay?" I managed to wheeze out a moment later.

"Yeah. You?"

"Fine."

I crawled forward a little and sighted over the sides of both boats, still rocking close together on the incoming tide. Gerard or whoever it was had waded farther out into the water. He gesticulated wildly, waving his arms over his head. He shouted again. Though I still couldn't pick up any of the words, it was pretty plain he wanted us out of there. I watched his right arm come level.

"Get down!" I yelled and flattened myself on the deck.

This time the bullet seemed a lot closer.

"Let's get out of here," Erik shouted, and I felt the engines rev to a screaming whine.

I risked another look back. "I don't see him."

Erik didn't wait for any more updates. He sent our sleek craft veering sharply away from Jericho Cay. When we'd put considerable distance between ourselves and the crazy man with the gun, I touched his shoulder.

"We need to get back to the dock. I'm going to call Mike Raleigh and report this. I draw the line at people shooting at us."

I looked back and saw Gerard's boat still rocking at anchor and pulled my phone from my pocket. As I flipped it open, it rang. In spite of having just dodged a couple of bullets, the caller ID lifted a massive weight from my chest.

"Where the hell have you been?" I snapped into my cell. "I've been picturing you dead by the side of the road."

"Yes, honey, I'm fine, thanks for asking."

"Well, God, Red. You can't just drop off the face of the earth like that and not expect me to worry. What happened?"

"A double whammy. My phone died, and then the Bronco decided to throw a rod. It's going to cost a fortune to get the engine repaired. I'm having it towed back to the island."

I glanced up to see Erik watching me over his shoulder.

"Red's fine," I said and turned my attention back to my husband. "So where are you?"

"I'm on my way home. I was lucky a state police car came by right after I coasted off the highway. He called triple A for me. I rented a car and had to get the chip replaced in my phone."

"I'm glad you're okay."

"Well, that's a relief. You sounded like you wanted to shoot me yourself there for a minute."

I winced at the reference to gunshots. I decided my husband didn't need to know about my own recent brush with flying bullets. "What happened at the funeral home?"

I heard the sharp intake of breath a moment before he answered. "I'm sorry, honey, but there was no way to tell if it's Wolfe or not.

Well, if it's whoever was impersonating him. You know what I mean." He swallowed audibly. "The face was just too . . . damaged. The body is about the right size. And there's the briefcase. But there was just no way to be certain. I'm afraid the sheriff up here isn't real happy with me for complicating his life. He was counting on me to make a positive ID. He doesn't quite know where to go on it from here."

"Join the crowd." Quickly, I filled Red in on our discovery of the local phone number on Wolfe's cell, and the fact that Terry Gerard had answered when we called.

"Where are you?" my husband asked. "It sounds like you're in a wind tunnel."

I paused for a moment, not sure how much to reveal about our chase out to Jericho Cay. And about the fact that someone had taken shots at us. I decided to save that until I could look him in the eye, and he could see for himself that Erik and I were unharmed.

"We're in a boat just coming back from Jericho. I think Gerard's on the island. At least, his boat's anchored offshore. We're headed back to Skull Creek to wait for him."

I could sense his almost pathological need to cross-examine me, but he managed to swallow it down. "Be careful. I'll see you in a couple of hours. Don't do anything crazy until I get there, okay? Just try to keep Gerard in your sights."

"Got it." I breathed a sigh of relief. "See you when you get back."

I shoved the phone back in my pocket and filled Erik in on Red's part of the conversation, almost shouting to be heard above the rush of the wind.

"It's a real mess," he said, letting his speed drop as we approached the no wake zone around the massive pillars of the bridges.

I jerked around at the distant *whomp* of the explosion and gaped in disbelief at the huge ball of flame and roiling black smoke rising out of the water behind us.

CHAPTER THIRTY-FIVE

$\mathcal{I}$NSTINCTIVELY BOTH ERIK AND I DUCKED, AND HE let the speed of the Grady White drop back to idle. In an instant I flashed back to Rob's plane disintegrating on takeoff and flung my arms over my head in anticipation of a rain of hot metal and debris. I cowered there in the well of the boat until I felt Erik's hand on my shoulder.

"It's okay. We're far enough away."

Slowly I lowered my arms and raised my head. "Gerard's?"

"I'd lay money on it. We should go back."

"No!" Again the visions of the exploding plane—and its aftermath—bloomed inside my head. "If it's him, there's nothing we can do." While I spoke, I pulled my phone from my pocket. "I'll call nine-one-one."

Erik laid a hand on my arm. "I know this must bring back terrible memories, but we can't just walk away. Gerard could be injured in the water. We can't just leave him out there to die."

I forced calm into my voice. "I'm sure they heard it all the way to Beaufort. The coast guard or somebody will be on it. Besides, he was on shore last time we saw him."

Erik didn't reply, simply powered up the engine and turned the boat in a wide, sweeping arc. In a moment, we were racing back toward Jericho Cay. It took just a couple of minutes before we began encountering debris floating on the water, along with the outer edges of the oil slick.

I turned my back and locked my eyes onto the shore on the opposite side of the water, but that couldn't stop the smell of scorched metal from wafting to me on the stiff breeze. I tried not to breathe in too deeply, afraid that the sickly sweet odor of burned flesh would be the next thing to assault my senses. A moment later, I felt the boat slow.

Without turning around, I asked, "Is it him?"

"Looks like it," Erik said. "His boat's not where we left it."

I could feel his eyes on the back of my head.

"There's already some other boaters in the area. I'm sure someone's called it in."

When I didn't reply, he spun the wheel and headed us back toward the boathouse. In a few minutes, Erik had edged us up to the pier and was securing the ropes to the stanchions. Almost immediately, the teenager was on top of us.

"Holy shit! I thought that might be you guys."

"As you can see, we're fine," Erik replied.

"God, I'm glad to see you. I'd have to join a commune in Outer Mongolia if you'd blown up my dad's boat."

"We wouldn't have been too thrilled about it, either," I snapped, accepting his hand to climb out onto the dock. Erik jumped out behind me.

Faintly, in the distance, I heard sirens. Erik handed back the keys to the boat, and we walked slowly toward the road. A few minutes later we were sliding into the Expedition.

"Now what?" my partner asked, cranking the engine.

"We have to pick up my car down at Coligny. Then let's rendezvous at the office." I could feel his eyes on the side of my face. "What?"

"You don't want to stick around? Find out for sure if it was Gerard's boat that blew up?"

I cupped my forehead in one hand. "I can't deal with it right now. We'll know one way or the other soon enough."

I let my eyes drift closed, the fireball from the explosion seeming to have imprinted itself on my retinas. When Rob was murdered, there hadn't been enough of his body recovered to warrant a casket, although we had buried what remains could be identified in the family plot in Newberry. I couldn't deal with reliving that horror. I just couldn't.

When the car finally eased to a stop in front of the Market Street Café, I pushed open the door. "I'll meet you back at the office."

I watched as Erik wheeled the big SUV back onto the street before I turned and entered the small restaurant. I waved at a couple of the waitstaff and made my way to the single bathroom. Inside, I locked the door and leaned against it for a moment. Swirls of flame and smoke seemed to dance in front of my eyes a moment before I leaned over the toilet and threw up.

I drove slowly, and it was probably half an hour before I finally turned into the lot and shut off the Jaguar. I'd taken the time to order an iced tea to go, and the cool liquid had helped to calm my roiling stomach. I slid out of the car and walked resolutely toward the office.

Both Erik and Stephanie looked up when I stepped in.

"Everything okay?" my partner asked.

I nodded and held up a hand before crossing the carpet and easing myself down into my chair. I drew in several deep breaths and rubbed the still-cold Styrofoam cup against my forehead. Time to shake it off and get busy.

"Stephanie," I called, and the young woman materialized in the doorway. "Get Maury Lance on the phone. See if he'll talk to me again."

"Sure."

I managed a half smile. At least she hadn't said *yes, ma'am*. I slipped off my shoes and leaned back in the chair. My mind whirled with a dozen possibilities, none of them verifiable, all of them bad. If the real Wolfe was in some loony bin or drug rehab clinic for the rich and famous, then he couldn't be the charred corpse in Winnsboro. On the other hand, if our guy was someone impersonating Wolfe . . . I couldn't get any farther down that road. Why? That was the critical question. Someone had spent a lot of money—for our retainer, to rent a plane, the limo, the suite at the Crowne Plaza. All that to convince us we were dealing with the real crime writer. To what end? We didn't have a hope in hell of proving whether Morgan Tyler Bell was alive or dead. Certainly not with what scant information we had, and for damn sure not by Friday. So what was the game? And where did Terry Gerard fit into the scheme? What did he have to gain? Or lose? Or did it matter, since I had no doubt it had been his boat being blown to kingdom come? Had he been on it? Had he disappeared from view because he was already in the water swimming back?

I could feel the knots tightening in my chest when Stephanie cleared her throat.

I opened my eyes and focused. "You have Lance on the line?"

"He's out of the office. I told his secretary it was urgent that he return your call the second he comes in. She said maybe fifteen or twenty minutes."

"Thanks." I toyed with trying to contact Wolfe's editors, but I had the feeling they wouldn't know about his breakdown or whatever it was. The agent had been pretty concerned about keeping the author's crackup from becoming common knowledge in what I guessed was a pretty small community in New York publishing.

"Anything else?" Stephanie still hovered.

"Not right now. Close the door, will you?"

She complied on her way out, and once again I settled back in the chair.

So where did that leave us? One body in Fairfield County. Another maybe in pieces scattered all over the coastal waters of the Lowcountry. And I couldn't forget Anjanette Freeman, Ty Bell's housekeeper. Suicide or murder? Three bodies, all tied in some way to the reclusive man who had quite literally barricaded himself off from civilization on Jericho Cay. Was he another victim to add to the body count? Or . . . ?

I snapped out of my daze and buzzed Erik on the intercom. "Come in here. Both of you."

The door slid open on two anxious faces.

"I'm okay. Sit down."

Stephanie had brought her laptop, and she flipped it open, her fingers poised over the keyboard.

"I've been thinking," I said, forcing a smile. "And I've got some things to run by you. I'm open to comments as we go, because it's pretty far out there. Feel free to tell me I've lost my mind." When neither of them responded, I pushed ahead. "I've been trying to figure out why someone would go to all this trouble to create such an elaborate hoax. The phony Wolfe, the plane, the retainer, all of it. You know, I started out at USC in pre-law, mostly to mollify my father, and there's a phrase that keeps popping into my head from some law book or other: *Cui bono?*

"Who benefits," Stephanie said without looking up from her typing.

"Exactly. Ty Bell was rich. Very rich. No one, so far as we know, has touched his fortune in the years since he disappeared." I paused and repeated myself. "So far as we know, right?"

"What about Gerard? If he was Bell's personal assistant, maybe he had access. Maybe he's been bleeding the estate without anyone catching on," Erik said.

"Yes, but then why is he living like a homeless guy, carrying everything he owns around in that beat-up satchel? And why the photos of him in different airports or wherever?"

Stephanie spoke softly. "But you don't know for sure the guy in the photos *was* Gerard, do you? I mean what if the guy you've been chasing is another imposter? The pictures could be fake, too."

"*Two* phonies?" I groaned. "I don't even want to consider the possibility." I massaged my temples. "I feel as if someone has taken an eggbeater to my brain."

"You said you had an idea to run by us." Erik leaned in and rested his elbows on my desk. "What is it?"

"It's almost too crazy to put into words."

"Try us."

I sighed. "Okay. Gerard and Wolfe—the real ones—hatch a plan to knock off Bell and somehow steal his fortune. They kill the housekeeper, make it look like a murder-suicide, and then take off. The phony Wolfe said there was no will. But what if Gerard had concocted something, a fake will, or gotten Bell to sign something without knowing what it was? They knock him off, wait for the bodies to be discovered, then swoop in and take everything."

Erik broke in the moment I paused for breath. "But they couldn't have killed him. There wasn't any body."

"Because they screwed up," Stephanie said, excitement making her voice crack. "They thought he was dead but he wasn't. And somehow he got away and—"

"Then why hasn't he shown up?" Erik asked. "Where has he been? Why didn't he call in the cops the second he got clear of Jericho Cay?"

"Sorry, I guess it was a stupid idea."

"No, it wasn't." I smiled at her. "It makes about as much sense as anything else we've been kicking around here. But Erik's right. It doesn't really jibe with what we know about Bell. Unless . . ." A thought darted through my mind and skittered away into the darkness.

Erik looked from his fiancée to me and back again. "But it doesn't fit with the facts. And why would all this be going down now? I mean, they've had years."

I felt the stirrings of another idea. "It has to have something to do with the cousin—what was his name?"

"Harold something. I can look in my notes." Erik half rose from his chair.

"Never mind. It doesn't matter. Wolfe said the cousin wanted to have Bell declared dead so they could settle the estate."

"Do we believe him?" Erik asked.

"Maybe. Let's say my crackpot idea has some merit. If Harold Whatever gets his cousin declared dead, the estate would go into probate. I think. How would it look for Gerard and Wolfe to suddenly show up with a will that leaves everything to them? I mean, where have they been all this time? Why didn't anyone know about it before? Why the secrecy? It would certainly raise eyebrows, maybe get the lawyers looking at Wolfe and Gerard in a different light."

"And if they thought they'd killed him and he somehow survived, they'd be tried for attempted murder." Stephanie slumped back in her chair. "But you're right. If he isn't dead, where has he been all this time?"

Something clicked in the back of my brain and shot immediately to the front. "But what if he *is* dead? And no one ever found his body."

CHAPTER THIRTY-SIX

*I*T COULD FIT." ERIK ROSE FROM THE CHAIR IN FRONT of my desk and began pacing. "Okay. Wolfe and Gerard kill the woman and think they've killed Bell. They get out of there and wait for someone to find the bodies. Except when the sheriff shows up, there's only the housekeeper. Weeks go by, and there's no news of Bell, alive or dead. They're basically screwed. They can't try to insist he's dead. That would point the cops directly at them."

"And," I said, warming to the theory the more Erik talked, "Gerard has to get out of there because he's immediately under suspicion of having something to do with the death and the disappearance. He can't just show up and say he was on vacation. Well, he could, but that would still have the cops sniffing around him. With Jericho laid out like a fortress, he'd be the logical suspect. Who else could have gotten onto the island with all the rocks and that dock that rolls up? He couldn't take the chance."

"We should run this by Red." Erik looked as if he expected me to challenge him.

"I agree. There's something else that's been bothering me. Why would Cousin Harold enlist Wolfe's help in finding out if Bell were alive or dead? That's bothered me on some level right from the start. I mean, how did the two of them hook up? I'm betting the phony Wolfe contacted him, offering a cut of the book or something like that."

"But Wolfe—or whoever—keeps insisting that Bell is alive. That can't be what the cousin wants to hear." Erik ran a hand over his face. "There are so many threads hanging out on this, we could make ourselves crazy trying to figure them out."

I nodded at my partner. "You're right. And if the corpse in Fairfield County is the Wolfe imposter, we're never going to know exactly what went down."

"Yeah, I almost forgot about that. But . . ."

"But what?"

"If it's the phony Wolfe up there, who killed him?"

"And Terry Gerard's boat just blew up, so who—"

The ringing phone interrupted Stephanie. I reached for it a moment ahead of her.

"Bay Tanner."

"Ms. Tanner? Please hold for Mr. Lance."

"Lance," I said to the other two, briefly covering the mouthpiece with my hand.

"Ms. Tanner? Maury Lance. My secretary said it was important."

I took a moment to gather my thoughts. "Sir, I urgently need to speak with Winston Wolfe. Can you put me in touch with him?"

"Impossible. He sees no one, as far as I know, including me when he's in this state, and they see that he doesn't have access to a phone. I get periodic reports from the clinic. It's a very expensive, very exclusive private facility. They know how to keep their mouths shut."

"I understand your wanting to protect your client, sir, but I'm not going to be the only one that wants to speak with him. I expect you'll be hearing from the local authorities before long." Inspiration struck. "If I could talk to him first, I might be able to hold them off. At least for a while."

I could hear the concern in his voice. "I don't understand. Why would the police want to bother Winston? If it's about this imposter thing, he doesn't have anything to do with it. He's the victim more than anything else."

"There have been two deaths connected with the scam I told you about earlier, both of which will no doubt turn out to be murders."

"Murder? My God! Who? I mean, I don't . . ." His voice trailed off into silence.

"It's too complicated to go into on the phone. If I could just clear up a couple of things, I might be able to deflect the investigation away from your client."

It was complete bullshit, but I hoped the New York literary agent would buy the bluff. I waited him out, shrugging my shoulders at Erik and Stephanie.

"I'll tell you what I'll do," Maury Lance finally said. "I'll get in touch with the clinic and insist on them putting Winston on the phone. If he agrees—and if his doctors say it's okay, I'll have him call you. I'm afraid that's the best I can do."

"I appreciate it. Let me give you my cell in case I'm away from the office."

"Got it," he said after I recited the numbers. "I'll get on this right away."

"Thank you, sir." I was ready to hang up when a thought struck. "Before you go, could you tell me the name of Mr. Wolfe's secretary? I'd like to check something out with her."

"I have no idea. He uses some sort of service when he needs it. Winston doesn't have any full-time staff." He paused. "But there is an old friend of his. Sort of down on his luck when he first met him, but a good researcher. At least that's what Winston told me."

I felt my whole body stiffen. "Do you know his name?"

"John . . . something. Sorry, I don't recall right now."

"Do you know how to get in touch with him?"

"No. I only met the guy once, at a launch party for one of Winston's books."

"Can you describe him?" I fumbled a pen out of the right-hand drawer and held it poised over the desk pad.

"God, I don't know. It's been a few years. Let me think. Tall, thin. Midthirties, I'd guess. Sort of nondescript, if you know what I mean. Not the kind of guy who stands out in a crowd."

"Do you remember anything else about him?"

"Is this important? I mean, I only talked to the guy for a couple of minutes. As I recall, he seemed uncomfortable. We held the party at the publishing house. Lots of high rollers in attendance. You know, money-and-power people. This John guy was definitely out of his depth."

"Hair or eye color?" I asked.

"Brown hair, I think. Look, I just don't remember."

I didn't want to antagonize the agent before he'd had a chance to connect me with the real Winston Wolfe. "That's fine, Mr. Lance. I appreciate the information. And you'll let me know as soon as you've talked to your client?"

"I'm only doing this to try and keep Winston's name out of it. You understand that? If he cooperates with you, I don't want to be reading about it in the *Enquirer.*"

"I'll do everything I can to keep that from happening," I said. "Thank you so much. I'll wait for your call."

Neither of us bothered to say good-bye.

We hashed it around for another half hour, but none of us could get a handle on any concrete way we could prove or disprove our theories.

"I'm going to call Mike Raleigh and see if I can verify that it was Terry Gerard's boat that blew up," I said, reaching for the phone.

Erik swigged down the last of his Sprite and tossed the empty bottle at the wastebasket beside my desk. It bounced off the side and dropped in. That brought his trademark smile back to his boyish face at last.

"Do you think he'll tell you?" he asked.

"Maybe. He might actually be glad to get some direction on where to start investigating." I swallowed hard. "There might not be enough of anything left for him to use as a jumping-off point, if Gerard made it back to the boat."

"He's going to want to pick your brain down to the bone, you know," my partner said.

"He's welcome to try. Besides, what's the point of holding back anything now? We're as good as out of this entirely. Our client—dead or alive—is obviously a con man. We don't owe him any loyalty."

"Do we get to keep the money?" Stephanie spoke softly as if she were afraid I'd bite her head off for asking the question.

"Good point. If the guy who gave it to us is dead, we'll have to wait and see who comes crawling out of the woodwork trying to get it back," I said. "We'll just transfer it over to a CD or something like that and let it sit. Wait and see what shakes out."

"So what do you want us to do?"

"You can get back on the women's shelter," I said to Erik. "Anything you need from me on that?"

"Nope. I'm just waiting for one of those clowns to try and hack into their system again, and I'll have him. The program will alert me, either on my computer or on my phone. I've got a trap set up that will allow me to follow him back to his own machine. Once I have the IP address, I've got him."

"Well, do what you have to do short of actually committing violence on anybody," I said, picking up the receiver. "Stephanie, I shoved all the paperwork on this case in the file cabinet." I jerked my thumb over my shoulder. "Will you please drag it all out? Try to get it into some order. Make some folders. I want to go through it all again."

She might have asked me why, but she didn't. I was glad, because I wasn't sure I had a reasonable answer for her, other than my insatiable curiosity and a burning desire to put all the pieces back together. Maybe I wouldn't be able to, I thought as I waited for the dispatcher to locate Mike Raleigh. Red would probably tell me to forget about it and move on. But one—and probably two—people had died, both of them tied to my agency. I'd sat across from both of them, looked them in the eye, tried to assess whether or not they were telling the truth. It was beginning to look as if I'd been conned by both of them, and I didn't like it. Mine wasn't the kind of business in which I could afford to be that wrong that often. I needed to find out how they'd both been able to suck me into their convoluted scheme to try and steal—

"Detective Raleigh."

His voice sounded as if he were already harried and none too happy about being interrupted. I could also hear other people talking in the background and the unmistakable sounds of motors churning.

"It's Bay Tanner. Thanks for taking my call."

"They patched it through to me. I'm a little tied up right now. How can I help you?"

"I think I can help you. Erik and I were tailing a man named Terry Gerard this afternoon, and his boat was anchored off Jericho Cay, right where the explosion occurred. I thought you might want to know he was in the area." I gulped down the bile I felt rising in my throat. "In case the body wasn't . . . that you couldn't . . ."

"There isn't one."

That stopped me cold. "Isn't one what?"

"Body. Not even any parts, at least not that they've found so far, but we're still looking. The boat is pretty much toothpicks. We may not locate any . . . You know what I mean."

"Pieces," I said softly.

"Right. But you think the boat belonged to this Gerard? Isn't he the one the sergeant was telling me about, that used to work for that Bell guy that disappeared?"

"Yes. You should check with the boathouse at Skull Creek. By the restaurant. That's where he picked up the boat." I thought a moment and made the decision. "Here's the thing, Mike. We came alongside Gerard's boat, and I hopped on board. It was empty. But Gerard's wallet and his belongings were there. Then someone, I'm assuming Gerard but I can't say for certain, fired a couple of shots at us from the beach, and we took off. I'm not sure, but he may have been in the process of swimming out to his boat."

"Jesus! Why didn't you call us right away?"

I thought about trying to explain to him that that had been my intention, that Red's call had interrupted me, and that the explosion had come just a moment after I'd hung up. Would he be able to understand the terror that had engulfed me, how the memory of that other explosion had shaken me to my bones? I didn't think so.

"I should have, and I apologize for that. But I'm telling you now."

He didn't respond for a moment. "So what the hell happened out there?" he finally asked. "Any ideas?"

"No. We were almost to the bridge when the explosion occurred. We went back, but there didn't seem to be anything we could do. I don't know if Gerard or whoever had time to get back on board before it blew up. I don't know a lot about boats. I guess this kind of thing can happen if you don't know what you're doing with them, right?"

"We'll see." The cop wariness was back in his voice. "Seems like too much of a coincidence, though." He paused, and I could almost hear him thinking. "Listen," he said after a few moments, "thanks for calling in."

"Will you—?" I began, then cut myself off. What else was there to say? "You're welcome," I murmured and hung up. I sat and stared off into space, contemplating what the detective had said. And what he hadn't. Erik had been wrong about his wanting to pick my brain. Or maybe he was saving that for a face-to-face meeting. The sharp ringing of the phone made me jump. Out in the reception area, I heard Stephanie pick up. A moment later, she stood in my doorway.

"There's a man on line two. He said his name won't mean anything to you, but he said you'll want to talk to him. It's about Mr. Wolfe."

"I'll take it." I picked up the receiver and punched the blinking light. "Bay Tanner."

"I hear you want to talk to Winston Wolfe."

"That's right. Who are you?"

"My name is John Wingo. I'm Wolfe's research assistant."

I perked up and whipped out a pen. "And where are you calling from, Mr. Wingo?"

"What difference does that make?"

I made frantic motions with my hand, leaning over my desk to the limit of the phone cord. Finally, Stephanie looked up and spotted me. I pointed at the screen shielding Erik's desk and jabbed at the space in front of my own. She nodded and jumped from her chair.

"It makes a difference, Mr. Wingo, because I've just spent the past week dealing with people who claim to . . . represent Mr. Wolfe. I'd like to be sure I'm talking to the genuine article this time."

Erik materialized, and I pointed at what I had scribbled on the desk pad: *Find out where he's calling from.* He nodded and sprinted back to his desk.

"I'm in Westchester. New York. At the . . . facility where Wolfe is staying. What do you mean, people who claim to represent Wolfe? What kind of people?"

"I'm only prepared to discuss that with Mr. Wolfe himself."

"That might not be possible."

"Why?" I asked a moment before Erik hurried back in.

"New York area," he mouthed, and I nodded.

"I'm not saying any more until you tell me what you want."

"I have no intention of using you as an intermediary, Mr. Wingo. Mr. Lance told me he would put me in touch directly with Winston Wolfe. I'm not going to discuss my business with anyone else but him."

The silence lasted about thirty seconds. "Look, Lance told the people at the clinic some cockamamie story about a couple of murders. Was he just screwing with them, or is that for real?"

"It's the absolute truth. One man was shot in the head and his car set on fire. The other was involved in an explosion just this afternoon. So I'd appreciate your cutting the crap and getting Mr. Wolfe on the phone. Believe me, it's to his advantage to speak with me." I fired my final salvo. "Unless he'd prefer to explain to the police."

Again he waited, and I could hear him breathing heavily. I was just about to demand he get his employer right that instant, when he finally spoke.

"I'm afraid I can't do that."

"Why the hell not?"

"Because Mr. Wolfe checked himself out of here last week, and no one—including me—has a clue where the hell he is."

CHAPTER
THIRTY-SEVEN

OW CAN THAT BE?"
Erik had stayed poised in my doorway, and I looked across to see his face scrunched up in concern.

"Hold on," I said before John Wingo could answer. "I'm going to put you on speaker so my associate can participate in the conversation."

"No! It's bad enough that you're onto this story. I don't want to see it splashed all over the Internet or the tabloids. Wolfe would have a fit."

"I'm going to tell him everything you say anyway. It'll save us both a lot of time."

I didn't wait for him to agree but punched the necessary buttons on the phone. I snapped the fingers of my other hand and pointed to Stephanie. Erik nodded and urged her into my office. Without being asked, she brought her laptop, ready to transcribe.

"Okay, Mr. Wingo, suppose you start at the beginning. If you tell us the truth—all of it—we might be able to help you. You said Mr. Wolfe checked out of the clinic a week ago. When, exactly?"

"Last Wednesday. See, I usually drive up every few days or so, but I hadn't been able to make it up here for almost two weeks. Sometimes he'll see me, and sometimes he pitches a fit, and I just go away. No one told me he was gone until I showed up this afternoon. I about had a heart attack. Wolfe had sworn he'd sue them into oblivion if they told anyone he'd checked out, but I got it out of one of his regular nurses."

"But no one knew he was there except for you and Maury Lance, right?"

"Supposedly. But you don't know Wolfe. At least not the way he's been for the last couple of months. He was whacked out, and that's the truth. Sometimes when I came to see him, he wouldn't know who I was. Thought I was a reporter one time, and he started telling me all this stuff about his childhood. Another time he was going on about some guy who got killed. Thought he'd come back to haunt him. It was creepy."

Both Erik's and my heads snapped up, and we eyed each other across the desk.

"Winston Wolfe said he was involved in a death?"

"Oh, you have to know him. Even when he's in his right mind he comes up with all this bullshit about how he'd run with the bulls over in Spain and sailed solo across the Atlantic when he was younger. I never take any of it seriously. When he's drinking—or on this prescription stuff—he gets mixed up a lot. Can't tell what's real from what he writes about in his books." He laughed, a short bark that held more derision than humor. "I used to tell him he has himself confused with Ernest freaking Hemingway."

"I understood from Mr. Lance that you've known Mr. Wolfe for a long time."

"Ten years or so. We sort of . . . ran across each other back when he was working on one of his books. I helped him out of a jam."

It didn't sound as if John Wingo wanted to expound on his history with Winston Wolfe. I wondered if it involved something illegal, but it really wasn't germane to the subject at hand.

"Where can we reach you, Mr. Wingo? At this number?"

"Why?"

"Because there's a possibility that we know where Mr. Wolfe is. If we can verify that, I think—" I swallowed and continued in a steadier voice. "I think you may need to come down here. To South Carolina."

"I don't get it," Wingo said, but he recited his cell number.

I couldn't blame him for being overwhelmed. I felt as if my own head were about to explode. "Just sit tight. I may have some answers for you soon. If it becomes necessary for you to travel south, can you do it? I mean—forgive me—do you have adequate funds?" I thought about the huge chunk of money sitting in our account from Wolfe's retainer. "I'd be happy to transfer whatever you need to make the trip."

"I got it covered. I have to tell you, though, I'm so damn confused I don't know which end is up. Is Wolfe down there? Is he okay?"

"I'll call you back as soon as I have news. Thank you."

I disconnected before he had a chance to ask any more questions.

"This is crazy!" Erik slumped in the chair and rubbed both hands over his face, as if his action could somehow wipe out the last few minutes.

Without conscious thought, I reached out to the corner of my desk where, up until a couple of years ago, I'd kept my cigarettes and lighter. Muscle memory, I told myself, jerking my hand back. To compensate, I picked up the pen from the desk pad and twirled it in my fingers.

"Do you think we've been dealing with the real Wolfe all the time?"

Erik's question dropped into the silence and hung in the air, all of us trying to wrap our heads around it. John Wingo had set all my harebrained theories on their ear. If the man who had sat in my office was in fact Winston Wolfe, was his the body up in Fairfield County, too? I tried that on for size, but there were still too many unanswered questions.

"Okay," I said, straightening my shoulders and leaning forward, my elbows on the desk. "When you come right down to it, there are really only two possibilities, though I'm damned if I can see how we're going to prove either one of them."

"You mean, we were either dealing with the real Wolfe or an imposter."

I looked across at my partner. "Right. And then there's Terry Gerard. He recognized Wolfe's cell number on the caller ID, and he answered. He was expecting it to be Wolfe, right? I mean, it was his phone he'd left the voice mail on. But he never used Wolfe's name."

"So you think there's a *third* guy involved somehow?" Erik asked.

"You said it yourself. If Wolfe and Gerard are both dead, who killed them?"

He didn't answer.

I leaned back and let my mind drift a little. "Gerard and Wolfe knew each other. If nothing else, they would have run across each other at Bell's. Wolfe certainly knew his way around the house on Jericho Cay when he took us out there. Remember? He led us straight to the housekeeper's room. There's no way he could have—"

I cut myself off, recalling my surprise at the time that a guest— and a famous, egotistical one like Wolfe—should be familiar with the servants' wing of the house.

"What?" Erik asked, and I told him. "I never thought of that," he added when I'd finished. "What does it mean?"

I realized I'd been flipping the pen around in my fingers again and slammed it down on the desk. "I don't know! None of this makes sense." I took a calming breath. "Where the hell is Red? We need him here."

"I'll try his cell." Stephanie set the laptop on my desk and scooted out of the room.

"Sorry," I said, running my hands through my hair. "I think all this speculation is pointless. What difference does it make? Gerard is probably dead, and Wolfe is stretched out on a slab in Winnsboro. Mike Raleigh isn't going to let us within fifty yards of the investigation, and we don't have a client. John Wingo should be able to get them something with Wolfe's DNA on it so they can positively identify his body. We should just chalk it all up to a bad experience and move on."

Over the years, Erik had come to know me almost as well as Red did. He leaned back in his chair and laid one long leg across his knee. "You don't mean that for a second. This is going to eat at you for the next ten years if you don't figure it out."

"Probably. But we've pretty much used up our collective brain power, and we're still no closer to a solution. I think I can give all this information to Mike and let him run with it. The sheriff will be thrilled if it leads to wrapping up the Bell disappearance. Fairfield County can at least identify their corpse—"

"If it really is Wolfe."

"Enough!"

This time his smile reached his eyes. "I know. But if you're right, both the major players are dead."

"So?"

"So the question remains—who killed them?"

Before I could lay hands on something sufficiently hefty to throw at him, Stephanie walked back into my office.

"I have Mr. Tanner on the phone."

"Thanks."

As I reached for the receiver, Erik stood and pointed toward his desk. "Let me know if you need me to do anything."

I nodded and picked up. "Hey. Where are you?"

"Just past Point South. I should be there in an hour or so. What's up?"

I toyed with just dumping the whole mess in his lap. But, on further reflection, it didn't seem like a good plan while he was whizzing down I-95 at probably eighty-plus miles an hour.

"We'll talk when you get here. I just wanted to make sure you were okay."

"I'm fine, honey. You sound kind of down, though. Anything I should know about?"

"When you get here," I repeated. "Be careful."

Leaning back in my chair, I folded my hands in my lap and forced my heart rate back to its normal pace. I did my best to clear my mind, the soft chatter of computer keys out in the other room making an almost hypnotic backdrop. I'd rarely been willing to admit defeat when it came to a case, believing that my own accountant's logic and innate puzzle-solving abilities would inevitably lead me to a solution to any conundrum. Perhaps it was a function of age—or maybe even the beginnings of wisdom—but I had to let this one go. I'd get it all organized in some sort of order and present it to Red. Then he could take it all and dump it on Mike Raleigh. We'd give him everything this time, from that first phone call from Winston Wolfe, real or imposter, right through John Wingo's revelations. If no one popped up to claim the retainer—and if Wolfe really was dead—we'd deduct our time and expenses and return the balance to his estate. I wondered if the famous crime writer had any family. Maybe not, if his sometime researcher and his agent were the only ones who knew about his breakdown. Sad, really, when you thought about it. Family could be a pain in the ass, but you always knew you could count on them when things went bad. . . .

A vision of Julia and Lavinia, their somber faces staring at me across Elizabeth Shelly's coffin, slipped into my head. Though it had been only the day before, it seemed as if a month had passed. I reached for the phone just as it rang, and I hesitated. I sent up a silent prayer to Whomever that it wasn't more bad news. A moment later, Stephanie buzzed me.

With a heavy sigh, I picked up and punched the intercom button. "Yes?"

"I just took that call, but there was no one there. Well, I mean, there *was*. I could sort of hear them breathing."

"Maybe a wrong number," I said absently, my mind still lingering on Julia, my one remaining blood relative, and how she was coping with the loss of her caretaker.

"I wrote it down just in case. The caller ID number. Do you want me to check it out?"

"Sure," I said, not really interested, and hit the button for an outside line.

A moment later, Lavinia answered.

"Hey," I said, mustering as much cheer as I could. "Just checking in to see how y'all are doing." When she didn't respond immediately, I sat up straighter in my chair. "Lavinia?"

"Oh, we're fine."

I glanced up to see Stephanie hovering just outside my door, and I waved her away. I swung around in my chair until I faced the window that looked out onto the strip of shrubs and trees that bordered the back of the building. "You don't sound like it. Is something wrong?"

Lavinia sighed. "I'm a little worried about your sister, that's all."

"Why?"

"I don't know how to explain it." She lowered her voice as if she were afraid of being overheard. "It's just a feeling."

I frowned. "I don't understand."

"I know, honey. I'm not makin' much sense. Only . . . she just lost the one person in the world who took care of her, looked after her. She should feel bad. But she's flittin' around here, asking all kinds of questions about the house and who lived here, wanting to know about all the portraits and who's who." She sighed. "And she keeps telling me she loves me. It just doesn't feel right somehow."

I thought about it for a moment, remembering how I had expressed something of the same concern to Julia's psychologist about her lack of emotion at Elizabeth Shelly's death.

"Neddie said to give her time. Do you think we should call her?"

"No, of course not. It's probably nothing to worry about. I'm just being an old woman, in more ways than one," she said with an unconvincing laugh.

"Would you like us to come over? Red should be back in a little while."

"No, honey, you've got enough on your plate. You said you had that big case you were working on."

I almost laughed myself. "That's pretty much a bust. We could make it right after dinner."

"You just stay right where you are. We'll be fine. I'll call you if I need you."

"Promise?"

"Tell Redmond I said hello." And she was gone.

Before I had a chance to process the strange conversation, I heard a soft rap on the doorframe. I swiveled back around and hung up the phone. Erik stood there looking grave, Stephanie a step behind him, one hand on his shoulder. My heart dropped into my feet.

"What's wrong?"

"That phone call Steph just took? With someone breathing?"

I nodded.

"I checked the number." For once, he didn't keep me hanging. "It was Terry Gerard's phone."

CHAPTER
THIRTY-EIGHT

"WE SHOULD CALL MIKE RALEIGH. NOW."

Erik spoke before I had a chance to digest the bombshell he'd just dropped.

"Wait a minute! Hang on." I flashed back to my few minutes rifling through Gerard's belongings on the boat. "His phone was there. Sitting on top of his clothes."

"So how did it keep from getting blown up?"

"He had two of them, remember? The one with the 440 area code and the one he used to leave the voice mail with Wolfe."

"Right." Erik moved inside the office and sat down in one of the client chairs. "So one of two things: either someone else has his second phone, or—"

"Or Gerard is still alive. Mike Raleigh said they hadn't found any remains. Maybe that's because there aren't any."

The phone rang again, and I grabbed for it. "Bay Tanner."

The faintest whisper of breath sighed down the wire, and I looked at the caller ID.

"Gerard? Is that you? Where are you?" I managed before the line went dead.

I slammed the receiver back in the cradle. "Stephanie, get Mike Raleigh. And Red." I pointed to where I'd scribbled on the desk pad. "Erik, is this the same number? From the first call?"

He moved around so he could see. "Yes. Definitely."

"So it's Gerard's phone. If he's not dead, that has to mean he never left Jericho."

"Detective Raleigh," Stephanie called from her desk. "On one."

I stabbed the button. "Mike, it's Bay. I just had a phone call from Terry Gerard."

"Are you sure?"

"It was his phone."

"What did he say?"

"Nothing."

"That's weird. Any clue where he might have been calling from?"

"Unless he was a really powerful swimmer, he has to be on Jericho. No way he made it to the mainland." I thought for a moment. "Unless he had another boat stashed somewhere, maybe a dingy or a johnboat."

"Listen, thanks for calling it in, but you stay put, understand?" He paused. "And be careful. Is Red back from Winnsboro yet?"

"No. And he wasn't able to identify the body."

"Yeah, I heard. I gotta go. You take care."

"You'll let me know?" I asked. "About Gerard?"

"Sure. When I can."

I hung up and noticed the second line blinking. I picked it up. "Red?"

"Hey, honey. Just can't stay away from me, is that it?"

"Are you close?"

"Coming through the light at Spanish Wells. I'm five minutes out."

"Hurry," I said.

———

I looked up when my husband burst through the door. He ignored Stephanie and was in front of my desk in three long strides.

"What's wrong?" His head swiveled from side to side as if he expected armed intruders to be lurking in the corners.

"Sit down, Red. We're fine. But all hell is breaking loose on the Wolfe thing."

He ran both hands through his hair, just as his brother used to do. As always, the gesture did as much to calm me as any verbal or physical reassurance he might have offered. I buzzed Erik on the intercom.

"Will you come in, please? And ask Stephanie to hold the calls." I paused. "Unless it's Gerard again. She'll recognize the caller ID."

A moment later, my partner pulled up the second chair. He and Red exchanged nods. I'd taken the opportunity to grab some sodas from the fridge, and I passed them around.

"What the hell's going on?" my husband asked.

I took a long swallow of Diet Coke and began.

Between the two of us, Erik and I managed a generally coherent recap of everything that had happened since Red had left for Winnsboro that morning. It hardly seemed possible that so many bizarre things could have occurred in such a short amount of time, but the facts were the facts. Red flinched when Erik described the shots whizzing over our heads and nearly jumped from his chair when I told him about the explosion. He and I exchanged a look that spoke volumes about the painful memories we shared. I finished with the strange series of phone calls, from Maury Lance to the mysterious John Wingo to the frustrating, whispery breaths that had come from Terry Gerard's cell.

When Erik and I finished, I leaned back in my chair and swiped the sweating bottle of Coke across my forehead where the faint beginnings of a headache had blossomed into a full frontal assault.

"So Mike's on it?" Red asked, his shoulders relaxing just a little.

"I assume so. There really isn't anything for us to do now except wait to see what happens out on Jericho. Do you think Mike will let us know?"

"I'll talk to him when it's all wrapped up. Off the record." He smiled across the desk at me. "I'm proud of you for not jumping into this mess with both feet. Letting the sheriff handle it was the right call."

I nodded. "I was thinking earlier that I might just be gaining a little wisdom."

"More than a little," my husband said. He rose and stretched. "How about we all knock off a little early? It's been a hell of a day."

I glanced at my watch. "Not early at all. It's after five."

Erik headed for his desk, stopping to speak to Stephanie on the way. A moment later she stuck her head in the door.

"Do you want me to take those files home and work on them tonight?"

I remembered then that I'd asked her to get all the myriad papers relating to Jericho Cay sorted into some kind of order. "No, that's okay. It can wait until tomorrow. You and Erik go have a nice dinner and try to forget about all this craziness."

"Okay. You guys have a good night."

"Switch the phone over to my cell before you go, will you?" I glanced at Red, who was frowning at me. "Just in case Gerard calls again. We should let Mike Raleigh know if he does."

A few minutes later they both left. I realigned everything on the top of my desk and took a moment to down a couple of aspirin with my last swallow of Coke.

"Ready?" my husband asked, holding out his hand.

I took it and followed him out the door. The only two vehicles left in the parking lot were my Jaguar and a little blue compact with a dent in its right front fender pulled up alongside. I turned to Red and smiled.

"That's your rental?"

He grimaced. "All they had at the only place in town. It felt like I was riding on a skateboard."

That made me laugh. "Want to leave it here? You won't be going out anywhere else tonight, will you?"

We slid into the Jag and cranked the engine. "Jump and Phil's?"

"Works for me."

I backed the big sedan around and headed toward the Cross Island Parkway. Out over the mainland, the sun had begun its retreat, sending fingers of orange and pink light reflecting off the few wisps of cloud that hovered over the horizon. In little more than a couple of weeks, we'd be back on standard time, and five o'clock would find us facing full darkness. The final days of October always seemed to me like the end of something, the longer nights signaling a winding down, a respite from the bustle of tourist season and the scorching heat of summer. I smiled to myself, remembering how much I'd hated this time of year when I was growing up. Even the cooler temperatures couldn't compensate for the loss of those lingering hours of twilight between dinner and bedtime, a magical space in which rules were relaxed and adventures were free to happen.

We rode in silence, and I did my best to put the frantic happenings of the day out of my mind. As we rolled through the Palmetto Pass lane and onto the bridge, a flicker of something caught my eye. I glanced to the right and saw smoke and flashes of red mingling with the spectacular colors of the sunset.

"What's that?" I asked, pointing across Red toward the mainland.

He turned in his seat. "Looks like a fire. Big one, too."

I slowed below the forty mile per hour speed limit and coasted to the wide shoulder at the crown of the bridge. We watched for a moment without speaking. Then my husband's head swiveled, and his eyes met mine.

"Jericho Cay?" he asked softly.

"Damn," I whispered back.

CHAPTER
THIRTY-NINE

"WHERE ARE YOU GOING?"

I could feel his eyes on the side of my face as I slid into the left-hand lane at the foot of the bridge. I made the turn before I answered.

"The marina."

"Why?"

"We might have a better vantage point from there."

He didn't reply, and I sneaked a glance across at him. His eyes were closed, his head thrown back against the headrest, and he massaged his forehead with his right hand. I eased over the speed bump and into the cramped parking lot, which served not only the marina but the row of restaurants and shops along the tiny harbor. Either everyone was doing a brisk business, or I wasn't the only one who wanted to rubberneck the fire.

I had to circle twice before I found a pickup backing out at the far end near where the boats were lined up for repair. When I shut off the engine, Red didn't move. I laid a hand on his shoulder.

"I know it's been a hell of a day," I said softly. "Especially for you. Why don't you just sit and relax? All I want to do is find out if it's for sure Jericho that's on fire. Then we can go on to Jump and Phil's." When he didn't respond, I added, "We'll have big, fat steaks. On the company. I think we've both earned it today."

My husband lowered his hand and opened his eyes. "It's okay, honey. Let's go check it out."

He opened the passenger door and stepped onto the gravel of the parking lot. Outside, I reached for his hand as we walked toward where a small crowd had gathered along the dock. I scanned faces but didn't recognize anyone, so it surprised me when I heard Red speak.

"Hey, Bobby, how's it goin'?"

"Hey, Sarge. Long time no see."

The man was shorter than my husband and me by several inches and built like a small tank. The sleeves of his T-shirt had been ripped out, and the well-defined muscles on his arms were covered in tattoos. His head had been completely shaved, and a sheen of perspiration glistened there in the waning rays of the sun reflecting off the water.

"Bay, this is Bobby Sanchez. My wife."

We nodded and shook hands, and I wondered where Red had encountered the bodybuilder.

"Ma'am," he said, "a pleasure." He glanced back toward the billowing smoke that rose behind the row of palms that delineated the very end of Brams Point across the way. "Hell of a fire going over there. Shame."

"Is it Jericho Cay?" I asked.

"Hard to tell." He held up an electronic device I couldn't identify. "Got the local news on. I been waiting to see what they've got on it."

Behind me, I heard someone say, "Oh, yeah, it's that little island, the one where the rich guy disappeared."

I turned to see who had spoken and came face-to-face with a tall black man, his white hair a soft cap against his wrinkled face. "You're sure?" I asked.

"Yes, ma'am, I sure am. My boy is with the fire and rescue. He got called out about a hour ago."

I tugged on Red's hand, and he followed me out of the crowd. We walked a little way until we were out of earshot of any of the onlookers. "Do you think this is something the sheriff's guys did?"

He glanced around him before replying. "You mean set the place on fire? Why? That doesn't make any sense."

"I don't mean on purpose. Maybe they got into a firefight with Gerard. He was certainly armed. Didn't you say there was a generator out there? They could have hit the gasoline storage tank."

Red smiled. "That only happens on TV. Besides, I didn't see one when I was snooping around outside that day."

I thought about my first foray into the amateur detecting business, in that summer after I came out of hiding following Rob's murder. Sometimes, in the deepest dark of the night, I could still see Geoff Anderson's hands clawing at the unreachable window of the welcome center as the inferno raged around him. *Not just on TV.* I could have argued the issue, but what was the point?

My husband must have read the pain on my face, because he reached for my hand. "Look, honey, let's just leave it for now. Enough speculation. Deal?"

I looked over his shoulder. As twilight darkened the clouds hanging over the mainland, the flames seemed to dance in the air, as if the whole sky were on fire. "I want to go out there."

Red's hand jerked in mine. "Don't be ridiculous. First of all, it's too dangerous. And second, they wouldn't let us within a mile of the place. We'd just be in the way." He shook his head. "Why would you want to do that anyway? What's the point?"

I didn't have a reasonable answer. "What if Terry Gerard is out there? What if that's where he was calling me from?"

"Mike's on it. It's not our problem."

"I know it doesn't make any sense, but I feel . . . like I need to *do* something."

"Come on, honey, take it easy. You did everything you could do. We all did. Leave it to Mike now."

The fire was dying, billowing gray smoke replacing the flickering flames against the spreading sunset. I drew in a deep breath and let it out slowly. These were exactly the kinds of situations that had led, in the past, to our big blowups. A part of me knew he was right. Another part of me wanted to tell him to quit patronizing me, to go straight to hell, do not pass Go, do not collect two hundred dollars. I chose the high road.

"Okay. Fine. Let's just go eat."

Red squeezed my fingers and turned us toward the car. Even with the fire apparently under control, a faint hint of its distinctive odor wafted to us on the cool night air. I walked around to the passenger side of the Jaguar.

"You drive, will you? I can't seem to shake this headache."

Red slid in and cranked over the engine. "You'll feel better after a rare steak and a pile of French fries. Then we'll get you a hot shower, and I'll tuck you into bed." He turned in the seat and grinned at me. "Maybe I can think of a way to make you forget about all this craziness, at least for a while."

He waggled his eyebrows at me, and I had to laugh.

"Maybe you overestimate your powers of distraction," I said lightly.

"We'll see," my husband said with a leering grin, and, for the first time in several days, I felt myself relax.

The drive from Jump & Phil's to Port Royal Plantation took less than fifteen minutes, Red choosing to take the long way around down the business arm of Route 278. Traffic was light, as it usually was after

Labor Day when most of our summer visitors had returned to their normal lives in Ohio and Pennsylvania and New Jersey and New York. *New York.* The voice of John Wingo popped into my mind. He'd said that, even when he was sober and off the pills, Wolfe had thought of himself as some sort of Ernest Hemingway successor, the quintessential macho guy of twentieth-century literature. That made me smile. The fastidious man in the yachting cap, his trousers rolled up over skinny white legs, couldn't have been farther from the images of the great man in safari gear, a big gun broken over the crook of his arm.

Another mental picture, this one of the revered writer blowing his brains out in a cabin in the Idaho woods at the end of his career, made me shudder. I wondered if maybe Wolfe had decided to go out in a blaze of glory himself by putting Jericho Cay to the torch. But that couldn't be right. I shook my head. If Wolfe had really been here, he must now be lying in a freezer somewhere in Fairfield County. *Right?* I asked myself. "Right?" I murmured.

Red reached over and squeezed my upper arm. "You're talking to yourself," he said softly.

I jerked. "Sorry. Just thinking."

"You need to let this go, honey."

A couple of minutes later we approached the plantation gates and were waved through. I rested my head against the back of the seat and closed my eyes. Red was right. Obsessing about the conflicting reams of information was pointless. I breathed in deeply and let it out in a long exhale. Red made the turn into our driveway, and I reached for my bag.

"What's that?" I jerked upright, pointing through the windshield to the seaward side of the house.

"Where?" Red slowed and flicked the headlamps to high.

"Over there. Beside the deck."

"I don't see anything. A raccoon?"

"No, it was bigger." I forced myself to speak calmly. "A person, I think."

Red's shoulders tensed. "Damn, I left my gun locked in the rental. Forgot all about it. Do you have your pistol?"

I pulled it from my bag. "Let's check it out."

He reached for the Seecamp, but I jerked my hand away. "I'll go," he said in a terse voice. "You stay here."

I tightened my grip on the gun and jumped out. "I've got it. Leave the lights on." I moved around the back of the car, unwilling to make myself a target in the headlamps, and joined Red. We spoke in whispers. "You want to try and flush him out?"

Red shook his head. "We'll stay together. You take the point. I'm on your right, one step behind. Slowly."

In the dark that enveloped us the moment we moved around to the ocean side of the property, I smiled. For once my husband hadn't argued, for once trusting me to hold my own. We crept closer to the stairs that led up to the deck that spanned three sides of the house. A breeze rippled through the palmettos, the clacking of their razor-sharp leaves making it impossible to hear any other movement. Red tapped my shoulder, and I turned my head. He pointed to the left, toward the short boardwalk that led across the dune, flattened by Hurricane Kitty a couple of weeks before. I moved cautiously in that direction.

My foot *thunked* against the first of two steps, and I stopped. Red moved closer.

"We need more light. Let's get back to the house and hit the outside floods."

Any reasonably sane burglar would have fled down the beach by then, but his suggestion made sense. I nodded, and we backed away slowly before turning toward the driveway. A moment later, I heard movement off to my left, and I swung the pistol in that direction. Red stopped, and in the dim light of the headlamps reflected off the garage door, I saw his head swivel around. I leveled the Seecamp, my left hand supporting my right, just as Red had taught me.

I opened my mouth to demand the intruder show himself, when the doe broke from cover and bounded right toward us. Instinctively, I lowered my gun and dived to the left, away from the frantic rush of the terrified animal. I heard Red let out a loud *oomph,* and the deer disappeared past me and into the night.

"You okay?" I asked, willing my heart rate back to normal.

"No," my husband said from somewhere below me. "The damn thing ran right over me."

I shoved the pistol in my pocket and knelt next to him. "What's hurt?"

"Besides my pride?" I breathed a sigh of relief at his low chuckle. "I think I jammed my wrist. It hurts like hell, anyway."

"Come on." I helped him to his feet while he cradled his left hand in his right. "Let's get inside and take a look."

We walked back around to the front of the house. I reached into the Jaguar and hit the remote for the garage door, grabbing my bag along with the car keys from the ignition. I followed my husband up the steps. He had just pushed open the door to the entryway when I felt the hand grip my ankle a moment before I tumbled sideways. I think I might have yelled something, but I'm sure it was cut off the second my head connected with the smooth wood of the handrail, and I dropped like a stone.

CHAPTER
FORTY

I CAME TO ON THE SOFA IN THE GREAT ROOM, WHICH swam in waves the moment I forced my eyes open. I quickly closed them again at the stabbing pain of the light from the floor lamp in the far corner of the room. I took a few short breaths and tried it again, this time with only one eye. For the second time that day, I felt like throwing up. I swallowed a couple of times and willed myself not to.

"Bay? Honey?" Red's soft voice sounded like a jackhammer.

I felt his cool hand on my forehead before it slid down to brush a tentative caress against my cheek. "Don't talk," I tried to say, but it sounded like a garbled croak even to my own ears.

I think I might have drifted away again. When I next became aware, I could hear voices. I forced myself to stay perfectly still and squinted through eyelids opened only to slits. I saw Red's shoulder and his left hand, turned palm up, resting gingerly on the sofa cushion. He seemed to be leaning forward, tensed, as if ready to spring, but my feet and legs lay spread across his lap.

He must have sensed some change in my body. His good hand moved to pat my bare foot, almost absently, but it seemed to me as if it were a signal of some sort. I let my eyes drift closed again and tried to focus in on the other voice in the room. Some of the pain receded, and I remember thinking that maybe I didn't have a concussion after all. I kept my breathing even and concentrated.

"She coming around?"

The voice was familiar, but my brain refused to let me put a name to it. I waited.

"You could have killed her, you son of a bitch." Red continued to stroke my foot.

"Shut up."

It sounded, by the tone of his voice, as if they'd already been over this ground. In the silence that followed, I tried to put the pieces together: The movement by the garage. Our stealthy approach. The doe breaking from cover. And my tumble on the steps. I tuned back in to hear the other person say, "None of this would have happened if that crazy old man had just left it alone."

And I had it. Terry Gerard. I flexed my foot a little to give my husband some warning, then moaned softly. Slowly, I turned my head to see the man who'd accosted me in Jarvis Park—and probably taken two shots at Erik and me on the boat—leaning forward in one of the wing chairs that flanked the fireplace. One of his elbows rested on his knee. A large pistol dangled from his right hand. I slid my legs from across my husband's lap, and Red was immediately at my side.

"Don't try to move, honey," he said, cradling my pounding head in his good hand. "Just lie still."

"I'm okay." Gingerly, I swung my feet to the carpet and let my husband help me to sit up. Again the room swam, but a moment later it settled into focus. I looked across at Terry Gerard. "You're a mess," I said without thinking.

His hair was matted to his head, and his clothes looked as if he'd showered and slept in them. The unpleasant odor of dried pluff mud, tinged with a hint of smoke, clung to him.

"It hasn't been my best day."

I snorted. "Let's see . . . I've been shot at and tossed down my own steps. It hasn't exactly been a red-letter day for me, either." I turned to Red. "Can I have a drink of water? And could you bring me my bag? I need a couple of aspirin."

Our eyes held, and I prayed he got my meaning. There was aspirin in the cupboard next to the sink, but that wouldn't serve my purpose.

My husband glanced across at the man with the gun, who nodded once.

"Stay away from the phone," he said.

Red moved toward the kitchen. I took the opportunity to run my arm along the right leg of my slacks. As I suspected, my pocket was empty, the Seecamp no doubt somewhere on Gerard's person. No one spoke until Red returned and handed me my bag. Across the room, I could feel our captor tense as I stuck my hand inside, his gun fixed directly on me. I fumbled around before pulling out the small plastic bottle. I handed it to Red, my eyes hopefully conveying that I had managed to locate and activate the alarm system's panic button I carried on my key chain. He shook out two tablets and handed them to me. I swallowed them with the icy water before rubbing the glass across my forehead. The shock of it seemed to bring me back to full consciousness. I wondered how long it would take before the security company notified the sheriff's office. I'd never used that particular device before. If it generated a verifying phone call, the fact that no one answered should get the ball rolling. Our job was to keep this guy talking until the cavalry arrived.

"I wasn't shooting at you," Terry Gerard said, as if the last few minutes hadn't interrupted the conversation. "I'm an excellent shot."

"So if you'd meant to hit us, you would have?" I asked.

His chin came up a little. "Yes. I—we used to target practice out on Jericho. Ty and I were both pretty good."

It was almost a save, but the fall hadn't totally scrambled my brain. Beside me, I felt Red tense as well. I forced myself not to look at him.

"What happened out there?" I took another drink and set the glass on the coffee table. Red moved closer and put his injured arm around me. I could feel his pulse racing as fast as mine.

"It's not important. The question is, what am I going to do about you two?"

We had to keep him calm. I stretched out my legs on the low table. "Why don't you put that damn gun away? Neither of us is in any shape to take it away from you."

Silently, he met my gaze, but the muzzle remained pointing directly at my chest.

"Did you kill Anjanette Freeman?"

He flinched, his eyes closing momentarily. I wondered if either of us could make it across the room and grab the gun before he had a chance to react. Red seemed to sense my intention and tightened his hold on my shoulders.

"Poor Anjie," he said.

"Did you kill her or did Gerard?" I spoke harshly, with no effort to disguise the contempt in my voice. I waited a beat, then added, "And speaking of Terry Gerard, where is he, Mr. Bell?"

CHAPTER
FORTY-ONE

I DON'T KNOW WHAT I EXPECTED—OUTRAGE? DENIAL? I tensed, waiting for some sort of outburst from the man with the gun pointed at my heart. Instead, Ty Bell shrugged.

"Well done, Mrs. Tanner. I thought I had you convinced back there in the park. Obviously I underestimated you."

I knew Red had caught his slip as well as I had, and he took his cue from me. My husband's voice, when he spoke, stayed calm and reasonable.

"So you've been alive all this time. What the hell kind of game have you been playing?"

Ty Bell shrugged. His face once again darkened, and his leg jiggled up and down. "I don't expect you to understand."

"Try me."

He went on as if I hadn't spoken. "Anjie shouldn't have done it. She should have known I'd take care of things."

"Are you saying she really did commit suicide?" I asked.

In answer, Bell jerked forward, the gun wavering a little in his hand. "Of course she did! I would never have hurt Anjie. She'd been with me for years." He paused, and sadness clouded his eyes. "She may have been the only person alive who really cared about *me*."

Again, the muzzle of the pistol dipped a little, and Red planted his feet more firmly on the floor. I leaned away from him, and his arm slipped from around my shoulders. Bell noticed, and his hand steadied.

"But why?" I asked, as much because I wanted to know as to keep him off balance. "No one's ever been able to figure out why she killed herself."

"Because she knew I had to go." He sighed and shook himself. "And I couldn't take her with me. But none of that matters now. What is it going to take to get you to let me walk away?"

Red and I exchanged a look.

"Walk away from what? What exactly is it you've done, Mr. Bell?"

He didn't answer me. "I have more money than God. I can set you up for the rest of your lives."

Red eased forward and spoke calmly. "Do you really think you can put a bullet in Wolfe's head, nearly kill my wife, and set your own island on fire, then just stroll back in and pretend like nothing happened?"

Bell squirmed in his seat, and his gaze shifted momentarily away from us. "What are you talking about? Wolfe's in New York. I haven't talked to him since I left."

"Nice try. Maybe you ought to start at the beginning," I said. "If you expect us to let you just waltz out the door, you're going to have to convince us you had a damn good reason for all this mayhem."

I tried not to glance out the French doors into the darkness surrounding the house. Where the hell were the deputies? I'd expected the alarm company to have alerted them by now, and a phalanx of armed men to have been pounding on my door long before this.

Bell checked his watch. "I have no idea what you're talking about. Just tell me how much it's going to cost me to get you off my back." He almost smiled. "I can be very generous to my friends."

"Like Terry Gerard? Where is he? Buried somewhere out on the island? Is that why you torched it?"

His head snapped up, on alert, and I wondered if he'd caught the first sounds of our rescuers. We needed him distracted. I jabbed a finger in his direction.

"You killed him, didn't you?" I shouted. I jumped to my feet and shook off Red's restraining hand on my arm. "What was it? Was he blackmailing you? Stealing from you? Messing around with your woman?"

I saw the muscles in his jaw tighten and knew I'd hit the mark.

"Shut up," Ty said.

"Come on, Bell. You caught him with Anjie. You killed him on Jericho Cay and dumped his body somewhere. Then you stole his identity, and you've been on the run ever since, just like the murderous coward you are. And Wolfe found out, didn't he? Or he suspected. That's why you had to kill him, too."

The gaping hole of the gun barrel moved with me, maintaining its fixation on my chest. Again Red tried to yank me back down, but I could hear the faint rustling in the palmettos that had nothing to do with the wind. I angled my body away from the windows so that our captor was forced to shift his gaze as well. A moment later, I heard the first soft footfall on the wood decking.

"You killed all those people, and for what? So you could take a vacation from your poor little rich boy life?" I yelled.

"Sit down!" Bell shouted back.

Slowly, I lowered myself back onto the sofa. "Then tell me I'm wrong. Let's get Wolfe on the phone and prove you didn't whack him and set his body on fire to cover it up."

He ran his free hand through his hair. Little flakes of dried mud tumbled down and settled onto the pristine white carpet. Then Morgan Tyler Bell really smiled, and it changed his whole demeanor. Beneath the layers of mud and sweat and smoke, I could glimpse the handsome, charming man he must have been in his prime. He'd had a life that almost every man on the planet would have envied, and he'd thrown it away. But for what? I still didn't understand.

"I can see you're not going to be reasonable, Mrs. Tanner, not that I'm surprised. And I regret that, I truly do. Wolfe just couldn't leave it alone."

"So you killed him?"

"He didn't leave me any choice. Somehow he became convinced I was alive, and he's been trying to track me for the last few months. And he stirred up Harold, my nitwit cousin, to begin proceedings to have me declared legally dead. He knew I couldn't let that happen, let that moron take everything I've worked for. I assume he brought you in to stir up the pot even more. He thought his little scheme would smoke me out." His grin had turned ugly. "I guess you all succeeded— maybe more than any of you bargained for. And all for a damned book." He shrugged. "God knows I tried enough times to scare off Wolfe. Damned drugged-up old fool just wouldn't get the message."

Red and I looked at each other. Bell had all but admitted to first-degree murder. There was no way he could leave us alive now.

Bell took a step in our direction. "I've had enough of running around the world posing as a nobody. I'll admit it was intriguing at first. Let me enjoy some of the more interesting sides of life I usually didn't get a chance to experience. Thank God I had some money stashed away from the IRS in the Caymans. But I'm ready to come back and take up my life again. And nothing—including your meddling—is going to stand in the way of that."

I took a moment to shift everything I'd assumed about the case

Winston Wolfe had brought us barely a week ago, and suddenly enlightenment dawned. "You knew I was tracking you. You deliberately led us on that wild-goose chase to the boathouse."

Bell laughed, a brittle sound that had no humor in it. "I did everything but throw myself in front of you down at Coligny. I was afraid for a moment you weren't going to be able to keep up." His smile was almost attractive. "I have to admit I was surprised you were able to get a boat so quickly. I didn't factor in that possibility."

"You expected us to back up the assumption that Terry Gerard died in the explosion. And you could blame the fire on him, too. You waltz back in as the long-lost Bell, explain away your sabbatical as the whim of a quirky millionaire or some temporary mental lapse and take up right where you left off. And no one goes looking for Terry Gerard's body because we all assume he died today on the water. Pretty ingenious, Ty." I forced myself to smile. "I mean, really. I'm impressed. Why didn't you just let it play out that way?"

"Because you kept showing up where you shouldn't have been. You ought to thank me, you know. If I hadn't scared you off with those shots, you and your husband here would be shark bait by now."

So he thought it had been Red and I, not Erik, who had ruined his scheme by chasing him down on the water. We could have testified that he wasn't onboard when he detonated the explosion, probably by some kind of remote control from the island. It was a small comfort that this madman wouldn't have any reason to go seeking out my partner for retribution.

"Why didn't you?" I asked. "Let us go up with the boat?"

"It was a knee-jerk reaction. I thought I needed you alive. It was only later that I realized my mistake." Again he shrugged. "I'm really not very experienced at all this."

"So now what?" I asked, staring across at the man who literally held our lives in his hands. "You're going to finish us off right here? We haven't given you an answer yet. About the money."

"Nice try, but I think I knew all along you couldn't be bought off. And I have a sneaking suspicion you've got copies of all those files I took out of Wolfe's briefcase. Some of the stuff in there might interfere with my plans. We'll just stop at your office and pick those up on our way out."

"Way out where?" I asked, although I already knew the answer.

"We're going on a little boat ride. I'm afraid your bodies will be discovered in the ruins of Jericho Cay. You have a reputation for not being able to keep your nose out of things that don't concern you. No one will be surprised." He paused, and again he smiled. "Perhaps they'll assume that was good old Terry's doing, too. Really, the man has been more use to me dead than he ever was alive."

"We're not going anywhere with you." Red pulled me closer, shifting his body in front of mine. "It all ends, here and now."

"I don't think so." He took another step closer. "Terry thought he could screw with me, too, you know, and look where that got *him*. I think if I put a well-placed bullet in one of you, I'll get the other to cooperate." He waved the gun back and forth between the two of us. "Do you have a preference? Arm? Leg?"

Bell's gaze shifted momentarily toward the French door, and I shouted at him again. "I don't believe Anjanette Freeman committed suicide! I think you killed her, too, because she realized you were just a garden-variety murderer!"

The barrel of the gun rose, the muzzle now pointing directly at my forehead.

"You and Wolfe should have just left it alone," he said. "You have no idea what I'm capable of."

"I think I do, Ty," I shouted. "I think you're a lying, murdering, son of a bitch who thinks he can buy his way out of anything. Wolfe knew it. So did your precious Anjie. She killed herself rather than face the truth about you. In the end, all you've got is your stinking money, and I hope you choke on it!"

It seemed to happen in slow motion. It was as if my husband and I had choreographed our moves. Red shoved me away from him and leaped at Bell. The gunshot sounded like a cannon in the confined space of the living room, and Red crumpled. It was followed a moment later by another report. Glass shattered, and Ty Bell's head exploded.

I crawled across the shards of glass that littered the carpet, oblivious to the pain as they cut into my hands and knees. Bell had fallen across my husband's body. I shoved at his weight, heedless of the blood and brains running over my arms, just as other hands rolled him away.

Red lay facedown, his head and neck covered in gore. I wiped it away a moment before his eyes fluttered open.

"Where are you hit?" I screamed, jerking away from someone trying to pull me back.

"Shoulder," he managed through clenched teeth. "You?"

"Fine. He's dead."

"Good," my husband mumbled and passed out.

CHAPTER
FORTY-TWO

EARLY A WEEK LATER, WE SAT AROUND THE HUGE mahogany table in the imposing dining room at Presqu'isle, raising our flutes of champagne to Erik and Stephanie. The weather had taken a cold turn, and a small blaze flickered in the old fireplace.

My partner had finally gotten around to giving his fiancée a ring, and Lavinia had insisted on hosting a small celebration in their honor. We'd dined royally on Coquille St. Jacques, a scallop recipe handed down through my mother's family and only trotted out on extremely special occasions. Preceded by lobster bisque and accompanied by fresh greens and vegetables from her own garden, Lavinia's meal had concluded to rave reviews over angel food cake and coffee.

Now my husband stood to offer his toast. I smiled up at him as he lifted his glass in his left hand, his right arm being held tightly to his side by a navy blue sling. Bell's bullet had passed through with only minimal muscle damage, missing the bone by a fraction of an inch. A couple of weeks of immobility and a few more of rehab and Red would be as good as new.

"Marriage is an honorable estate and one not to be entered into lightly," he said solemnly a moment before I burst into laughter.

"Please, Red, spare us the sermon."

He smiled down at me. "Shut up, woman. I'm trying to give these two children the benefit of my wisdom."

I faked a punch to his damaged arm, and he flinched. "Get on with it, then."

"We wish you happiness always," he continued, "although that won't be the case. So here's to ups and downs—and to surviving them with grace and humor." He sat back down to mild applause.

A moment later Julia stood, her champagne glass of ginger ale glinting in the candlelight. "Can I say something?"

"Of course." Lavinia smiled up at her.

"Well . . . It's just that you're my family, my *real* family now, just like I've been dreaming about ever since I met you, and . . . I love you. That's all." She ducked her head and started to sit a moment before she popped back up. She raised her glass again toward Erik and Stephanie. "And I hope you'll have lots of babies."

I caught Lavinia's quick look in my direction, and the little frisson along my spine dissipated on a wave of laughter. My partner blushed, and his fiancée linked her arm through his.

We lingered over our tea and coffee, chatting about nothing, while Lavinia and Julia cleared the table. Both Stephanie and I had offered our help but had been sternly told to sit still and enjoy ourselves. When the room had been left to the four of us, my husband broached the subject we'd been avoiding all evening.

"I heard from Mike Raleigh today." Red spoke softly, and instinctively everyone leaned in a little closer. "They've cleared the deputy who took out Bell. Justifiable shoot."

"That's great," I said. "I was afraid they were going to hang him out to dry for going for a kill shot."

Red shook his head. "It's instinct. Larry is a veteran. Once the subject opens fire, you have to go for taking him down. I knew they'd rule in his favor. It's a shame, though."

I tried to come up with a scenario in which I felt bad that Ty Bell was dead, and failed. "No it's not. He would have found some way to wiggle out of going to jail. You know he would. He said it himself: the man had more money than God."

Erik spoke for the first time. "It would have been nice to have some more answers, though. I still feel as if there are a lot of loose ends we're never going to tie up."

"It's not the first time, and it probably won't be the last." I reached for the teapot and poured myself a fresh cup. "When will they be able to get out to Jericho and start looking for Gerard's body?" I asked my husband.

"It's still a smoldering mess out there. I'd guess maybe a couple of weeks. Although we're supposed to get some rain over the next few days. That might help."

"I still don't get why he set his own house on fire." Stephanie leaned forward, her elbows resting on the snowy white damask tablecloth.

Red and I looked at each other, and he tilted his head in my direction.

"Well, it's only speculation, based on what little he told us that night. I'm guessing he wanted to obscure any trace of Terry Gerard's corpse. It doesn't make a whole lot of sense to me. The sheriff's guys were all over the place after they found Anjanette Freeman's body, so Gerard's couldn't have been right out in the open."

"I'm guessing either the cistern or that old well I found when we were out there. Mike's going to give those special attention," my husband said.

I shrugged. "Could be. You know, I would have liked to have Neddie Halloran's opinion on what exactly drove Bell to do what he did. Complete narcissism would be my guess."

"Mr. Wolfe did say that he'd been acting strange in the months leading up to his disappearance," Stephanie said. "Hiding out in his own wing of the house and never showing himself."

The mention of Wolfe made me shake my head. He'd set in motion a series of events he could never have imagined would lead to his own death. Just the day before we'd learned that, thanks to a hairbrush John Wingo had forwarded to SLED in Columbia, the burned body near Newberry had been positively identified as the missing crime writer. Bell had admitted to Red and me that he had terrorized Wolfe over his few days on the island, had somehow scared him off from the airport, ransacked his room, and sent him running for his life from the Holiday Inn. With both of the players dead, though, we were never going to know for certain how it had all played out. Maybe he really had intended to convince Wolfe to back off, but the end result had still been murder.

"Strange is one thing." I stirred sweetener into my tea. "But even if he killed Gerard in a fit of anger or something, I'm convinced he couldn't leave Anjanette behind to deal with the authorities and all their questions. He must have believed that she'd crumble under the pressure."

"So you don't think she killed herself?" Stephanie asked.

"No. And neither did your father."

The mention of Ben Wyler brought a silence that Red broke after a few moments.

"You think what you want, honey, but the facts are still the facts. The coroner took another look at his findings back then and still maintains it was a suicide."

I let it go, but I would be a long time shaking the image of Anjanette Freeman's systematically stabbing herself to death out of grief over Ty Bell and his actions. Guilt maybe, for her role in Terry Gerard's death. That I might be able to buy. Maybe.

"But he killed Wolfe in cold blood," my husband said. "Even if he suffered from some kind of mental breakdown when he murdered Gerard, he knew exactly what he was doing when he took out Wolfe."

"You're right," I said.

Red squirmed a little in his chair and readjusted the sling. "It's over now, anyway. One way and another."

Erik reached for Stephanie's hand. "I'm just glad everyone here came through okay."

I remembered my promise to my partner that I wouldn't involve his soon-to-be wife in any of the dangerous aspects of our business. I shivered a little in the warm dining room, hoping that I'd be able to keep it. Winston Wolfe and Ty Bell had both brought that danger and ugliness into what had initially seemed like the most straightforward of cases, but not all of our work ended in death or injury. I tried to hold on to that thought as I looked across the table at the two young people who had become such an integral part of our family. We'd experienced both losses and gains over the past year, and I sent up a silent plea to Whomever that those we had left would be safe and—

Julia interrupted my gloomy introspection by bouncing into the dining room, a beautifully wrapped package held tightly in her hands. Lavinia followed, her smile almost tentative. She glanced across at me, and I nodded.

"Go ahead, honey," she said, urging Julia forward.

"We have a present for you," my sister said, extending the box in Stephanie's direction. "It's a really, really good one, too."

We all laughed, and Lavinia put her arm around Julia's shoulder. I was probably the only one who caught the fleeting look of concern that passed over her wrinkled face a moment before she resurrected the smile.

"All of us wish you and Erik every happiness as you anticipate your new life together," Lavinia said. "It's a beginning, but we believe that you also need a grounding in the past, a reminder of those who have come before and shared the same hopes and dreams."

"It's something from the family. *My* family." Julia's face had taken on a smug, satisfied look, tinged with something darker that I couldn't immediately put my finger on.

"That's enough," Lavinia said sharply, then modulated her tone. "We don't want to spoil the surprise, do we, honey?"

Julia flashed her a look of anger that was almost immediately replaced by that same self-satisfied smile. Over her head, Lavinia caught my eye, her expression a mixture of confusion and pain.

My mind shot back to her hints about Julia's unusual behavior after Elizabeth Shelly's death, and a horrible thought exploded into my consciousness. I flinched when Red's hand reached across to cover mine.

"What's the matter?" he whispered under cover of Stephanie's excited tearing of the paper that covered her gift.

"Nothing," I said, which was true because it wasn't possible. Julia had been outside. Hadn't she? I wouldn't think about it. I wouldn't! Not now. Not ever.

I lifted my gaze back to Lavinia's. And saw reflected on her anguished face the same question. One I prayed neither of us would ever ask.

"Oh, it's wonderful!" Stephanie lifted the small red leather book from its nest of tissue and opened it gingerly.

I forced a smile. "It's one of our ancestor's recipe books," I said, slipping my hand out from beneath my husband's. "Although they called them 'receipts' back then. I don't know how much you're into cooking, but we wanted you to have something that will remind you of us."

"But this is your family's. I couldn't possibly—"

"Of course you can," Lavinia said, her voice steady. "Even though you aren't officially members, you'll always be family to us." She looked at me and pulled my sister's body more closely against her own. Her eyes challenged me. "Just like Julia."

I closed my eyes and lowered my head as Red slipped his good arm around my shoulders. I felt his love and concern flow into me, giving me strength. I leaned into his comforting embrace and smiled up into his face.

"Amen," I whispered.

Amen. So be it.

EPILOGUE

CREPT UP THE STAIRS, THE OLD WOOD COLD BE-
neath my bare feet. I carried my sneakers in my hand as I
hugged the outside of the steps, avoiding the creaky boards in the
center. I eased open the door to the attic, careful to make certain
the old hinges didn't betray me. I flipped on the flashlight and left the
door ajar.

I worked on my shoes and followed the dim beam of light across
the dusty floor, the jumble of footprints from my last visit leading me
unerringly to what I sought. I propped the light on a stack of boxes
and pulled the humpbacked trunk into the center of the aisle. Outside, one of the remaining high branches on the old live oak scratched
against the eyebrow window.

The storm had kicked up just as we were finishing dinner. Nothing to compare to Hurricane Kitty's fury of a few weeks earlier, but
bad enough for Red and me to decide to spend the night. Erik and
Stephanie—younger and braver—had headed back to Hilton Head.

I'd tossed and fretted for the first hour after Red and I had settled
into one of the guest rooms. We'd chosen one with twin beds so that I
didn't inadvertently knock against my husband's wounded arm. Finally,

about two o'clock, I'd given up, pulled on one of my old robes I'd moved from what was now Julia's room, and tiptoed out into the hallway. Gusts of wind whistled around the chimneys, and rain beat unceasingly against the windows, covering my stealthy movements. Around me, the rest of the house had slept.

I lifted the lid on the trunk and removed the clothing I'd hastily piled inside just before I'd raced down the stairs to take the call that had set the whole Bell nightmare in motion. I pushed that thought away and gathered together all the small, moldy journals into a stack. With the flashlight balanced in my lap, I skimmed the first few pages of each one, searching for the beginning entry that might give me some clue as to which of my ancestors might have spent her days recording her thoughts and the events of her life in such detail.

I recognized one or two names as I flipped through the pages, a couple of Baynards whose portraits hung in the gallery downstairs. I shifted around on the box I'd chosen for a seat and thought about turning on the lights overhead, dim as they were. Maybe I could decipher the flowery script a little better. . . .

I let the thought trail away as my gaze lit on what had to be the first entry, dated April 23, 1860. Across the top of the page, in beautiful copperplate, was written:

Madeleine Henriette Baynard
Her Book

I clutched the journal to my chest and shot the light around the vast expanse of attic until it settled on a dilapidated, overstuffed chair in a hideous flower pattern. Some of the padding had fallen victim to mice, but the frame looked sturdy enough. I wove my way to it, brushed off as much of the dust as I could, and eased myself down into it. I opened the journal on my lap and focused the flashlight on the first page. Without conscious thought, I found myself reading out loud.

" 'I was fourteen when Papa and Boy were taken by the fever, and Mama began to lose her mind.' "

The barest whisper of a footfall brought my head snapping up to find my sister Julia watching me from the open doorway.